D.B. AXTELL

Edited by: Erica Rogers @ Logophile Editing Services

Cover design and formatting by : Kate @ Kate Decided to Design

www.katedecidedtodesign.com

CONTENT WARNING

The FMC has severe anxiety and depression. It's talked about throughout the book and there is an on page mention of a brief anxiety episode. I understand attacks and episodes are different for everyone. These descriptions are based on my own experiences.

There is also mentions of:

- Parental Death - not shown, just discussed.
- Suicide attempt - not shown, just discussed.
- Harm to animal - on page scene.

This book is for me.

For the people who want to give up, but keep pushing forward.

You matter.

You are important.

Also, for Dodger, my very own Bruno. He was my savior at 13 and I thank him every day for it.

And for myself. Like Amelia, I've suffered through the dark days, the hard days, and still battle with my mental health.

So to me, and you, always remember:

Your anxiety is a lying hoe!

TAKING THE Pitch

PLAYLIST

1 CONTROL // BRYCE SAVAGE
2 SLAYER // BRYCE SAVAGE
3 BOM BIDI BOM // NICK JONAS & NICKI MINAJ
4 YOU // CHASE RICE
5 GONNA WANNA TONIGHT // CHASE RICE
6 UNSTEADY (ERICH LEE GRAVITY REMIX) // X AMBASSADORS
7 ISLAND // FLORIDA GEORGIA LINE
8 COME BACK TO BED // SEAN STEMALY
9 YOU ARE IN LOVE(TAYLORS VERSION) // TAYLOR SWIFT
10 ALL OUT OF FIGHT // P!NK
11 INTRUSIVE THOUGHTS // NATALIE JANE
12 GUILTY AS SIN? // TAYLOR SWIFT
13 CRY // GRYFFIN & JOHN MARTIN
14 LOVE IN THIS CLUB // USHER (FEAT. YOUNG JEEZY)
15 SO DO I // TENILLE ARTS
16 SNAP // ROSA LINN
17 IF YOU LOVE HER // FOREST BLAKK
18 BIRTHDAY CAKE // DYLAN CONRIQUE
19 PRAY // JESSIE MURPH

PROLOGUE

Judd

I FUCKED UP.

Bad.

Like the most ultimate fuck up I could ever pull right now fuck up.

How?

Oh, let me tell you.

It all started at my brother's engagement party.

CHAPTER 1

Judd

"CHEERS TO THE HAPPY COUPLE," I say, finishing my speech, holding up my beer.

Shouts of *Cheers!* go up around me and we all take a drink with me, finishing mine off.

I make my way to the open bar and order another. While I'm waiting, I turn around and lean my elbows against the bar, looking around at everyone who showed up for my brother and Lucy. It's not a huge crowd, but they wanted to keep it small, just the important people in their lives. Tony and his whole family are here. Lucy's best friend, Kara, and her son, of course. Garrett, who isn't fooling anyone with the way he's giving Kara looks from across the room.

We see you, buddy.

Reese, Brent, Duke...which is surprising, he never comes to these things; the recluse that he is. A few other guys from the team Kessler's friends with and their dates, wives, girlfriends, whatever.

Coach Dixon and his wife and daughter Charlie, who also runs the team's PR department.

Coach raises an eyebrow at me from across the room and I tip my head towards him.

The bartender sets my drink on the bar, and I turn and grab it, taking a swig while I finish my perusal of the room.

Aunts, uncles and cousins from our side round out the body count. Apparently, Lucy's family disowned her when she got pregnant with Hudson. What fuckheads do that to someone? Especially someone as sweet and amazing as Lucy?

Jared Cox, that's who.

Shaking my head, I take another drink of my beer as I think about the guy who I used to call my friend. The things he said about Lucy when he and Kessler got into that fight during their league game last season were shocking. I knew he was known to go through women.

It's not a secret. A lot of ballplayers sleep around, but abandoning your kid? And to toss Lucy to the side like that? No. I told that motherfucker where he could go the last time he called me up. Then I blocked his number.

Dad comes over and claps me on the back. He orders a beer for himself and a white wine for my mom.

Leaning on the bar, he looks out over the crowd with me. "Good turnout," he notes, tipping his head towards everyone.

"Yeah, everyone they invited showed up for them," I say, taking another drink.

Feeling Dad's gaze on me, I turn towards him. "What?"

"You good, Son?" He looks at the beer in my hand and back at me.

Reaching out, I clap his shoulder. "Yeah, Dad. I'm fine, just celebrating the happy couple."

He grabs his drinks from the bartender. "Okay, but ease up on the drinks, yeah? Maybe switch to water?"

"Sure, Dad," I tell him. He nods his head and heads over to where Mom is fussing over Lucy.

Oh yeah, fun fact. Lucy is three months pregnant. With twins. Which is another reason we're here tonight. They wanted to get married before the babies were born and Lucy wanted it to happen before she's as big as a house. Her words, not mine. So, in true Lucy and Kessler fashion, they decided to get married on Christmas...which is in two months. Their reasoning being everyone who they were going to spend Christmas with would be at the wedding anyway. Honestly, I can't argue with that logic, not that I would. Lucy has gotten a little scary with all the extra pregnancy hormones coursing through her body.

Something hits me between the ribs, and I absently rub at it.

One of Tony's daughters comes over. Marie, I think, I don't know. They all look similar, and I'm not as close to them as Kess is. After she orders a glass of wine, she looks over at me, giving me a shy smile.

I return the smile, but don't pursue it from there. She's pretty, dark brown eyes, the color of whiskey, dark chocolate-brown shoulder length hair, beautiful really, but I don't feel an attraction there.

Giving me one last look, she takes her drink and heads over to Kara and the girl group that's formed around Lucy.

Seeing my brother has finally peeled himself from Lucy's side, I make my way over to his little group. He's been a little... over-protective of Lucy since finding out she's pregnant. Mom thinks it's adorable. Lucy is slightly annoyed, but grateful to actually have her partner with her this time.

Squeezing in between my brother and Brent, I clap Kessler on the back a few times. "I thought Lucy was going to have to pry you off her side with a crowbar," I joke.

"I'm not that bad," Kessler grumbles, looking over at Lucy with a mixture of adoration and concern. Feeling his gaze on her, Lucy looks over and gives Kessler a wink, making him smile and his body relaxes slightly. "Okay, maybe I'm a little... protective."

I scoff. "A little? I recall Lucy telling Mom at the last Sunday dinner she had to sneak out of the house the other day so she could go on a run."

Kessler rolls his eyes like I'm the one being dramatic.

"Then, *then,* when you couldn't find her, you. Tracked. Her. Phone." Kessler's face turns a slight shade of red. Driving my point home, I finish, "Then *drove* to her location and insisted she get in the truck so you can drive her back."

Brent and Reese snicker beside him. Duke rolls his eyes and Garrett just takes a drink of his beer.

Kessler grips the back of his neck like he does when he's stressed. "I was concerned about her jostling the babies around." Pulling his hand from his neck, he waves it around in the air. "How was I supposed to know that's not what happens? I've never done this before. I know *nothing* about babies, or pregnancies." He stops and takes a drink of his own beer.

Feeling a twinge guilty for giving him a hard time, I lay my hand on his shoulder. "You're going to be a great dad, Kessler; you already are to Hud. Plus, we've had a great role model. You have nothing to worry about."

Kessler nods and takes another drink of his beer. Trying to lighten the mood, I turn to Brent, who has been eyeballing Lucy's group. "So, Brent, who are you eye fucking over there?"

Brent chokes on the drink of beer he was taking. Reese smacks his back hard a few times. "What?" he chokes out. "I'm, no, I." He coughs a few more times, then takes another drink. "I'm not *looking* at anyone," he says, his voice a little higher than normal.

I grin. "Riiight. That's why you haven't taken your eyes off Lucy's little group over there," I say, pointing with my bottle to Lucy's girl gang. Brent looks over again, right as Marie looks up. Their eyes lock and they both turn red and look away.

Oh...

"She's cute man, you should go for it," I tell him.

Brent shakes his head and moves off, muttering something about needing another drink. I chuckle and Kessler just shakes his head. "Always have to stir up trouble, don't you?"

I shrug. It's always been my duty as the younger brother to cause trouble. Why stop now?

"Sooo Garrett," I start, turning to him.

"Nope," he says, staring me down, blue eyes blazing into me.

I laugh, but don't push it. Garrett is a retired Navy SEAL. I may like to cause trouble, but I don't have a death wish. Holding my hand up in surrender. "Okay, chill. Just thought there was a certain BFF over there that caught your eye."

He cocks his eyebrow at me in warning, but there's a hint of a smile on his lips.

I smirk back, but decide to keep quiet, not wanting to push my luck.

"What about you?" Reese asks, looking at me.

"What about me?"

He tips his chin at me. "You seem invested in everyone's love life. What about yours?"

I shrug. "Don't have one." Another twinge hits me between the ribs, and I try to ignore it. "You know me. I'm not the relationship type." Apparently, I'm not the hook-up type anymore, either. It's been longer than I care to admit since I've been with anyone. Not that I'm going to tell them that.

"Mmm hmm," Reese responds, knowing I'm full of shit, but not calling me on it.

I tip my beer and finish it off. I excuse myself and go to the bar to grab another one. I know I told my dad I would switch to water, but one more won't hurt.

Fresh beer in hand, I spot my favorite nephew, or soon to be nephew, I guess, and head over to where he and Kade, Kara's son, are sitting at a table playing on their Nintendo Switches. Hudson looks up from his game and gives me a wide grin. "Hey Uncle Judd, wanna play?"

A warm feeling spreads through my chest when he calls me Uncle. I return his grin and sit in the chair next to him. "Sure, what are we playing?" I ask, holding out my hand for his switch.

"*Mario Kart*," he says, handing me his game system. "I'm kicking Kade's ass, and I think he needs a break from me winning." His eyes widen when he realizes he said the word 'ass', making me chuckle.

"Don't worry, Hud, I won't tell if you don't." I give him a wink.

He relaxes back into his chair and nods.

I lace my hands together and crack my knuckles. "Alright boys, prepare to lose."

I suck...

Twenty minutes and several lost rounds of *Mario Kart* later and Hudson has dubbed himself king. He wiped the floor with both Kade and me.

"Re-match," I say, motioning to Kade for the switch. He's holding it out for me when Kara comes up to the table, grabbing it.

"Sorry boys, no re-match, the party is over," she says, motioning to the room. I look around and realize that only our families are left and getting ready to head out themselves.

Standing up with the boys, I take my phone out of my back pocket and check the time. 8pm. Shit, it's still early. If I go home now, I'm just going to sit in my apartment and mindlessly flip through the channels. I make the decision to stop by my favorite club for a while before heading home.

I walk with the boys and Kara over to where Kessler, Lucy, and my parents are getting their coats on. October in Oregon is usually pretty wet, and this year is no exception. It's currently dumping outside the event space they rented for the party.

"Great party guys," I tell Kessler and Lucy, grabbing my jacket.

"Nice speech," Lucy says, slipping her coat on that Kessler is holding out for her.

I blow on my nails and buff them against my shirt. "Thanks. Only the best for my favorite future sister-in-law."

Lucy laughs and gives me an eye roll.

"Hey! What about your favorite brother?" Kessler asks, shoulder bumping me.

"I don't have one of those."

"If it wasn't for me, you wouldn't have a favorite sister-in-law," Kessler argues, handing Hudson his jacket before putting his own on.

I lift a shoulder. "You're right." Placing my hands on Hudson's shoulders, I stand behind him before adding, "There's still time to change your mind, Luce. I could have a favorite fiancée instead," I say, giving her a wink.

Lucy barks out a laugh while Kessler says something about being an only child under his breath. An elbow digs into my ribs, and I turn to see my mom giving me a pointed look.

"Quit teasing your brother."

"What? I'm just letting Lucy know that she still has options."

Lucy pats my arm and gives me a sweet smile. "Sorry, Judd, but I only have eyes for Kessler."

"That's right baby," Kessler says, looking down at Lucy like she's the only woman in the world. He leans down and connects his lips with hers. Mom makes a soft hmm and places a hand over her chest, grinning.

"Ugh, gross," Hudson mutters.

I laugh and pat his shoulders. "One day, Hud, you're not going to think it's gross."

He shakes his head in disagreement, making us all laugh.

A few seconds later when the rain lightens up and Kessler releases Lucy's lips, a decision is made that Dad and Kess will go pull the cars around so Mom, Lucy, and Hudson don't have to get completely soaked. Me, being the lone wolf, will just leave from the lot. I say my goodbyes and make a beeline to the only three cars left in the lot. Lifting my hand to my dad and brother, I get in the car and head off to the club.

Two hours and a couple of drinks later, and I'm beginning to think I made the wrong decision. The thumping of the music is giving me a headache, and the girl that attached herself to me as soon as I walked in isn't helping. Apparently, she's a chatty drunk, and she's sucking down the drinks like they're water.

I let my eyes wander her body again and wonder how she's still upright. She maybe weighs 120 pounds soaking wet. Her clothes have left little to the imagination. It's basically two scraps of fabric covering, and I use that word loosely, her important parts. To top it all off, she's wearing heels that make *my* feet hurt just looking at them.

"Want to get out of here?" she asks hopefully, noticing my gaze.

Yes, but not with you.

Leaning forward in the booth, I set my half empty beer down on the table. "Actually, I have a headache. I think I'm going to head out," I tell her, hitching my thumb over my shoulder.

She gives me a pouty lip, and then her eyes light up. "I can help you with that," she says, scooting closer to me. Any closer and she'll be in my lap. "You know, take your mind off the pain," she says suggestively, with a wink.

I pry her hands off my arms and scoot towards the outer part of the booth. "As fun as that sounds, I'm going to have to take a rain check. Maybe next time," I tell her, standing. She shimmies her way out of the booth. I have no idea how her clothes stay where they are, but she manages to keep all her important parts covered.

Once she's standing, she digs in her purse that's no bigger than my fist and extracts a folded piece of paper. "Here's my number." She reaches forward and tucks the paper into my front pocket, letting her hand linger there for a minute. "Give me a call when you want to continue this," she says, looking up at me through her lashes.

Pulling my keys from my other pocket, I give her a wink and nod to Nate behind the bar. He gives me a wave and I leave out the back.

Once I'm in my car, I reach into my pocket and take out the paper and unfold it.

Huh, I totally thought her name was Sandra. Crumpling the paper, I toss it onto the passenger floorboard and start my car. Pulling out of the lot, I start the 10-minute drive to my apartment.

I'm lost in my thoughts of why I didn't take that girl home when I normally would. She was beautiful. Blonde hair, blue eyes. Except she was a little too skinny for my taste. I like a woman with more curves, something I can grab onto while I'm driving into her, preferably from behind. I reach down and adjust myself, trying to remember the last time I got laid. It's been a while.

I'm trying to remember exactly how long it's been when all of a sudden blue and red lights flash and the whoop of a siren sounds.

Fuck.

The siren whoops again and I hit my blinker, seeing a space on the shoulder to safely pull over. I blow out a breath once I'm stopped and try to figure out what I did.

After what feels like an eternity, the officer and his partner get out of their car and make their way over to my car. One taps the window and I roll it down, squinting against the rain that's blowing in and the light from his flashlight. "Officer..." I look at his nameplate. "Blackstone, what seems to be the problem?" I ask, holding my hand up slightly against the light.

"Son, do you know how fast you were going?" he asks, holding his light down now that he got a good look at me.

I blink a few times, letting my eyes adjust from the assault of his flashlight, then look up at him. He's older, salt and pepper hair at the temples. His eyes look like they've seen some things, and the wrinkles at the corners suggest long and stressful days on the job. I respect the hell out of law enforcement and I'm not looking to make this guy's night hard. "Uh, no officer, I'm sorry I don't. Was I speeding?"

"Does 40 in a 25 sound like speeding?" he asks, raising his bushy eyebrows.

Shit.

"Uh, yes sir. It does. I'm sorry. I'll pay better attention next time."

"License and registration," he says, indicating he's not done with me.

I grab my wallet from the cup holder and pause. "Uh, my registration is in the glove box. Can I reach for it?"

He nods and I move across my car, getting into the box and pulling out the paper he asked for. I blow out a breath and hand over both items. He reaches for them, then stops. "Son, have you been drinking?"

Fuck.

I stare at him, trying to decide if I want to lie or tell him the truth. I opt for the truth, since he obviously smelled it on me, or he wouldn't have asked. "Uh, yes sir, I had a beer at *Ignite.*" I don't add the drinks I had before that. That was hours ago, they have to be out of my system by now. Right?

His eyes flick from me to his partner, then back to me. "Do you mind stepping out of the car and coming to the back to do a voluntary test for me?"

Son of a bitch.

I nod and move to get out. He steps back, keeping his flashlight on me. Opening my door, I slowly get out, keeping my hands where he can see them, and walk to the back of the car where the other officer is waiting.

He looks at me and does a double take. "Holy shit, you're Judd Davis."

I nod and hold out my hand. "Nice to meet you..." I look at his nameplate. "Officer Thompson." He takes my hand and gives it a quick shake.

"Thompson!" the other officer bellows from behind me, making me jump a little. "Run these while I start his field test."

Officer Thompson gives me a weak smile and grabs my cards from the other officer and heads back to the patrol car.

Officer Blackstone comes and stands in front of me. Raising his flashlight, he points it back at my face. "Are you sick or injured?"

I shake my head no.

"Diabetic, or any major medical issues?"

"No, Sir."

"Great. Place your feet together for me and stick your hands down at your side." I do as he asks, and he holds a finger up to my face. "See my finger?" I nod. "I need you to follow it with your eyes, and only your eyes. Don't turn your head. Understand?"

"Yes, Sir."

He moves his finger first to the left, almost out of my line of vision. I almost turn my head to follow it, but catch myself. He moves it to the other side of my face and repeats the motion a few times before pausing on each side of my head.

"Now follow it down and up," he says, motioning up and down in front of my face a few times. "Okay, now we're going to do the walk and turn. For this test, I'm going to have you stand with your right foot in front of your left, heel touching your toe. Your hands need to be at your side and you're going to walk in a straight line counting nine steps out loud. Understand?"

I nod while he demonstrates the movements.

"Upon completing the ninth step, leave your front foot planted and make a series of small steps to turn around and make nine steps back. Once you start this test, you cannot stop it. Got it?"

Fuck, do I?

I nod anyway and start the test, as Officer Thompson comes back with my cards. I complete the first nine steps with a few wobbles, but nothing I couldn't correct, but as I start to turn around, I feel myself tilt and lose my balance. I stop and correct myself before completing the turn and finishing my nine steps back. Or what I thought was nine steps, maybe ten?

Officer Blackstone's face remains impassive as he gives me instructions for the final test. "Last test. For this one, you're going to stand with your feet together, hands at your sides again, only this time you're going to raise your left or right leg off the ground and parallel to it. I'm going to ask you to count one, one thousand, two, one thousand, etcetera until asked to stop." He demonstrates for me. "Do you understand?"

I nod and lift my left leg. Fighting the urge to hold my arms out, I start counting. "One, one thousand, two, one thousand, three, one thousand…" I make it to 11 one thousand before I start wobbling.

"Ok, that's enough." Officer Blackstone sighs. "Signs indicate that you're impaired and shouldn't be operating a vehicle. Turn around and put your hands behind your back for me."

I close my eyes and let my head fall back. "Fuck," I mutter to the sky.

"What was that?" Officer Blackstone asks, taking his cuffs out of his utility belt.

"Nothing, sir," I say, turning around and placing my hands behind my back. He reads me my Miranda Rights as he secures the first cuff around my wrist. The cold metal bites into my skin. The second cuff locks around my wrist and he guides me to the back of the patrol car. Officer Thompson opens the door while Officer Blackstone puts a hand on the back of my head as I duck down into the back. Sitting on the hard bench seat, I look out the window and wonder how much I just fucked up my life.

I blew a .09 on the breathalyzer. I'm charged and booked with driving under the influence. Then I'm fingerprinted, photographed, and allowed my phone call. It's well past midnight when I called Kessler. After he got over the initial shock that I was, in fact, calling him from jail and not pulling a prank on him, I'm wondering if I made the right decision by calling him instead of our parents.

I take the envelope that holds the stuff I had on me when I was arrested from the booking officer and head out through the doors to what looks like a waiting room. Kessler is sitting in a chair with his arms on his knees and his head in his hands, staring at the floor. I clear my throat and his eyes shoot to me.

Instantly I feel like I'm 12 years old again and Kessler is pissed at me for letting it slip that he snuck out after curfew to take Sadie Green to the lookout. Mom was pissed when she found out, and he wasn't allowed to drive anywhere but school and practice for a month.

Without saying a word, he gets up from the chair and heads to the door leading outside. I follow him like a puppy who was punished for peeing on the floor.

Once we're inside the truck, the silence is almost deafening. Kessler doesn't make a move to start the truck, just grips the steering wheel, turning his knuckles white. After a few uncomfortable minutes, I finally speak up. "Are we just going to sit here, or?" I don't even finish my sentence before Kessler explodes.

"What the fuck were you thinking, Judd? Driving drunk? What the hell do you have to say for yourself?"

"Okay, Dad," I start, but he cuts me off again.

"This isn't a joke, Juddson. This is your fucking life! What if you crashed? What if you had hit someone? Or worse, killed someone or yourself?" His voice echoes inside the cab of the truck as his voice gets louder the angrier he gets.

I can count on one hand the number of times I've seen Kessler lose his shit. Most recently, when he found out about Jared and Lucy's past and told Lucy he wanted a break, resulting in one very smashed coffee table. So him screaming at me tells me I fucked up big time.

I sit there in silence, letting the reality of the situation wash over me. "Kess, I'm, I-" I stop and run my hand over my jaw and mouth. "I didn't realize I was drunk. I thought I was good to drive, man."

Kessler blows a breath out through his lips and lets his head fall back against his headrest. He turns his head and looks at me with eyes that match mine. "Judd, it's not just about you. You have to think about how your actions affect others. I had to convince Lucy to stay home and not come with me. Hudson idolizes you. What if something had happened? He would be devastated. We all would."

Those words are a hit straight to my heart and I rub at the ache in my chest. I don't consider myself a selfish person, but my actions tonight have said otherwise. Running my fingers through my hair, I tug at the ends in frustration. "You're right Kessler, I wasn't thinking. I'm sorry for worrying all of you."

Kessler nods and sits forward, turning the key in the ignition. The truck roars to life. "You have to get your partying under control. You're thirty two, Judd, time to grow up."

I clench my teeth together. I know he's right, but it doesn't make hearing it any easier.

Kessler pulls out of the lot and heads in the direction of my apartment. "You need to call Dale first thing in the morning, too. You know this won't stay quiet for long."

I nod, even though the darkness in the truck prevents him from seeing it and lay my head back against my own head rest. The events of the day catching up to me. Dale is not going to be happy about this, but if anyone can handle this, it's him. He's been our agent from day one and we trust him with anything. He handled Kessler's media shit show with ease, and I'm hoping mine has the same outcome.

Neither of us speak during the drive to my place. When Kessler pulls up to the front of my building, I turn to him before getting out. "I'm sorry for taking you away from Lucy on the night of your engagement party. Tell her sorry for me?"

Kessler sighs and rubs his eyes with his thumb and pointer finger. "You can tell her at family dinner tomorrow." He looks at the clock on the dash. "Or should I say today?"

Shit.

I know there's no way mom would let me skip dinner, especially after what happened tonight. Oh no, it'll be all hands on deck to figure out how to fix Judd's fuck up. I release a sigh of my own and nod. "Guess Mom wouldn't let me skip this one, huh?"

Kessler snorts. "Yeah, maybe if hell froze over." He gives me a slight smile. "Better get some sleep, little brother. Mom is going to be all over your ass tonight."

Grabbing the handle, I open my door and slide out of the truck. "Thanks again, Kessler."

He nods. "We'll figure this out, Judd. Everything will work out."

I close the door and tap it a of couple times, giving Kessler a wave as he pulls away from the curb. Turning to my building, I make my way up the steps and into the lobby. "Good evening Mr. Davis." I tried correcting Marty my first two months here to call me Judd, but it never stuck, so I gave up trying.

"Evening Marty. How's your night?"

"Can't complain Mr. Davis."

I nod my head at him and give him a wave, heading to the elevator. "Have a good rest of your night, Marty."

"Thank you Mr. Davis, you too."

Once I'm in the elevator, I hold my phone up to the screen and hit the button for the Penthouse. Slouching against the wall, the reality of the day hits me in full force. I fucked up, bad.

Entering my apartment. I toss my keys onto the entry table and sag into the couch, my eyes instantly grow heavy. Before I drift off to sleep, my mind replays the events of the day and I pray tomorrow is a better day.

CHAPTER 2

Judd

TODAY HAS NOT STARTED off as a better day.

I woke up with a raging headache, thanks to last night's events, and was barely able to choke down my first cup of coffee before Kessler picked me up at the ass crack of dawn to take me over to Dale's house to meet with him and my lawyer. After they both read me the riot act on how 'destructive' my behavior has gotten lately, they informed me that the Silverbacks front office is also not happy with the picture their new star pitcher is painting.

Charlie, our PR manager, was also on a conference call with us and suggested now may be the perfect time to start looking into outreach programs for my foundation I want to start like we've been talking about. I balked at the idea at first. I hate doing things just for the PR, but I might be able to kill two birds with one stone this way. She requested I send her a few of my interests so she can at least look around for some programs that I'd be interested in, instead of just doing it because I'm forced to. Not that I'm being forced exactly, but it was heavily recommended that I do something for my *image*.

Now I'm sitting at Kessler's house playing video games with Hudson while we wait to go to my parents' house for

Sunday dinner. Hanging out with Hudson has been the highlight of my day.

Being driven around like a teenager without their license has not. Having my driving privileges suspended until my court date is the turd on top of this shit sundae. I've been driving myself everywhere since the very day I turned sixteen. Having to rely on someone else to take me places does not sit well with me, but I'm trying not to let my mood ruin my time with Hudson.

"Uncle Judd, what's a DUI?" Hudson asks.

I whip my head to the side and look at Hudson, who has paused our game and is now staring back at me expectantly. Grabbing my glass off the table, I take a drink of my water, trying to collect my thoughts.

Kessler was right. My actions don't just affect me anymore. Shame burns through my stomach that I even have to have this conversation. I set my glass back down on the table and clear my throat. "Why do you ask?"

He lifts a shoulder, then drops it. "Mom was talking on the phone with Aunt Kara about it this morning, but when she saw me walk in the kitchen, she changed the subject."

Ah, so he thought he'd come to cool Uncle Judd for answers. I'm in enough trouble with my brother and his wife-to-be. I don't need to add to it. "Well, Hud, I think if your mom wanted you to know, she would have told you."

"Know what?" Kessler asks, coming into the game room with a very thick book I can't read the title of and sitting in the recliner next to the couch Hudson and I are sitting on.

Hudson turns in his seat slightly to look at Kessler. "I asked Uncle Judd what a DUI was."

Kessler shoots me a quick "I told you so" look, before turning his attention to Hudson. I can see the internal struggle on his face about how much he really wants to tell him. Kessler has taken to being Hudson's dad, like a fish to water and I only hope when I eventually have a family, I'm half the dad Kessler has become. Blowing out a breath, Kessler runs a hand through his hair, tugging at the ends. "It's something a person gets when they have had too much to drink and decide to drive and a police officer pulls them over."

"Okay... But why was Mom talking to Aunt Kara about it? She seemed pretty upset about it."

Kessler raises a single eyebrow directly at me and tips his head, giving me a "This one is on you" look.

It's my turn to blow out a breath. "Well Hudson, that's because I got a DUI last night."

After a few beats of silence, Hudson nods his head slowly, and I can see the wheels turning in his brain, trying to figure out what that means. "Did you have to wear handcuffs?"

I nod and try to shove down the shame that rises in my chest. I'm supposed to be someone Hudson looks up to and I feel like I've failed on an epic level.

Kessler clears his throat and sits forward, resting his elbows on his knees. "This doesn't mean Judd is a bad person, though." He looks at me for a beat before turning his attention back to Hudson. "Sometimes, good people make bad decisions. It's what they do after their mistake that matters."

Hudson nods again and un-pauses his game, now focusing on the screen. "Is there anything else you want to ask me?" I ask him. I want to make sure he has the right answers to any of the questions he may have.

Hudson shakes his head. "Not right now, but if I have more later, can I ask?"

"Anytime Hud," Kessler says, leaning back in the chair and opening the book he brought in with him.

"Whatcha reading?" I ask, still not able to see the cover. Kessler holds up the book and I squint, trying to make out the words, but all I can make out is a picture of a pregnant woman on the front. "I don't have my glasses. Is that a pregnancy book?"

Kessler lays the book back down on his lap and scratches

the back of his neck. "It is. Lucy got it for me after the–" He pauses and gives me a sheepish look. "Jogging incident. It's called *What to Expect When You're Expecting*. It tells you what is happening in the woman's body each month, and what development is going on with the fetus, or in our cases *fetuses.* It's...eye opening and has actually been really helpful."

I look at my brother as he looks back down at the book and continues to read. Awe and, if I'm honest, envy runs through me. I can't believe he's going to be a dad. Well, he's already a dad to Hudson, but he's going to have *babies.* I never realized until he met Lucy, how badly he wanted a family to call his own, and now here he is only six months later, and he not only has a fiancée and a son already, but he has two more on the way.

Something in my chest pangs, and I rub at it, willing it to go away. I'm not ready for that yet. I still have oats to sow. Not that there's been much of that going on lately, but still, I have plenty of time to set down roots.

I turn back to the screen and watch Hudson play *Mario Kart* when my phone pings with a text. Unlocking it, I see a text from Charlie.

CHARLIE

How do you feel about kids and dogs?

Charlie must have found a couple of programs for me already. Damn, she's fast, but she wouldn't be head of PR if she wasn't good at her job.

ME

I love being around both.

CHARLIE

Do you read?

If she only knew how extensive my book collection is. It's

not something I brag about, though; I keep the fact that I read under wraps. I was picked on in middle school and the first year of high school because I always had my nose in a book. The only people who know my love of reading is my family. Now if I'm on the road for away games, I read on the kindle app on my phone, so I can easily hide it. So instead of giving her the answer I want to give her, I play it cool.

ME

I read that message you sent me just fine.

Being a smart-ass has always been my go-to deflection.

CHARLIE

Some days I feel like I don't get paid enough to handle you jocks. Books Judd, do you read books?

Excitement builds inside of me. How awesome would it be if Charlie found me a program where I can be around books all day? *Play it cool, Judd, no one knows.*

ME

I mean I've read one or two.

Or hundreds....

CHARLIE

I think I found the perfect fit for you. Let me finalize details and I'll send you an email with all the information you need. Once you read it, just text me back if you think it's something you'd be into.

ME

Sounds good Charlie, thank you for doing this.

CHARLIE

No need to thank me, Judd, it's literally my job.

"What are you so giddy about over there?"

I look up from my phone to see Lucy padding into the room in black leggings and one of Kessler's old Silverbacks T-shirts that's tied at the side. She has dark rings under her eyes and her hair is a little disheveled. She looks exhausted. Guilt grips my chest. She's had enough to deal with being pregnant with twins. Now I've added to it with my stunt last night.

"Uh, Charlie was just texting me about a possible outreach program she thinks I would be a good fit with. Aren't you supposed to be taking a nap before we head to Mom and Dad's?"

Lucy rounds the chair Kessler is in and he opens his arms, lifting the book in one, without her even having to say a word. She sits next to him and pulls her legs up, draping them across his lap. Laying her head on his chest, she lets out a heavy sigh and closes her eyes. "I tried, but I couldn't seem to get comfortable. This is the only way I have been able to take naps lately."

Kessler lays the book on her legs, still reading, and drapes his other behind her, rubbing her upper back in small circles. "The doctor said her energy levels would get better in the second trimester, but that hasn't seemed to happen yet." He looks over at me, worry lines litter his face. Lucy had a rough first trimester, to say the least, with debilitating bouts of morning sickness. She even had to go into the hospital to get IV fluids, twice, because she couldn't keep anything down. The doctors said it was common with twin pregnancies, something about double the hormones.

"I'm literally only like a week and a half into the second trimester. Give it some time." She mumbles, already halfway asleep.

Common or not, Kessler has been a wreck and I know they've had a few disagreements about Lucy continuing to work, even if her workload has lightened a bit since going down to part time. Thankfully, since starting the second trimester, her nausea has calmed down a bit, but she's still in a perpetual state of exhaustion.

Soft snores erupt from where Lucy has taken residence in the oversized chair. Kessler's worried face transforms into one of pure adoration as he looks down at his now sleeping fiancée and places a kiss on the top of her head. "Can you text Mom and let her know we'll be over as soon as Lucy is up? I want her to get some sleep. I would do it, but my phone is currently under Sleeping Beauty."

"Sure thing Broski." I take my phone out and open my text thread to my mom.

ME

Lucy just fell asleep. Kessler wanted me to let you know we'll be over when she wakes up.

MOM

Not a problem. She needs her sleep.

That's the first text she's sent me that hasn't had the tone of yelling since this morning when she found out what happened. Maybe she's calmed down after having some time to mull it over.

MOM

And don't think you're off the hook Mister, this is just a minor delay in our talk.

Or not...

Lucy ended up only being able to sleep for 30 minutes before the urge to pee woke her from her slumber.

Now we're sitting around my parents' massive oak dining room table finishing up the pot roast Mom made. Nothing has been said about my 'incident' last night. Everything has either been about the party and how Lucy's feeling today, or about the wedding. I'm guessing my parents want to chew my ass out in private.

As soon as Hudson finishes his second helping of roast and mashed potatoes, Mom stands and starts clearing the table to make room for the dessert she's made. Lucy gets up to help but is immediately told to sit down by not only Mom, but Kessler, too.

"I'm pregnant, not an invalid," Lucy says, crossing her arms and sitting back in her chair with a huff.

"We never said you were dear." Mom tells her, in her reassuring mom voice. "I just know how tired you've been lately. The boys can help," she adds, nodding to Hudson and I.

Taking the hint, we both get to our feet and start piling dishes on top of one another, clearing the table in record time so we can get to the good part, dessert.

Mom brings out not one, but two pies.

"I wanted to try some new recipes out before Thanksgiving." She sets one pie down on the table that's chocolate with dollops of white cream piled into mountains around the rim. "That is a peppermint hot chocolate silk pie with marshmallow whipped cream." Setting the other one down, she says, "And this one is a pumpkin pecan pie with a caramel drizzle."

My mouth floods with drool at not only the sight of these masterpieces, but at the smell of them, too.

Come to daddy.

I reach forward to grab a plate when Mom slaps my hand, making me jerk it back. "What the hell, Mom?" I say, rubbing my stinging skin.

"You don't get pie until *after* our talk," she tells me, giving me a pointed look.

Kessler snickers from across the table and reaches for the chocolate pie. I kick my leg out, my foot hitting my target. He lets out a groan, and a muttered curse and reaches down to rub his shin.

"Boys!" Mom shouts, giving us both a pointed look. "I will take the pie from *both* of you if you don't knock it off."

"More pie for me," Hudson comments, swooping in and taking a piece from both pans before anyone can blink. This kid fits right in with us.

Lucy barks out a laugh and hands her plate to Kessler. He dishes her up one of each and hands it back to her, placing a kiss on her temple while running his hand over her barely there bump. God, they're adorable. I love it and hate it at the same time.

Mom watches them, a contented sigh escaping her.

Dad clears his throat and I turn my attention towards him. While Mom has been voicetress in her displeasure with me, Dad has been...quiet. He nods his head to the door that leads to the den and gets up from his seat. Taking that as my cue, I follow him in, Mom bringing up the rear.

Once all three of us are in, Mom shuts the door and takes a seat beside Dad on the well-worn sofa. I take the chair opposite of them and look around at the various pictures on the wall. Most of them are of Kessler and I throughout the years playing baseball. There's some from the family vacations we rarely got to take because both Kessler and I not only played baseball during school, we both played on summer and fall travel teams. Our parents never pushed us to play, only nurtured our drive and love for the game.

I take my eyes from the wall and settle them on the people who raised me, who sacrificed everything to make sure we were able to pursue our passions. Guilt consumes me and suddenly, pie doesn't sound so good.

How could I have done this to them?

Dad clears his throat again and sits forward on the couch, resting his elbows on his knees and steepling his hands. "Judd," he starts, but I stop him.

"Can I say something? Before you give me a well-deserved ass chewing?"

Mom and Dad look at each other, then back at me, both giving me a nod. Mom loops her arm though Dads and Dad turns his hand over, taking her hand. They've always been so in love, so together. Their love reminds me of Lucy and Kessler, and I wonder if I'll ever find something like that for myself.

Rubbing my hand across my chest to ease the never ending ache that has taken residence there, I take a breath and start, looking them both in the eyes. "I want to apologize to you both. I don't have any excuse for what I did. You raised me better than that, and to disappoint and embarrass you the way I did is inexcusable. I hope you can forgive me because I know it's going to take me a while to forgive myself for being that reckless."

Mom's the first one to break the silence that follows my apology. "Judd, Honey, we're not embarrassed. Disappointed? Yes. But not embarrassed. We just want to know what's going on."

I wish I had an answer for them, but I don't. Mainly because I have no idea what's been going on with me lately. "I'm, I, I really don't know. I guess I'm just feeling a little lost." And if I'm really being honest, lonely. But I decide not to tell my mom that because then it would be mission: Find Someone for Judd. And let's be honest, the last thing I need is for my mom to set me up.

"It'll happen for you too, Judd."

My eyes snap to my dad's. He's sitting there with a knowing look after giving me an answer to my unspoken question.

"What will happen for him?" Mom asks, curious eyes bouncing back and forth between us before realization crosses her face. "Oh Juddson, is that what this is about?" she asks softly.

Dad pats her hand and gets up from the couch. "Let's not get into this now, Mar. Let the boy tackle his demons before you start playing matchmaker." Mom looks at me. "Now, I don't know about you two, but I could use some pie." He gives me a wink and heads to the door. Mom stands with a concerned look, like she wants to say something more, but Dad pulls her along with him.

She reaches the door and turns to look back at me. "Everything's going to be alright Judd, we'll take on whatever happens next together."

My shoulders droop in relief and I release a breath I feel like I've been holding since seeing those red and blue lights last night. "Thanks, Mom."

"You coming? There might not be any pie left if we don't hurry."

My phone buzzes in my pocket. "I'm coming, I just need a minute," I tell her, reaching for my phone.

Once she leaves, I open the email Charlie promised to send. Reading through it, twice, I feel a spark of excitement. Opening my text thread to Charlie, I send her a text.

ME

I'm in.

CHAPTER 3

Amelia

TWO WEEKS LATER

"LENGTH OR GIRTH?" Hazel asks, handing me my as large as you can get, pumpkin spice cold brew and apple cider donut. Hazel opened Latte Daze three years ago, and I have been a regular since day one. We hit it off right away, and the rest is obviously history. While I love almost everything Hazel makes, her fall and winter menus are my favorite.

I love fall, and these seasonal sweet treats are just a bonus to the reasons why. Walking in the crisp air, watching the leaves change from green to vibrant, yellows, reds and oranges, honestly what's not to like? I don't even mind the ridiculous amount of rain we get, because on days like this, when it's sunny, beautiful and cold...the rain is worth it.

Taking a sip of my coffee, I hum with delight. "Hazel, you are a godsend." I just got back from a two-month book tour two days ago and jet-lag is still kicking my ass. Taking a bite of my donut, I moan in ecstasy. "Neither–everything is disappointing compared to this delightful, confectionary blessing," I tell her around a mouth full of donut.

Hazel snickers, "You can't fuck a donut." She wrinkles her nose. "Well, *you* can't." She pauses and looks over my shoulder at the only other person in the café at the moment. I follow her gaze, looking at the guy with a plain black baseball hat pulled low over his eyes, earbuds securely in his ears. He's messing around on his phone and doesn't seem to be paying attention. She looks back at me. "Anyway, answer. Which is it?"

I finish my donut and tip my head back and forth in thought. "As long as it doesn't have me questioning if it's in yet and faking my way through the whole thing, I'm not picky."

The guy behind me sputters and starts coughing. I turn around and see him mopping up what I assume is his coffee he spit out. I shrug and turn back around. Guess he was listening, after all.

"Such high standards," Hazel says dryly.

"Hey, it's not like I've been having mind blowing, make you forget your own name, sex like someone else," I tell her, giving her a pointed look.

Hazel smirks and pops a shoulder. "Don't hate the player, hate the game."

I laugh, rolling my eyes. I glance at my watch and realize if I don't take off soon, I'm going to be late. I'm going to the library early to meet with Gladys and Irene and the person who is supposed to help bring more eyes to my program. "Hey, can you put two more in a bag for me to take to Gladys and Irene? I'm sure they would appreciate it."

"Sure thing," Hazel says, popping two donuts in a bag and handing it to me.

"Thanks, Haze."

Taking the leash out of my belt loop, I look down at Bruno, my four-year-old blue merle Australian Shepherd I adopted when he was six months old. "Ready to go, buddy?" Bruno's ears perk and he looks up at me with his one blue eye, one brown eye. "Come on lazy bones, time to work." Bruno stands up and arches his back, stretching like a cat. He extends his neck up in another stretch, then sits back on his haunches with a grumble and a yawn.

"Oh, poor Bruno, do you needs a cookie to make it all better?" Hazel baby talks to him.

I roll my eyes and laugh. "You spoil him. No wonder he has such a complex."

Hazel reaches into the smaller case next to the main one and pulls out an oatmeal and pumpkin flavored bone shaped cookie, because not only does she serve humans, she caters to our four-legged friends too.

Coming around the counter, Hazel stands in front of Bruno, whose attention is now one hundred percent on the redhead holding his delectable treat.

"At least make him do something to earn it."

"He is. He's being undeniably adorable," Hazel argues, handing Bruno his cookie. Bruno takes it gently in his teeth, like the gentleman he is, and munches happily.

I shake my head but laugh. "Alright Bruno, we gotta beat feet. See ya tomorrow, Hazel."

Hazel waves and we head out the door, turning left in the direction of the library. It's only a few blocks away, and it's a nice enough day so we can walk.

A block in and I get the feeling of being followed. I glance over my shoulder and notice the same guy who was in the coffee shop is only a few feet behind me. He's looking down at his phone again and not at me, so why do I get the feeling he's following me? There's plenty of reasons he would be going the same way as me... right? Trying not to let my overactive imagination get the best of me, I keep trudging ahead.

When I finally reach the library steps, I take a quick look over my shoulder to see if the man is still following me. Not only is he behind me, but he's climbing the steps, too.

"Can I help you?" I ask, raising both my eyebrows at this man who seems to be following me.

He stops a couple of steps down from me and looks up. Forest green eyes meet my gaze. "No, but it sounds like you could use some help," he replies, not affected one bit by my attitude.

"Excuse me?"

"I heard you talking to your friend in the coffee shop back there. No one should settle for mediocre sex."

My cheeks instantly heat, and I take in the stranger in front of me. Dark-brown hair the color of espresso, curls out from under his baseball hat, like he's in need of a trim. His eyes have a tired appearance to them, like he's had a few sleepless nights lately. *Join the club.* Dark-brown scruff matching his hair covers his face, long enough to not qualify as a five o'clock shadow.

Who the fuck does this guy think he is? I'm about to ask him as much when he steps forward and offers me his hand.

"Judd Davis."

I look down at the hand he offered and see ink peeking out at me from beneath his sleeves. I stare back at him, but don't take his outstretched hand.

This is Judd Davis? Wow, he looks... different out of uniform–hotter, if that's possible.

"Did you follow me here to...offer me sex?"

The guy... Judd...snorts and drops his hand. "Honey, you would know if I was offering you sex."

What a cocky asshole.

"Don't call me Honey."

"You're right, honey is sweet."

Over this conversation and this guy, I turn and stomp up the rest of the steps. Bruno trotting happily at my side like nothing is wrong. Before I reach for the door, a body appears out of the corner of my eye and Judd moves past me and opens the door instead.

I stop and pop a hand on my hip. "Seriously, are you following me?"

"Don't think so highly of yourself," he says dryly. "I'm supposed to be here for a reading program."

A puzzle piece slides into place, and it dawns on me. "You're the ball player Charlie told me about."

Surprise passes through his face. "How do you know Charlie?"

I lift a shoulder and walk through the door he's still holding open for me. "Charlie and I have been best friends since college."

He follows me in, then stops, looking around. We're standing in the vestibule where the library branches off into different sections. He's obviously never been here before. I internally roll my eyes and take pity on the man. "Follow me. The children's area where my program is ran is this way."

His eyebrows raise in surprise before following me down the short hallway. "Your program? I thought this was the library's program."

I pause at the entrance and turn to him. "The library runs it, but I'm the one who created it."

He reaches past me and grabs the handle, opening this door for me too. His scent smacks me in the face, making my insides do a little flip.

Jesus, he smells good. Like coffee, cinnamon, and something else I can't quite put my finger on–pine maybe? Whatever it is instantly brings Christmas memories I've long forgotten rushing back to me.

"You okay?" he asks, staring down at me. At 5' 3", I'm an average-ish height for a woman, but the fact that I have to tilt my head up as far as I do says something.

A *big, tall, hot* something.

Bruno's cold, wet nose bumps against my hand, knocking me out of my trance. Giving myself a mental shake, I tear my gaze away from his and walk through the door. Needing to create some distance.

Get a hold of yourself Millie, he's just a man.

A very *attractive* man.

I can feel his gaze on my back as we make our way to the desk that's in the middle of the open room, where Gladys and Irene are prepping for the weekly reading session. Reaching the desk, I set the peach pastry bag down between the two women.

Gladys' eyes light up. "Is that what I think it is?" she asks, reaching for the bag and peering inside.

"Two apple cider donuts made fresh this morning," I announce, reaching down and unclipping Bruno's leash so he can wander about.

"You are a godsend," Irene says, peering over her sister's shoulder.

Gladys and Irene have been running the children's section of our town's library for the last six years. Both women are in their 60s and decided that they didn't want to retire and do nothing. So, when the library was threatening to close the children's part of the library due to the lack of funds and interest, Gladys and Irene stepped in and contacted me, hoping as a local and successful author, I'd help drum up interest. Which it did. The children's section became even more popular after I founded RUFF, Reading with Furry Friends. Don't ask what the 'U' stands for, it just sounds better with it.

A throat clears from behind me and both women look up from the pastry bag, eyebrows shooting up.

Judd comes around from behind me and offers his hand to the women. "I'm Judd Davis. Charlie arranged for me to come and help out here."

I suppress a groan. The funding for my program has been less than normal. Donations are down and one of the major grants we rely on just went to a different program. It's not cheap to take dogs from the shelter and put them through a training program so they can come read with kids. There are several factors that go into it, and while it makes them more adoptable, the shelter can't afford the training without our program.

So unfortunately, the ridiculously attractive man standing beside me is a necessary evil. When I confided in Charlie about my program not only unexpectedly losing funds, but my hesitation to continue with expanding said program, I never expected her to do something about it. I was coming to her as my best friend, not Charlie the PR goddess. So when she texted me a couple of weeks ago saying she had a solution that will not only hopefully solve my problem, but hers as well… I jumped on it, no questions asked.

I should have asked questions.

"Well, hello there," Gladys says, taking Judd's hand and giving it a shake. "I'm Gladys; this is my sister Irene. We run the children's part of the library and Millie's program."

Blushing, Irene moves up and takes Judd's hand after Gladys finally lets go. "Thank you so much for doing this, Mr. Davis. When Millie told us she might have a solution, we never thought it would be you."

That makes three of us, Irene.

"Please call me Judd," He says, releasing Irene's hand. Turning to me, he gives me a devilish grin. "Millie, huh?"

"My *friends* call me Millie. You can call me Amelia, or better yet, Ms. Morgan."

His grin grows wider, and I don't like what it's doing to my insides.

"Now Millie, I know you're stressed about this, but that doesn't mean you need to be rude to Mr., uh, Judd. He's here to help us," Gladys chastises me.

Knowing Gladys is right, I take a deep breath and let it out. "You're right," I tell her.

Plastering a smile on my face, I look up at Judd. "I'm sorry. That was rude of me. Let's try this again." I hold out my hand to him. Still looking amused, he takes it, and a tingle shoots up my arm and through my body.

Whoa.

A surprised look appears on his face, and I imagine it mirrors the one I'm currently sporting. Mentally giving myself a shake, I continue, "Hi, I'm Amelia. You can call me Millie. Thank you for taking the time out of your busy schedule to help us save RUFF."

I try to keep the sarcasm out of my voice for that last part. I know he's in his off season and probably has nothing going on. But Gladys is right, we do need him and his "celebrity status" if we're going to save RUFF. This program is too important to me to let my snarkiness get in the way.

Still holding my hand, Judd replies, "Pleasure to meet you, *Millie.*" Amusement twinkles in his stupidly beautiful eyes. "I really hope I can help bring some attention to your program." Even though he's a smart ass, I also know he's serious about helping the program.

An unspoken truce has been called between us, and he finally lets go of my hand when Irene clears her throat. "Now that we have all the...pleasantries out of the way. Shall we go over things before the kids and dogs get here?"

After going over the brief history of the program, and answering all Judd's surprisingly thoughtful questions, there's about ten minutes left before the dogs are scheduled to arrive. When we first started, the kids and dogs arrived at the same time and it took both groups so long to settle down, it cut into their actual reading time.

So, after a few tweaks, we decided the dogs should arrive first and settle in and then the kids follow suit about a half hour later. It seems to work better for both parties this way.

"I'm going to let Bruno out before the other dogs get

here." I tell no one in particular, standing from my chair and stretching. Hearing his name, Bruno's ears perk up and he jogs happily over to me from where he was laying and sits nicely in front of me, waiting for me to clip his leash onto his collar.

Once he's sniffed and done his business multiple times, we head back to the side door just as the van from the shelter shows up. Hoping out of the front of the van and greeting me with his megawatt smile is Jeremy, who runs the shelter side of the program. Without him, we wouldn't have the dogs we need for it.

"Millie! You're back!" he says excitedly, kneeling down and giving Bruno some attention. "How was the book tour?"

"It was great, but we're happy to be home," I tell him, watching Bruno continue to lap up the attention he's getting. "Some of us more than others, apparently."

Jeremy laughs his deep baritone laugh, bringing a smile to my lips. I've always thought Jeremy was attractive with his sandy-blond hair that always looks like it's in need of a trim, and his cornflower-blue eyes. He looks up at me, giving me his boyish smile, and I expect the butterflies I normally feel when he smiles at me. But nothing takes flight.

Must be the jet lag.

After giving Bruno one last pat, he gets up and heads to the back of the van and opens the doors, revealing six dogs waiting excitedly in their kennels to be let out.

Letting Bruno back into the fenced area, I walk over and grab two of the dogs Jeremy just put leashes on and take them to sniff around and do their business. Hearing the side door open behind me, I turn to hand the dogs off to Gladys or Irene, only to see Judd standing at the entrance.

"Need some help?" he asks, holding his hand out for the leashes.

"Uh, sure," I say, handing off the dogs. "Just let them sniff around for a few minutes. If they go number two, bags are there," I tell him, pointing to the bags near the gate to the fenced area.

Judd nods and takes the dogs. Returning to the van, I grab the next two dogs Jeremy hands me and he follows me out with the remaining two. When we enter the little grassy area, I see Judd kneeling down and giving belly rubs to Ruby, a beautiful tan and white 3-year-old pitty-mix and my favorite dog of the group.

My heart stutters at the sight and my feet freeze. While Ruby is a complete mush ball for the kids, she has a hard time trusting men. It took Jeremy months to get her to come to him without her cowering with her tail between her legs, which is why she hasn't been adopted yet.

Something slams into my back, and I stumble forward, almost tripping over the dogs, knocking me out of my trance.

"Oh shit, sorry Millie!" Jeremy exclaims, reaching out and grabbing me by an arm before I tumble to the ground.

Righting myself, I huff a laugh. "Thanks Jeremy. Sorry, I shouldn't have stopped so quickly."

"That's..." he starts, but the words die off as he looks ahead of me. "Holy shit, is that, is that Judd Davis?"

"Unfortunately," I mutter, letting the dogs pull me ahead.

Jeremy follows beside me, still in awe over the baseball god, his words not mine, in front of us. When we reach Judd, he looks up at me and smiles a wide, carefree smile, and my heart does a little flip-flop.

Stop that.

His eyes flick to Jeremy and he stands, much to Ruby's disappointment. He towers over Jeremy, dwarfing his almost six-foot frame. Holding out a hand, he introduces himself. "Jeremy, right? Judd. Nice to meet you." Realizing she's not going to get anymore belly rubs, Ruby rolls back to her feet and shakes.

Jeremy snaps to his senses and returns the shake. "Jeremey, uh, I guess you already knew that, though," he says with a little chuckle. He nods down to Ruby. "That's impressive. She's never let a strange man pet her, let alone rub her stomach. It took me months to earn her trust."

"I have a way with the ladies," Judd says, looking right at me and giving me a wink. A fucking wink. Who the fuck does this guy think he is?

Rolling my eyes, I turn and head back toward the door. Needing to be far away from this man.

CHAPTER 4

Judd

JESUS. *She's beautiful.*

No, not just beautiful. She's fucking *enchanting.*

The thought keeps popping into my head since the moment I saw her walk into the coffee shop. Ashen-blonde hair, long enough for me to wrap around my hand a few times. Blue eyes so sharp and bright; I feel like she's staring straight into my soul. And *fuck*, her smile? Her real smile, not the fake one she plastered on when she 'apologized' to me. No, the one she gives the people who mean something to her. That one would light a whole town on the darkest night.

I wonder if this is what Kessler felt when he first saw Lucy? Because fuck, I've never felt this before. Like she stole the breath right out of me. But I can't seem to stop saying stupid shit. Which is the reason she's storming off right now, giving me an amazing view of her tight little ass.

Jeremy chuckles. "Don't bother."

Prying my eyes from Amelia, I look over at Jeremy, who's smirking at me. "I'm sorry?"

He tips his head towards Amelia. "With Millie. I said don't bother. None of her relationships last more than a few months." He shrugs. "And if they do, they don't last past

Christmas. She's got some baggage and seems like no one can handle it."

We start back towards the gate where Amelia stormed off, all dogs having done their business. "What kind of baggage?" I noticed Bruno is wearing a service vest, but I haven't had the chance to ask why. Everyone has some type of baggage, some more than others, but what kind of baggage does that blonde firecracker have that seems to drive men away?

Jeremy shrugs and opens the gate. "I'm not sure. She's never told me. Whatever it is, seems like a deal breaker for everyone."

We head through the door leading to the library, and I tuck that information away to think about later. Once we get inside, it's all hands on deck, getting things ready for the kids to arrive. After setting out the dog beds, getting the refreshment table set with drinks and Halloween cookies, and making sure there are a variety of books for the kids to choose from based on their reading level, we have only a few minutes to spare before the kids arrive.

Earlier, when Amelia was explaining how the program works, she said they like to keep the groups small to limit distractions and for better one-on-one help. So, we're expecting six to eight kids tonight. Since tomorrow is Halloween, the library is decorated with pumpkins on the tables, bats and witches on brooms hanging from the ceiling, and a string of purple and orange lights is draped around the main desk.

Voices at the entrance catch my attention while I'm giving Ruby another belly rub. I wish I could have a dog, but my travel schedule during the season really doesn't allow for one. And it wouldn't be fair to the dog to have me practically abandon it nine months out of the year. Disappointing Ruby yet again when I stop the belly scratches, I get to my feet just as a handful of adults come in with kids in an array of different costumes.

There's Spiderman and Iron Man, a black cat with a sparkly black tutu, a cop, Harry Potter and a... Ninja/Ballerina? They all bustle in, happily chatting with one another. When they get to the main desk, Amelia claps her hands, quieting the group.

"I am so excited to see everyone, and what amazing costumes. Katie, I'm loving the Ninja/Ballerina combo." Her voice is soft and cheerful, completely the opposite of the tone she used with me. "Now, we have a special guest today," she says, gesturing towards me with a wave of her hand. "This is Judd Davis. He is a pitcher for the Salem Silverbacks and he's here to help with the program. Isn't that exciting?" she asks enthusiastically.

I have to give her credit. She sounds so excited, I almost believe it.

Only one of the kids, Iron Man, seems to recognize me. His eyes widen and his mouth opens a fraction after Amelia introduces me. His mom nudges him and whispers something into his ear. He reddens slightly and shoots his eyes away from me and back at Amelia.

"Parents, after we get the kids settled, Judd and I will talk to you about a journalist coming next week." The parents murmur their agreement and Amelia continues. "Alright guys, you know the drill! And we have a special treat for you after your 20 minutes of reading time is up!" she says excitedly.

The kids' voices rise, trying to guess what it may be, and Amelia raises a hand, making bunny ears with her two fingers and raising a finger to her lips with her other hand. Once the kids quiet back down, she continues, "Read first, surprise after. Now, go find your books."

The kids split off with their parents to the table with the books. Earlier in my meeting with the ladies, they explained each child has a specific reading level, and they make sure there are multiple options in each level for the child to choose from.

While the kids choose their books, the remaining adults

take the dogs to the beds laid out among the room and wait for the kids to join their assigned dog. Honestly, it's a really cool program and I'm really impressed with how it's run and organized.

Kneeling next to Ruby, giving her yet more scratches, Katie, the Ninja/Ballerina, joins me, sitting on the opposite side of the bed. Ruby moves from me and crawls across the bed, lying her head in the girl's lap. Releasing a giant sigh, like it's what she's been waiting for all week, Ruby closes her eyes as Katie begins to scratch her big head, not paying an ounce of attention to me.

"This is her favorite day of the week," Katie's mom comments, coming up beside me. I stand and she holds her hand out to introduce herself. "Jane, I just want to say thank you for coming to help. This program means everything to us." She looks at Katie, who is telling Ruby all about her day at school, and lowers her voice. "It would be such a shame if they had to shut it down. Katie has gained so much confidence in her reading, which has helped her self-esteem too. I'd hate for her to regress."

I return her shake. "I'll do everything I can to make sure that doesn't happen." Even if it means donating money myself, which I already planned to do. But if I can start a foundation that specifically supports the needs of this program, they could expand so other kids can benefit. I already know there's a waiting list for kids to join. There's just not enough funding to support them yet.

Once the kids are settled into their reading, Amelia gathers the adults at a table away from the kids. I take the seat next to her and she shifts slightly away from me, but not enough to be noticeable. I fight a grin and act like I don't notice. "Okay, so I wanted to chat with you all really quick while the kids are reading," she starts. "As you know, we've run into some funding issues as of late, especially with us not getting the grant we rely on to fund the training part of the program for the dogs. So that's where Mr. Davis–"

"Please, call me Judd," I interrupt.

Amelia gives me a tight smile. "That's where Judd comes in. His PR agent Charlie, who happens to be my best friend, connected him with my program in hopes Mr. uh, Judd's foundation would be a good fit and a new source of funding for us. In order to bring attention to the budding foundation *and* the program, Charlie suggested an article be published. We wanted to speak to you all first before just moving forward with it." She pauses to pass out papers to the parents. "These are consent forms giving the reporter permission to speak to and publish photos of your child for the article. There is absolutely *no* pressure to have the kids do this, but it would be beneficial."

Amelia pauses, just as Bruno pops up from his place on the floor beside her and thrusts his head into her lap. She lays her hand on his head and gives it a couple of strokes, while taking a deep breath and letting it out. Dots start to connect as Amelia gathers herself. "Sorry, I–" She clears her throat before continuing, "I wouldn't ask this of any of you if I didn't have to, but I really have exhausted every other resource I can think of."

Jane covers Amelia's hand with her own. "Of course we want to help. I think I speak for everyone when I say we would do anything to keep RUFF running." Jane looks around the table at all the parents, who are nodding their heads in agreement. Turning back to Amelia, she gives her a smile and squeezes her hand. "See, nothing to be anxious about. We're happy to help."

Blinking furiously, Amelia gives the parents a watery smile. "Thank you," she whispers.

Jane pats her hand again before changing the subject, asking everyone where they're taking the kids to Trick or Treat tomorrow, taking the attention Amelia is clearly uncomfortable with off her.

After the kids and parents leave, with special cookies Amelia had made courtesy of her friend from the café, and the dogs are loaded up with special cookies of their own, we finish cleaning up the refreshment table before Gladys and Irene shoo us out of the library despite our protests to help.

Amelia and Bruno head out the doors and down the steps first and *surprise* turn the same direction that I need to go to get to my apartment. Falling back and slowing my steps, I decide to enjoy the view of the fiery little blonde in front of me as she struts down the sidewalk with her dog. I could have driven today since I got my license back yesterday thanks to RUFF also serving as community service but seeing as it's one of the last nice days for a while and the fact that I only live ten minutes from here, I decided to walk and let my mind wander.

Up ahead I see Amelia and Bruno disappear around a corner, the same corner I have to turn at too. You know the feeling you get when you realize something that you can't believe is happening, but. It. Actually. Is.

Yeah, that's the one I'm getting too.

I turn the corner and look ahead through the throngs of people ahead of me, but I don't see the tiny blonde and her hairy sidekick. A small wave of disappointment rolls over me and I give myself a shake.

Get it together Davis. She doesn't even like you.

I chuckle to myself; wouldn't that be a hilarious coincidence though? Well, I would think it's hilarious. Her, not so much. I reach the intersection and wait for the little crossing guy to make his appearance before I cross. Once I'm safely across the street, I dig my phone out and see a text from Charlie waiting for me.

CHARLIE

Well, how did it go? Do you think this program will be a good fit for you and your foundation?

ME

I do. I think it's a brilliant idea. There's only one problem.

CHARLIE

What's that? Tell me how I can help.

I snort. I don't think there's any helping the hate Amelia has for me. I tell Charlie just as much.

ME

I don't think you can fix this, Charlie. It seems Miss Morgan has taken a disliking to me.

Dislike is an understatement.

CHARLIE

Oh, Um. I'll talk to her. She's been under a lot of stress lately. I promise, it's probably not you.

I can guarantee it's me.

ME

Don't stress it, Charlie. I can deal with Amelia's attitude. And I'm absolutely all in with the program, so let's get that reporter booked for next week.

CHARLIE

You're a Godsend Judd. This will take a huge stress off of Amelia's shoulders. She'll be in better spirits next week. You'll see.

I doubt that, but I decide to let Charlie believe it will. Pocketing my phone after confirming a few more details with Charlie about the interview next week, I enter my building and look up. That feeling I was talking about earlier? Yeah, it's back and confirmed.

Standing right in front of the doors I just walked through is none other than Amelia Morgan, and she does not look happy to see me.

CHAPTER 5

Amelia

"YOU HAVE GOT to be fucking kidding me," I growl when I see the infuriatingly hot baseball player I thought about the entire walk home saunter through the doors of my building like he owns the place. "Seriously? Are you stalking me? Do I need to call the police?"

Judd's lips tip up into a smile. "As much as I enjoy handcuffs, I prefer to be the one using them."

I stare at him, not only because I'm shocked that came out of his mouth, but because I'm surprised at the way my body perked up at the suggestion.

I open my mouth to tell him off when Marty, my doorman, comes over from the desk.

"Miss Morgan, Mr. Davis, is there a problem?"

"Marty I–."

Wait, *Mr. Davis? No.*

"Marty, do you *know* this man?" I ask, praying that what I'm thinking isn't true. The universe wouldn't be that cruel, right? *Right!?*

Marty visibly swallows and looks between the baseball god, *Fuck, stop. No Amelia.* Judd, his name is Judd. He looks between *Judd* and me before continuing. "Well, yes, Ms.

Morgan. He lives in the penthouse. He moved in while you were on your book tour."

I swear I hear brakes screeching and the world coming to a stop as the truth bomb Marty just dropped settles over us.

No, there's no way. I must still be asleep, and this is just some twisted dream I'm having because I'm still jet lagged. There is absolutely no way this infuriatingly gorgeous man with 'fuck me' eyes, who is not only good with kids but also good with dogs with major trust issues, is living in *MY* apartment building. Does God really hate me this much?

"What's the matter, Sugar? Cat got your tongue?" Judd asks, grinning down at me with a sinful smirk.

And what is with his damn pet names? "I thought you said I wasn't sweet. Sugar sounds awfully sweet to me," I shoot back. Jesus, *why* am I even engaging in this conversation?

Marty's eyes volley back and forth between us, worry creasing his brow. Bruno also looks between us before he lets out a soft whine.

"Is he signaling you for something?" Judd asks suddenly, his playful tone gone. He takes a step forward and stares at me with...concern?

"What? Oh, no. He's just sensitive to confrontation." I reach down and pat Bruno's head. "It's okay buddy. Nothing to get upset about," I reassure him.

Yeah, Amelia, nothing to get upset about.

Judd takes another step forward and kneels down. "May I?" he asks, looking up at me. An image of Judd on his knees, *naked,* pops into my head and my mouth goes dry. I give him a nod, not trusting myself to speak.

He holds a hand out to Bruno and lets him sniff it. "I'm sorry buddy, I didn't mean to upset you," he says softly. Bruno sniffs his outstretched hand before nosing it and pushing his head into his hand for a scratch.

Traitor.

Judd runs both hands down his neck and roughs up his

scruff, letting out a deep laugh that makes my stomach flip when Bruno's tongue snakes out of his mouth to lick his cheek.

"What do you say, big guy? Am I forgiven?" Bruno licks his cheek again, getting another laugh out of Judd.

Marty clears his throat, making me jump. I forgot he was standing there. "Is everything okay, then, Ms. Morgan?"

I eye Judd as he stands and tucks his hands back into the front pockets of his jeans, looking at me expectantly.

Turning to Marty, I give him a smile. "Yes Marty, we're fine. Thank you. Sorry for the disruption."

Marty dips his head and gives us one last look before he heads back over to the desk.

I turn and head to the elevators, with Bruno reluctantly following along, without giving Judd another look. I need a hot bath and a large glass of wine. Maybe I'll just bring the whole damn bottle with me. Turning the corner where the elevators are tucked into the back of the building, I stop and suppress a groan. I'm definitely going to need the whole damn bottle.

One elevator has an 'Out of Order' sign strewn across the entrance. Which means I'll now be sharing an elevator with the sexy man that just appeared at my side.

Giving me a smirk, he hits the call button on the wall. "Going up?" he asks, leaning his shoulder against the wall and crossing his arms. It should be illegal for someone to look that good in a simple black henley. His muscular arms stretch the fabric to within an inch of their life.

His chest rumbles with a chuckle. "My eyes are up here, Cupcake." I feel my cheeks flame while I drag my eyes from his arms, up over his defined chest and to his warm green eyes that are dancing with humor.

Busted.

The elevator pings, indicating its arrival, knocking me out of my trance.

The doors open and Judd motions me in. "Ladies first."

Mentally giving myself a shake, I lift my chin and walk straight into the elevator and tuck myself into the corner, trying to keep as much distance as I can in this tiny box. Judd follows me in and turns to the panel. "What floor?"

"Ten," I say, pulling my phone out of my pocket, so I have something to do other than stare at Judd.

Judd hits the ten and puts his phone up to the screen and taps the PH button, then turns towards me as the doors close, sticking his hands back in his pockets and leaning against the side of the elevator. "So, what type of service dog is Bruno?" he asks, nodding towards him. Bruno's ears perk up at his name and his tongue flops out of his mouth as he happily pants beside me.

I pull my bottom lip into my mouth and bite down. I hate this question. Most people roll their eyes when I tell them he's an emotional support animal, like I'm just using it as an excuse to take him everywhere with me, when in fact he's not a regular support animal. "He's, uh, an emotional support animal," I tell him, looking him in the eye, wondering if he'll do the same. But to my surprise, he doesn't.

"What's he trained to indicate?" he asks, completely shocking the hell out of me.

"He, uh. I–" I stumble over my words, my mind trying to process the fact that Judd's not judging me like so many people have before. I take a breath before trying to answer him again. "I have anxiety, severe anxiety, and he can sometimes stop me from going into a full-blown attack by bumping me with his nose."

Judd nods again. "So when he bumped you at the library, he was trying to prevent an oncoming attack?"

I drop my eyes and nod. Embarrassment taking over that I was on the brink of an attack at the library and that Judd of all people noticed. Usually the library is a safe space, but between the stress of my program being at risk of shutting down and the stress of traveling for my book tour, my nervous system was already maxed out.

Judd closes the short space between us and reaches out, gripping my chin and tipping it up to make me look at him. His delicious scent invades the small space between us. "Don't ever be embarrassed about that," he whispers. "Do you understand?"

My breath catches in my chest and my heart rate skyrockets like it does when I'm anxious, but this time it's not the anxiety making it race. It's the zap of energy I feel when Judd touches me.

"I need to hear you say it, Amelia. Do you understand that is *nothing* to be embarrassed about?"

"Y-yes," I manage to whisper.

"Good." He drops my chin and steps back to his place against the wall just as the elevator comes to a stop. The elevator dings and the doors open, waiting for me to make my exit.

On wobbly legs, I convince my feet to move and leave the elevator, turning around just in time to see Judd give me a wink before the doors close completely and continue its ascent to the penthouse.

Leaving me wondering,

What the hell just happened?

A half bottle of wine later, I'm soaking in the tub, still replaying what happened in the elevator.

What the fuck *was* that?

I take a sip of my wine when my phone pings, announcing a text. Wiping my soapy hand on my towel, I set my wineglass down and grab the phone off the table next to the tub and unlock the phone, reading the group text.

CHARLIE

So how did today go? Judd mentioned you not liking him? Did he do something?

I sit up so fast, water threatens to slosh over the edge. He tattled on me to Charlie?

ME

He tattled on me? Wow, I did not expect that. Was his ego damaged?

I set my phone back down and pick my wine glass back up as my phone pings again.

HAZEL

Uh-oh, did the meeting at the library not go well?

CHARLIE

He didn't tattle. I asked him how it went and he straight up said you didn't like him. And knowing you, something set you off. Sooo, what happened?

ME

He looks… different out of uniform.

HAZEL

Oh do tell.

HAZEL

GIF eating popcorn

CHARLIE

uh, yeah I guess? I don't really notice? Or see how this has anything to do with you having an issue with him. He's a really nice guy Millie, besides his brother, he's probably one of the kindest guys in the league. So, what gives?

Great, of course he is.

ME

Hazel, remember that guy that was in there this morning when I swung by?

HAZEL

chokes on pretend popcorn NO! It wasn't!

ME

Oh, it was.

CHARLIE

I feel like I'm missing something... Video chat!

ME

I'm in the bathtub.

CHARLIE

We were roommates in college. I've seen it all, Millie.

I'm just about to send a text telling her Hazel hasn't, when my phone rings requesting a video chat.

I sigh and gather as many bubbles as I can to cover my boobs before accepting the call.

"Ladies," I say before I'm cut off by Charlie.

"Spill, woman, what happened at Hazel's this morning?"

"Well, hello to you too," I say, taking a sip of my wine.

Beep, beep, beep sounds from my phone making me look at Hazel's half of the screen. "Hazel, are you actually making popcorn?" I ask and I see her pulling a bag out of the microwave.

"What? It sounded good after I sent that text." She shrugs.

My stomach rumbles at the suggestion of food and I realize I haven't eaten anything since this morning. I also realize I'm going to have to order in because I still haven't gone grocery shopping since getting back into town.

"Are you going to answer my question?" Charlie asks, pouring her own glass of wine.

"Let me order dinner first. I still don't have food in the apartment, and I haven't eaten since Hazel's." Clicking over to my browser, I type in the name of my favorite Chinese place and order enough food to feed a family of four. I have about 20 more minutes of soaking time before my food should arrive.

Clicking back over to my video chat, I see both women staring at me, waiting for me to spill the tea.

"So where were we?" I ask innocently.

"You were going to tell Charlie about how you announced you have a shitty sex life while at the café to none other than Judd Davis."

I sink down further in the tub as Charlie chokes on her mouthful of wine. "You did WHAT!?"

Hazel and I spend the next couple of minutes telling her about our conversation at the counter this morning and how we didn't think he was listening, which fun fact, apparently, he was.

"So, is that the problem?" Charlie asks, sounding like it's not much of a problem.

"Wellll, not exactly," I say, taking another sip of wine. "I might have accused him of offering me sex."

Hazel barks out a laugh and Charlie stares at me like I have three heads.

"To be fair," I explain before Charlie strokes out. "What are the odds the guy in the café turns out to be the same guy I need help from? Plus, like I said in my text, he looks different out of uniform," I explain the rest of the events that happened on the library steps before stopping to finish off the rest of my wine.

"I have to give you that, Millie. I served the guy, and I didn't even recognize him. You can't fault her on that, C," Hazel says in my defense before shoving another handful of popcorn into her mouth.

Charlie pinches the bridge of her nose and blows out a breath. "Okay, besides all of that. What seems to be the *actual* problem? Are you embarrassed? Is he mad? I'm still lost here Millie."

You and me both sister.

"The problem is *Charlie*, he fucking lives in my building! I found that gem out after getting back from the library today and threatened to call the cops on him for stalking before I knew he lived *in the penthouse*. To which he told me *he* prefers to be the one to use the handcuffs."

Both women stare at me with matching shocked looks on their faces.

"No one's going to say anything?"

"You lucky bitch," Hazel says finally, while Charlie still stares at me in silence.

"I don't see the lucky part of this Haze."

"He wants to fuck you," she says, like it's the most obvious thing in the world.

"I don't think so. I think he just enjoys fucking *with* me. There's a difference." I don't tell them about the elevator. I hold that piece of information back until I can wrap my head around it more.

"Do you want me to find him a different program? I know it would leave you back at square one, but I don't want you to be uncomfortable," Charlie says, worry lacing her voice.

I sigh. "No, despite us butting heads, I can tell he actually truly cares about it and is a really good fit for it." I sit up and reach for the wine bottle, dumping the rest into my glass.

"Plus, he made friends with Ruby." Both women gasp. They know all about Ruby and how much it pains me I can't adopt her and haven't found her the absolute perfect home yet, either.

"Maybe he can adopt her!" Hazel says excitedly.

I lean my head back against the tub. "I just don't think that would work with his travel schedule during the season. Plus, how would Ruby feel to get adopted, then sent somewhere else off and on throughout the year? It's just too chaotic for a rescue dog, especially one with trust issues like hers."

Charlie nods in agreement. "Our schedule is insane and it truly wouldn't be fair to her."

Hazel sighs. "Well, it was a good thought, at least."

"Look on the bright side Hazel, maybe this means she's coming out of her shell more and can be adopted soon."

My phone pings with a text. Opening it, I see it's Marty from the front desk, letting me know my food is here.

"Ladies, my food is here. I'm going to go eat my weight in Chinese food now."

"Hey Millie, before you go, are you sure you're okay with this? I can find something else for both of you if it's too much."

I don't even need to think about it. "I'm sure, Charlie. I feel better after talking with you guys. After the interview next week, maybe he'll just be one of those silent investor types and all I'll have to do is avoid him at my apartment."

Really, how often could we run into each other? After the other elevator is fixed and if I use the stairs more than I currently do, I bet I hardly see him.

CHAPTER 6

Judd

I FUCKING LOVE THE HOLIDAYS. Yeah, I know, Halloween isn't *technically* a holiday, but it really is like the kickoff that starts the entire season. This year's Halloween looks a little different with me not going out, but at least I still get to dress up.

I hit the button to call the elevator up to my floor and check out my costume in the mirror in the hallway. Hudson chose the theme this year after watching *Pirates of the Caribbean* last month and I'm not mad about it. I adjust the parrot on my shoulder because what is a pirate without his salty parrot? The doors open and I walk in, hitting the button to the parking garage. As the doors close, I can't help but wonder if Amelia is going out tonight too, and who she's going with, and does she take Bruno?

Consumed with too many questions and no answers, I'm jerked out of my thoughts when the elevator dings and stops at the next floor. I look to see where we stopped, only to be slightly disappointed it's not the floor I'd hoped it was. The doors open revealing a woman standing there with a princess and a Ninja Turtle. The mom gives me a warm smile as I move over to make room as she ushers them inside and hits the button for the lobby.

"What are you?" the Ninja Turtle asks. He has to be around six or seven, and I can see he's missing one of his front teeth when he talks.

"Arrrgh, I'm a pirate," I say, kneeling down so I'm at his level. "And what might you two be?" I ask in my best pirate voice. The princess hides behind her mom and peeks out to look at me, but doesn't answer. Her brother, however, is much braver and answers me loudly.

"I'm Donatello the Ninja Turtle. My sister's a princess," he says, pointing to his sister.

"Inside voice baby, we don't want to make everyone deaf," she says, giving me an apologetic smile.

"Sorry," he says, lowering his voice and dropping his chin like he's embarrassed.

"Ah, it's ok buddy. I'd be excited too if I had a costume as cool as yours," I reassure him, giving him a wink.

He brightens up and points at my parrot. "What's his name?"

"You know, I didn't give him one. Do you think you could help me with that?"

The kid's face brightens, and he turns to his mom like he's asking permission. She nods encouragingly, and he turns back to me. "Can my sister help?"

"Of course, bud."

He turns to his sister, and they whisper back and forth, not so silently, until they seem to agree on a name.

"We like Petey."

I chuckle and nod. "Arrrgh, Petey's a fine name for a parrot."

The kids both giggle. "Why do you talk like that?" the boy asks.

"That's how we pirate's talk."

The kids giggle again and the elevator dings indicating

we've made it to the lobby. I stand and gesture for the mom and kids to go first when the doors open. She thanks me and ushers her kids out. They both yell "Happy Halloween!" at me as they leave the elevator.

"Happy Halloween! I hope you get lots of candy!"

I look around the lobby before the doors close and see it's packed with kids and parents, all getting ready for an evening of mischief. I smile to myself as the elevator takes me down to the garage, at the memories of many Halloweens I enjoyed as a kid.

A level later, I'm out of the elevator and making my way to my blacked-out Jeep Gladiator. Kessler told me it's one of the ugliest vehicles he's ever seen when I came to their house after purchasing it to celebrate signing my contract with the Silverbacks. I told him it was a good thing I didn't value his opinion on my vehicles, because he's never liked any of my cars.

A beep of a car echoes throughout the garage as I'm walking to where my car is, and I look up to see my favorite little blonde bombshell making her way over to me. She hasn't noticed me yet as she carries on a conversation with Bruno. She's dressed in a pair of black workout pants that look like they were painted on, and a sweater that says, *"There's nothing I can't do except reach the top shelf. I can't do that."*

A laugh erupts from my chest, startling Millie. She looks up and her face morphs from startled, to annoyed, to...heated, once she lays her eyes on me. I look down to where she's staring and notice my ruffled pirate's shirt has gaped open more than I intended it to, showing off the top of my hard-earned abs. Instead of fixing my shirt, I leave it, liking the way her eyes rake over me hungrily. "Like what you see, Muffin?"

My voice breaks the trance my body seemed to have over her, and she wrinkles her nose. "Muffin? Ew, please don't use that one again."

My eyebrows lift in surprise. "Oh, so you *do* like the pet names I call you?"

"No, but out of all of them, that is the worst one so far. Come on Davis, you can do better than that."

Challenge accepted.

Striding across the garage until I'm next to her, I lower my voice, "You're right, I can do *much* better." She visibly shivers at the suggestion in my voice before regaining her composure, a cool unbothered mask slipping into place.

"That's yet to be proven," she tells me before continuing her path towards the elevator. "Nice sword. by the way," she shoots over her shoulder.

"Probably the nicest one you've ever seen," I shoot back, liking this game we're playing.

She shrugs and looks at me over her shoulder, giving me a playful smirk while she waits for the elevator to arrive. "I've seen better."

Oh, I highly doubt that.

"Unlikely."

The elevator doors open, and she steps in, turning around to face me. "Awfully sure of yourself, aren't you, Davis?" she says, before pressing a button on the panel.

"You know it, Sweet Cheeks," I tell her and she wrinkles her nose again and shakes her head before the door closes, telling me that one's off the table too.

I laugh and head to my Jeep. Climbing in, I realize one thing I *am* sure about is that I'm one hundred percent committed to seeing if this playful banter between us is the start of something more.

I walk into Kessler and Lucy's about twenty minutes later with a smile still on my face from the run in with Millie.

"Hey Judd," Lucy greets me from the massive island in the

kitchen. When Kessler had this house remodeled, he kept it a secret from Lucy and asked Lucy's best friend, Kara, for help. Kara sent Kessler a link to Lucy's Pinterest board that she had made over the years of what her dream house would look like, and even during their 'break', made sure every dream off of her board came true.

"Hey Luce, how are you feeling?"

"I'm fine, Judd. I wish everyone would stop asking me that damn question," she snaps.

My eyebrows shoot up and I involuntarily take a step back, slipping my foot back into my shoe. I've never heard Lucy snap, ever, at anyone, in the six months that I've known her.

Sighing, she throws the dish towel she's holding onto the counter and rests her elbows on the counter, propping her chin up with one hand. "I'm sorry, Judd, I didn't mean to snap. These pregnancy hormones are no joke, and I have *twice* as many coursing through me. But I swear if your brother doesn't back off a little bit, I'm going to be a widower before I can even say 'I do'."

I snort and finish taking my shoes off, setting them onto the rack. No need to have Lucy pissed off at me for not putting my shoes away. "Just say the word Luce, and I'll marry you right now," I joke.

"Quit trying to steal my fiancée," Kessler grumbles, coming into the kitchen, dressed similar to me, sans the parrot and partially unbuttoned shirt. He rounds the island and places a kiss on Lucy's temple. "Feeling–" he starts, and I stop him before he can finish.

"I wouldn't finish that question if I were you!" I yell, startling him.

"Jesus Judd, why are you yelling at me?" he says, looking between me and Lucy, who's laughing. "What did I miss?"

"I was just telling Judd that I might take him up on his offer," Lucy says, smashing her lips together, trying to keep a straight face.

Never missing a chance to fuck with my brother, I join in on the fun. "Sorry brotato, I think I've finally convinced Lucy who the better looking, funnier, smarter brother is," I say, walking into the kitchen and throwing my arm around Lucy's shoulders, who to my surprise, snuggles into me and turns her face into my chest. I can feel her shoulders shake and I do my best not to break character by placing a kiss on the top of her head. I look up at Kessler, who is giving us a shocked look. Deciding to dig in a little further, I add, "Not to mention who has the bigger–"

"Ooookay, no," Lucy says, moving out of my embrace and back into Kessler's. "I don't want to hear about my future brother-in-law's dick."

I hold my hands up in surrender. "Fair enough. I just wanted to see how far I could get before Kessler lost his shit."

"Always the instigator, aren't you?" she says, lightly backhanding my arm.

"Yeah, he's always been a little shit," Kessler says, pulling Lucy into him more.

"Oh, don't get your panties in a bunch, we were just messing with you. Actually, you should be thanking me," I tell him, moving to the fridge and grabbing a bottled water.

Kessler snorts and turns both him and Lucy towards me, leaning his back against the counter. "For trying to steal my fiancée...*again*?"

"No, for *saving your marriage.* Lucy told me if you don't stop asking her every five minutes about how she's feeling, she's going to be a widower before she can even say I do," I tell him and give him a pointed look. "Back off the little mama."

Kessler looks over Lucy's shoulder. "Is that true?"

Lucy sighs and leans back against him. "I know you mean well, but how would you have felt if I had known you when you first injured your shoulder and I asked you day in and day out, *multiple* times a day, how you were doing?"

"Annoyed," Kessler mumbles.

"Exactly. Now, I know you're doing it because you love me and these babies, but can we limit the amount of times you get to ask me that question to like three times a day? Is that acceptable to you?"

Kessler nods and leans down, giving Lucy a kiss. He moves his hand down to Lucy's slight bump and she covers his giant hand with her much smaller one; her ring glittering back at me under the lights. I catch myself staring at them and feel like I'm intruding on an intimate moment.

"I'm going to go find our other deckhand," I say, moving out of the kitchen and down the hall to give Kessler and Lucy some privacy.

"He's in the game room," Kessler calls to me.

Making a left instead of a right, where Hudson's room is, I find him playing *Mario Kart*.

"'Sup broski?" I say, plopping down on the couch next to him, jostling Petey around. I twist the cap off my water and guzzle down half of it.

"Hey, Uncle Judd," he says, pausing his game to look at me. "Nice parrot."

"Thanks. I felt like it was a nice touch." I nod to the screen. "Wanna play teams until Kade gets here?" Kessler and I are taking Hudson and Kade Trick or Treating tonight, while Lucy and Kara stay home to have a girl's night.

"Sure!" Hudson exits out of his screen, and I grab the other controller off the charger. We end up playing three rounds before Kade joins us in the game room and we turn everything off to head out.

Lucy and Kara take tons of pictures of us before shooing us out the door so they can start their movie.

We settle into Kessler's truck and head off to one of the neighborhoods that apparently has the best candy.

"So," Kessler starts, looking at the boys in the rearview mirror and seeing they're occupied with their own conversation. "How was the thing at the library yesterday? Is it something you're interested in?"

An image of a feisty Amelia pops into my head, and I smirk. "Very."

Kessler cocks an eyebrow at me. "Why do I feel like you're not talking about the foundation?"

I look over my shoulder and lower my voice. "I am...for the most part."

"Fuck Judd. *Please* tell me you didn't chat up one of the moms. That's a conflict of interest."

I huff a laugh. "Says the guy who pursued the coach of the Little League team he volunteered to help. Pot meet kettle."

"That was different. I volunteered to help because she wouldn't let me take her to dinner to thank her for getting me out of my batting slump. I was already interested in her *before* that."

Kessler slows down and flips on his blinker, waiting to turn into the housing development just a few miles down the road from their house.

"You know, you never really told me what drew you to Lucy and how you knew she was the one."

Finally, there's a break in the traffic and Kessler turns down the street, stopping behind a line of cars letting kids out. Turning around, he addresses Kade and Hudson. "Boys, I'm going to let you out here so you can start. We're going to go find a place to park and then we'll come find you, okay?"

"Okay!" the boys parrot back in unison, both bailing out of the truck and slamming their doors. Kessler watches them for a second, making sure they both make it to the sidewalk before driving ahead, looking for a spot to park.

"I should have taken Lucy's car. It'd be easier to park." He whips his head to me and gives me a pointed look. "Don't tell her I said that. She suggested it earlier, and I told her I'd be fine."

I shake my head and chuckle as we slowly follow the trail of cars, who are probably also looking for spots to park.

"And to answer your question, there was an unexplainable energy that I felt when I touched her. Still is."

"What?"

"You asked what drew me to Lucy."

"Oh." I think back to yesterday and the zap of energy I felt when Amelia and I shook hands. "That's it? There's just energy?" Not convinced that's all it was.

He scrubs a hand down his face, scratching his beard. "No. When I was around her, every unsettled feeling I was having about baseball just...stopped. She calmed me, made me want things I didn't think I'd ever have." He chuckles. "Plus, she wanted nothing to do with me and what man doesn't love a little challenge?"

I nod my head, thinking about how Amelia also wants nothing to do with me.

We make it another block before we finally luck out and come upon someone pulling out of their spot. Kessler puts the truck in park and turns to me. "So, *is* it one of the moms?"

I shake my head. "No, it's the woman who founded the program. Millie, she–" I can't help but chuckle. "She's not really a fan of mine. Although we did have a better interaction in the parking garage today than at our first meeting."

Kessler gives me a confused look and I decide to explain everything that happened leading up to today's conversation with her in the garage.

"Oh shit," Kessler says when I finish telling him everything.

"Yeah, I'm not sure where to go from here, but I do know she's the first woman to catch my attention in a long while, and I want to explore that. I'm tired of the one-night stands and women who only want me for my status."

"Aww, is little Juddy growing up?" Kessler asks, reaching over and pinching my cheek.

"Fuck off," I tell him, slapping his hand away from my face and getting a laugh out of him.

"Don't ignore that feeling though," Kessler tells me, turning off the truck and pocketing his keys. "But don't move too fast either."

"Says the man who practically told Lucy a week into knowing her you loved her."

"That wasn't me, that was Mom," he says, sounding a smidge defensive. "Anyway, why don't you talk to Lucy when you come over for poker night? She might be able to give you some insight on how to proceed with this, get her version of things, and why she felt the way she did. I'm not saying that Millie has the same reservations as Lucy did, but she might be able to help you figure out where to go from here."

I nod. That might not be a bad idea at all. I clap Kessler's shoulder. "Thanks man, I'll do that."

He nods and we get out of the truck and start walking back towards where we left the boys. "Who gave you your advice when you didn't know how to proceed with Lucy?"

Kessler looks at me, and a huge shit-eating grin breaks out over his face. "Duke fucking Keller."

Duke? Color me shocked.

CHAPTER 7

Amelia

THE DOORS close on the image of the sexy pirate I leave standing there smirking at me in the parking garage.

So much for not running into him.

Not even twenty-four hours into finding out we live in the same building and boom, there he is in all his sexy pirate glory. Abs and all. *And* he caught me looking, so I had to deflect the fact that he is the sexiest fucking man I have ever laid my eyes on with what I deflect everything else that makes me uncomfortable in my life, humor.

Ok and *maybe* there was a little flirting, but honestly can you blame me? I haven't had sex in *months,* and the things that man does to my body with just a look. I pinch the front of my sweater and pull it from my body a few times to get the air flowing. He makes me hot and bothered without even touching me.

But I can't let him know I'm attracted to him.

One, because he is *way* out of my league.

Two, he's now involved with my program for the library, and I would *never* do anything to jeopardize that.

Three, because... I'm broken.

I've never been able to make a relationship work for longer

than eight months. But we're not going to get into that right now.

The elevator opens on my floor, and I step out, Bruno following happily beside me. I took him for an extra-long walk this afternoon to make up for him having to stay home tonight while I go out with Charlie and Hazel to *Ignite* for their annual Halloween party. I don't usually go out, *thank you anxiety*, but I feel safe with Charlie and Hazel and the alcohol I will be consuming won't even give my anxiety a chance to flare its ugly head. Plus, I really need a night to just let loose after months of stress over the library and book tour.

Unlocking my door, I enter my apartment and unclip Bruno's leash and take off his vest. Tossing my keys on the counter along with my shoulder bag. I look at the clock and see I only have an hour until Charlie and Hazel arrive so we can get ready together. We're not even leaving for the club until nine, but we're going to pregame before we go. Mostly *I'm* going to pregame before we go. We figured out if I have a couple drinks in me before we go out, the less likely I am to back out or freak out before we leave.

Is it the healthiest way to cope? Probably not, but my therapist advised me not to drink when I take my 'emergency panic pills' as I like to refer to them as, and if I'm going out, I'm drinking. So, this is my compromise to be able to be a somewhat normally functioning twenty-nine-year-old and go out with my friends. Seeing I'm going to be short on time if I don't get moving, I give Bruno his dinner before I jump in the shower to get ready for a night of drunken festivities.

Showered, shaved, and still in my robe. I hear obnoxious knocks on my door as I finish blow drying my hair. Knowing those knock's, I head to the door and open it to reveal Charlie and Hazel, both loaded down with their bags and costumes for the night.

"The fun has arrived!" Hazel announces, coming in and

setting her arm load down on my couch before collapsing into the empty space next to it.

Charlie shakes her head and laughs as she follows her in with her much smaller yet still impressive arm load of stuff.

"Ladies, it's one night. What did you bring?"

"Just the necessities," Hazel says, digging through one of her bags and pulling out a bag of dog treats she makes at the café for Bruno.

"You spoil him too much," I tell her, heading towards my kitchen and grabbing three shot glasses along with the whiskey.

"There is no such thing." She croons to Bruno, giving him a cookie.

I roll my eyes and pour out the whiskey. Charlie takes a seat at the bar, and I slide a shot to her. "Hazel, get your cute ass over here so we can take a shot and start this night off right," I tell her, setting a shot in front of the empty chair beside Charlie.

Hazel takes the empty seat and picks up the shot. "What should we toast to?"

"Hot, meaningless sex," Charlie says, holding up her shot.

"Nope, something that benefits us all," Hazel chimes in. "Because I'm already having the hot sex part."

Charlie and I boo, and I throw a napkin at Hazel. She grabs it mid-air and sticks her tongue out at me. Don't get me wrong, I'm happy Hazel is having crazy hot sex with her boyfriend. That doesn't mean I can't be a little envious.

"How about no panic attacks for the rest of the year," I say, knowing damn well I'm the only one graced with that issue.

"Oh honey, are they getting bad again? I know this time of the year is hard on you," Charlie says, setting her shot glass down and covering my hand, not holding my alcohol.

I shake my head. "No, my med change has helped. I'm just afraid it's not going to last." Not wanting to bring the mood down, I continue, "But enough about me. Tonight's about fun. Oh! I know!" Thinking of a toast, I give the girls a mischievous grin. "Ladies, raise your glasses." They raise their glasses to mine and I announce, "To a night of fuckery."

Laughing, they both cheer, "To a night of fuckery."

We clink and down our shots, all of us making faces from the burn that travels down our throats.

"So, how's everything going on the friendly neighbor front?" Hazel asks, hopping down from her seat and going over to the couch to grab her makeup bag, before heading into my bedroom.

I sigh, following in behind her to finish my hair. "I don't know. Fine, I guess? I ran into him in the parking garage and had a total out-of-body experience." I plug my curling iron in as Charlie comes in behind us and takes a seat on the closed toilet lid. "I, I think I flirted with him."

Hazel gasps and jumps up and down, clapping her hands, her dark-red hair bouncing along with her. "That's *amazing* Millie! Did he flirt back?"

I scrunch my nose, thinking back to earlier. "Yeah, I think he did."

Hazel lets out a squeal and Bruno tears in from the living room to see what the fuss is about, making us all laugh.

"So why don't you sound more excited?" Charlie asks, rummaging through her own bag.

Sectioning off my long hair, I grab a chunk and wrap it around the curling iron. "I have too much going on right now. The last thing I need is to add to my stress."

Hazel looks at me in the mirror, concern wrinkling her brow. "Still having writer's block?"

I tip my head and grab another chunk of hair. "Unfortunately. I don't know what I was thinking, giving myself a deadline at the beginning of January."

"You thought it'd distract you from your heavy feelings you get around the holidays," Charlie says matter-of-factly.

It's true. I did it specifically to try to divert the darkness I usually experience during the holidays since losing my parents eight years ago. We all know that. However, I didn't take into consideration that the heaviness I usually experience may prevent me from writing *anything*. Specifically, the witty and steamy scenes I'm known for. How can I be creative when I feel nothing inside?

I let out a heavy sigh. "Yeah, well, I think I fucked up with that one. I may just have to push the release back a month or two, which will screw up my whole release schedule for the next year."

Hazel bumps her shoulder into mine. "But isn't that the benefit of being your own boss? Deciding what works for you on your own terms?" She would know, being the badass boss bitch she is.

"Yeah, but my readers will be disappointed, and I don't like letting them down."

Charlie gets up from her spot and walks over to me, setting a hand on my arm, and stares back at me in the mirror. "You know they would understand and completely support you if you told them *why*."

I release the hair from my iron and set it down on the counter, shaking my head. "I can't," I whisper, staring back at her in the mirror. No one, besides my very close group of friends and Charlie's parents, is aware of my past, and I intend to keep it that way. It's not that I'm ashamed of what happened. Well, not now anyway thanks to years of therapy, but the image I portray as an author is the fun version of myself and that's who I want the world to see me as. Not the depressed and broken version I actually am. Whose anxiety is so bad she has to take two different medications to even function as a semi-normal person and have another one on hand for extra bad days.

Noticing the shift in my mood, both Hazel and Charlie wrap their arms around me and lay their heads on my shoulders as we stare back at ourselves in the mirror. "We love you no matter what. Nothing is going to change that," Charlie tells me softly.

Hazel tugs on one of my curls. "You're never alone in this. We got you, Boo."

Sensing my mood, Bruno squeezes his body in between Charlie and me and takes a seat, leaning his whole body against me. "See, Bruno's got your back too," Hazel says.

I bend over and give Bruno a scratch, who in turn gives me a lick on my nose, extracting a small laugh from me, and the pressure in my chest eases a bit.

Standing, I throw my arms around my best friends and give them side hugs. "Thanks, babes, I don't know what I'd do without you."

They hug me back. "You'll never have to find out. You're stuck with us," Charlie says and Bruno gives a small woof, like he agrees.

"We need another shot!" Hazel announces, extracting herself from the group huh and beelines it for the kitchen.

"None for me!" Charlie calls to Hazel as she leaves. "You guys are going to be drunk before we even leave," Charlie mutters.

"That's why you're going to stay sober enough to get us into the Uber and to the club," I say, cheerily giving her a cheeky grin. "Plus, this is my last one until we get to the club. They won't let us in if we're already trashed, and I need this."

She rubs my arm. "I know you do, babe."

Hazel comes back and hands me a shot. "Drink up bitch, we're getting our freak on tonight."

"Lord help me." I hear Charlie mutter under her breath as Hazel and I knock back our shots.

I savor the burn of the alcohol as it makes its way down my throat, pushing thoughts of my past down with it.

"Bye Bruno, Mikey will come take you for a walk if I'm not home by midnight!" I tell him as I close the door and lock it, not that he understands, but it makes me feel better thinking he does. I hate leaving him, but he loves Mikey, Marty's seventeen-year-old nephew who lives on the second floor. I pay him to walk Bruno from time to time when I'm going to be out late.

Hazel hits the down button for the elevator, and I send up a small prayer that Judd doesn't appear when the doors open. "Why did I think this costume was a good idea?" I grumble, pulling down the skirt to my *very* short costume.

"Because you look hot as fuck," Hazel says, adjusting the top of her sexy nurse's outfit.

"Yeah, but now I'm going to be tugging at my skirt all night hoping I'm not flashing anyone my ass cheeks."

Charlie snorts and is the first one in the elevator when it arrives, sans Judd, *thank God.* "Babe, you're going to be too drunk to notice or care in about another hour or so, and so will everyone else. Stop worrying about it."

"Easy for you to say! You're wearing a jumpsuit," I say, motioning up and down at her costume that's skintight, but covers everything.

"You can 'arrest' anyone who says anything? That could be fun," Hazel suggests as she follows me into the elevator. I snort and my mind jumps to what Judd said to me yesterday about liking to be the one who uses the handcuffs. The thought sends a round of shivers through me.

"Earth to Millie," Charlie calls to me, waving her hand in front of my face and snapping me out of my thoughts.

"What? Did you say something?"

Charlie raises an eyebrow at me just as the elevator dings

announcing its arrival at the lobby. "I said that all the Ubers are backed up," she tells me as we leave the elevator and head to the front doors. "Which is not shocking, considering it's Halloween."

"Soooo, what does that mean?" I ask, doing my ritual of checking my purse for my keys and phone, even though I already know they're in there.

"It means," Charlie says, stopping by the front desk and leaning against it. "We either wait," she checks her phone, "about thirty to forty minutes for a car to be available, *or* we can try a group ride share?"

We scrunch our noses at that suggestion, but it would still be a better option than waiting close to an hour.

"Or I can take you," a voice says behind me, sending chills down my back. I don't even need to turn around to know who that voice belongs to because in the last two days, I've learned the sound of that voice well.

"Judd!" Charlie announces like he's the lord and savior himself. "Happy Halloween! Were you going out too?" she asks, gesturing at him.

I still haven't turned around, but I'm sure he still looks the same as he did when I ran into him earlier in the parking garage.

Tall, hot, and muscly.

Delicious.

Stop it.

I can feel him come closer and I tug at the back of my skirt as he stops next to me.

"Hi, Shortcake. Nice costume. I'm really digging your handcuffs." An image of what Judd could do with those handcuffs pops into my head, and I feel my cheeks heat. I cock an eyebrow up at him and send him a side glare, extracting a low chuckle from him. "Where's Bruno?" he asks, looking around for my sidekick.

"In my apartment, he's not the club type," I tell him, looking over at the girls.

Hazel looks at Charlie and mouths, "Shortcake?" Charlie shrugs and looks at Judd as he answers her question. "No, just coming back from taking Hudson Trick or Treating with Kess."

Kess must be his older brother Kessler. I remember him and his now fiancée being plastered all over the gossip sites not too long ago when their relationship went public. And again, when Kessler got into a fight during a game after Hudson's bio dad said some unsavory things about Lucy and her son at the plate.

"Oh, how fun! Did you get pictures?" Charlie asks. Judd takes his phone out of his pocket and unlocks it, bringing up a picture and handing his phone to Charlie.

"Aaawwww," both Hazel and Charlie croon, looking at the picture.

"Hudson and Kade look so adorable," Charlie says, handing Judd his phone back.

"You wanna see too?" he turns to me, holding his phone up.

Not wanting to be rude, I nod my head once and he hands me his phone. Two tall pirates with identical green eyes have their arms slung around two much shorter pirates who are holding their fake swords out towards the camera. Wide grins grace all four faces. Seeing Judd being so 'domestic', the opposite of what his reputation is known to be, gives me a funny feeling I'm not used to in my stomach.

"Cute," I tell him, trying to play it cool that he turned my insides to mush with just a picture, handing the phone back to him. Our fingers brush when he takes his phone back, sending a jolt through my hand like the same jolt I felt yesterday when we shook hands. My eyes connect with his, seeing that he felt it too.

A throat clears, making us both jump and look at the two

women that we forgot were standing in front of us. Taking my hand back, I cross my arms and shift to my left, trying to create a little distance between us without being noticeable.

"Anyway," Charlie drawls out, looking between us and giving me a look that says 'we'll talk about this more later'. Cool, just what I needed. "We wouldn't want to impose, Judd. We can just find a group ride share," Charlie says, holding up her phone and shaking it.

"Absolutely not," he argues, crossing his arms as if that's final. "You're not imposing. I was just going to go upstairs and turn on *Hocus Pocus*."

"Ooh, I *love* that movie!" Hazel exclaims. Looks like someone's still buzzing. Mine has unfortunately died down since freaking *Jack Sparrow* has joined us.

Judd holds out his fist for a bump, and Hazel enthusiastically returns it. "Judd," he says to her.

"Hazel, nice to officially meet you!"

"Same," he says, giving her his playboy smile. "Anyway," Judd continues, "there's no imposition. I'll take you." He pulls his keys out of his pocket and shakes them.

Charlie and Hazel look at each other and shrug. I, however, protest. "That's unnecessary. Thanks, but no thanks. We'll just wait for an Uber to free up," I tell him, grabbing my phone out of my purse and bringing up the Uber app, which now shows that there's nothing available for *at least* an hour.

Awesome.

"I found a group rideshare that could be here in fifteen minutes," Charlie says, looking at her phone.

"Perfect!" I yell at the same time Judd says, "No."

I whip my head to look at him, and he gives me a pointed look. "It's not your decision," I tell him, matching his look.

He takes two steps towards me, closing the gap, towering over me. "It is when you look like that," he says in a low voice.

I narrow my eyes at him. "What's wrong with how I look?"

His eyes quickly drop to my cleavage, then back up to my

eyes. His stare a little more heated than before. "Not a damn thing."

I squirm under his gaze, fidgeting with the strap on my purse, but not breaking eye contact.

"Okay, you know what, we accept," Charlie says, breaking our stand-off.

"Charlie!" I start, but Judd interrupts me.

"Great, cars in the garage. Let's go," he says, turning on his heel and making his way back to the elevators. Hazel looks between me and Charlie before taking off after Judd, whose long legs have him half-way back to the elevators in a few strides.

"What the fuck, Charlie?" I whisper, following behind her.

"I could ask you the same thing, Millie," she shoots back. "What was that?"

"What? I told you we didn't get along."

Her lips tip up and she snorts. "Looks like you guys get along *just fine*."

I stop and put my hand on her arm, stopping her with me. "What's that supposed to mean?"

"It means Hazel was right. He wants to fuck you." I let go of her arm and she trudges ahead, leaving me standing there with my mouth gaping open, watching her join Hazel and Judd.

"Coming, Gumdrop?" Judd asks when the elevator opens, and he sees me still standing in the hallway.

I'd like to punch him in the gumdrops. I think to myself as I trudge down the hall and walk into the elevator, not saying a word.

CHAPTER 8

Judd

I DIDN'T THINK it was possible, but Amelia is even hotter when she's mad and right now she's downright pissed. We get to my Jeep, and I hit the unlock button, jogging ahead and opening the doors for the girls. To my surprise, Amelia throws herself into the front passenger seat and buckles up, staring ahead. She must notice my surprise because she rolls her eyes and says, "I get carsick, so I have to sit up front if I'm not driving." Still not looking at me.

I close the doors and hop into the front seat, turning the engine over. "Where to, ladies?"

Charlie's the one who answers. "Ignite." *Shit.* I haven't been back since the night I was arrested. I look in my rearview and Charlie's eyes meet mine. "You don't have to stay. We can just reserve an Uber ahead of time."

"No, I'll stay and drive you drunkies back when you're ready," I tell her, giving her a wink in the rearview and putting the Jeep in reverse and turning to look behind me, placing my hand behind Amelia's seat.

"You have a rearview camera." Amelia nods to the screen.

I lean closer to her and move my hand from the headrest to

play with a lock of her hair. "Maybe I just wanted an excuse to look at you."

Her eyes flick to mine briefly before she rolls them and looks away, biting her bottom lip. She crosses her legs, making her already incredibly short skirt ride up even further. She uncrosses her legs and pulls her skirt back down, huffing out a sigh and crossing her arms over her chest, pushing her breasts up higher.

I adjust slightly in my seat as I drive us out of the underground garage, trying to ease the pressure of my erection that's formed against my pants since seeing her standing in the lobby. I had every intention of grabbing my mail and heading upstairs to watch a movie like I told the girls, but as soon as I overheard them talking about getting a ride share and saw Amelia in that costume that leaves little to the imagination, I knew I wasn't letting them go anywhere alone, especially since I know they'll be drinking.

No one speaks as we exit the garage, taking a right onto the street, the music from my playlist filling the space. The song ends and Taylor Swift's "I did something bad" comes across the speakers.

"Oh, fuck yeah!" Hazel yells from the back. "Turn that shit up Millie," she says, dancing in her seat.

Amelia reaches for the dial, her hand pausing halfway. "Do you mind?" she asks.

I look over at her quickly, liking the way she looks in my passenger seat, maybe a little too much, and shake my head. "Not at all Princess, go for it."

"I'm no one's princess," she mutters, cranking the volume up before I can respond.

Hazel lets out a whoop and raises her arms up in the air, as far as the roof lets them at least, and shimmies in her seat. Charlie even joins in singing along with Hazel and Tay-Tay. Amelia looks back at them and barks a laugh.

"Come on Millie! Dance with us!" Hazel says, scooting as close to the middle as she can and bopping to the beat.

I start drumming my hands on the steering wheel. "Yeah, come on Amelia," I say, singing along with the music.

A look of shock crosses her face. "You're a Swiftie?" she yells over the music.

"Game recognizes game."

She gives me the first genuine smile I've seen since we met yesterday and my heart stutters in my chest. She laughs a genuine laugh and starts moving to the beat in her seat, singing along with the music and the other girls in the back and a sliver of hope blooms in my chest that maybe she likes me more than she's letting on.

The normally ten-minute drive takes twenty, thanks to the influx of Halloween traffic. After the first Taylor Swift song, there was an unspoken decision made between the girls to continue this mini-Era's tour. I unlocked my phone so Amelia could control the lineup, and I didn't mind one second of it.

When we pull up to *Ignite*, we see a decent line formed outside the entrance. I get into the valet line while Amelia turns the music down and turns back to talk to the girls. "It's going to take *forever* to get in."

"No, it won't," I say, giving her a wink.

She raises a brow at me. "Have you seen the line?" she asks, gesturing out the window. "We're going to freeze our asses off before we can even shake them. I don't know if you've noticed, but this costume doesn't provide much warmth."

Running with the excuse she's inadvertently given me, I run my eyes over her costume, or lack thereof, finally bringing my eyes up to hers. I say, "Oh, I've noticed." And give her a slow grin.

She rolls her eyes and turns her head back to the line of cars in front of us, crossing her arms back over her chest and sits back in her seat.

I chuckle. "If you play your cards right, you won't even have to wait."

Amelia narrows her eyes at me. "What's that supposed to mean?"

"It means," I say, leaning on the console, closing the distance between us. "I have VIP access, and if you say please like a good girl, I'll get you guys in without having to wait."

Her blue eyes flare, burning brightly. She sits up and leans into me, leaving only a few inches between us, whispering, "Good thing I'm not a good girl, huh?" A slow, devious grin spreads across her face.

Can't hear that enough.

I chance another inch forward and match her unspoken challenge. "We'll see about that."

Seconds tick by, neither of us willing to back down, when we hear Hazel's voice erupt from the back seat, "Damn! Is it hot in here? Or is it just all the sexual tension I'm feeling?"

Chuckling, I back away from Amelia. Whatever moment we were having between us, broken. Her face flushes and she breaks eye contact, retreating to her side of the Jeep. I'll let her off the hook for now, but there's no way I'm not revisiting whatever that was later.

The line ahead of us moves and a valet driver rushes to my door. I put the Jeep in park and turn to the girls. "That's our cue, ladies. Ready to get your party on?" Amelia exits without even saying a word and Hazel gives me a wink before getting out. Charlie, however, stays.

"You don't have to stay if it's going to be too much for you, Judd," she says, and I know she's talking about being around all the alcohol and drunk people and being one of the few sober ones. But really it doesn't bother me. Not drinking was never my problem. Not knowing when to stop was.

"I'm good, Charlie. It won't be a problem."

"You'll let me know if it is, though, right?"

I nod. "I promise."

We exit, and the valet guy hands me my ticket and hops in, driving off. I hold my arm out to Charlie, and she loops hers through mine as we meet Amelia and Hazel on the sidewalk. I offer Amelia my other arm once we reach them, but she doesn't take it. Instead, she walks to Charlie's other side and takes her arm. Chuckling, I raise my eyebrows at Hazel. "Are you going to play hard to get to?" I ask, offering my arm.

"Nope, who doesn't want to hang off the arm of a gorgeous baseball stud?" she says loudly, aiming her eyes at Amelia.

Amelia peaks around Charlie. "Someone who has *standards*, Haze," she shoots back, chancing a quick look at me before turning her head back to watch where she's walking.

Charlie bumps her shoulder into Amelia's. "Put the claws away Millie, thanks to Judd, we didn't have to wait for a ride, *and* we get VIP access."

I hear Amelia mumble a "Whatever" as we get to the entrance, making my grin grow wider. The more she resists, the more amused I become. I can't help but wonder just how much I can push her until she gives in to the attraction that is clearly between us.

When we get to the VIP entrance, I see my favorite bouncer is running it tonight. "Deny! How's it hanging, man?" I hold out a fist with Hazel's arm still weaved through mine and Deny gives me a bump back. Deny's an intimidating dude at 6'7". Not only is he a fucking giant, he's also built like a damn linebacker. His arms are easily the size of one of my thighs. He has a serious resting bitch face, too. But underneath all that brick and brawn, is a soft teddy bear, not that he wants anyone to know that.

"Judd! Not bad man. Haven't seen you here in a while. Everything good?"

I can feel Amelia's eye on me, silently waiting for my answer. "Ah, everything's good, bro, just been hanging out with my nephew and helping Kess with things around the property." It's not a lie. I *have* been doing those things since my arrest. Trying to keep myself busy and out of trouble.

Deny nods. "Cool man, well, enjoy yourself tonight." He moves and pushes the door open for us. Before we can even walk in, the base of the music smacks us in the face. Hazel lets out a whoop as she disentangles from my arm and enters the club first, dancing through the entrance. Once she's in the doorway, she turns back and grabs Charlie's arm that was connected to me and pulls her through with Amelia, who shoots me a quick side eye before following behind.

"Looks like you have your hands full tonight, Juddman," Deny says to me as I follow them through.

I watch the sassy blonde that has completely entranced me make her way to the bar with the other girls. She peaks over her shoulder, looking back. When she sees me staring at her, she whips her head back around and pretends to pursue the bottles that are displayed on the shelf behind the bar. I look at Deny with a wide grin. "You have no idea Deny, no idea at all."

I give him one more fist bump before making my way to the bar. Nodding my head at a couple of people I know as I make my way there. Amelia is ordering her drink when I reach them.

"An amaretto whiskey sour please," she yells to Seth over the loud music. Seth nods to her then sees me and gives me a chin raise.

"What about you, Judd? The usual?"

"Nope, not drinking tonight. I'm the devilishly handsome designated driver for these angels tonight. I'll stick to water," I tell him, giving Amelia a wink. She rolls her eyes while Hazel and Charlie giggle.

Seth places the girls' drinks in front of them and Amelia sucks half of hers down before I even get my water. "Woah there Angel Cake, might want to pace yourself," I tell her, leaning in closer so she can hear me.

She gives me a look from the corner of her eye that screams 'Fuck Off' before taking her straw out of the drink, laying it on the bar and tossing back the rest, slamming the glass down on the bar. My eyebrows shoot up and I look at the two women on her other side, making eye contact with Charlie, who's trying to hide her smirk behind her cocktail glass.

Seth comes back to the center, and I hear Amelia order another drink *and* a shot. If she keeps this pace up, she's gonna be passed out or sick as hell before the night is over.

Seth places the shot in front of her and moves to make her drink. Amelia grabs the shot and turns her body towards me, leaning an elbow on the bar. She raises the shot in an air salute to me and downs it, keeping her glacier blue eyes on me the whole time, challenging me to say something.

Yeah, I'm not that stupid. I give her a smirk instead, and she smirks back before turning to the girls.

CHAPTER 9

Amelia

"WHO THE FUCK does he think he is? Telling me to slow down," I grumble as the girls and I make our way to the dance floor. Honestly, the fucking audacity of that man.

"What!?" Hazel yells from behind me. The music is getting louder the closer we get to the dance floor, and I can barely hear myself complain. I shake my head, letting her know that it's nothing.

Charlie is in front, leading the charge to find a free space on the packed floor for us to dance. Even in the VIP section, there are bodies everywhere. Finally, a space opens up and we slide in, bumping along to the music and sipping our chosen poison of the night.

"You like him!" Charlie yells over the music.

"What!? Who?" Hazel yells.

Charlie tips her head towards the bar where Judd is leaning back against it, one elbow propped on the top, watching us. Looking sexy as fuck. The asshole.

"Millie likes Judd."

"No, I don't! He's insufferable." I yell back at her.

Charlie's grin grows. "If it's any consolation, it seems like the feeling is mutual."

"You should go for it!" Hazel yells over the building tempo of the music as her body follows along like a cobra dancing to a flute. The girl can move, and it doesn't seem like I'm the only one who notices. A trio of guys eyeball us and make their way over.

"Absolutely not. He's not my type," I say as the guys get closer.

"Sexy as sin isn't your type?" Charlie asks, also noticing the tripod coming closer behind Hazel.

I scrunch my nose. "He's not *that* good looking," I say, taking a drink.

Hazel lets out an unlady-like snort. "And I'm a virgin."

I roll my eyes, but the subject is dropped when the group of guys finally reaches us. Without uttering a word, the guys slip in and start dancing with us. At first, they keep a respectable, yet danceable distance, but soon into the third music transition, the guy I'm dancing with decides to get a little...handsy.

It's subtle. A little slip here, bump there, easily mistaken for just accidents. But apparently because I don't say anything about him 'accidentally' touching me, that's an 'all systems go' in his mind. Before I know what's happening, I feel his hand slide low, very low, almost too low, over my stomach and pull me back against him on a very prominent body part.

I let out a gasp, but no one notices over the music. No one except him apparently, because he leans down and says into my ear. "There's more where that came from, shorty."

Gag me.

Utterly annoyed and disgusted, I turn and try to push away from him, but my tiny build has me at a complete disadvantage. He takes my trying to get away from him as 'playing hard to get'. Taking his other hand, he places it on my ass along with the first one and pulls me closer, pushing his boner into my lower stomach. Since I still have my now empty glass, I can only push at his chest with one hand. "Not interested," I say as I push against him again.

"Come on baby, I can show you a real good time."

"Doubtful," I retort. I'm fucking over this shit. I shove harder and his face changes from amused to pissed in a flash.

He reaches up and grabs my wrist, squeezing it painfully. "Don't be a fucking bitch," he says into my ear.

Fuck this.

I pull back just far enough to create a little distance, then bring my knee up swiftly, making contact with the fuck wads pathetic excuse of manhood.

He releases my wrist and doubles over with a loud, "Fuck!"

His shout gets the attention of the other members of our group and a few others and they finally turn towards us.

"What happened?" Charlie asks, looking from him to me.

"She's a fucking tease." The guy I was dancing with coughs out.

"And you're a fucking twat, what part of 'No' didn't you understand? I'd spell it out for you, but I'm afraid that would be too difficult for you to read."

"You fucking–"

I sense him come up behind me before I hear, "Is there a problem?" in that deep rumble I recognize as Judd's voice.

Unconsciously, I take a step back, towards the safety of Judd's body, colliding with his front. He steadies me but doesn't release me. Instead, he pulls me to him, tucking me into his side. My body instantly relaxes, knowing it's safe.

"Yeah, this bitch led me on, then kneed me in the balls." I feel Judd's body stiffen when the idiot calls me a bitch.

By now Hazel and Charlie have both left the guys they were dancing with, joining me at Judd's side. The guy's friends look both uncomfortable and annoyed.

Judd looks over at Charlie and passes me to her, then strides forward and towers over the asshole. "Wanna try that again?"

The guy opens his mouth to speak, but Judd interrupts him. "I suggest you think before you speak. I watched the whole thing from the bar and from what I saw, she was trying to get away from you, but you wouldn't take 'no' for an answer."

The guy snaps his mouth shut and shakes his head once.

"Good, now I suggest you call it a night and get the fuck out of here before I get the bouncer. Deny's looking a little bored." The group looks over at the bouncer we met earlier and Deny tips his chin up at Judd in acknowledgement.

The idiot's friends finally come to their senses and pull him away. We watch as they shove him through the crowd towards the door. Deny stares them down the entire way through until the door shuts.

Relief washes through my body, and I sag slightly against Charlie. Judd turns back to us, eyes running over me. "You okay?" His gaze is soft, tender. Completely opposite of the one he gave that ass hat.

I nod.

"You sure?" he asks, reaching up and brushing a lock of my hair away from my face.

I suck in a breath as a wave of heat hits me in my core.

Is it me, or did he just get...hotter?

"Mills, did you hear me? Do you want to go home?" he asks, concern in his voice.

Mills? No one's called me Mills since...

No. Not here. Not now. Suck it up Amelia.

I take a breath, steadying myself, then give him a quick nod. "I'm sure. Thank you for standing up for me. I'm sure I could have handled it, but I'm glad I didn't have to."

"No need to thank me, Amelia. Men shouldn't assume just because they're lucky enough to get a beautiful woman to dance with them they're entitled to anything else." He gives that devilish smile of his. "And I have no doubt in my mind that you could have handled it. You just shouldn't have to."

My cheeks heat and I turn to the girls, who have matching looks of curiosity on their faces. "I'm fine, I promise. I'm not gonna let some asshole ruin our night." I give them my best smile and loop my arms through theirs. "Come on, girls, I think another drink is in order." I glance over my shoulder to see Judd right on our heels.

When we hit the bar, I feel the heat from Judd's body wash over my back as he towers over me and orders us all another round. The bartender nods and grabs fresh glasses for our drinks.

"We're heading to the bathroom! Be right back!" Hazel yells to us, grabbing Charlie and hauling her to the bathroom with her before I can even acknowledge her.

Turning my back to the bar, I lean against it and let my eyes roam over Judd.

I'd have to be an idiot not to admit how sexy he is. Especially in his pirate costume. His white shirt is unbuttoned down to the base of his sternum, showing off his smooth, chiseled chest. No tattoos have graced his skin there yet, but I know he has a full sleeve down his right arm and a few on his left. Not that I've had the pleasure of seeing them in person. In a moment of weakness, when I couldn't sleep last night, I googled the man standing before me, and I was not disappointed.

Well, that's not true. I *was* disappointed, but not because he's not impressive to look at. I was disappointed to find that I *enjoyed* what I was looking at... Immensely.

My eyes finally make their way up to his and I find he's staring back at me with a hunger I've only written about in my books, never experienced myself.

"Like what you see?"

I roll my lips inward, biting at the bottom one, and shrug. Because there is no way I'm admitting how much I actually enjoy what I see to this man.

His green eyes darken, and he closes the small gap between

us. Towering over me, he leans down and whispers into my ear. "I think you do." His breath tickles the hair on my neck, sending chills down my spine.

When he leans back, my drink is in his hand. I reach up to grab it, but he pulls it back out of my reach. He brings it to his lips and takes a sip. He raises his brows in surprise and hands me my drink. "Not bad, a little sweet, a little sour, a little burn at the end. Fits you perfectly." There's a little drop on his lip from the drink. Before I know what I'm doing, I'm watching my hand as it reaches up and my thumb swipes at the corner of his mouth. His hand grips my wrist before I can pull back. He sucks my thumb into his mouth, teeth grazing the pad of my thumb.

My lips part as I suck in a breath. *Fuck, that was...hot.*

The girls come back breaking whatever the fuck that was between Judd and I.

Looking from Judd to me, Hazel asks, "Did we interrupt something?" Mischief in her voice.

Deflect, deflect, deflect. "Not at all." I tip my head at Judd as I pull my hand away, instantly missing the contact with him. "He's a slob, so I was just helping him out."

Hazel's smile widens and Charlie rolls her eyes, giving me a 'yeah right' look.

Needing to change the subject, I grab their free hands and pull them away from the bar, leaving Judd. "Now that we have drinks, let's go dance."

Making our way back out into the crowd, we find a free spot on the dance floor and start moving with the music. But when I turn around, Judd is no longer just watching from the bar. No, he's followed us out onto the floor and is watching my every move. Turning back around, I decide to try to just ignore him. I take a sip of my drink, also trying not to think about his perfect lips that were on my glass moments ago.

That idea is quickly tossed out the window when one of my favorite songs comes on and I start moving with the beat. I can feel my backside graze Judd's jeans, just barely, just a whisper of contact, indicating he's moved closer to me. With alcohol coursing deliciously through my veins and more promised to come, I'm feeling brave, adventurous even.

Taking a half step back, my ass connects with Judd's front as I shimmy down his body, throwing my free hand up above me. His hands skim down my sides as I make my way back up. I cup my hand behind his neck while his fingers graze down to my hips. Closing my eyes, I lean into him, letting myself get lost in the beat and his touch. One of Judd's hands snakes around my middle and I feel his body moving perfectly in rhythm with mine.

He leans down, lips grazing my ear, sending shivers through me. I'm so lost in the sensation of our bodies moving together, I let out a shocked gasp when his teeth nip at my ear, sending delicious heat down to my center.

I take another drink of my liquid courage and turn around in his grasp. Looking up at him, I lock eyes with his almost black gaze. Want and desire reflect back at me, matching my own. My hand on his neck laces through his shaggy hair and I give it a small tug. He growls and tightens his grip on my back, bringing me impossibly closer.

Everyone around us fades away as we stare at each other, dancing to the hypnotic beat of the music. I feel the pull to be closer to him, to have his lips on mine. He must feel it too, because his face inches closer. The scent of mint and whiskey mingling together.

I move closer, completely entranced by him. Our lips are impossibly close and still not close enough. I close my eyes, expecting him to close the distance. I feel his breath on my lips just as I'm jostled from behind and my half full drink spills all over Judd's back.

He lets out a "Shit!" and pulls away from me, breaking the moment.

I hear a 'sorry' yelled over the music from behind me, but I don't turn around to acknowledge them. I'm too busy ogling the Greek God in front of me who just pulled his wet shirt over his head, revealing the body of a very tattooed Adonis himself.

Fuck me.

CHAPTER 10

Judd

IF THIS IS what it feels like to be completely entranced by someone... I get it now. I get the obsession, the want, the *need* to be near that person. Watching her dance with that douchebag from across the club earlier drove me insane. I almost said 'fuck it' and started drinking just to keep myself from storming over there and punching his smug face in for dancing with what I want as mine.

And now that I have her in my arms, her looking up at me with her crystal-blue eyes full of the same desire I'm sure is reflected in mine, I'm not sure I can let her go. I move closer, breathing her in. I can almost taste the whiskey on her lips when she suddenly jolts forward.

"Shit!" I yell as cold liquid splashes down my back, causing my shirt to immediately stick to my back and the ice that was in her glass clatters to the floor.

Not thinking about where I'm at, I reach behind me and pull my shirt over my head, needing to get the sticky feeling of wet fabric off me.

I look up at Amelia and see her staring at me, lips parted and eyes dilated. She's jostled from behind again, and I catch her in my arms as she stumbles forward. Her soft delicate hands landing on my chest. She stares at her hands for a second, then looks up at me through her lashes. Licking her lips, she glides her soft hands up the rest of my chest and over my collarbone, tracing the prominent lines with her fingertips.

Fuck, that feels good. I want to kiss her badly, but not here and especially not on the dance floor. Truth be told, I'm glad we were interrupted, because the first time I feel her lips on mine, I want it to just be us.

I feel droplets of what's left of Amelia's drink slide down my back. Making a decision, I take Amelia's hands in mine and guide her off the dance floor, not even knowing or caring where Hazel and Charlie are at the moment. We weave through the crowd until we finally reach the bar. "Hey Seth!" I call to the bartender. He looks up from the other side of the bar, where he's handing someone a beer, and cocks an eyebrow at me. Making sure no one needs anything else, he comes to where we're standing.

"What happened to you?" he says, nodding to my bare chest.

"Dance floor mishap. Do you mind if I use your employee bathroom? There's a line for the other ones." I take the empty glass Amelia's still holding and place it on the bar. "And another drink for her when we come back out?"

Seth walks around to the side and unlocks the little half door they have that leads to the back. He nods his head for me to come on through. "No funny business with the girl in the back, Davis," he says through a grin as we pass by him.

I feel Amelia pull back for a second and I gently tug her forward. "Just getting cleaned up man, I have her drink all down my back and can't reach it myself."

Seth reaches under the bar and grabs a towel and rifles through another pile before finding what he was looking for and tossing both things at me. "Bathrooms to the right and there's an employee shirt for you to change into."

I give Seth a fist bump. "Appreciate it man."

Hand still in mine, I lead Amelia down the short hall and to the door on the right marked bathroom. I open the door and guide her in first before closing and locking it behind us.

I turn back to see Amelia standing there worrying her lip.

"What's wrong?" I ask, tossing the towel and shirt onto the small counter and moving until I'm in front of her.

"I'm so sorry, Judd," she says quietly, staring down at the floor.

I tip her chin, making her look up at me. "It's not your fault, Sugar Pie, that dance floor is beyond crowded. It was bound to happen." She nods, but stays quiet. "Besides, I'm glad it happened."

Shock crosses her face. "You are? Why?"

I step closer, taking her in my arms. "Because, when I kiss you, and it will happen, I want it to just be you and me," I tell her.

She sucks in a breath and searches my eyes. "Why?" she whispers.

"Because Amelia, I am so goddamn attracted to you, I don't want anyone else to witness me getting to taste your lips for the first time. That moment will be for us, and us only."

We stayed at the club for another hour before the girls decided to call it quits. Hazel claiming she strained something in her booty from all the moving and shaking that was going on. After revealing to Amelia how I felt in the bathroom, she's been a little on the quiet side. I hope I didn't push too hard too fast, but fuck, I needed her to know how I was feeling.

Everyone's quiet as I pull into my parking spot and turn off the engine. I look over at Amelia to see she's fallen asleep, one of my Silverbacks hoodies practically swallowing her body. She was cold when we got the car from the valet and because I always have a hoodie handy; I gave it to her to wear. I look over my shoulder to see Hazel also passed out in the back. Glancing in the rearview to see if Charlie is in the same state, I'm met with emerald-green eyes staring at me through the dark.

"You good Char?"

She nods and gives me a soft smile. "You like her," she whispers, eyes glancing at Amelia, then back at me.

"I do," I tell her, deciding there's no reason to hide it.

She nods and holds my gaze. "Just...be careful with her, Judd. She's my best friend and if your intentions are just to fuck around, please find someone else. She's been through enough."

"It's not," I tell her immediately. "I like her. I don't want to hurt her."

Charlie nods again and releases her seatbelt just as Hazel snorts. "One pumpkin latte!" she yells, startling herself out of her sleep. "What happened?" Hazel asks, rubbing one of her eyes and smearing makeup, making it look like she got in a fight with all the colors around her eye.

Charlie chuckles. "We're back at Millies. Come on, let's get all this shit off our faces so we can go to sleep." She looks at me again in the mirror. "Thanks again, Judd."

Hazel stretches, then looks over at me too. "Thanks for driving tonight, Judd. We had a blast." She looks at Amelia's seat, then back at me, giving me a wink. "All of us."

"Anytime, ladies," I tell them as they open their doors. Hazel pauses before getting out. "Want me to wake Millie?" she asks.

I shake my head. "You two go ahead. I've got her."

"Thank God, Millie can be a grouch when she's woken up." Hazel smirks at me and twiddles her fingers at me. "Good luck with that," she calls over her shoulder before shutting her door and heading towards the elevators with Charlie, leaving Amelia and me alone in the car.

I sit there for a few minutes, watching Amelia sleep, letting Charlie's words replay through my head. *'She's been through enough.'* I know she has a story. Between talking with Jeremy yesterday, Charlie's words today, and the fact that she has to have a service dog because of her anxiety, something terrible and traumatic has happened to her. The overwhelming desire to protect her washes over me and I make a silent promise to her to do anything possible to gain her trust.

She stirs in her seat before her eyes pop open, and she slowly looks around. Sitting up quickly in her seat, she looks around again, then notices me in my seat. She relaxes back in her seat before a yawn escapes her perfect mouth and she stretches. "Sorry, I didn't mean to fall asleep." She freezes and whips her head to the back, noticing the empty seats. Turning back to me, she asks, "Where are Hazel and Charlie? How long was I asleep? Why didn't you wake me?"

I chuckle. "We just got here." I nod to the elevators. "As for Charlie and Hazel, they just headed up. I told them I'd bring you up."

"Oh, uh thanks." She pauses and looks at me, narrowing her eyes. "Wait, were you going to carry me?"

I shrug. "Hazel mentioned something about you being a grouch when woken up, so I figured that might be my best bet."

She crosses her arms across her chest and huffs. "I'm not a grouch."

I laugh and open my door. "Whatever you say, Peach. Are you ready to go up?"

She crinkles her nose at the nickname and shakes her head, opening her own door and getting out. She rounds the front, and we walk to the elevators, my hand dropping to her lower back.

"Don't like Peach?"

She shakes her head again and hits the call button before crossing her arms over her chest. My hoodie looks like a dress on her and I fucking love it. The elevator dings announcing its arrival and as she walks ahead of me to enter, blood rushes straight to my cock. Because the hoodie I gave her is one that has my name on the back. An image of her naked with nothing but my jersey pops into my head, making my cock even harder.

"Are you coming or what?" she asks, sounding slightly annoyed that I'm still not in the elevator.

"Yep, coming," I say, getting into the elevator and sliding my hands in my pocket, hoping to disguise the major hard on I'm now sporting.

She hits the button for the tenth floor and looks at me, eyebrows raised. "You gonna do the phone thingy for your floor?"

"No. I'll walk you to your door first."

"That's not necessary," she protests. "I'm a big girl. I can get myself home."

Something shifts inside of me, and I take my hands out of my pockets, softly gripping her upper arms and backing her into the wall of the elevator. When her back hits the wall, she gasps and I bring my hands up to both sides of her head, caging her in.

Reaching down with one hand, I grip her chin and tilt her face to look up at me. "I know you can take care of yourself Mills; I never said you couldn't. But my momma raised a gentleman, and I will be walking you to your door. Understand?"

I see her throat bob as she swallows and nods her understanding.

"Good," I whisper, tracing my thumb over her plump bottom lip. "Now, remember what I said at the club earlier?"

I flick my gaze up from her lips to her eyes and see that they're dilated with desire. She gives me a small nod.

"Well, it's just us in here," I tell her, lowering my head.

I can hear her breath catch as my lips get closer to hers.

"Tell me to stop Mills and I will. I won't take something you're not willing to give me."

She stares at me for a heartbeat before I feel her hands run up the front of my borrowed shirt. One hand grips the front of my shirt and tugs me closer, the other roams over my shoulder to the back of my neck, fingers tangling into my hair.

Taking that as permission, I crash my lips to hers. Eliciting a soft moan from her. Her fingers tighten in my hair and tug softly. I hear a growling noise and realize it's coming from me. Fuck, this woman makes me feral.

Needing more, so much more, I angle my head and trace her lips with my tongue, seeking permission. She opens willingly and I dive in, the taste of whiskey strong on her tongue. She pulls at my shirt, trying to bring me closer. Taking my hand from the wall, I run it down her body and over the curve of her ass, lifting her easily and pinning her to the wall. She wraps her legs around my waist and gasps when her core slides over my length. I press my body into her, catching her soft whimper with my mouth.

I pull away from her lips and trail soft kisses over her jaw and down her neck. God, she tastes so good. She arches into me when I hit a spot on her neck, her legs clamping down harder around me. Softly biting the spot, a deep moan erupts from her, making my already rock-hard erection painful. I'm moving further down to her collarbone when the *Ding!* of the elevator startles us.

We both stare at each other, chests heaving before I set her down just as the doors open. She pulls my hoodie back down that rode up when I had her delicious body pinned up against the wall. Running a hand through her mussed hair, she looks at me sheepishly. "Guess we should get off before the doors close."

"I was trying, but the elevator interrupted us," I tell her jokingly and not at the same time. I don't think I've ever wanted someone as much as I want the five-foot nothing spitfire in front of me. If I didn't witness how much she drank tonight, I would suggest we go back to my place and finish what we started. But tasting the whiskey on her reminded me she is under the influence, and I don't want anything impairing either of us when I make her mine.

Her cheeks redden at my comment and a soft chuckle leaves her. Placing my hand on the small of her back, I guide her out of the elevator. She turns to me, fidgeting with the sleeve of the oversized hoodie when we reach her door.

"Thank you... for everything tonight," she says, ducking her head.

Her hair falls forward when she dips her head down. Without even thinking, I push the lock of hair out of her face and trace my finger along her jaw. I can't help myself. Touching her is like breathing, it just feels so natural. I drop my hand from her jaw and stuff it in my pocket. "There's no need to thank me. I enjoyed going out with you three."

A little crease forms between her brows when she looks back up at me and my hand fists in my pocket. It's all I can do to keep myself from reaching up and smoothing it away. "You enjoyed watching us get drunk and dance with other guys while you had to stay sober and play bodyguard?" she asks skeptically.

I shake my head and take a step forward, leaning against the hand I place above her head. "I enjoyed watching you let loose and have fun. Something tells me you don't do it often, and that's a damn shame because you looked sexy as hell out on that dance floor."

Her teeth graze her bottom lip, pulling it into her mouth. Reaching with my other hand, I tug it free, running the pad of my thumb over it. Her heated gaze falls to my lips, then back to my eyes, silently pleading with me for another kiss. Just as I'm about to fulfill her wishes, a loud *thump* followed by giggles, then not so quiet *shhh*, sounds from the other side of her door.

Amelia covers her face in a groan and thumps her head

against the wall. Chuckling, I gently grab her wrists and pull her hands from her face. "Guess that's my cue to leave."

I drop her hands and step back, giving her room to move. She turns towards the door and reaches for the knob, but stops and turns around. "I still have your hoodie," she says, turning around and reaching for the hem.

Placing my hands over hers, I stop her. "Keep it."

"No, I couldn't. It's yours."

"Keep. It. I have more." Closing the short distance between us, I grip the back of her neck, extracting a gasp from her and whoever is on the other side of the door. I cover the peephole with my other hand and lean down, whispering into her ear. "Besides, I like seeing you wear my name."

I give her a kiss on her flaming red cheek and back away, giving her a wink before turning and heading back to the elevator before I'm tempted to do more. "Goodnight, Amelia," I call to her over my shoulder.

I hear a faint "Goodnight" before reaching the elevator. Hitting the call button, I rock back on my heels, waiting for the car to reach the floor.

Goodnight indeed.

CHAPTER 11

Amelia

FOUR DAYS.

I've been able to successfully avoid Judd for four days. I woke up the day after Halloween full of self-loathing. How could I have let him slip past my defenses like that?

Because he's safe. A little voice chimes in.

I snort to myself while lacing up my running shoes. More like I was drunk and had a momentary lapse in judgment.

But he rescued you.

Shut up!

I let out a huff and grab my water bottle, phone, and keys off the kitchen island. I need to get this anxious energy out and since Mother Nature has decided to give us a big 'fuck you' and dump three to four inches of rain on us over the next couple of days, I have no choice but to use the gym that's located on the main floor down the hall from the front desk. It's either that or I drive myself crazy in my apartment, replaying that kiss over and over.

I lock up my apartment and head to the stairs with Bruno in tow. I've been avoiding the elevator at all costs. Allowing myself to kiss Judd was a monumental mistake, but one I can't get myself to regret, no matter how hard I try. Because I have *never* been kissed the way Judd kissed me. His lips were surprisingly soft, and it took everything in me not to bite down on his full bottom lip.

When he hit that delicious spot on my neck, my knees nearly buckled at the jolt of pleasure he extracted from me. If it wasn't for the elevator announcing the arrival to my floor, I can't say I wouldn't have stripped him down right there in the elevator and had my way with him. I blame seeing him shirtless at the club and my utter weakness for tattoos, and *Jesus,* is he tatted. The black swirls and designs of ink running up his entire right arm and half of his left nearly made me combust on the spot. What I wouldn't give to run my tongue all over them.

The bang of a door brings me back to the present and I look around, realizing I'm already out of the stairwell and at the gym door.

I've been doing that a lot lately. Spacing out and not noticing I've arrived somewhere until I'm actually there. It's disturbing, and I blame Judd. I was fine until he entered my life. Okay, so I wasn't *fine*, but at least I wasn't this distracted.

I set my stuff down on the bench closest to my treadmill and give Bruno the down command. He plops down and watches me with his brown and blue eyes while I stretch. I have the entire gym to myself, seeing as it's only four o'clock in the morning.

Thank you, insomnia.

After I'm stretched, I hop onto the treadmill and start at a walk, letting my leg muscles warm up. The last thing I need is an injury. While I'm walking, I place my headphones into my ear and find my latest workout playlist, letting myself get lost in the music.

Two songs later and I've picked up my pace to a nice steady jog, feeling my shoulders relax slightly as my anxiety starts to melt away. A faster paced song comes on and I increase the speed slightly on the treadmill, pushing myself, running from all my problems and uncertainty until my legs burn.

I should stop, or at least slow down, but I can't. My brain and leg muscles are at war. My brain screams at me to keep going, that I can outrun the pain, that the pain is all in my head, while my muscles are threatening to give out at any moment.

The song ends and switches to something that has a slower tempo, breaking my focus, making my feet falter. I try to hit the stop button, but it's too late. I'm already behind. I feel my feet near the edge of the treadmill and make the decision to try to hop backwards, but I have no idea how I'm going to do that with my feet moving forwards. I'm about to give up and just let fate take its course when I see a figure out of the corner of my eye. I whip my head to the side to see who it is. My feet falter as a strong arm grabs me around the middle and tugs me to the side.

I throw my hands up to brace myself, and they land on a solid wall of muscle. Lungs burning, I gulp down air before looking up and seeing the main problem I was running from in the first place.

Judd.

Of course.

Looking down at me with his mischievous smile, he says, "No need to throw yourself at me. I'm already interested, Shortcake."

Something pulls low in my belly, but I pull away before it goes any further than that. Ignoring his comment, I say, "Uh, thanks for catching me. I was ready to just take the hit." Turning back to the treadmill, I hit the stop button and grab my towel off the arm, wiping the sweat that's dripped down my face.

"I'll always catch you, Amelia."

My eyes snap to the mirror and see his green eyes blazing back at me. "Why?" I breathe out, asking his reflection.

"Because I think you're worth holding on to." Taking a step forward and crossing his arms across his chest, he leans against the post my body would have flown into if he hadn't grabbed me, letting his words sink in.

No one has ever thought I was worth keeping, not with my...baggage.

My eyes travel over his reflection, taking him in. He has on a pair of gray basketball shorts, and I never realized how attractive calf muscles were until I saw Judd's very muscular ones. My perusal continues north over a slight bulge, and I quickly flick my eyes over it, not needing to be turned on any more than I already am seeing him in that damn backwards hat. He's wearing a black cut off shirt, exposing his beautiful tattoos and muscles that are totally doing it for me. Finally, I reach his face. His beard is shorter than it was the last time I saw him, making his jawline sharper. I can't help but wonder what it would feel like between my legs. Would it be too rough, or just enough friction?

I blink and mentally give myself a shake. Judd would eventually think my baggage isn't worth keeping me too, which is why I need to steer clear. But when he looks at me like that, like I'm the only one who matters, it makes it harder to resist him.

His smile widens. "Like what you see?"

I bite my bottom lip and pull it into my mouth, tearing at the skin. I do, I really fucking do, and that's the problem.

Pushing off from the post, he strides over, not taking his eyes off mine in the mirror. When he reaches me, he gently turns me around by my shoulders so I'm no longer looking at his reflection but the real thing. Gripping my chin, he tugs my lip out of my mouth and runs his thumb over it. His eyes move from my lips to my eyes. "Are you going to answer my question?"

"No," I whisper.

"No, you don't like what you see, or no, you're not going

to answer?" he asks, eyes bouncing back and forth between mine.

I force myself to take a step back, even though the last thing my body wants is to break contact with his touch. Turning, I walk to the bench where I left my stuff and Bruno. "No, I don't like what I see." I can't say the words while looking at him or he'll know it's a blatant lie. "I don't even like you, remember?" I remind him, grabbing my water bottle and chugging down half of it. Wiping my mouth with the towel I've draped over my shoulder when I'm done.

He chuckles and crosses his arms over his chest again. "I think you like me plenty. You're just afraid."

Fuck yes, I'm afraid. I'm more than afraid. I'm terrified. None of my relationships last. I'm too fucked up to love fully. They love the surface version of me, but once they get deeper, it's too much. It's always been too much. That's why I'm better off alone. You can't get hurt if there's no one to hurt you in the first place.

As if reading my thoughts, Judd closes the distance between us and sits on the bench, dipping his head to meet my eyes. "I would never hurt you, Amelia." He reaches for my hand and laces my fingers between his large ones, dwarfing mine.

I stare at our linked hands, wanting to believe him. "You don't know that." I finally look him in the eyes, letting him see my fear, my turmoil. "You can't know that."

"I do."

I shake my head and pull my hand away. Grabbing my phone and keys, I release Bruno and let him say hi to Judd. Bruno wiggles between Judd's legs while he pets him, yet not breaking eye contact with me. "I'm too broken, Judd. You might as well cut your losses now."

He shakes his head. "We're all a little broken, Amelia. It's about finding the right pieces to put us back together that makes the pain bearable."

"I'm not your missing piece, Judd." I'm the mangled puzzle piece that you have to throw away, never getting to complete the puzzle.

"I think you could be." He gives Bruno one last pat before getting up from the bench and coming to stand in front of me. "Can I touch you?" he asks.

Knowing it's a bad idea, I nod anyway.

Judd cups my cheek, brushing his thumb back and forth. I close my eyes and give into the touch, releasing a sigh.

One last time.

"What do you feel?" he whispers in the silence of the room.

"You," I tell him, opening my eyes to look into his.

He huffs a small laugh. "Yes, but what do you feel *when* I touch you?" He tips his chin at me. "Close your eyes again."

Taking a deep breath, I reach up and grab his wrist with my free hand and close my eyes.

"Tell me what you feel."

I stand there for a second, trying to figure out what he means when it hits me. My eyes fly open meeting his.

"It's all quiet, isn't it? The thoughts, the fear, the anxiety? All the thoughts turning in your brain, driving you crazy are–"

"Quiet," I finish for him.

He nods.

"How? Why?" I ask, trying to figure out why I didn't notice this before.

Because you were too busy fighting your feelings to notice.

He shrugs one shoulder. "I don't know, but I think it's the same thing my brother Kessler felt with his fiancée when they first met. I asked him how he knew and what we're feeling is what he described. That and undeniable energy."

I think back to a few days ago at the library when we shook hands and felt that zap, and then again on the dance floor on Halloween. And now with his hand cupping my face. It's true, I've never felt the way I do with anyone like I do with Judd. But we've only known each other for a few days.

That fact pours over me like cold water and my body jolts. Needing to break contact, I step back out of his touch and shake my head. "This is crazy, Judd; we've only known each other for what? Six days. I'm not your puzzle piece. I'm not your soulmate. I'm just someone who's trying to save their library program, and you just happened to be the person who can help me. There can't be anymore to it." I call Bruno and turn towards the door.

"Amelia wait–"

I shake my head and keep my pace. "No Judd, I'm sorry, but I can't be the person you want me to be."

I exit through the door and to the door leading to the stairwell. Yanking it open, I run up the stairs as fast as my feet will take me, Bruno hot on my heels. Once again, running from my problems.

ME

I think I need to move.

CHARLIE

Why? What's wrong with your apartment?

HAZEL

Is it because of the HOT baseball daddy?

ME

OMG Eww Hazel, don't call him daddy. That's just...no. And Yes, I don't think I can live in the same building as him anymore.

CHARLIE

snort baseball daddy, Judd will love that.

CHARLIE

Also, what happened now? You kissed him in the elevator, which btw still jealous about that. Not the kissing Judd part, because I don't see him that way, but the elevator part. That's fucking hot.

HAZEL

GOD! SAME! I want a hot elevator kiss.

ME

Can we focus here please? I'm having a crisis.

CHARLIE

No, you're over analyzing something and your anxiety has worked it into a bigger deal than it probably is. Tell us what happened.

ME

I was in the Gym yesterday morning. At 4am might I add, because we're avoiding. And Judd came in as I almost face planted off the treadmill. He saved me and then basically told me I was his missing puzzle piece.

CHARLIE

Wait, he saved you then said you're his puzzle piece? Just like that?

HAZEL

OMG THAT'S ADORABLE! 😍

ME

Ok well no not just like that. Other things happened, but that was basically the gist of it.

ME

It's not adorable Hazel, it's.... scary.

CHARLIE

What's more scary though Millie? Not taking a chance and missing out on something great? Or taking that chance and realizing it was worth it.

HAZEL

Sometimes you have to take the pitch to find the right one.

CHARLIE

Nice baseball analogy Hazel. Someone's been studying their terminology.

HAZEL

takes a bow Thank you. I thought it was a good one.

ME

sigh I hate you, both of you.

CHARLIE

No you don't, you just hate that we're right.

HAZEL

^ what she said.

ME

🖕

CHARLIE

💋

HAZEL

💋

CHAPTER 12

Judd

IT'S poker night at Kessler's house and I've shown up early to talk to Lucy. I haven't seen Amelia since the gym incident yesterday and I don't know how to proceed with her from here without going to her apartment and making her talk to me. Which probably wouldn't go over well. I don't want to push her. I'm afraid I did that yesterday, but I couldn't stop myself from telling her how I felt.

I know it's too soon to have those feelings. Too soon to think of a future with the tiny blonde spitfire every time I think of her. But I can't help it. Every time I close my eyes, I see Amelia's gorgeous face and the word 'mine' pops into my head. Kessler says it's a Davis family trait. Apparently, my dad's side of the family has a history of 'love at first sight.' I mean, I've heard the story of how my parents fell in love while I was growing up and witnessed Kessler and Lucy's relationship. I just never figured it'd happen to me.

Throwing my Jeep into park, I turn off the engine and sit for a minute, staring at the house my brother had remodeled for Lucy in secret. When Kessler told me he bought a house for a woman he *just* started dating, I'll be honest, I thought he had completely lost his mind. But now? Now I can totally see what drove him to do it. I scrub my hand over my face and get out. I hope Lucy can give me some insight on what to do next because I've got nothing.

Opening the front door and kicking off my shoes at the entry, I holler a 'hello'. When I first came to their house after moving back, I knocked and waited for someone to answer the door. When Lucy answered, she asked if I knocked at my parents' house. I told her I usually just walked in or went to the backyard. Lucy just shook her head and told me I was family and that I never needed to knock because I was always welcome. I decided then that she was my favorite sister. It didn't matter that she's my *only* sister. When I look up from putting my shoes on the rack, I see Lucy's blonde head poke up from behind one of the couches in the living room.

"Oh, hey Judd," Lucy says before a massive yawn takes over her face.

"Did I wake you?" I wince, hoping I didn't. "Where's Kessler?"

She shakes her head and waves me off. "No, it's fine. I was just resting my eyes for a minute. He took Hudson to Kara's. He and Kade are having a sleepover."

Which means she was, in fact, sleeping. "Shit, Luce. I'm sorry. If I would have known, I would have been quieter." Walking over to the couch, I sit on the opposite end of the couch Lucy is on. Angling my body so I can look at her. Her long blonde hair is mussed from sleep, but other than slight shadows under her eyes, she looks good, maybe even better than when I saw her on Halloween.

"You're fine, Judd," she says before another yawn takes over her face. "I was reading and must have fallen asleep." She looks around for her book. Lifting the blanket on her lap, we hear a *thud* as the book hits the floor.

"I got it," I tell her, leaning forward and scooping the book up from where it fell. I look at the cover and chuckle. Amelia's name is on the cover.

"Are you laughing at my book?" Lucy asks as I give her back her book.

"No, not at all."

"Because I'll have you know, Kessler has read some of her books too, and he says they're pretty good." She points a finger and narrows her eyes at me. "Don't make me sic your brother on you, Juddson."

Raising my hands in surrender, I tell her, "No judgment here, Lucy." I don't mention that Amelia is, in fact, the woman I came to get her advice on. I want to keep that information to myself just a while longer.

Seeming to believe me, Lucy tosses her book on the reclaimed wooden coffee table Hudson and Kessler built this summer from old boards we saved after tearing down one of the dilapidated outbuildings on the property. Watching Kessler do things with Hudson our dad did with us when we were his age brought up feelings I didn't know I had. Like jealousy because Kessler gets to have this experience and fear that I never will.

Hearing a throat clear, I pull myself out of my thoughts and look at Lucy, who's looking at me expectantly. "I'm sorry. Did you say something?"

Lucy rolls her eyes like she's annoyed, but gives me a smirk. "I asked what exactly you wanted my advice about. Kessler said you met a girl that you're interested in, but apparently, *she's* not interested in you, but really couldn't give me any more information than that."

I tip my head. "Yeah, well at the time, there wasn't any more information than that."

She raises an eyebrow. "And now there is?"

I nod. "Now there is."

"Well... Give me all the details and I'll see if I can help." Lucy settles back into her pile of pillows behind her and tucks the blanket back around her, getting comfortable while I start at the beginning of the story about how I met Amelia.

"You kissed her in the elevator? Fuck, that's hot," Lucy says, fanning herself. She's sitting up, attention fully on me. Her blanket was discarded halfway into me, telling her about the events that happened in the club. She props her chin up on her hand and sighs, a far off look in her eyes. "That's the stuff romance books are made of."

If she only knew the person I'm interested in, is in fact her *favorite* romance author.

I run my hands through my hair, tugging at the ends. "So now that you know everything, what do you think I should do? She's obviously interested, right?"

Lucy tips her head back and forth, chin still in her hand. "I mean, yeah. It sounds like she's interested, but it also sounds like she's stopping herself from letting it go any further than it has. She could just be afraid that if she starts something with you and it doesn't work out that her program would suffer." She shrugs and sits back, tucking her legs underneath her. "It's a valid worry. *We* know you would never revoke assistance even if things went sideways with you guys, but she doesn't. Like she's pointed out, she's only known you for a few days. Sounds like you need to show her who Judd Davis is." Lucy points at me and gives me a pointed look. "The *real* Judd, the Judd we all love, not the playboy player the trash magazines write about."

We both know the magazines she's talking about. She and Kessler were prime targets in one particular magazine that is owned by the dad of one of the kids on Hudson's baseball team. Unfortunately, scandal sells, and my past isn't exactly pristine. Being the top pitching prospect of my year put me in the spotlight. My series of one-night stands kept me there, when my talent should have been what people focused on. It's only been in the last year that I've started to realize I wanted more than what I was allowing myself to have and slowly my sex life faded out of the harsh spotlight. Which in turn has kept my latest transgression out of the spotlight, so far.

"What made you finally give in? The moment that you finally decided Kessler was worth taking a chance on? Trust that he wouldn't hurt you?"

Lucy sits quietly, staring at the coffee table, eyes unfocused, like she's playing a movie in her head. She breathes out a small laugh and her eyes flick up to mine. "It wasn't just *one* moment. It was a series of moments. Him texting me every day just to let me know he was thinking of me, making sure I had my favorite coffee delivered to me from my favorite café, coming back early from a stretch of away games, and making it to Hudson's championship game." She pauses and quickly wipes a tear from her eyes. Voice cracking when she says, "He was there when he didn't have to be, claimed Hudson and I as his, and made sure everyone knew it too. Even before he found out I had been thrown to the sidelines all my life by people who I thought loved me."

Fuck. I rub my chest, trying to ease the ache that's appeared. I knew Lucy had a rough past, but damn when she puts it like that... I'm glad she and Kessler found each other.

She lets out a huge sigh. "Anyway, enough about us. What are you going to do to show Millie you're in it to win it?" she asks, wiggling her eyebrows.

I bark out a laugh and scrub a hand down my face, rolling my head to look at the spunky blonde who will soon be my sister-in-law. "Fuck, I don't know Luce. What do you think I should do?"

Pulling her top lip into her mouth, she nibbles on it while she thinks. Her lip pops out from between her teeth when she says, "Maybe, just try to be her friend for now."

The sound of a door opening has us both turning to look as Kessler comes through the garage door, tossing his keys on the counter. "Hey baby," he says, a smile breaking out over his face as he looks at Lucy.

Lucy gives him a matching smile. "Hey."

"Did you just want Kessler as your friend?" I ask, watching them give each other eyes from across the open concept house.

Lucy snorts and a look of hunger passes over her face as Kessler walks from the kitchen to the couch we're sitting on. "No, I wanted to jump his bones. Still do if I'm being honest."

"I don't know what we're talking about, but I agree," Kessler says, bending over and giving Lucy a deep kiss. Lucy hums contentedly, running her fingers through Kessler's hair.

"God, get a room," I groan, throwing a pillow at them and hitting the back of Kessler's head.

Kessler flips me off with the hand that's not currently tangled in Lucy's hair, making me chuckle. Breaking the kiss, he looks up at me. "Last time I checked, this was our house and all these rooms are ours."

Lucy laughs and lightly hits Kessler in the chest with the back of her hand. "Be nice. Judd was just asking me for advice before you rudely came over and mauled me."

Kessler looks down at her and wiggles his eyebrows. "I didn't hear you complaining."

Rolling my eyes, I tap the top of Lucy's feet and stand from my seat. "Thanks for the advice, Lucy."

"Anytime Judd. Keep me updated."

I give her a salute with two fingers and make my way down the hall towards the game room where the poker table is set up. Leaving the two lovebirds to make out before all the guys get here.

"Okay assholes, the name of the game is high card flush," Reese says, flicking out the cards to us.

Since moving back and joining the Silverbacks, Kessler and his close group of friends, my teammates and Garrett, have taken me into the fold, including me in their monthly poker nights. I really never clicked with any of my old teammates. Not that I really cared. I liked my team well enough, and we played well together, but I've always wanted to play for the Silverbacks and grew up watching them and going to games with my dad and Kessler. What kid doesn't grow up dreaming of playing for their home team?

To say I'm finally where I want to be is an understatement. The only thing missing is someone to share it with. But I'm working on that.

Pain shoots up my right leg and I reach under the table to grab my shin. "Ah, fuck." I look around and all four sets of eyes are on me. "What the fuck was that for?" I ask, shooting a glare at Kessler.

"I asked you twice if you wanted to keep your cards," Reese says.

"Okay, but did you have to fucking kick me so hard? I have to pitch with Sanders this week, and I don't need to explain to him why I'm not extending forward in my stride."

Austin Sanders is the best pitching coach I've ever worked with, but he has zero tolerance for excuses. If my leg is sore from fucking around and affects my pitch, he will not give a fuck.

"Don't be a little bitch," Kessler says, not looking up from his cards. "When you squat for a living and have the knees of a 60-year-old, then come complain to me. Until then, fuck off and decide if you want to keep your cards or change 'em out."

Garrett snorts from Kessler's other side. "I wouldn't brag about making your living on your knees, bro."

Kessler backhands Garrett in the chest but pulls his hand back and shakes it. "Fuck man, you got armour under there?"

Garrett flexes. “Nope, I’m just a man.”

Snorts of laughter erupt from around the table. “If that’s the case, why haven’t you asked Kara out?” Reese asks, raising his eyebrows at Garrett.

“What the fuck does that have to do with anything?” Garrett asks, setting his cards down on the table and narrowing his eyes at Reese. He may be Ex-Navy, but it seems even SEALs get embarrassed judging by the red creeping up his neck from under the collar of his signature black T-shirt.

Reese either isn’t scared or doesn’t give a shit about breathing air because instead of backing off, the dumbass keeps going. “Well, last time I checked, men have balls,” he says, “and if you had said balls, you would have asked Kara out by now.” Reese shrugs. “But, since as far as we all know, you haven’t, that must mean you, in fact, are not a man.”

Silence surrounds the table as we all look from Reese’s smug face to Garrett’s progressively red one until Reese breaks the silence by barking out a giant belly laugh.

“I’m just fucking with you,” Reese says, slapping a hand on Garrett’s shoulder and giving him a shake. “Man, you shoulda seen your face. I thought you were going to stroke out.” Wiping moisture from the corner of his eye, he adds, “Plus, we all know Kara’s out of your league.”

The tension around the table is broken as Garrett chuckles and slaps Reese’s back, a little harder than normal judging by the way Reese winces. “Ain’t that the truth,” Garrett says, picking his cards back up off the table.

With the beat-down averted, we get back into the game. Changing out cards and making our bets. “I fold,” Brent mutters, tossing his cards onto the table and picking up his phone. He’s been on it non-stop since he got here and he’s not his normal chatty self.

I tap him with my foot, tipping my chin at him when he looks up. “Everything good, dude? You’ve been quiet since you got here.”

He releases a heavy sigh and scrubs at his face. "Just sister drama."

"Which one this time?" Kessler asks, flicking his eyes from Brent back down to his cards. Brent has four sisters. Two older and two younger. Leaving Brent smack dab in the middle to deal with them all.

"Cass," he says with a sigh. I see Reese tense out of the corner of my eye as Brent continues on. "Her dickwad of a boyfriend dumped her, *again*." He runs his hand through his hair, tugging at the ends. "I don't know why she keeps going back to him. It's like he gets off on fucking with her emotions. We've all told her he's a piece of shit and that she deserves better, but she never listens to us. She just sticks up for him and tells us he's just *misunderstood*." He snorts. "He's just a fucking prick who gets off on belittling people and stringing my sister along."

I've met Cass a few times. She's the one who helped Lucy and Kessler plan their engagement party and is also planning their wedding. She seems sweet, if not a little shy.

"Want me to help you kick his ass?" Reese asks from across the table. His posture seems relaxed, but I can see the tendon popping in his jaw as he pretends to look at his cards. "He doesn't even have to know it's us." His eyes bounce to Garrett, a bit of an unhinged gleam in them. "Seal boy can give us some pointers on how to do it quickly and quietly."

"Call me Seal boy again and I'll show you firsthand what I can do," Garrett mutters, still looking at his cards.

Kessler shakes his head and rolls his eyes, tossing his cards down. "Fold. I don't have shit." He stretches and gets up from the table, heading to the mini fridge in the corner. "Anyone want anything while I'm up?"

Everyone shakes their heads, mumbling their responses. "I'll take a water," I tell him, before turning my attention back to Brent. "So, what are you going to do?"

"Nothing I really can do. She's a big girl, and as much as it sucks to see her hurting, she's old enough to make her decisions, whether we agree with them or not." He releases another heavy sigh. "I just have to stand by and watch and be there for her when she needs it." He turns in his seat and looks over at Kessler. "You know what? I changed my mind. I'll have a beer."

Kessler grabs two beers and my water out of the fridge and sets them down in front of us. Brent twists the top off and downs half of his before coming up for air.

"Okay Garrett, it's just you and me. What are you packin'?"

"Three hearts, queen high," Garrett says, revealing his hand.

"Fucker," Reese says tossing his cards down, revealing three spades, with the highest card being an eight.

"Who's the man now?" Garrett asks, collecting his winnings and stacking the chips.

"Whatever, the night's still young," Reese says, shuffling the cards to be re-dealt.

CHAPTER 13

Amelia

FUCK, my head feels like it's going to pop right off my neck. Shutting my car door and opening the back hatch for Bruno, I clip his leash on and wait for him to hop out of the back before stabbing the close button on my compact SUV.

If it wasn't for the interview being today, I would have called and told Gladys or Irene I wouldn't be making it today. But here I am, later than normal, but here, running up the steps of the library with Bruno hot on my heels to avoid being completely drenched, making my migraine worse with every step.

Once I reach the landing, I wrench the door open and dart inside. Dropping my oversized bag to the floor, I grab the towel I tucked inside and throw it over Bruno before he can shake everywhere. Getting him dried off to the best of my ability and cleaning up the slight puddle we made in the entrance, I fold the towel over my arm and proceed to the children's room.

Walking in, I see a couple of the dogs are already settled into their beds, the sounds of licking echoing throughout the space as they dry themselves off more. I unclip Bruno's leash and stow my stuff in the back room, laying the towel over the back of the chair to help it dry.

"Millie, there you are. I was just about to call you," Gladys says from the office door.

Slowly turning around because I've moved way too fast for my body's liking the past few minutes, I face Gladys. "Sorry I'm late. I have a terrible migraine and if it wasn't for the interview, I wouldn't be here at all."

"Oh dear, well, as soon as the interview is over, don't you worry about anything and just go on home. I know how bad these can get for you," she says softly. "Why don't you sit in here with the lights off until the reporter gets here?"

Mustering a small smile, I thank her and slump into the chair. Folding my arms across the desk, I lay my head down as Gladys flips the lights off and leaves the door cracked. My eyes immediately take solace in the darkness, and the pounding in my head eases slightly.

A few minutes later I hear Judd's deep voice just outside the door, making my heart rate skyrocket and the pounding in my head increase. I haven't seen him since the gym, and I don't know how I'm going to face him today. It's one of the reasons I have a migraine. I've been playing out different scenarios in my head about how today could go. I'm also incredibly behind on my next novel and I'm falling further behind every day. At this rate I won't make my deadline, which will put me behind all next year. I had panic attacks all night about it.

Just another perk of my anxiety.

Yay me.

The door creaks open and light from the library leaks in. Squinting my eyes, I look up and see Judd's tall silhouette in the doorway. He closes the door behind him until there's just a sliver of light sneaking through. "Hey," he whispers, coming over to crouch next to me, resting a hand on my back. "Gladys said you had a migraine. How bad is it?"

My eyes glide over his barely visible face, but even in the dark I can still see how handsome he is...asshole.

Filling my lungs with Judd's signature christmassy scent, I decide to downplay just how much pain I'm in. "I'm fine, just a little headache. Already feeling better." The lie feels thick and sticky on my tongue, but to drive the point home, I roll the office chair back and stand. "See? Feeling..." The words die on my tongue as the dark room tips on its axis.

Judd grabs me by the shoulders and shoves me back down into the chair before I topple over. "That's what I figured. Mills, there's no way you can do this interview today," he says, using the nickname I secretly love. The name only my dad used for me. Tears prick at my eyes, and I will them away, blinking rapidly. Thankful that we're in the dark.

Judd takes his phone out of his back pocket. "I'll be right back. Sit tight and whatever you do, don't try to get up," he tells me before stepping out of the room.

I'd roll my eyes, but honestly, that would even hurt too much at this point. Every movement is too much and I'm wondering how I'm going to drive home after this. A wave of nausea hits me, and I pull a slow breath through my nose. I've officially hit the point of no return. Nothing but an ice pack, a dark room, and a massive amount of Tylenol and ibuprofen can help me now. I've taken meds for my migraines off and on throughout the years, but they really don't seem to work any better.

I'm reclining back in the chair, trying to breathe through the nausea when Judd comes back in and crouches back down in front of me. He places his hand on my knee, and I'm surprised at how quickly the spot warms under his touch. Looking down at him, I have to convince my hands not to reach forward and run my fingers through his thick, dark hair.

"I'm taking you home. I called Jules and rescheduled the interview. She said to tell you she hopes you feel better soon."

I blink slowly at him while my brain processes the information he just told me. "Jules? Julie? The reporter? Wait, how? You know her?" Apparently, full sentences are no longer a thing for me today.

"Yes, Julie, the reporter. We go way back to my rookie year. I was one of her first athletes she interviewed after she graduated." He shrugs and I know there's more to the story than he's letting on. An irrational streak of jealousy burns through my stomach, increasing my nausea.

No, I am *not* jealous. I have nothing to be jealous about.

"Alright Sweetheart, grab your stuff and let's head out."

Hold up. "Uh, what?"

"I'm taking you home. Grab what you need and let's get Bruno and get you home."

I blink slowly at him, trying to ignore the flip my stomach does when he says *home*. "But I drove here," I tell him.

He chuckles lightly and leans down, bracing himself on the arms of the chair, towering over me. "I know, but there is no way I'm letting you drive home like this." Judd reaches up and cups my face, running his thumb over my cheek, eyes gazing into mine "I would never forgive myself if I let you drive home, and something happened to you."

Oh.

"But, uh, what, what about my car?" I ask, trying to wade through the migraine induced fog.

Judd lifts a shoulder and removes his hand from my face to stand. "We can come back and get it tomorrow."

Panic eats at the edge of my pain, making the thumping in my head worse. "No, I, I can't leave my car. What if I need it? I'll just drive, it's fine. I'll be fine." I honestly don't know if I'm trying to reassure him or myself at this point.

"It's not really a big..." he trails off. "It's an anxiety thing, isn't it?"

I nod and drop my gaze, grateful for the millionth time in the last five minutes the room is dark enough to hide my reddened expression. Judd's fingers pinch my chin and lift my face to look at him. "What have I told you, Amelia?"

I stare at him blankly, not knowing what he's talking about.

He sighs and traces his thumb below my bottom lip. "You have nothing to be embarrassed about. Now that I know being without your car gives you anxiety, I'll figure out how to get your car back to the apartment after I get you home. Okay?"

I nod again, and he releases my chin and holds out his hand to me. "Let's go."

Without hesitation, I take Judd's hand and he pulls me up. After tucking the towel back into my oversized bag, I grab Bruno's leash and clip it back on him before we say our goodbyes and head back out of the library. Judd has me wait at the entrance while he pulls his Jeep up to the bottom of the stairs, trying to keep my movement to a minimum. I think he'd carry me if I let him. Which I won't because that would just be embarrassing.

Tempting, though.

I'm soaking in a hot bath with my Epsom salts and an ice pack behind my neck, trying to remind myself why I've been avoiding Judd in the first place. I'm not doing a very good job. When we got back to my apartment, Judd asked if he could come in to help me get settled. The short car ride made me even more nauseous than I was to begin with, so I just waved him in as I unclipped Bruno's leash and headed to my bedroom.

Judd found me sitting on the edge of my bed, staring into my bathroom. When he asked what I needed, I told him I usually take a hot bath with an ice pack behind my neck and that I was just trying to psych myself up to get my bath ready. He left the room and came back with one of my blue moldable ice packs. He handed it to me and asked how hot I liked my baths.

When I told him 'Hot enough to make a man cry', he just laughed and rolled up the sleeve of his sweater and went into the bathroom. I laid on the bed with my ice pack while I watched him run me a bath, checking the water frequently and adjusting the nobs to make sure it was just right.

Fun fact: it was perfect.

Before I got into the bath. Judd asked if I needed Bruno or if he was okay to take him with him to go get my car. The rain had stopped by the time we reached our building, and according to his weather app, it wasn't supposed to start up again until later tonight. He said a walk would be good for both of them. It had been a few days since I had been able to take Bruno for a long walk, so I told Judd to take him. With a wink and a promise to be back soon, I watched the man I don't want to have feelings for take *my dog* with him to go get *my car* so I wouldn't worry about it being left in the library parking lot overnight.

I feel like an absolute bitch for running from him the other day. I think I owe him an apology.

With the bathwater getting cold and my migraine now at a more tolerable pain level, I flip the drain and get out of the bath. Toweling off, I wrap the towel around me and move into my bedroom. I walk to the dresser and grab the softest pair of leggings I own and a camisole and pull them on. Not wanting to wear a bra, I snag the hoodie I borrowed from Judd on Halloween night and pull that on too, so it's not obvious I'm braless.

Grabbing the ice pack off the side of the tub, I walk into the kitchen to swap it out with a new one. My stomach lets out a growl, reminding me I haven't eaten anything since convincing myself to choke down a slice of peanut butter toast and a banana this morning. Looking at the time on the stove, and deciding it's close enough to dinner time, I open the fridge to find a yogurt, two eggs, and a bunch of random condiments.

Take out it is.

Taking my hair down from the claw clip and laying out on the couch, I tuck the ice pack behind my neck and pull up the website to my favorite Chinese food place. I'm ordering hot and sour soup and trying to guess what Judd would like too when I hear the jingle of my keys on the other side of the door. The door pushes open and Bruno jogs in. When he sees me laying on the couch, he wiggles his body and comes over to greet me, snout crinkled in a smile.

"Hey buddy, did you have a nice walk with Judd?" I croon to him. He wiggles his butt faster in response, so I take that as a yes.

Judd comes in next with an arm full of bags. Peaking over the bags, he sees me laying on the couch and gives me a grin. "You look better. How's the pain level?"

I return the smile and give Bruno one last scratch before sitting up, pulling my feet up and resting my chin on my knees. "Better. Manageable," I tell him, watching him go into the kitchen to set the bags he's carrying on the counter. I'm about to ask him what he has in the bags when the smell of Chinese food hits my nose. I inhale a deep breath, and my stomach rumbles in response.

Judd pauses amid unloading the bags and stares at me, eyebrows raised. "Was that your stomach?"

My face heats and I mumble a 'Yes' from where my face is hidden behind my knees.

"Well, it's a good thing I called Charlie and asked her what you normally eat when you have migraines and don't feel like eating." I sit in stunned silence as I watch him pull out a large container of what I'm hoping is my hot and sour soup, along with various other containers.

Looking up from the food, Judd tilts his head at me and

says, "Tell me where the bowls are and I'll dish you up so you don't have to get up."

Where the hell did this man come from? I've never had anyone offer to get me a plate so I can relax on the couch.

Feeling awkward that he even offered and not really understanding why, I rise from the couch and walk into the kitchen, grabbing a plate and a bowl from the cabinet and set them down next to the containers and handing the plate to Judd. "I can do it, but thank you. You are a lifesaver. I was actually just getting ready to order food from here when you came in." Grabbing the soup container, I lift the lid and pour a generous amount into my bowl. Feeling Judd's gaze on me I look up and see him staring. "What?"

Caught in the act, Judd shakes his head and laughs. I spy a little red poking out from under his beard, like he's embarrassed. "Nothing," he says, grabbing a container and dumping some onto his plate.

"No, not 'nothing'. Why were you staring at me like that?"

Grabbing a smaller container, Judd opens it and reaches in, grabbing what looks like barbecue pork and putting it on his plate. He shakes his head and smirks. "Has anyone ever told you that you're short?"

"Yeah, well, not everyone can be a jolly green giant," I grumble, bumping him with my hip, which hits him mid-thigh. Chuckling, he moves, and I dig out spoons and forks, setting them on the counter. Grabbing a spoon and napkin, I turn to leave when he stops me.

"Wait," he says, rummaging around in a reusable bag I recognize from my car. "Here, chug this before eating," he tells me, handing me a light blue sports drink.

"Why?" I question, setting my bowl down to twist the top off, taking two big gulps.

"The electrolytes help ease headaches." Pointing a fork at me, he adds. "You're probably dehydrated, drink up."

I roll my eyes but do as I'm told because he's not wrong. I

have a tendency to forget to drink anything other than coffee when I'm on a deadline. Finishing the bottle, I hold up the empty container and shake it, showing him it's empty.

"Good girl."

I roll my eyes again and grab my bowl, trying to quiet the butterflies that took flight in my stomach at those words. The only women who like that are the ones I write about...right?

Turning away from him, I stop at Bruno's food bowl and scoop his dinner into his dish before I head to the couch and take a seat, grabbing the remote from the side table. "Want to watch a movie or something? I mean, no pressure. We don't have to if you don't want to," I babble.

Smooth Amelia.

Plate piled high with more food than I could probably consume in two meals, Judd grabs a napkin from the food bag and comes into the living room, joining me on the other end of the couch. "Sure, what do you have in mind?"

I shrug and flip on the TV. My recently watched list pops up.

"Do you like *The Office?*"

Judd snorts and holds up a finger to me as he chews his mouth full of food. "Does telling you I dressed up as Gold Face for Halloween two years ago answer your question?"

"Pictures or it didn't happen," I tell him, pointing my spoon at him.

Chuckling, he pulls his phone out of his pocket and swipes across his screen until he finds what he's looking for. "Here," he says, handing me the phone.

I take it and look at the picture. Judd is dressed in a suit with a gold tie, wearing what looks like a wig, holding up plastic handguns in each hand with a wide smile across his glittery gold face.

"That is epic," I say, handing the phone back to him. Our fingers brush when he takes it back and I pull my hand back quickly when I feel a little zap. He must feel it too because he's staring at me with what I assume is a matching expression to mine.

Judd clears his throat and puts his phone back in his pocket. "Must be static from the next storm rolling in," he says before going back to his food.

That has to be it, because there can't be any other reason why, I tell myself.

CHAPTER 14

Judd

WE'RE two episodes into *The Office* when Amelia pauses the show and turns to me, hugging her legs to her chest. She looks nervous. "I owe you an apology," she says quietly, eyes flicking to mine, then back down to her hands where she's picking at her cuticles.

"For what?" She doesn't owe me anything, least of all an apology. When I was heading to the library today, I decided to take Lucy's advice and just be Amelia's friend, to show her who I really am.

"For my behavior. For how bitchy I've been lately, especially towards you." She pauses and shakes her head slightly. "I promise I'm not usually a miserable person. I just..." She sighs, flicking her eyes back up to mine. "I have a lot going on and I'm not handling it well," she admits and rubs at her temples. I take her appearance in quickly. Even in the dim light, I can see the dark circles under her eyes are even darker than they were at the gym the other day.

"You don't need to apologize for anything, Amelia."

"No, I do. Especially after taking care of me tonight and rescheduling the interview. You didn't have to do any of that, but here you are. Coming to my rescue."

I shift on the couch and turn my body towards her, coming up with an idea. "I'll tell you what. I'll accept your unnecessary apology if you agree to accept my friendship."

One eyebrow quirks up. "You want to be my friend?" she asks slowly, like she's trying to comprehend something impossible.

I nod.

"Why?"

I shrug. "You can never have too many friends." Deciding to keep my conversation with Lucy to myself. "So, what do you say? Friends?" I ask, sticking my hand out to her.

She eyes my hand before extending her own, connecting with mine. A tingle shoots up my arm as her cold hand connects with my warm one and her eyes snap to mine.

She feels it too.

"Friends," she whispers, shaking my hand slightly. Not uttering a word about what I know we both just felt.

"Friends," I repeat.

We stare at each other for a few heartbeats before she pulls her hand back and tucks it inside the sleeve of the hoodie I gave her. Seeing her in my hoodie when I walked into her apartment did things to me that had me reciting baseball stats in my head to calm myself down. I've never asked a woman to wear my jersey, but I hope one day that will change.

Collecting our plates, I watch as she heads to the kitchen and dumps them into the sink. I make a mental note to wash them before I leave. Moving to the fridge, she pulls open the freezer and extracts another ice pack. "Do you need anything while I'm up?"

I shake my head. "I'm good. Do you still have a migraine?"

"Unfortunately," she mutters, coming back to her spot on the couch while she wraps a towel around the ice pack and places it behind her neck. "The pain is better than earlier, but it's still there." She lets out a heavy sigh. "Depending on how bad they are and what triggered them, they can come and go for a few days."

"What triggered this one?"

"Lack of sleep, too much coffee and not enough water, stress...honestly a combination of things," she says, hitting the play button.

"Is there anything I can do?" I ask, hating that she's still suffering, even though she's trying not to let on that she is.

Amelia rolls her head to the side and gives me a small smile. "No, I'll use my neck massager after I take Bruno out one more time to help ease the knot I have. That should help."

"I can rub your shoulders." The words leave my mouth before I realize what I'm saying. "I mean...if you want? I've been told I have great hands." I close my eyes. "Not like that. I mean, like that too." *Shut up.* "But that's not how I'm offering to use them." Scrubbing a hand down my face. I look to see Amelia's shoulders shaking and her face buried in my hoodie.

I stand. "You know what? I'm just going to show myself out," I say, walking past her. A hand shoots out and grabs my arm and I look down to see Amelia's face contorted in a laugh, eyes shiny from tears.

"No, please," she says, wiping her eyes. "Stay. That was truly entertaining."

"I think I'd rather go be awkward in the comfort of my own home."

"That was impressive," she says, letting go of my wrist and patting the couch. "But please, don't feel like you can't be yourself around me. That's what friends do, right? Let their guard down around their friends. Shed the facade of having to be perfect all the time?"

"Okay, fine. I'll stay," I tell her, but point a finger at her. "*If* you let me rub your shoulders. I guarantee I can do a better job than a machine."

She purses her lips, fighting a laugh, but doesn't do a good job holding off her laugh as one bubbles past her lips.

"Get your mind out of the gutter, *Miss Morgan*."

She snorts. "Have you read *any* of my books? My brain *lives* in the gutter." She gives me a wicked smirk. "Buckle up Davis. This friendship is going to be a hell of a ride."

Something tells me I'll enjoy every second of it.

"Fucking Roy," Amelia mutters to the T.V. from her spot on the floor in front of me where I'm currently rubbing out a series of gnarly knots from her shoulders and neck. I don't know how she functions with these. I'd be crying like a baby. In fact, I *did* cry like a baby the last time one of the team's massage therapists got their hands on me.

"How do you even function with this many knots?"

She shrugs, tracing her finger from Bruno's nose to the top of his head and back down. He came over and plopped down next to her as soon as she sat on the floor, laying his head in her lap. "I guess I just adapted after a while. I used to get massages every other week, but when my massage therapist moved. I just quit going. It gave me too much anxiety to find a new one."

Running my thumbs up her neck and digging into the base of her skull, Amelia lets out a long moan, not helping the semi I'm sporting from listening to her moan off and on for the past fifteen minutes. I'm running out of stats to recite.

"Have you ever tried booking a group massage with Charlie and Hazel? It might help ease the anxiety of going for the first couple of times?" I suggest.

"We actually did once, but Charlie is so crazy busy most of the time our schedules usually don't align with hers or what the spas had available. Hazel and I don't want to go without her and make her feel left out."

I make another pass with my thumbs, then run my fingers

over the back of her skull, entangling my fingers in her hair as I increase the pressure.

"Oh, fuck," she whispers, melting into my hands.

Her breathy voice sends a jolt straight to my cock, making me bite my lip to keep my own groan at bay.

"I think I'm dead," she mumbles.

I clear my throat and drag my thoughts from a naked Amelia spread in front of me, moaning my name as I feast on her. I'm beginning to think this was a bad idea.

"Uh, is it helping?" I croak out as I continue to rub her skull.

"Immensely. Can I just hire you? We can add personal masseuse to your resume in the off season," she jokes.

Extracting my hands from her hair, I hold one hand out and twiddle my fingers. "Give me your phone. I'll put my number in it and you can text me anytime you need me to release some tension," I tell her, choking back a snort at the double innuendo.

She slaps my hand away. "I was joking."

"I'm not. Give me your phone," I tell her, holding my hand out again.

"Seriously, Judd. It was a joke. I'll be fine," she says, tapping Bruno to move him and scooting away from me, slipping her hoodie back over her head, indicating she's done. "I really appreciate you working those knots out, though. It's true, you really do have great hands," she says, smirking at me.

I chuckle. "Anytime Amelia. I mean it."

She looks from my hand to me and back. Sighing, she grabs her phone off the floor and unlocks it, placing it in my palm. "Don't make me regret this," she grumbles.

I quickly input my number before she changes her mind and send myself a text before handing it back to her. One of her eyebrows quirks up when she sees the screen and looks up at me with a small smirk.

"Sexiest man alive?"

"I wanted to make sure you knew who it was."

"Because I have so many other Judd's in my phone," she deadpans. "Anyway, it's getting late. I should take Bruno out."

Bruno's ears perk up at the mention of his name and he goes to the door, spinning twice before sitting down and waiting.

"Do you want some company?" I ask, not ready for the night to be over yet and not wanting her to be out in the dark alone.

Shrugging, she slides on a pair of shoes. "If you want. We're just going to the grassy spot in the park next door." She jerks her thumb over her shoulder towards the park that borders this side of the apartment building.

"I'll go with you. It's dark out."

Amelia snorts. "It's a really well-lit area. Plus, I do this every night. Nothing has happened to me yet."

"And nothing will tonight either," I tell her, following her out the door.

After she locks her door, we make our way to the elevator. Hitting the call button, I lean up against the wall and tuck my hands into my pockets, waiting.

Amelia chews on her bottom lip and peeks up at me out of the corner of her eye.

"What's on your mind, Shortcake?"

She shakes her head, lips twitching in a smile. "Why do you call me Shortcake?"

I chuckle at her question. The elevator arrives and we shuffle in, my hand falling to the small of her back as I enter behind her. She hits the lobby button, and she turns toward me as the doors close.

"Well?"

I rub my hand over my beard. "Well, if it's not obvious, you're pretty short." She rolls her eyes and I laugh. "Plus, out of all the names I've called you, you seem to balk the least at that one."

She hums and nods her head.

"So, you approve, Shortcake?" I joke, nudging her with my arm.

She snorts and rolls her eyes. "I guess I do."

I know she's approving of the nickname, but maybe it means she's approving of me, too.

CHAPTER 15

Amelia

THE BELL above Latte Daze jingles, announcing my arrival. Hazel peeks over her shoulder at the sound. "Hey girl, get us a table and I'll be over in a jiff. I'm just putting the last of the scones in the oven."

"Please tell me they're your cranberry white chocolate ones," I beg, my mouth already watering at the prospect of tart cranberries and rich white chocolate blessing my tastebuds.

"'Tis the season," she says, giving me a wink.

"Thank you, baby Jesus," I mutter, claiming a table near the back close to the counter so Hazel can still chat with Charlie and I while she putters around behind the counter. Even though Hazel has employees to run the counter when we have our coffee dates, she still has a hard time sitting down and just relaxing, so Charlie and I sit and enjoy our coffee while Hazel bounces around the back like a rabbit on crack.

I'm settling into my seat when my phone buzzes in my back pocket. I set my bag on the table and pull it out, seeing a text from Charlie.

CHARLIE

Be there in 5! Don't start without me.

ME

Hurry up! I can't promise there will still be scones left. I'm starving.

HAZEL

I'll save you some scones Char. You want the usual?

CHARLIE

THANK YOU BEST FRIEND HAZEL! Yes, the usual please.

I smirk at my screen and set my phone down as Hazel sets my large gingerbread cold brew and a plate of cranberry scones in front of me. "Bless you," I tell her, picking up the coffee and taking a sip. "It's like Christmas came in my mouth."

Hazel snorts. "I thought you didn't like to swallow?"

I shrug. "If it tasted like this, I would."

Hazel laughs and goes back behind the counter, busying herself with making Charlie's drink. I look around and see there's a handful of people spread out among the tables and couches. One person is sitting in the little reading nook Hazel put in last year at my suggestion. I always imagined myself opening up a little café/bookstore. I even majored in business in college, where I met Charlie. But after losing my parents, I found myself lost. At the suggestion of my therapist, I started writing down my feelings because voicing them was too much. Writing seemed to be the only thing that helped me process my emotions and escape from my reality.

My thoughts became short stories, which became books. One of my professors read a short story that I wrote for class and suggested I submit it in a contest where the top ten submissions would be published. I hesitated at first. I didn't think it was good enough, and I wasn't sure I wanted people reading my inner thoughts. When I told Charlie, she said the worst that could happen was that it didn't win. No harm, no foul. I voiced my fear of people reading my thoughts and she said people didn't need to know my writing was my inner dialogue. To them, it was just a story someone wrote. So, I submitted it.

I ended up winning the contest, and my first piece was published. Turns out using humor to process my pain worked, not only for me, but for other people, too. Even though there were nine other stories published, mine was the one readers resonated with the most, resulting in publishing agencies contacting me for book deals.

But winning the contest sent me into a downward spiral. Don't get me wrong, I was happy that I won, excited even. I opened my phone to call my parents and realized I couldn't... because they were gone, and their deaths were the reason I had won in the first place. That was the first time in almost a year that I had forgotten, just for a second, that I was an orphan.

What happened after that is what led me to being hospitalized and in an intense therapy program for six months. It's not something I'm proud of, but it's a part of my journey and I had to learn to accept that I have to take the bad days with the good.

The bell brings me out of my thoughts, and I see Charlie hurrying over. Short, wavy dark brown hair mused from the wind. She pats her hair down as she makes her way over to me.

"Sorry, I'm late," she huffs out, plopping down in the empty chair and giving Bruno a pat when he stands and sticks his head in her lap. "What did I miss?"

I reach forward and pluck a leaf out of her hair. "Nothing, Hazel's busy making her confectionery goodness, so I've just been sitting here sifting through my emails." It's not a complete lie. Hazel is busy baking. I'm just not telling her what I was thinking about. I don't need to worry her; I've done enough of that for one lifetime.

Hearing her name, Hazel pops out from the back, bringing Charlie her coffee and carrying one of her own. She eyes the plate and looks up at me. "All the scones are still here. Are you sick?" she asks, putting her hand on the back of my forehead.

I knock her hand away and laugh. "I was checking my emails and got distracted," I tell her.

"Mmmm," she hums, not believing me but letting it slide.

"So, I heard the interview was rescheduled to next week," Charlie says, peering over her cup at me while she sips on her coffee.

"Hello to you too, Charlie. How have you been? Me? Great, great, just living the dream," I tease.

Charlie rolls her eyes. "Good morning. How is everyone? Great? Awesome. Now tell me why Judd texted me, asking what you ate when you had a migraine and were sick."

Busted.

I forgot Judd did that. Knowing I won't get out of explaining what went down, I gulp down a fourth of my drink and sigh. "He drove me home from the library. Ran me a bath that was the perfect temperature by the way and then went and got my car that we had to leave behind. All without complaint. *Then* he brought me hot and sour soup, made me drink a Gatorade because he just somehow knew I was dehydrated and gave me the best shoulder massage I've ever had in my life. Oh, and we agreed to be friends."

The girls stare at me in varying degrees of surprise.

"Friends?" Hazel asks, like the word is foreign to her tongue.

I nod.

Charlie picks up a scone and bites the corner. "I give it a week," she says around the pastry.

I raise an eyebrow at her. "A week for what?" I ask, grabbing my own scone, biting into the flaky, buttery goodness. Tart cranberries making my taste buds dance.

"A week until the sexual tension between you two is so great that you can't deny it anymore."

Hazel tips her head to the side and looks at me. "Nah, I think Millie will make him wait at least two just to spite us."

"No. We're friends. Friends don't bone."

"Friends with benefits do," Charlie suggests.

Hazel points her scone at Charlie. "Yes, agreed." She turns to me. "Use all his benefits. I bet he has a lot of benefits."

I pinch the bridge of my nose, sighing. "No, no benefits. And can we stop saying benefits, please?"

"Come on, Millie. You can't tell me having his hands on you last night didn't bring up some feelings?" Hazel challenges.

That's the problem. Having his hands on me brought up too many feelings. Feelings I haven't had for someone in a long time, if ever. Imagining his hands venturing beyond my shoulders left me achy and needy. Let's just say my vibrator got a good workout after I went to bed.

"That's what I thought," Hazel says, taking my silence as an admission.

"Okay, fine. I *may* have felt...things, but that doesn't mean it has to go anywhere beyond friendship. It can't go anywhere beyond friendship. I'm not interested." I sit back and cross my arms, almost believing the lie myself. "Look, can we just drop this, please? I don't want to talk about it anymore. Judd and I are friends. End of discussion."

Charlie sets her scone down and brushes the crumbs from her hands. Leaning forward, she lays one hand across the table and grabs my free one. "It's ok to be scared, Millie," she says softly, giving my hand a squeeze.

"I'm not scared. I just don't have time. And this is a bad time of the year for me to be getting involved with anyone, anyway." I look between my two best friends, my constants, the only ones who have never given up on me, even in my darkest times. "No one ever stays, and I don't blame them. I'm a lot."

Hazel's hand darts forward and lands on top of mine and Charlie's connected ones. "No one *worthy* ever stayed," she says, bright-hazel eyes boring into mine. "And that's their loss. You're amazing Millie, and I think Judd sees that too. You just have to decide if you want to let him in."

"What if I do and he decides *I'm* not worth it?"

"Then he wasn't the right one for you, but you'll never know unless you try," Charlie chimes in.

I take a deep breath and blow it out. "I don't have enough coffee in my system to be making these decisions right now, but I'll think about it." They both give my hand a squeeze and pull away. "Enough about me. What's happening with you two?" I ask, needing a change of subject.

"Nothing really with me, just trying to get ahead of all the holiday orders I'm going to be hit with in the next few weeks," Hazel says, sipping on her coffee. Hazel's holiday treats sell out every year. She already has a preorder list a mile long.

"When do you sleep?" I ask, knowing she's working long hours.

Hazel snorts. "I don't. I got home at nine last night, fell asleep in the middle of sexting Jason, and was up and out the door by three. My sex life is suffering," she pouts.

Charlie and I both snort. Hazel has the most sex out of all of us. "A day or two without an orgasm isn't going to kill you," Charlie mutters.

"It might! An orgasm a day keeps the doctor away." She points her finger between Charlie and me. "You two bitches are just jealous I'm getting it on the regular."

"Yeah, we are," Charlie and I say at the same time. We all erupt in giggles, like high schoolers talking about our crushes, earning a few quizzical looks from other patrons in the shop.

Once we recover from our giggle fit, I turn to Charlie, who's wiping tears from under her eyes. "What about you, Char?"

"Nothing new really, just packing for the cruise and making sure nothing implodes at work while I'm gone for almost three weeks." She looks at me and scrunches her nose. "I still wish you could come. It's going to be weird not spending Thanksgiving with you."

After I lost my parents, Charlie's mom and dad took me in, even though I was twenty-one and an adult. Charlie's mom, Diana, helped me with my parents' funerals, settling their estate, everything. I still have a room at their house. I spend every holiday with them, except this year. Diana has been wanting to take a cruise for years. But because baseball is from February through October, and Chuck is the manager for the Silverbacks, she's never been able to book one. So when Charlie found a cruise that runs through Thanksgiving, she showed her dad and they bought tickets and gave them to Diana for her birthday this last spring. Charlie asked if I wanted to go, but there's no way I could leave Bruno for that long and having a dog on the ship wouldn't work. So this year I'm flying solo for Thanksgiving.

"I know. But it'll be fine. I'm already planning on spending the day in my pajamas, binge watching *Sweet Magnolias* on Netflix, and ordering way too much Chinese food. It'll be great," I say cheerily, trying not only to convince Charlie, but myself.

"You could always come and spend it with us," Hazel chimes in with her offer again. She usually spends Thanksgiving at her aunt's in Eastern Washington, with her dad and Jason. I love Hazel's dad, but I'm not a huge fan of Jason. He makes Hazel happy, but there's something about him I just don't like, and I'd rather not spend more time with him than I already have to.

"Thanks Haze, but I need to do this on my own. I can't rely on you guys forever. Plus, I booked a session with my therapist for that Tuesday, so I'll be good."

"You can always rely on us, no matter what," Charlie says.

"Yeah, we're ride or die bitches for life," Hazel adds,

holding up her scone. Charlie and I each grab another scone and tap them together in a cheers.

I truly hit the jackpot with these ladies.

My thumb hovers over the contact I swore I wouldn't text first, but here I am, texting him first. Damn him.

ME

I have a question for you.

SEXIEST MAN ALIVE

Shoot, Shortcake.

ME

How much does getting a tattoo hurt? Like on a scale of 1-10. 1 being not at all and 10 being fuck it's excruciating.

SEXIEST MAN ALIVE

It really depends on where you get it and what your pain tolerance is. Based on the boulders you call knots I massaged the other night. I'd say you have a high pain tolerance so it probably wouldn't hurt as much as it might other people.

SEXIEST MAN ALIVE

Why? Are you wanting a tattoo?

ME

Yes, thanks for the information.

SEXIEST MAN ALIVE

Wait, that's it? You're not going to tell me what or WHERE?

ME

NOPE, *twiddles fingers*

SEXIEST MAN ALIVE

Tease.

ME

CHAPTER 16

Judd

POP!

The sound of the baseball hitting the glove echoes off the walls of the Silverbacks training facility.

"Better. Again," Austin Sanders commands from where he's standing with Hudson behind the backstop. Sanders has been the pitching coach for the Silverbacks for the last five years and he's one of the best. I've only been working with him for the last four months and I've already seen a difference in my pitching.

Kessler tosses the ball back to me and I set up, taking a breath and releasing it as I launch the ball towards the plate.

Pop! Echoes through the facility again.

"Good, good, that's enough for today, Davis," Sanders calls out, waving me over. I wipe my forehead on the back of my sleeve and walk over to where Kessler has joined Hudson and Sanders. Picking up my water bottle, I chug half before taking a breath.

"How does the arm feel?" Sanders asks, arms still crossed over his chest, looking me over.

I rotate my shoulder and shake my arm out. "Feels good, like I could keep going."

He nods. "Good. That's what we want. Cool out and we'll call it a day. No need to push before season starts. Pitches looked good today, Davis. Keep it up." He turns to Kessler. "Your kid here knows his stuff." He tips his head towards Hudson, whose face tinges pink. "Better watch out, or he'll be gunning for your job."

"Couldn't ask for a better replacement." Kessler says, ruffling Hudson's hair. The pink on Hudson's face deepens, and he reaches up to smooth down his hair.

Sanders holds out his fist to Hudson for a bump. "Hope to see you around more often, kid," he says and Hudson returns his bump. Giving us a two-finger salute, he takes off towards the offices in the back, calling over his shoulder. "Get jogging Davis!"

"Yes, sir!" I call back. "Come on, Hudson, keep me company while I jog around the field a couple of times. We'll bribe Kessler to stop and get us ice cream on the way home."

"From Uncle Garrett's?" Hudson asks, walking around the fence to join me.

I scoff. "Of course, there's no better place." I look at Kessler. "You coming?"

"Nah, you two go ahead. I'm going to go talk to Paul. I'll meet you back here."

I cock a brow at him. Paul is our head physical therapist. He and Kessler worked closely together last season after Kessler came back from his injury. "Everything good?" I ask. Kessler would tell me if he was having issues, right?

"Yes, nothing like that," he tells me, hearing my concern.

I nod and clap Hudson on the back, turning him around to the exit where the field is. "Let's go, first one to the door gets a double scoop," I tell him. He takes off like a rocket and I laugh, letting him get a few strides ahead of me before I take off after him. I pull up just slightly at the last minute, letting him beat me.

"Yes! Double scoop here I come!" Hudson shouts, opening the door.

I chuckle at his enthusiasm. I would have gotten him a double scoop anyway. I'd do anything for this kid. Kessler says I spoil him, I can't help it. A part of me feels guilty that his sperm donor is such a piece of shit. I know it doesn't make sense because I didn't even know Jared had a kid, but that doesn't make the feeling any less real.

"Hey Uncle Judd?" Hudson says when we're about halfway into our first lap.

"What's up, big brotato?"

"Uh, never mind," he says quickly, giving his head a little shake.

I reach out and lay my hand on Hudson's shoulder, bringing our slow jog down to a walk for a minute. "You know you can talk to me about anything, Hudson, right?"

Hudson chews on his lip and nods. "So, I was thinking... Do you, do you think Kessler would mind if I called him Dad?"

My feet falter, bringing me to a stop. Hudson stops a few steps in front of me and turns back when he notices I'm not beside him. "I should just stick to Kessler, huh?" he mumbles, dropping his eyes to the ground and kicking his toe into the red dirt. "It was stupid. Forget I mentioned it."

I shake myself out of my shock and walk up to him, clapping my hands down onto his shoulders, bending slightly to look him in the eyes. "Hudson, I think Kessler would love nothing more than if you called him Dad."

His face brightens, and his bright smile appears. "You really think so?"

The bridge of my nose tingles and I rub at it, trying to rub away the emotion I'm suddenly hit with.

Jesus, get it together, Davis.

"Yeah, bud, I really do," I choke out before wrapping my arms around him and giving him a hug.

He squeezes me back fiercely and I'm hit with another round of hatred towards Jared. After Hudson lets me go and we continue our jog, I make a silent promise to Hudson to always be there for him. No matter what.

It's dark by the time Kessler drops me at my place. After my cool down, we went to Garrett's shop and got ice cream as promised. Kessler made Hudson swear to secrecy that he wouldn't tell his mom that he let him get two scoops before dinner. I took a picture of Hudson licking his giant waffle cone and sent it to Lucy. I'm sure I'll hear about it when Kessler gets home.

I say a quick hello to Marty as I pass the front desk, heading to the elevators. Once inside, I tap the screen with my phone and hit the button for my floor. I briefly think about swinging by Amelia's, but I really need a shower first. Besides, she hasn't texted me since asking me if getting a tattoo hurts and I'm secretly hoping she makes the next move, friends or not. I don't want to push myself on her anymore than I feel I already have.

I enjoyed spending time with her the other night, even though the noises she was making while I was massaging her shoulders gave me a massive hard on. One I had to take care of as soon as I got into my apartment.

I adjust myself in my sweatpants. Her sweet moans replaying in my head, making me hard again.

Christ. It's like I'm a teenager all over again and can't control myself.

I strip off my clothes as soon as I enter my room and head straight for the shower, needing to take care of my growing frustration. Turning the water to warm, I climb in and brace an arm against the wall, letting the water pour down my head as I fist the base of my cock. Picturing Amelia on her knees in front of me, sucking me down her throat, big blue eyes peeking up at me through her lashes.

I don't last more than a few minutes with that picture in my head and the sounds she made last night on a loop. After milking out the last of my orgasm, I scrub a hand over my face. I need to get a better handle on this before I become a walking erection.

I quickly wash my hair and body before turning the knob on the wall that controls the jets in my shower, focusing on my upper back. I stand there for a few minutes, letting jets melt away the rest of the tension left in my body before switching off the water.

I'm running a towel over my head when I hear my phone ping with a text. Tying the towel around my waist and grabbing my pants off the floor, I fish the phone out of my pocket and unlock it.

It's a text from Amelia.

SHORTCAKE

I'm going to take Bruno out for his nightly walk... Do you want to join us?

SHORTCAKE

I mean, if you're not busy. Or even home. Are you home? Cause if not, no big deal.

SHORTCAKE

Ok, I'm going to shut up now.

God, she's so cute when she's flustered. I hit reply.

ME

I just got out of the shower. Give me 5 minutes and I'll meet you at your door.

SHORTCAKE

I'm actually in the lobby. But please don't feel like you need to join me. I was just texting you like you asked me to.

When I asked her to text me when she took Bruno out in the dark, she rolled her eyes and said she would, but I'm actually surprised she did. I figured she was just saying it to appease me.

ME

Don't move. I'm on my way.

Moving to my dresser, I whip my towel off and toss it onto the bed, quickly pulling on my briefs, sweatpants and a long-sleeved shirt. When I get to the living room, I grab a sweater and pull it on, then grab my favorite baseball cap and tug it on over my wet hair, flipping it backwards. My phone pings in my pocket while I'm tugging on my shoes.

SHORTCAKE

OK, we're by the front desk.

I hit the lobby button on the elevator and tap out a reply.

ME

Good girl.

SHORTCAKE

Bite me Davis.

I chuckle, watching the elevator tick down the floors.

ME

That can be arranged.

I exit the elevator and turn the corner towards the desk. I spot Amelia before she sees me. She's looking at her phone and biting the corner of her lip, a slight pink tinge to her cheeks.

"You okay, Shortcake? You're looking a little flushed," I tease when I reach the desk. She startles and looks at her phone again before putting it in her pocket and looking back at me. Her eyes widen slightly when she sees me.

"Yep, all good. Just warm in this jacket. Let's go, Bruno's tired of waiting on you," she shoots back, dropping her eyes and striding ahead towards the door.

I bite back a laugh and take my time following her out the door, enjoying the view of how her ass looks in the forest green leggings she's wearing.

I jog ahead and open the gate to the park next door. She mutters a thank you under her breath as she leads Bruno through. We walk in silence for a few minutes, our breaths mingling together in the frosty air.

"So," I start, breaking the silence. "Were you able to get any writing done today?"

She mentioned the other night that she was planning on writing after she had coffee with Hazel and Charlie.

She lets out a frustrated groan. "Not as much as I would have liked. I'm just," she flails her free hand around in the air, "Stuck."

"Stuck how?"

Amelia lets out a sigh and dodges a giant puddle, brushing against my arm as she does. My hand drops to the small of her back as I guide her in front of me and I hear her suck in a breath. I drop my hand once she's back beside me, my hand instantly missing the contact.

"Stuck as in nothing's flowing, everything feels...forced."

"Maybe because you are forcing it?"

"I know! But my characters aren't talking to me, and the deadline is getting closer by the day and I have nothing to show for it," she says, plopping down on a bench that's across from a lighted stretch of grass. I sit next to her while she unclips Bruno's leash and extracts a ball from her pocket. She tosses it and we watch as Bruno tears after it.

"What's it about?" I ask, bumping my leg into hers. "Maybe talking about it will get the juices flowing?"

Bruno trots back, dropping his ball at our feet and backing up, waiting for the next throw. I bend over and pick it up, tossing it back out again.

Amelia sighs and tugs at her cream beanie. "I guess it couldn't hurt. So I have a baseball romance series and in this book the main female character is a single mom and her kid plays baseball. The main male character is obviously an MLB player. I'm just having trouble coming up with a realistic-ish way they could cross paths and meet. Like they're not from the same world. How am I going to make them cross paths?"

"How about a meet and greet after one of the games?" I suggest, thinking about how Kessler and Lucy met.

She tosses the ball for Bruno again when he returns it and tips her head to the side, scrunching her nose. "I mean, the scenario crossed my mind, but," she shakes her head, "Honestly, what are the odds of an MLB player noticing someone at a meet and greet and pursuing things from there?"

I snort and take off my hat, running my fingers through my still damp hair.

"I'm glad my dilemma brings you joy."

Setting the hat back on my head, I turn to her. "No, I'm not laughing at you. It's just that's how my brother met his fiancée."

Amelia lifts an eyebrow at me. "Really?"

I nod. "Yeah, it's actually a pretty crazy story. I'm surprised you didn't hear about it."

We watch Bruno as he comes trotting back, plopping down at our feet, panting. "Actually, now that I think about it, I remember reading an article about them when they first started dating." She shakes her head. "I completely forgot about it."

"I'm sure Lucy would love to talk to you about it," I offer.

"She's a huge fan of yours and even got Kessler into your books."

"Shut up, Kessler Davis reads my books?" she says with a shocked expression.

A jolt of jealousy courses through me. "I didn't realize you were such a big fan of my brother," I say dryly.

"Are you kidding? He's one of the best catchers in the history of the MLB. I thought for sure he was done after that injury, but he proved everyone wrong and came back better than ever. It's really too bad you guys didn't make it to the World Series this year. That would have been icing on the cake for his comeback," she gushes.

"I didn't realize you were such a huge baseball fan."

She looks at me with a guilty expression. "I might follow it a little bit."

"Mmmhmm."

"Anyway, I'd love to talk to Lucy. If you think she'd be willing to?"

"I'm pretty sure she'd think about giving you one of the twins for a chance to even meet you," I joke.

"Oh, that's right. She's pregnant with twins." She laughs. "I don't want one of their kids, but I'd love to set up a time to talk to her."

An idea hits me, and I look over at her petting Bruno with a wide grin. "Come to Sunday dinner with me."

She freezes and peeks at me from the corner of her eye. "What?"

"Come to Sunday dinner with me," I say again. "We have dinner at my parent's every Sunday unless we're out of town. It's Mom's way of taking care of us, even though we're grown and out of the house." I shrug. "Lucy, Kessler, and my nephew Hudson will be there. It's a perfect time to get both Lucy and Kessler's side of the story."

Amelia pulls her bottom lip into her mouth and bites at the skin.

Reaching over, I grip her chin, using my thumb to gently pull her lip from the punishment of her teeth, and turn her face to look at me. "It's just dinner, Shortcake."

"With your family." Her eyes nervously bounce back and forth between mine.

I shrug and pull my hand away. "It doesn't have to mean anything. Friends have dinner with their friends' families all the time."

"I don't know," she says quietly, looking down at Bruno.

"You can bring Bruno if that's what you're worried about. Hudson has been begging for a dog for a while now. He'd love it."

She huffs a laugh. "Who am I to deny the chance to convince someone's parents to get them a dog?"

My heart speeds up and I sit forward a little. "So, does that mean you'll come?"

She nods and I mentally give myself a high five.

ME

I'm bringing a friend to dinner Sunday. Don't be weird.

LUCY

👀

LUCY

Is it Millie?

MOM

We're never weird dear. Who's Millie? And why does Lucy know about her?

ME

Millie is a FRIEND. Please don't make a big deal out of this. She has anxiety and you being extra will not be helpful. She needs to talk to Lucy about something for her research and I figured Sunday dinner would be the best place.

LUCY

Research? For What? Doesn't she run a library program?

MOM

Yes, I would still also like to know who this Millie is?

MOM

and I am not 'Extra'. ALSO you still didn't tell me why Lucy knows and I don't. Lucy, I thought you loved me.

ME

It'll make sense when you meet her on Sunday. I promise.

LUCY

Sorry Mom, future brother-in-law sister-in-law confidentiality.

ME

Marry me Luce.

KESSLER

Stop trying to steal my fiancée.

CHAPTER 17

Amelia

I SHOULD CANCEL.

It's his *family* dinner.

I have no business being there.

These are the things I keep telling myself as I pace back and forth in my room in nothing but my towel. I pick up my phone to text Judd that I can't make it but see there's already one from him.

Maybe he's having second thoughts and is canceling on me.

The thought should make me happy, but it doesn't. I'm actually beginning to enjoy spending time with him. He's not the arrogant playboy the press has made him out to be. He's kind, thoughtful, and so... Fucking. Hot. that part the press definitely got right.

But that's not what I should be focusing on. Shaking my head at myself, I click on Judd's waiting text.

SEXIEST MAN ALIVE

Stop overthinking this.

How the fuck did he know that's *exactly* what I've been doing all morning?

ME

I'm not. I'm currently standing in my towel fresh from the shower, trying to figure out what to wear.

Okay, so some of that's a lie. But he doesn't have to know that.

SEXIEST MAN ALIVE

pictures or it didn't happen 😉

ME

Perv.

SEXIEST MAN ALIVE

🤷 Worth a shot.

I snap a picture of my reflection in my full-length mirror and send it to him before I chicken out.

That'll show him.

SEXIEST MAN ALIVE

Ok, I believe you. Now get your cute ass dressed. I'll meet you at your door in 30 minutes.

At least he thinks your ass is cute.

I shake my head at myself. You sure showed him Millie. Now you *have* to go, or he's going to know he was right, and we can't have that.

Tossing my towel aside, I dig into my closet and pull out my favorite charcoal gray chunky knit sweater with the oversized buttons on the shoulders and pair it with my butter soft black leggings and black boots that come up mid-calf. Might as well be comfortable.

Heading back into my bathroom, I decide to keep my makeup simple with foundation and a little contour, adding a couple of coats of mascara to make my eyes pop. I take my hair out of my claw clip and shake it out, letting my long blonde waves fall around my shoulders.

"You can do this Millie," I tell my reflection. "It's just dinner with a friend and his family. No big deal." As I'm staring at myself in the mirror, I realize that while I'm nervous about meeting Judd's family, I'm not anxious about it.

Before I can analyze that revelation any further, though, I'm pulled from my thoughts by a knock at my door.

"Coming, coming," I mutter, making my way to the front door. I peek through the peephole and see Judd standing on the other side, looking like a damn snack in his dark wash jeans and black peacoat.

Fuck me.

Friends, Millie. Judd and you are friends. No more, no less.

Taking a final breath after my internal reprimand to my lady bits to behave, I pull the door open and Judd's cinnamon pine scent smacks me square in the face. My heart does a little flip that I'm not one hundred percent sure I shouldn't be concerned about.

Judd's eyes roam over me, causing goosebumps to break out over my body at the pure heat in his gaze. When his journey stops at my eyes, it's like time freezes as we stare at each other, neither uttering a word but saying so many things.

I want you.

I need you.

Fuck me.

Keep me.

That last one jolts me out of my trance. Never in my twenty-nine years have I wanted someone to claim me as much as I want Judd to. But friends aren't supposed to feel that way about each other.

"Like what you see, Shortcake?"

Yes.

I roll my eyes. "You wish, Davis." I look down at my smartwatch to check the time and look back up at him. "Aren't you early? You said thirty minutes. I still have ten minutes to spare."

He walks into my apartment and kneels down to give Bruno some attention, who is whining and shaking his butt uncontrollably, like he's his long-lost love.

Traitor.

"I figured if I came down early, it would give you less time to over analyze everything," he says, looking up at me with his devilish smile. "You look really nice."

I duck my face at the compliment, closing the door and turn to him, crossing my arms in front of me. "Thanks. But how? How did you know that's exactly what I would be doing?" I narrow my eyes. "Have you been talking to Charlie?" That's the only explanation to him knowing how my brain works.

He stands and takes his phone out of his pocket, tapping on the screen a few times and turning it towards me so I can read the screen. It's a website on how to support someone who deals with anxiety and depression.

The back of my eyes start to sting and I flick them back up to Judd's as he pockets his phone. I told him about the anxiety, but never about my depression. "Why?" I ask, my voice cracking just slightly.

"If we're going to be around each other more, I want to be prepared on how to help you if you ever have an anxiety attack while you're with me," he says, shrugging like it's no big deal.

It's a huge deal.

Not one of the boyfriends I've had since developing my anxiety disorder has ever taken the time to do something as simple as googling how to support me. And here Judd is in all his sexy glory, doing just that, and he's not even my boyfriend.

He could be. My inner voice chimes in.

No, he can't. And he's showing me another reason as to why. He's too good for me to bring him down with all my darkness.

"I really appreciate you doing that, Judd, truly," I tell him, clearing the emotion from my throat. "Should we go? I'll just grab my coat." I move to the closet, needing a minute to gather myself. When I turn back around, Judd has Bruno's leash clipped on him and his ball in his hand.

"My parents have a huge backyard. I figured we can tire him out there. That way, when we get home, he'll just need his nightly potty walk."

I nod and try to ignore the warm feeling I get in my chest when he says *home* while I lock my door. Once we're in the elevator, he hits the button for the garage and leans against the wall, watching me.

"So, is there anything I should know about your family before we get there?" I ask. We really haven't had a chance to talk much after Judd invited me, other than texting me yesterday to let me know what time he would pick me up today.

He lifts a shoulder. "Not really. My family is pretty cool. Mom is excited I'm bringing someone. I should probably warn you, even though I told her we're just friends, she's still going to think otherwise. Now that Kessler is settled down with babies on the way, she has been chomping at the bit for me to be next."

"She just wants her baby boy to be happy," I tease, reaching up to pinch his cheek.

He gently grabs my arm and turns it, kissing the inside of my wrist. My laugh dies in my throat as chills race down my arm.

"I am happy," he says, staring down at me, still gripping my arm.

The elevator stops and the 'ding' announces its arrival to the parking garage. I pull my arm out of his grip and step out into the garage. The cold air brings relief to my heated cheeks.

Judd hits the key fob to his Jeep, unlocking it. I climb into the passenger seat as he loads Bruno and when I look back; I see the seats are folded down and there's a cushy dog bed with a toy laying on it, which Bruno immediately picks up.

I look at Judd when he climbs in the driver's seat. "When did you do that?"

He looks back at Bruno and smiles at his soft growls as he plays with his new toy. "I went to the pet store while I was out running errands yesterday. I didn't want Bruno to be uncomfortable."

How am I supposed to resist this man when he keeps doing sweet shit like this?

Don't.

I have to. I'm not it for him.

Judd gives me a wink, turning back around and pulling out of the parking garage.

Lord, give me strength.

"Wow, it's so beautiful. You grew up out here?" We're about twenty minutes into our drive on the outskirts of the city. Neither of us really talking, but it's been a comfortable silence.

"Yeah, born and raised. You should see it before all the trees lose their leaves. It's one of the most beautiful things to see." Judd gives me a smirk. "Besides you, that is," he adds.

My cheeks heat and I roll my eyes. "Smooth, Davis."

"I thought so."

I shake my head, deciding to change the subject. "I've been meaning to ask...how did you know how to help me with my migraine? Did you research that, too?"

At this point, I wouldn't doubt that he did.

He shakes his head. "No, I get them if I read too much without wearing my glasses."

"You read?" The shocked comment flies from my mouth before I register what I'm saying.

Judd barks out a laugh and rubs his cheek. "Yes, Amelia. I can read."

"Shit, sorry. That was rude." I cringe. "What I meant to say is, what do you like to read?"

Nice save, Millie, not.

Judd shakes his head and looks at me when he brings the car to a stop at the stop sign, amusement in his grin. "Fantasy, mystery, thrillers..." He shrugs. "I'll have to show you my library sometime."

"Is that code for your dick?" I slap my hand across my mouth, horrified.

Why is my brain saying the first thing that pops into it today? Normally, my filter is solid. The only time I'm this candid around people is when I'm around Hazel and Charlie. Am I *comfortable* with Judd?

Judd's deep baritone laugh draws me out of my thoughts. "No, Mills. An *actual* library. I've built up quite the collection over the years."

"Oh." is all I allow myself to say as we turn into a driveway that has a beautiful sign on one side of the stone entrance that reads *DAVIS*, indicating we've arrived at his parents' house.

Butterflies take flight as we make our way up a long gravel driveway lined with various shrubs and bushes that are all dormant for the upcoming winter. The driveway ends guarded by two giant oak trees, revealing a beautiful two-story home with a stone chimney with smoke lazily billowing out the top.

"You grew up here?"

Judd nods, a faraway look in his eye when he looks out at the house through the windshield. "This is home."

We sit in silence for a few breaths, both staring at the cozy home that should be in one of those home design magazines with its cute black shutters that pop against the creamy exterior.

The front door opens and a woman with dark brown hair the same color as Judd's walks out onto the porch and waves at us, giving us a warm smile. Her inviting smile eases my nerves.

"Ready, Shortcake?" Judd asks, reaching across and giving my hand a squeeze. "If you get overwhelmed or anything becomes too much, just let me know and we can leave. Mom won't be offended, I promise." I look from the house to Judd, taking in his features. He has his mom's nose and hair color, but that's where the similarities end, and I find myself wondering if he looks more like his dad.

"Amelia?"

I shake myself out of my thoughts and nod. "Okay. I'm ready." I tell him and reach for my handle.

"No, don't move. I'll open your door," Judd says, getting out and jogging around the front and opening my door before I can even protest.

"I can open my own door, Judd," I grumble when I get out.

"I know you can, but my mom would have my balls if I wasn't acting like the gentleman she raised," he says, giving me a wink and closing my door.

Judd lets Bruno out next, and he darts into the front yard, zigzagging back and forth over the perfectly manicured lawn until he finds a spot worthy of his mark.

"Come on, Mom's dying to meet you," Judd says, placing his hand at the small of my back and guiding me over to where his mom is waiting for us.

"Mom, this is Amelia," Judd says, introducing me once we reach the porch. Now that I'm closer, I can see the glittering of silver weaved throughout her hair and I can't help but wonder if my mom would have gray or silver in her hair if she was still alive. I tuck that thought away. Now is not the time to dwell on what I'll never know.

"Amelia, it is so nice to meet you. I'm Marlene," she says, stepping forward and enveloping me in a hug. My body stiffens at the contact. It's been years since I've had what can only be described as a motherly embrace. I feel my body relax as it realizes it's safe and I melt into the contact, hugging her back. My eyes stinging.

I release a breath that feels like I've been holding in for years and an extreme sense of calm falls over me.

I don't know how long we stand there like that, but Marlene seems to know I need this because she doesn't pull back until I release her, stepping back into Judd. His hand falls to the small of my back and he swipes his thumb back and forth in a soothing motion. I quickly swipe at my eyes, embarrassed over the wetness I find there.

"I'm sorry, I don't know what came over me," I apologize.

Marlene brushes it away, giving me a warm smile. "You never have to apologize for your emotions to me, dear."

Bruno comes charging over and rudely pushes his head into Marlene's hands.

"Bruno!" I chastise. "You know better!"

"It's ok," she says, crouching down to pet him. Bruno takes advantage and licks her face, making Marlene laugh. "Nice to meet you too, Bruno."

"Bruno heel," I command. I swear he rolls his eyes as he hangs his head and mopes to my side.

"I am so sorry. He knows better than to behave like that," I apologize again.

Marlene chuckles. "It's fine, I love dogs. We just haven't had one since the boys were teenagers." She stands and brushes her hand down over her apron that says 'I'm not old, I'm well-seasoned'.

"I love your apron."

She shoots a smile behind me where Judd is standing. "Judd got it for me for Mother's Day. Now come on in out of the cold, Kessler called and said they would be over in a bit, sounds like Lucy was able to get a nap in," Marlene says, opening the door off to the side of the front door, ushering us inside a mudroom where we kick off our shoes and Judd takes my coat before hanging up his own. He looks incredibly good in a navy-blue and white flannel that looks like it was painted on. Judd grabs a towel out of a cupboard and kneels down to wipe Bruno's paws.

"I can do that," I say, reaching for the towel.

"I got it, Shortcake." He nods towards Marlene. "Go in with Mom, and we'll be there in a minute."

I turn to Marlene, and she looks between us quickly before rolling her lips inward like she's trying to suppress a smile, and opening another door that leads into the house.

I follow her through, pausing once the door closes behind me. I thought the outside was amazing, but it has nothing on the inside of the house. An enormous stone fireplace with a warm crackling fire greets us off to the left, surrounded by plush, oversized furniture. Various smells from the adjoining kitchen are the next thing that hits me, making my mouth water.

I follow Marlene into a kitchen that I've only ever dreamed of. Dark wooden cabinets line the walls. A copper farmhouse sink looks out over a huge picture window. Uneven, pearlescent subway tiles contrast with the charcoal granite countertops.

"Make yourself at home, dear. Would you like anything to drink?" Marlene asks, opening the giant stainless-steel refrigerator. "We have water, juice, wine, beer..." she says, trailing off.

"Uh, water would be fine," I tell her, still taking in the breathtaking kitchen as I settle onto the plush stool at the island.

She sets a glass of ice water down in front of me. "Thank you."

She gives me a wink and a smile and turns back to the stove to stir something.

"Smells good, Mom. What are you making tonight?" Judd

asks, walking in from the mudroom. Bruno tries to go into the kitchen, but I tell him to get out and he sulks over to where I'm sitting before plopping down onto the floor.

"Just roasted chicken with garlic mashed potatoes, corn, buttermilk biscuits, and of course two new desserts I'm trying out before Thanksgiving," Marlene tells him over her shoulder, still tending to things in the kitchen. Judd grabs a glass out of the cabinet next to Marlene and gives her a kiss on the cheek as he passes by.

My heart melts a little bit at the sight, and I feel like I'm getting to see a side of Judd only his family is privy to.

After filling his glass with water, Judd joins me at the island, taking a seat next to me.

"So," Marlene begins, setting potatoes on the island across from me. "Do you prefer Amelia, or Millie?

I shrug. "Doesn't matter, I respond to both. Can I help with anything?" I ask, feeling useless just sitting here watching. "I'm not much of a cook, but I can work a potato peeler." I say, nodding to her hands.

"No, you're a guest."

I hop off the stool and come around the island. "Honestly, I can help." I roll up my sleeves and wash my hands, drying them on a towel and going back to where Marlene is standing. "Put me to work."

Marlene gives me a wide smile and looks at Judd from the corner of her eye. "I like her," she says blatantly.

Judd's face reddens slightly under his scruff, no doubt matching my own blush. His eyes quickly meet mine. "Yeah, she has that effect on people."

"Do you want an apron?" she asks, moving to a door beside the mudroom marked 'Pantry', breaking the trance with Judd.

"Sure."

Marlene disappears into the pantry and returns a second later with a black apron. I don the apron and tie the strings.

Judd smirks at my apron. "Nice, Mom."

"What?" she asks innocently.

I follow Judd's eyes to my chest and read the words that are upside down. 'BITCH, I'm the secret ingredient.'

"It's perfect," I tell Marlene, chuckling.

I get to work peeling potatoes, while Marlene dumps apples on the counter next to me and extracts another peeler. We work in a comfortable silence, with just the sounds of the cracking fire and our peelers filling the space. I look up to see Judd staring at me, giving me a wink when our eyes connect. I drop my gaze back down to the potato I'm working on. Trying to ignore the warm, fuzzy feeling that's blooming in my chest.

"Where's Dad?" Judd asks, reaching across the island and snatching a slice of apple from his mom.

Marlene waves her hand to the sliding door that must lead out to their backyard. "Oh, he's puttering around in his wood shop. You know him. He always has to be doing something."

Judd nods and raps his knuckles on the counter. "I'm going to go see what he's doing." His eyes cut to mine. "You okay in here, Shortcake?"

I nod, grabbing another potato. "I'm fine."

He nods and slides off the stool, going into the mudroom and grabbing his shoes. He passes through the kitchen on his way back and stops between Marlene and me, stealing another piece of apple and placing another kiss on his mom's cheek before turning to me and dropping one on top of my head. "I'm going to take Bruno with me, if that's okay?"

I look up at him in stunned silence, nodding my head slowly. "Uh, yeah. Sure. That's, that's fine," I stutter out while my brain processes what just happened.

Friends don't kiss friends on the head like that. At least *I've* never kissed my friends like that, but then again, I've never just been friends with someone like Judd.

"So, how long have you and Judd been *friends*?" Marlene

asks after Judd and Bruno leave out the back door. Saying friends like there's more going on than there actually is.

I lift a shoulder. "A week?"

"Mmm," she hums, slicing up the rest of her apples and dumping them into a bowl where she mixes them with cinnamon and brown sugar.

"It's okay that he brought me to your family's dinner, right?" I ask, doubt creeping in that I'm welcomed here, even though I feel welcomed. "Judd told me he brings friends all the time."

Marlene snorts a laugh and wipes her hands on a towel before turning to me. "Of course, it's okay that you're here, dear. I didn't mean for it to sound like that. It's just that Judd has *never* brought anyone home before besides his teammates, and even then, it was only a few times."

I blink slowly at her words, trying to process what she's telling me. "You mean, Judd has never brought a girl home before? Not even in high school?" No, that can't be right.

Marlene confirms my doubts, shaking her head. "Not even in high school. Neither of my boys have. That is until Kessler brought Lucy home this spring."

As if saying their names summons them, the door to the mudroom opens, revealing Kessler Davis in the flesh, followed by a tiny blonde woman who I assume is Lucy and a boy who is almost as tall as her.

"Holy shit! You're Amelia Morgan!" Lucy yells, pointing at me. She looks up at Kessler, then back to me, mouth opening and closing like a fish out of water. She rubs her eyes. "Kessler, pinch me. I think I'm dreaming."

Kessler chuckles and closes the door behind him. "I assure you, Coach, you're not dreaming."

"What is Amelia Morgan doing in your mom's kitchen?" she asks, still shouting.

"No need to yell dear, we're standing right here," Marlene says, laughing and going over to Lucy, giving her a hug. When she pulls back, she sets her hand on Lucy's stomach and rubs it.

"Sorry. Sorry, it's just, you're just. How?" Lucy asks, looking from Marlene to me.

I set the peeler down and wipe my hands on my apron, walking over to Lucy. I hold out my hand to her and say, "Hi, I'm Millie. Judd's friend."

A look of realization crosses Lucy's face as she takes my hand. "Oh, *you're* the Millie he was talking about."

He's been talking about me?

"Uh, I guess?" I say, unsure of how to respond to that.

"Hmm," Lucy hums, letting go of my hand and tipping her head. "Of course, Judd would go for someone completely out of his league."

My cheeks heat at the statement.

Kessler laughs. "That sounds about right," he says, wrapping an arm around Lucy's shoulders and holding out his hand to me. "Kessler. Nice to meet you, Millie."

I give his hand a shake. "It's really nice to meet you too, Kessler. To say I'm not fangirling a little bit would be a lie."

Lucy giggles and lightly smacks Kessler's chest. "See, she's a fan too."

"I have your signed jersey hanging in my closet. My parents got it for me for my high school graduation present."

"Jesus, that makes me feel old. How old are you, Millie?" Kessler asks.

Lucy smacks Kessler harder in the chest.

"Kessler Davis, you do not ask a woman their age," Marlene chastises.

"Ow, what? It was a simple question," he says, rubbing at his pec.

I chuckle. "No, it's fine. I'm twenty-nine."

"At least my brother isn't robbing the cradle," Kessler mutters, receiving another smack from Lucy.

"Fuck! What did I say now?" Kessler exclaims, moving away from Lucy before she can hit him again.

"Kessler Davis, language," Marlene reprimands again. "I swear these boys."

"He's not robbing anything Kessler, they're just friends," Lucy says, rolling her eyes and shaking her head. "I am so sorry about this neanderthal."

"No need to apologize. I'm actually pretty entertained," I chuckle again. I thought I would feel anxious meeting Judd's family, but other than a few awkward mix ups about mine and Judd's relationship status, I actually feel at ease.

Kessler puts an arm around the boy who's been wordlessly watching our exchange and brings him forward. "Anyway, this is our son, Hudson."

Hudson holds out his hand, and I take it, returning the shake. "Hi, Hudson, nice to meet you."

"You too. Where's Uncle Judd?" he asks, looking around the room.

Marlene tips her head to the back door. "Out back in the wood shop with Grandpa."

Hudson takes off through the house and out that backdoor without another word.

"Sorry, we all take a back burner when it comes to Judd," Lucy apologizes with a laugh.

"It's fine. I totally get it. He's really good with the kids at the library."

They all give me a weird look, like they know something I don't. I really don't know how to describe it. "I should get back to the potatoes," I say, throwing a thumb over my shoulder.

Lucy and Kessler follow Marlene and I back to the kitchen. Both taking a seat across from us.

"I'm surprised Marlene is letting you help her. She never lets me help," Lucy comments.

"I uh, kinda didn't give her a choice. I just washed my hands and told her to put me to work," I say sheepishly.

"Guess I should try that next time."

Marlene sets apple slices and a bowl of what looks like caramel in front of Lucy and her eyes light up. "Ooh yes, come to mama," she says, dipping a piece of apple into the caramel. The amount of caramel she scoops up makes my teeth hurt by just looking at it, but Lucy shoves the whole slice into her mouth, moaning in delight. "So good," she mumbles around the mouthful.

Kessler looks to the ceiling and shifts in his seat. Marlene and I chuckle from the other side. Lucy's eyes meet mine and she gives me a wink before dipping another piece in, repeating her sounds. Kessler pushes back from the island, mumbling something about going to the shop and disappears out the back door, still in his socks.

We all burst out laughing. Lucy reaches for a napkin, wiping tears away. "I'm sorry. I know that was cruel, but I had to." She sighs and settles back into her chair.

"Is he still being overbearing, hun?" Marlene asks, putting the finishing touches on her apple dessert before sticking it in the second oven. Whatever she's making looks amazing, and my stomach rumbles in agreement.

"Not nearly as bad as he was. Judd helped me talk to him on Halloween, so it's been better. But you know Kessler. Always the worrier."

I cut the last potato up and take them over to the sink for a final rinse. After placing them into the pot Marlene gave me and filling it with water, Marlene takes it from me and thanks me for my help. "Anything else I can help with?" I ask, feeling like I should do more.

"No dear, now we sit and wait for things to cook." Marlene grabs a bottle of wine out of the fridge and pours herself a glass, then looks up at me. "Would you like one?"

Lucy whines, "I miss wine."

Marlene gives her a sympathetic look. "You'll be back to enjoying wine before you know it."

Lucy turns to me. "Have a glass for me. Please, I'm begging you."

I smirk and nod. "Well, when you put it like that, how can I say no?"

Marlene turns, grabbing another glass out of the cupboard and pours me a glass. "Let's go sit in the living room where it's more comfortable."

Lucy tucks her feet under her once we're settled in front of the fireplace and turns to me. "So, Judd said you wanted to talk to me?"

I take a sip of my wine and nod. "I'm working on the next book in my baseball series and I'm stuck."

Lucy sits forward. "Is it Dean's story?"

I nod.

She plops back into the pile of pillows behind her. "I'm going to be ruined by his story. I've been dying for it." She sighs. "But how can I help? I know nothing about writing."

"Well," I start, "I'm pairing him up with a single mom. I know nothing about being a parent, let alone having to do it on your own."

She raises her eyebrows and sits up. "Really? Oh man, he'd be such a good DILF." She pauses, eyes shooting to Marlene and cringes.

Marlene waves her off. "I was your age once too, you know, plus you've gotten me into these books, remember? I agree, Dean would be a good DILF."

My face flushes. Normally I'm not embarrassed with what I write, but knowing Judd's mother has read...scenes, has me taking a bigger drink of my wine.

"You're very talented, dear."

"Oh god," I groan, covering my face.

Lucy and Marlene both chuckle. "Nothing to be

embarrassed about. It's human nature," Marlene says before taking a sip of wine.

I do the same, then look at Lucy. "So, do you think you could help?"

"Absolutely, tell me what you need."

CHAPTER 18

Judd

"MILLIE IS AMELIA MORGAN, HUH?" Kessler's voice booms from behind me.

Dad and I turn around from the workbench at the sound of his voice.

"Yep."

"And you didn't think to mention that at all when you were asking me or Lucy for advice?"

I shrug and turn back to the workbench. "Would it have changed your advice?"

He sidles up next to us, looking at the new project Dad is working on for the twins' nursery. The one he's going to surprise Lucy with after we learn the genders of the babies. "Wow, Dad. These look amazing. Lucy is going to love this."

Dad carved two baseball diamonds out of slabs of wood off an old tree that fell on their property last year. There's a space in the middle for their names once they're picked.

"And to answer your question, no. It probably wouldn't have made a difference. But why the secrecy?"

I turn and lean a hip against the workbench. "I'm not really sure. It was just something I wanted to keep to myself until I got to know her better."

"And now that you have, you've decided to throw her straight into the fire?"

One side of my mouth quirks up. "Something tells me she can handle herself with Mom and Lucy. Plus, we're just *friends.* No fire with friendship."

"Mmm hmm. Let me know how that works for you." He turns to Dad. "Wanna take bets on how long it is before they're dating?"

Dad finishes putting his tools away and turns to me, gripping his chin like he's contemplating something. "What's the ante?"

The fuck?

"Dad, you're betting on my love life? I thought you liked me more than that?" I say, acting offended.

Dad claps me on the shoulder. "Yeah, but Kessler's giving me grandbabies. He's in the top spot now," he jokes.

Kessler tips his head back and forth in thought. "How about if you win, I will pay for your and Mom's next trip?"

I groan, knowing Dad will definitely be taking that bet now.

"And if you win?"

"Babysitting for a month, whenever we need it."

Dad holds out his hand to Kessler, and they shake. "I feel like that's a win-win for me, son. I'll take that bet."

Dicks.

"So how long?" Kessler asks.

"A week."

Kessler nods and looks back at me, tapping his chin. I flip him off, earning a laugh. "I'll say four days. Something tells me little Juddy has game."

"There's nothing little about me," I tell him, throwing my arm around his neck and getting him into a headlock. "I'm also taller than you, dick."

"You may be taller, but I'm stronger, shithead." His voice is muffled against my side. His arms tighten around my waist, and he tries to kick out one of my legs, but misses.

"Take it outside, boys. There's too much you can break in here," Dad says, opening the door. I let go of Kessler and move out to the yard. Just as I turn around, Kessler rushes me from behind, knocking me to the ground.

My back hits the ground and my breath whooshes out of me, stunning me and giving Kessler enough time to get me into a cradle hold, making it even harder for me to catch my breath.

I throw out my elbow in desperation to break the hold, but I don't have enough leverage to make much of an impact. Kessler laughs and tightens his hold on me. "Is that all you've got, little brother?"

I'm about to throw another elbow when a growling sound behind us makes us both freeze.

"What the fuck is that?" Kessler says quietly, loosening his grip on me.

"Bruno! Here, boy! Where'd you go?" I hear Hudson call from the other side of the property.

I never pegged Bruno as an aggressive dog. "It's Bruno. He must think you're hurting me," I tell Kessler. "Let go of me slowly."

When I feel Kessler's grip on me loosen, I roll to my knees and face Bruno. He's about ten feet back and staring Kessler down, lips curled slightly in a snarl. Kessler sits up, extracting another growl from Bruno.

"Bruno, come here. It's okay," I tell him, patting my thigh. One of his ears flicks at the sound of my voice, but his eyes stay on Kessler.

"Bruno! There you are!" Hudson calls while coming out of the trees and jogging up to him.

"Hudson, careful, he might bite," Kessler tells Hudson just as he reaches down to pat Bruno.

"It's just Dad and Uncle Judd, Bruno," he tells him,

shaking the ball in his face and throwing it, distracting Bruno from Kessler.

Kessler sucks in a breath and watches Bruno and Hudson run off again like nothing happened. "Did he, did I hear that right? Did he just call me Dad?" He turns to me with a glassy look in his eyes.

I get to my feet and clap him on the shoulder, offering him my hand to pull him up. "Yeah man, he did. He asked me about it when we were at the field house the other day. I told him you would love nothing more."

Kessler swipes at his eyes and clears his throat. "Shit, I thought Lucy was supposed to be the hormonal one." He gives me a pointed look. "Don't tell her about this."

"Tell me about what?"

We whip around and see Lucy and Amelia standing at the open sliding door with matching amused looks on their faces.

"Nothing," we say at the same time.

Lucy cocks an eyebrow at us. "Mmmhmm. So, what's with the wet eyes, Kessler Davis," she says motioning to his face.

"Allergies?"

"In November?"

Amelia stifles a laugh watching their exchange. She looks relaxed, leaning her head against the frame and peering out at the expanse of the property. Her eyes land on mine and her look is one I haven't seen on her before. Like she's seeing me differently.

Bruno's barking and Hudson's laughter breaks the moment as they come running back to the group. Dad comes out of the wood shop just as Mom reaches the space between Lucy and Amelia.

"Hope you guys are hungry because dinner is ready."

Laughter and chatter fill the space as we file into the house. I'm the last one in, standing behind Amelia in line. "Did you get to talk to Lucy?'

She peeks at me over her shoulder, pulling one side of her lip into her mouth as she nods her head.

"Did she give you what you needed for your book?"

She nods again. "And I have her number in case I have any more questions." She turns to me, the commotion of the room fading away. She places a hand on my chest, playing with the button of my flannel. When she looks up at me, my heart beats faster. "She definitely gave me something to think about."

"Is that good or bad?"

She releases my shirt, and I instantly miss the small contact. Smiling up at me, she lifts a shoulder. "I don't know yet, but I'll tell you when I do."

"I hope everyone saved some room because I have two new desserts to try," Mom announces, setting two dishes in the center of the dining table. Groans and a hooray from Hudson sound around the table.

"Give me five more minutes and I'm sure I'll be hungry again," Lucy says, leaning back in her chair and rubbing her baby bump.

"I have room!" Hudson chimes in, practically drooling over the desserts in front of him.

Chuckles sound from around the table as mom cuts into the desserts. Placing the first plate in front of Hudson, who dives right in.

"So good, Grandma. What's this one?" he asks around a mouthful of food.

"Hudson James, do not talk with your mouth full," Lucy chides, trying to hold back a smirk.

Mom chuckles while setting a plate in front of Amelia, then me. "Thank you, Hudson. That one is no-bake cranberry cheesecake with a graham cracker and pretzel crust. And the other is caramel apple crumble."

I watch as Amelia takes a bite of the crumble and closes her eyes, humming in delight. The sound goes straight to my dick. I watch as she puts another bite into her mouth, plush lips wrapping around the fork. I've never been so jealous of an inanimate object in my life, but here I am wishing my dick was a damn fork.

My hand reaches forward before my brain comprehends what it's doing, and I use the pad of my thumb to wipe away a drop of caramel at the corner of her lips. She turns to look at me, eyes dilating as I stick my thumb in my mouth, sucking the caramel off it.

Something has shifted between us. I caught her sneaking glances at me all throughout dinner. Laying her arm on the table next to mine so it's touching. Not enough to draw attention, but just enough to feel it. She even scooted her chair closer to me when she came back from the bathroom. I try to remind myself not to read into it, that it's nothing. But my heart is telling me a whole lot of nothings put together is something.

A throat clears from across the table, pulling me out of another Amelia haze. When I look over, I see Kessler and Lucy looking at us with amused expressions.

"So, which one do we all like better?" Mom asks. If she noticed the interaction between Amelia and me, she's doing a good job of not noticing, or at least not drawing attention to it.

"I like them both," Hudson says, piling the last bite of crumble into his mouth.

Kessler snorts. "Shocker."

"Honestly, Mom, they're both really good. I don't think I can choose," Lucy says while nibbling at her desserts. Kessler nods in agreement.

"I have to agree with Lucy, hun. I can't choose either," Dad says, finishing off his plate.

"You all are no help." She turns to Amelia and me. "What about you two? Are you going to help me narrow it down?"

I stretch and lay my arm across the back of Amelia's chair. "Sorry Mom, but I can't decide either. You're just too good of a baker."

"Flattery will usually get you somewhere, Juddson, but not when I need to narrow down what desserts to make for Thanksgiving." She turns to Amelia. "You're my last hope, dear."

Amelia sits up. "Oh, I don't think my opinion matters. I won't even be here."

"Your opinion matters, my dear. Whether you're here or not. Which one would *you* make for your family?"

Amelia bites her bottom lip and looks down at her plate, eyes unfocusing. The corner of her mouth lifts a little. "My mom always loved homemade cranberry sauce. We always made an extra big batch and ate it on everything. Biscuits, pancakes, toast." She huffs a small laugh and looks up at Mom. "Dad always said canned was best and, even though he knew he wouldn't like it, would try our homemade stuff every year just to appease Mom. Mom wouldn't get the canned stuff out until he tried it."

Mom laughs. "They sound like lovely people. Will you be with them this year?"

Amelia's smile falls, and she shakes her head. "No, they..." She pauses and clears her throat. "They passed away almost nine years ago." She lifts a shoulder. "Just me and Bruno this year."

Mom's chair scrapes across the floor as she gets up and sits in the empty seat next to Amelia, placing a hand on hers. "I am so sorry." Mom's eyes flick to mine and back to Amelia's. "I didn't know."

That makes two of us. I grab her other hand and give it a

squeeze. She gives it a small squeeze back. I expect her to pull it away after, but she lets me keep my hand on hers.

Amelia shakes her head. "It's okay. I don't really talk about it much."

"You are more than welcome to join us for Thanksgiving," Mom tells her. "In fact, I insist."

"Oh, no. I don't want to intrude on your family's day. I promise, I'll be fine. I have a day of binge watching my favorite show and eating Chinese food planned."

"Nonsense. We always have way too much food and it's not just our family who eats with us." Mom releases Amelia's hand and motions to Kessler. "Kessler's friends Reese and Garrett usually join us for dinner."

"And this year my friend Kara, her son Kade, and her mom are joining us too," Lucy chimes in.

Amelia gives Mom and Lucy a warm smile. "I really appreciate the offer. Can I think about it?"

Mom pats her hand again as she rises from her chair. "Of course, dear, take all the time you need. We'll save you a seat either way."

Amelia dips her head and whispers a thank you. I give her hand another squeeze and stand, helping Mom clear the dessert and dishes from the table.

I hear Lucy ask her a question as I dump the dishes in the sink and start rinsing them off.

"Do everything you can to make sure that girl doesn't spend Thanksgiving alone, Judd. Even if it means staying in with her," Mom says quietly while taking a Tupperware container out of the cabinet.

"I'll do my best, Mom. I can't force her to spend time with me."

She pats my cheek. "Use that charm I know you have to win her over."

A snort escapes me. "Trust me, Mom. My charm doesn't work on her."

Mom looks over my shoulder, then back up at me, giving me a wink. "I wouldn't be too sure about that."

I sneak a look over my shoulder to see Amelia watching me from the dining table. When she notices me looking back, she quickly looks away, focusing on something Lucy is saying.

Huh, would you look at that...

CHAPTER 19

Amelia

I. AM. *So. Screwed.*

After listening to Lucy talk about her and Kessler's story, watching Judd with Hudson, feeling and experiencing the love Marlene has for everyone in this room, I'm a goner.

I'm seeing Judd in a whole new light. Not only am I starting to fall hard for him, but his family, too.

And that scares the ever-loving shit out of me.

I don't know if I'm capable of loving someone the way Lucy loves Kessler or Marlene loves Henry. Judd deserves someone who can give him that.

Something inside of me broke the night my parents died, and I don't know if it can be fixed.

"Did you have a good time tonight?" Judd asks, reaching over and giving my hand a squeeze. Tingles shoot through my arm, like they always seem to do when we touch, before he pulls away and places his hand back on the steering wheel.

"Truthfully?" I ask, looking over at him in the driver's seat of his Jeep. It's dark enough that I can only see his profile.

"I always want the truth, even if it's painful. Hit me with it, Mills. Was Mom too much? Did she make you uncomfortable?"

"No, not at all. Your mom was perfect. And Lucy was hilarious. They made me feel right at home."

"Then what's the problem?"

I blow out a breath. "There isn't a problem, that's the problem."

"I'm not following."

Turning in my seat, I prop my arm on the center console and rest my chin on it, staring at him. "What I'm trying to say is that your family is amazing and loving and welcoming and I really, really like them and that's the most comfortable I've felt with strangers in I don't even know how long."

"Oooh 'kay. I'm sorry, still not catching on here."

I huff out a breath. "I was *hoping* that they wouldn't be this wonderful."

"Why would you want that, Shortcake?" Judd asks, turning into the parking garage of our apartment complex. Once we're parked, he turns to me. Green eyes I have grown to enjoy looking at me, shine bright under the fluorescent lights.

I bite my bottom lip and Judd's eyes flick to the movement. He reaches out, his thumb freeing my lip from the assault of my teeth, then tracing my chin. "Amelia?" he whispers, gazing into my eyes.

"Because it would make it easier to not want you," I whisper back to him.

Judd's pupils grow bigger. "Is that what you want? To not want me?"

I nod, my head moving in jerky movements like my muscles even know I'm lying.

Judd smirks and leans closer, enveloping my senses with the scent I've come to recognize as comfort. His hand slides from my chin and across my cheek to cup the back of my neck. Making a delicious shiver run up my spine. "Then tell me you don't want to see me any more. Tell me not even a small part of you wants to explore this energy between us. Tell me that all your fears and anxiety don't lessen when I'm around you and I'll leave you alone."

I suck in a deep breath, trying to calm my racing heart. My mouth opens, but words fail to come out.

Judd gives me a sinister smirk. "Can you tell me any of that pretty girl?" he asks, moving even closer until our faces are an inch apart.

"No."

"Good. Now, I'm going to kiss those perfectly plump lips like I've been wanting to since the moment I came to your apartment to pick you up. Any objections?"

I lick my lips and shake my head once, giving him permission because as much as I want to fight this, I can't. All the feelings Lucy talked about having with Kessler are exactly the way I feel when I'm around Judd. While that frightens me, I can't deny wanting to kiss him again any more than I can deny myself air.

I'm not sure who moves first, or if we both move at the same time, but when our lips connect, I swear I see stars.

His soft lips are gentle at first, caressing mine in a sweet embrace. Grabbing the front of his shirt and trying to pull him even closer, I open my mouth slightly, wanting, no *needing* more, swiping my tongue across his lips. He opens without hesitation, letting me in. Our tongues tangle together in a dance. Judd pulls back slightly and nips my lip, sending a rush of heat straight to my core, making me whimper.

"Mmm, I love that sound," Judd mumbles, moving from my lips to pepper kisses along my jaw and down my neck. He bites a spot on my neck, making me gasp at the sting. Then swipes his tongue over it, soothing my skin.

"Jesus," I whisper, moving my hands into his silky hair. When Judd reaches the space between my neck and collarbone, I tip my head to the side to give him better access. He pulls the collar of my shirt away and sucks hard. A long moan leaves my mouth, and I can feel a rush of wetness between my legs. If he can do that to my body from just licking and sucking my neck, I wonder what he can do to me in other places.

Just as I'm about to reach my hand under Judd's flannel, a very cold, very wet nose pokes my face from under Judd's chin, followed by a lick of a tongue that's not Judd's.

"Bruno!" I squeal, whipping my head back. Bruno takes that as an invitation and crawls from the back into the front seat with me, completely breaking the moment.

Judd's chest rumbles with a laugh, and he scrubs a hand down his face. "Nothing like a fifty-pound ball of fur in your face to break the moment."

I peek out over Bruno's back and see Judd adjust himself before reaching for the door. A sense of pride courses through me, knowing I made him react like that. Bruno and I both watch as he rounds the front of the Jeep to our door and opens it. Bruno leaps off my lap and sniffs around the cement. Judd reaches for the Tupperware container of leftover desserts his mom insisted I take home, then offers me his other hand. Taking it, he helps me out of the Jeep and closes the door. Removing his hand from mine, he drops it to my hip and backs me into the vehicle.

The chill of the parking garage fades as my body heats back up from the contact.

Jesus, Millie. Has it really been that long where a simple touch makes your body want to go up in flames?

Judd's hand moves up my body and stops at my chin, tipping it up so I'm looking at him. There's nothing simple about the way Judd is looking at me. Hunger, desire and something else I don't want to think about reflect back at me.

He leans down, kissing me again. This time it's slower, deeper, *more.* He pulls back way too soon and gives me that devilish smirk of his. "Come on, Shortcake. Let's get you inside before you freeze to death."

"I'm not cold," I mutter, grabbing the front of his flannel

and tugging him back to me. Surprise flashes across his face before he leans down again.

But instead of kissing my lips, he turns his face at the last minute and kisses my cheek, then whispers, "You're a greedy girl, aren't you?" into my ear. Clenching my thighs together, I close my eyes and suppress the moan that desperately wants to escape.

Why is that so fucking hot?

Chuckling, Judd straightens and steps back, making me shiver at the loss of his body heat. Okay, so it *is* cold in here. Wanting to get upstairs, I clip Bruno's leash onto his collar and take Judd's outstretched hand. Judd hits the button for the elevator when we reach it and the doors open automatically. Thankful we don't have to wait; I hurry into the elevator with Bruno. Judd follows and stabs the button for my floor. Turning to face me, he gives me a heated look that makes my insides dance. The doors chime, indicating they're closing, and he starts towards me, but before he can take another step, we hear someone yell, "Hold the door, please!"

Judd's hand snakes out, hitting one of the doors, stopping them from closing. A woman around my age comes into view, herding two young children into the elevator. "Thank you," she says once they're all inside.

"No problem," Judd tells her. He releases the door, and they proceed to close again. When he moves back, he hits the button for the eighth floor.

Does he know this woman?

The little boy looks at Judd and squints his eyes. "You look different without your parrot."

Judd chuckles and squats down so he's at the kid's eye level. "And you look different when you're not a Ninja Turtle." He looks at the girl glued to her mom's legs. "And a princess. How was your Halloween? Did you guys get lots of candy?"

The boy shakes his head vigorously and I'm afraid he's going to give himself whiplash. "*So* much candy," he exclaims, widening his arms to show us how much. "But mom says we can't eat it all because if we did, it would make us sick and give us lots of cavities," he says slightly bummed.

Judd's smile grows wider, and he chuckles. "She's right. You should always listen to your mom. They know best."

The little girl tugs on her mom's sleeve and she shifts her reusable bag to her other arm with her purse and picks her up, propping her on her hip. The girl whispers something into her mom's ear and points at Bruno.

"Oh, he has a vest on, honey. That means he's working, and we can't touch him."

Disappointment floods the girl's face, and she tucks it into her mom's shoulder, making my heart crack.

"What's that mean?" the boy asks, looking from his mom to Bruno and me.

"It means Bruno is a special dog that is trained to help me if I need it," I tell him, crouching down next to Bruno.

"Does he have powers!" the boy shouts.

Judd and I laugh. His mother shushes him and reminds him to use his inside voice.

"No, he doesn't have powers. He just knows how to calm me down if I get too nervous about something."

I look up at the girl who's peeking out from her mom's shoulder, watching Bruno. "Would you like to pet him? He really likes kids."

"Are you sure?" their mom asks.

"Of course."

She sets the girl down and she takes her brother's hand as they walk closer to Bruno. Bruno wags his butt in excitement, and I give him the command to sit.

"Put your hand out, palm down like this," I tell them, showing them with my hand. "That way, he can sniff you."

They both do as I show them and Bruno sniffs both their hands before pushing his head into their palms, making both of them giggle. Bruno sits patiently while they both stroke his head and ears. "He's soft," the girl whispers so quietly I almost don't hear her. Her eyes completely transfixed on Bruno like she's in a trance.

"I brush him a lot. He's *really* hairy," I say, making the kids laugh.

The elevator dings, announcing our arrival at their floor.

"Say thank you to the nice lady for letting you pet her dog."

Both kids say thank you and bye and high five Judd as their mom herds them out the doors and down the hallway. Once the doors close, we both stand and look at each other.

"How do you know them?" I ask.

Judd lifts a shoulder and tucks his hands into his pockets, leaning against the wall. "I really don't. They were on the same elevator as me on Halloween and named my fake parrot."

"That's cute. You're really good with kids."

"Mom says it's because I still act like one," he jokes, making me laugh.

The elevator dings again, making my heart rate increase. "Ladies first," Judd says, gesturing out the door with his hand.

I exit the elevator and Judd follows me out, placing his hand at the small of my back. By the time we make it the short distance to the door, my body is like a live wire humming with energy.

It takes me three tries to get the key into the door to unlock it. On the third try, Judd places his hand over mine, steadying it. Once I get the door open, I walk in and unclip Bruno from his leash and hang up my purse and keys. Turning, I notice Judd still in the doorway, hands above him, holding onto the frame.

"Are you coming in?" I ask.

"Only if you want me to, Shortcake. I'm not going to push you into something you're not ready for."

That right there means more to me than he'll ever know.

Walking to him, I hold out my hand. When he takes it, I tug him in and close the door.

Judd pulls me to his chest, caressing my cheek with one hand while his other sits dangerously low at the small of my back. He rests his forehead against mine, giving us a moment to just breathe each other in. "We'll go at whatever pace you want, Shortcake. Just say the word and we'll stop. Okay?"

His lips crash to mine as soon as I nod. His hands run down the length of my back and over the swell of my ass. When he reaches the backs of my thighs, he lifts me effortlessly without breaking our kiss, pinning me against the door. I wrap my legs around him tightly, loving the way his body feels between mine.

We hear a whine and break the kiss, turning to Bruno, who's watching us from his bed.

"We should probably go to the bedroom, or he's just going to keep interrupting us."

Judd nods, and I expect him to set me down. Instead, he carries me through my apartment and into my room, closing the door with his foot and pinning me against this door.

"Why are we standing when there's a perfectly good bed over there?" I ask with a laugh.

"Oh, don't worry, pretty girl, I'm going to fuck you there too. Now, take your sweater off so I can see those pretty tits."

Heat shoots to my core at his words and I do as he says, tossing the sweater to the floor.

He groans at the sight of my black lace bra. "Did you wear that for me?" he asks, tracing his tongue over the top of one of the cups. I lean my head back against the door, pushing my breasts out more. "Mmm, you like that, don't you? What about this?"

Judd sucks a nipple into his mouth through the lace, making my hips buck. "Yes, more, more of that," I beg, tightening my legs around him, pulling the huge bulge in his jeans to my center.

"More of what? More of this?" he asks again, licking a trail to my other breast and sucking the other nipple into his mouth.

"Yes," I hiss, arching my back and tugging at the hair at the back of his head.

He releases a hand from my legs and reaches up, pinching my other nipple while still sucking the other one, making me cry out.

"God Mills, you're so responsive. I bet you're soaked down there, aren't you, baby?" he croons.

I nod my head and whimper, relishing in the sensations his hand and tongue have brought to my body.

"Show me."

I freeze and open my eyes to stare at his dilated ones.

He gives me a wicked smile and sets me onto my unsteady feet. Kneeling down, he unzips one boot. Slowly tracing a finger along my leg as he goes, sending chills through my body before repeating the action with the other one.

After helping me step out of them, he sits back on his haunches and looks up at me. "Show me that pretty pussy, Amelia."

Holy. Fuck.

I've never been talked to like this during sex. Have I written about it? Yeah. But I have never experienced it. I've been missing out, because his words alone could probably make me come. I'm so turned on.

"Amelia, if I have to ask again, I'll have to punish you for making me wait."

I rub my thighs together, trying to ease the ache that's formed there. If I wasn't so desperate for release, I'd be tempted to find out what his punishment is. Instead, I hook my thumb into the tops of my leggings and shove them down and pull them off my feet, kicking them away. All that's left is matching black lace bikini cut underwear.

"So beautiful," he murmurs, ghosting both hands up my

calves and over the backs of my thighs. He stops just below where my ass begins and traces a path back and forth with his thumbs. "Are you achy baby? Do you need a release?"

I look into his eyes and nod, reaching up to cup both my breasts.

"Use your words, Amelia. I won't touch you unless you *tell* me what you want."

"Yes," I whisper.

"Yes what, pretty girl?"

"Yes, I need a release."

"Such a good girl using your words," he praises. Warmth spreads through my body at his words.

Holy shit, do I have a praise kink?

Judd skims his hands to the front of my thighs, his fingertips brushing the edge of my underwear.

I suck in a breath. The anticipation of what his next move is has me on edge.

"As pretty as these look on you, I'm afraid they're in the way," Judd says, hooking a finger under the lace panties and snapping them against my skin, making me gasp. He slides them down my legs and helps me step out of them, tossing them into the pile with my leggings and sweater.

Judd stands, looking down at me like I'm his last meal. "You're wearing too many clothes," I grumble and reach for the buttons on his flannel. He grabs my hand and tugs, pulling me into his chest.

"This isn't about me, Shortcake. This is about you and your pleasure. Just from the little I've done to you, I can tell you've never been with a man who knows how to please their woman. That changes tonight," he tells me, cupping my jaw and bringing his lips to mine. His tongue strokes mine and I swear I could spend hours just kissing this man. His other hand skims around my ribs to the back of my bra, flicking the clasp open in one try.

I pull back and smirk. "You're way too good at that," I tell him, tossing my final piece of clothing into the pile. Standing completely naked before him.

Normally I'm uncomfortable being so exposed like this, but the way Judd is looking at me, the way his eyes are drinking in my body like I'm water and he's been stuck in the desert for weeks, makes me feel sexy, wanted.

Judd grabs my hips and walks me back against the door. The wood is cool on my naked back, doing little to tame the heat that's built up inside of me. "You're so fucking beautiful, Mills," he whispers, staring into my eyes. My heart speeds up at his words. I've been told I'm beautiful before. But the way he says it makes me actually believe it.

He takes my lips again, his kisses turning hungry. He skims his lips over my jaw and down my neck, nipping and kissing as he goes. He pulls back, cupping my breasts and running the pads of his thumbs over both nipples. I gasp and arch into his touch. "So sensitive," he murmurs, repeating the motion.

"Judd," I whimper, threading my fingers into Judd's soft hair as he leans down to take a nipple into his mouth. His tongue flicks over my nipple as he rubs the other one with his thumb, making me see stars. I watch as he kisses his way over to the other breast and gives it the same attention, repeating the motion.

Looking up at me through his lashes, Judd takes his hand and skims down my stomach, and stops just above where I want him. I push into his hand, making him chuckle. He stops his assault on my nipple and detaches his mouth with a pop. "You want my hand on your pussy, baby?" he asks, sliding it half an inch closer. "Or do you want my mouth?" he asks, getting down onto his knees.

My mouth goes dry at the sight of Judd on his knees before me. "Which is it, baby? Hand?" He moves his hand closer, this thumb resting just above my clit. "Or mouth?" He leans forward and places a kiss on each of my hip bones, making me squirm.

"Yes, both," I force out, needing him to touch me before I combust.

Judd's deep rumble fills the space. "Such a greedy girl. But I won't give you anything if you don't use your manners."

"Please," I beg. "Please use both."

Judd hums with approval. "Good girl," he praises before sliding his thumb over my swollen clit.

Yep, I definitely have a praise kink.

"Yes," I hiss through my teeth, tightening my grip on his hair. "Just like that." Judd's thumb stops, and I quickly add a 'please'.

He circles my clit one more time before trailing his hand lower and swiping a finger through my slit. "Fuck, Mills. You're drenched for me."

My mouth parts slightly as I watch Judd take his finger and suck it into his mouth. "Mmm, you taste so sweet, just like I thought you would. Now put your leg over my shoulder. I'm ready for my second dessert."

Grabbing one of my ankles, Judd places it on his shoulder, then traces a path up my leg as he moves closer. Once he's satisfied with his position, he looks up at me. "Hold on, Shortcake. I'm starving."

His mouth is on me in an instant, licking a path from my clit to my entrance and back again, making my leg quake. "More," I beg. "Please. More."

Judd chuckles into my pussy. "Since you asked so nicely." Inserting one finger, Judd growls into my clit. "Fuck you're tight baby."

Words fail me and all I can do is whimper in response as Judd plays my body like a fine-tuned instrument. My head spins at the sensations Judd's making with just his finger and tongue. "H- how are you so good at this?"

Judd pulls back and stares up at me, mouth glistening from his feast. "Anyone who can't get a woman off using their mouth isn't doing it right," he says simply, before going back to eating my pussy like it's his job.

Tipping my head back, I reach up with my free hand and tweak one of my nipples, magnifying my pleasure.

"Eyes on me, baby. I want to watch you when you fall apart."

Prying my eyes open, I stare down at Judd, watching him insert another finger into me and nearly making my knee buckle.

"That's right, squeeze my fingers with that pretty pussy of yours."

My insides quiver, signaling my impending orgasm. "I'm cl-close."

Judd hums into my pussy, driving me wild. The sensation of his fingers and tongue overwhelms me, and it's almost too much. I tug on his hair, trying to pull him away. "I can't, Judd. It's, it's too much. I can't."

He pulls his mouth away from my clit and replaces it with the thumb of his other hand. "Yes, you can, baby. You're being such a good girl soaking my face. You're almost there," he croons, encouraging me.

I bite down on my bottom lip as my body tenses and my walls start to convulse. The wave of pleasure builds, higher and higher, until I don't think I can take it anymore. "Judd."

"That's it, baby. Come for me," he orders, pinching my clit and rolling it, sending me right over the edge.

"Fuck!" I cry out as I ride Judd's hand. He strokes me with his fingers, drawing out my orgasm until there's nothing left for me to give.

Judd lowers my leg from his shoulders after he licks me clean. My legs tremble and start to buckle until Judd swoops me up in his arms and takes me over to my bed to lay me down. "Holy shit," I breathe out, throwing an arm over my eyes.

The bed shifts with Judd's weight as he sits down on the edge of the bed, chuckling. "You okay, Shortcake?" he asks, fingers skimming across my stomach, leaving goosebumps in their path.

"I think I died." I peek an eye out from under my arm. "Is this heaven?"

"It could be," he tells me, leaning over me and giving me a kiss. It starts out soft, but quickly grows frantic with teeth and tongues clashing.

My stomach clenches when he bites that place on my neck I didn't know existed until he found it.

Seems like Judd has uncovered a lot of things I didn't know about myself before I met him, and I'm slowly starting to hope he uncovers more.

CHAPTER 20

Judd

SHE'S SO beautiful when she comes undone. When she lets all her walls down to feel. Her cheeks and chest are flushed red, and her thighs marked from my beard. I want to mark her all over. Claim her. But she's not there yet.

"I think I died," she says, peeking out from under her arm. "Is this heaven?"

I chuckle and lean down. "It could be," I tell her before taking her lips again. Fuck, I just can't get enough of these lips, of her. My kisses turn desperate. I move to the spot on her neck that drives her crazy and softly bite down. Her moan makes my already hard cock strain against my zipper and I reach down to adjust myself.

"Take your clothes off," she pants, tugging at my shirt but getting nowhere.

"Easy, Mills. We have all night, and I plan on using every minute of it." Standing, I unbutton my shirt and toss it to the floor. I reach for the button on my jeans, but Amelia's soft hands cover mine.

"Let me," she whispers, looking up at me through her lashes.

I drop my hands, and her fingers make quick work of my

button and zipper. The look she gives me has me discarding my pants in record time, leaving my boxers as the last thing between us.

Amelia's hand reaches forward, stopping halfway. "May I?" she asks, a look of uncertainty crossing her face.

I cup her jaw with one hand. "Baby, if you don't, I think I might combust right here on the spot. But good girl for using your manners," I praise. I had a feeling Amelia had a praise kink after spending some time with her and judging by the look she's giving me now, I was right.

Her hand continues forward. When she reaches me, she runs her palm firmly up my length from base to tip and back down again, repeating the motion. "Fuck," I growl when her thumb traces over my swollen head.

Encouraged by my reaction, Amelia scoots to the edge of the bed and pulls my boxers down, freeing my erection. "Holy shit," she whispers. She looks up at me with wide eyes. "I knew you were big, but not the fucking Hulk big."

My dick bobs once against my stomach as if it hears the compliment.

Mesmerized, if not slightly intimidated, Amelia takes my cock in her grip, pumping it a few times. Pre-cum leaks out of the top and instead of spreading it around with her thumb, she leans forward and licks the tip. "Mmmm, salty."

Sucking a breath through my teeth, it takes everything I have not to thrust my hips forward when she wraps her swollen lips around the tip and sucks. Pulsing her hand around my base, she sets a rhythm with her mouth and hand, taking me deeper each time.

"Damn, Mills," I whisper, voice strained. I'm barely keeping it together. Her mouth is like heaven, and I start reciting baseball stats in my head to keep from blowing my load early and embarrassing myself.

I can feel a tingle start in my balls and I pull back. Amelia's mouth coming off my dick with a pop. She looks up at me with watery eyes. "Why did you pull away? Did I hurt you?"

"No, baby. That felt so fucking good, I didn't want you to stop, but if you didn't, I was going to come embarrassingly quick. Besides, I want to come with your pussy pulsing around my cock."

Leaning over her, I cup her head with both my hands and get lost in her kiss. She skims her nails up the backs of my thighs, over my ass and up my back, sending shivers through my whole body. With a growl, I pick her up and toss her back onto the bed, crawling up after her.

"I wish you could see how beautiful you are with your hair mussed and lips swollen from my kisses," I murmur, peppering kisses along her jaw and down her neck, moving further south to worship her perfect breasts. "And these tits. God Amelia, it's like they were made to fit perfectly in my hands." She arches her back, thrusting them further into my palm. "Mmm, you like it when I play with your tits, pretty girl?"

"Y-yes," she moans as I tweak her nipple.

"Mmm, that's my good girl. Give me all your sounds. I want to hear you." I roll her nipple in between my thumb and finger, taking the other one in my mouth and giving it a suck before flicking it back and forth with my tongue, making her cry out with pleasure.

I switch breasts, repeating the pattern, making Amelia squeeze her thighs together. "Touch yourself, Mills. Show me how wet you are."

She opens her legs and moves one hand down to her pussy, circling her clit with one finger. I can feel her stomach clench before a long moan leaves her lips.

"Does that feel good, baby? Do you need more?"

"Yes," she whimpers as she dips her fingers into her pussy. I can hear how wet she is and when she looks up at me with her pupils blown with pleasure, I lose it.

The need to be inside of her becomes too much and I move

over her body, bracing my arms on each side of her head. She retracts her hand, and I position myself at her entrance. "Condom?" I ask in between kisses. "All of mine are upstairs."

She shakes her head. "No, I haven't been with anyone for over a year."

Over a year? I pause and pull back slightly, looking down at her. I mean, I've been in a dry spell, but over a year? "I can run upstairs really quick," I offer, moving to get off the bed. But before I can move, she places her hand on my arm, stopping me.

"I'm on birth control. I've been on it for years. And I've never been with anyone without a condom," she tells me. My heart thuds in my chest at her words. "I was also screened at my last exam and I'm clean."

Fuck, this woman is going to ruin me, and I'm crazy enough to let her.

"I'm clean too," I reassure her. "If you're sure this is what you want?"

She nods and I groan, taking her lips in mine, fucking her mouth with my tongue like I want to do to her pussy. "I want you so bad it hurts, Mills."

"Then take me, take all of me." Wrapping her legs around me, she pulls me in until my tip is at her entrance.

"You're absolutely sure you want this?" I ask again. I want to make sure she doesn't regret this, like she did when we kissed in the elevator on Halloween. Because once I have her, I'm never going to get enough of her.

She lets out a frustrated huff and squeezes her legs, pulling me tighter against her, the tip of my cock nudging her pussy. "I want to feel you, Judd. All of you, with nothing between us. Fuck me, please."

"Well, since you asked so nicely." Moving my hips slightly, I slide in an inch, making us both hiss. "You're so tight."

"Jesus, you're so big."

I chuckle. "Can't hear that enough."

I thrust forward another inch, her walls clamping down on me like a vise. "You have to relax, baby," I whisper.

"I can't," she whines, scrunching her eyes shut. "You're too big. I, it's not going to fit."

"Trust me, Amelia. It's going to fit," I reassure her. "Take a deep breath, relax your muscles."

She does as I say and I feel her muscles relax slightly. "Good girl, baby. You're doing so good," I tell her, inching forward again. Her body tenses slightly at the intrusion, but she closes her eyes and breathes through it.

Sitting back, I open her legs and look down at where we're connected, and fuck, does it drive me insane. "Look at your pretty pussy, taking my cock so well." Her eyes pop open, and she props herself up on her elbows so she can look. "You like watching?"

She nods, speechless, as she watches me thrust in and out, driving myself into her further and further. I reach forward and circle her clit with my thumb, thrusting forward again, finally fully seated inside of her.

"Judd," she whimpers. Her blue eyes have turned black with desire and her whole body is flushed red. "I'm so full."

Fuck, the way she says my name when I'm fully inside her makes me want to come on the spot. But I'm not allowing that to happen until I get another orgasm out of her.

"You're so tight, Mills. You feel so good," I tell her, leaning back over her to give her a kiss. Her mouth is hungry for mine and she lays back again, taking me with her. I pull her right leg up with me as I go, changing the angle, making her scream into my mouth.

Amelia pulls back from my kiss and arches her back. "Yes, ri-right there, Judd," she says, breathless. I thrust forward again and again, increasing my pace. Her nails dig into my back and I'm pretty sure I'll have marks there in the morning.

The sound of our bodies coming together fills the room, along with Amelia's sweet moans. "Harder," she begs as her walls start fluttering around me. I comply, thrusting into her harder, making her gray tufted headboard slam against the wall.

The pull of my orgasm starts, and I don't think I can hold it off any longer.

"Touch yourself, Amelia," I demand.

She reaches between our bodies and circles her clit, crying out in pleasure. Her walls clench around me again and again, indicating her orgasm is close.

"That's it, baby. You're right there, aren't you? Such a good girl you've been, giving me your tight wet pussy," I croon into her ear.

Amelia sucks in a breath before her body goes still, and she comes apart under me. "Judd!" She moans and her body trembles. Her walls squeeze me impossibly tight.

"I'm about to come, baby. Where do you want it?"

She moans again, riding another wave of pleasure. "In-inside of me. Please"

Her please does me in. I thrust one last time and feel myself fall off the cliff. I bite down on her shoulder, muffling my own sounds. Her pussy milks every last drop from me until I'm left trembling. Not wanting to crush her, I pull her with me as I roll over.

She lies on top of me, both of us panting, trying to catch our breaths. When her head finally lifts from my chest, she looks at me and I wish I could capture this moment and bottle it up so I could keep it forever. A freshly fucked Amelia is my new favorite look.

"Wow."

I chuckle. "Yeah, wow."

"Where have you been all my life?" she asks, giggling.

"I wouldn't have been worth your time, Amelia." It's true. I wouldn't have, not that I am now, but I'm a better person than I was even six months ago. And after the whole DUI thing, I never want to go back to being that person again. He wouldn't have been worthy of Amelia.

"Who says you are now?" She tries to keep a straight face, but the corner of her mouth quirks and she laughs.

I reach down and pinch her butt, making her yelp. "Ow! What? It was a simple question!" She smirks, smacking my chest.

I grab her wrist and kiss her palm. "Keep it up and next time I won't let you come twice," I warn.

"One, what makes you think this is going to happen again? And two, having more than one orgasm was a bizarre phenomenon. It won't happen again."

I frown. "Hold up. We'll circle back to that first one later. You're telling me no one's ever made you come more than once?"

She snorts. "If at all. I'm very surprised you were able to do it. Kudos to you buddy, I thought I was broken."

I sit up and pull her with me, so she straddles my lap. Amelia circles her arms over my shoulders, threading her fingers through my hair. Taking her face in both my hands, I look her in the eyes. "You are *not* broken, Mills. Those other guys you were with didn't know what the fuck they were doing. And to answer your first question. I don't think we'll be doing this again." Disappointment flashes through her face before I add. "I *know* we'll be doing this again. Fight it all you want, Amelia, but you can't tell me that you didn't feel something tonight."

She bites her lip and looks away, not answering me. But I decide to let it go for now. Whether she wants to admit it or not, some of her walls fell tonight and I'll be damned if I let her rebuild them.

CHAPTER 21

Amelia

GOD, *why am I so hot?*

That's the first thought that pops into my head when I wake up. The second, did last night really happen? I try to stretch, but an arm is pinning me down and there's a very large, very warm body spooning me, preventing me from rolling to my back.

Yup, it happened.

I replay the night in my head, expecting to feel regret, but all I find is contentment. Something I haven't felt in years.

After I avoided Judd's statement about me feeling something between us, he changed the subject, much to my relief. It's not that I don't feel something because I do. It just scares me that I do.

"Stop thinking so hard," Judd mumbles into my neck.

I suck in a startled breath. "Jesus, I didn't know you were awake."

"You woke me up with all that thinking you're doing," he says, stretching. His morning wood poking me in the back.

"I did not," I grumble, turning over to look at him. "How did you know I was thinking, anyway?"

He pulls me closer and tucks me into his chest, resting his

chin on my head. "Because your body tenses up and your breathing changes."

Shit, he's right. The fact that he already knows that means he's been paying attention to me more than I realized. And that he even noticed it to begin with? He cares.

"See, you're doing it again." His voice thick with sleep.

"Sorry," I apologize, snuggling into him more.

Judd runs his hand up and down my naked back. "You have nothing to apologize for, Mills. Just know you can talk to me about anything, ok?"

I nod into his chest and feel him give me a kiss on my head. "Good. Now, I'm starving. It's time for breakfast."

Judd tips my chin up and kisses me roughly. Snaking his arm around my waist, he pulls me on top of him without breaking the kiss. I grind my pussy against his already hard cock, making him growl.

"You. On my face. Now," he demands, breaking the kiss.

"Um, what?"

"Sit on my face, Amelia."

I'm sorry, do what now? No, there's no way I am sitting on his face. "Yeah, that's not going to happen. I'll suffocate you, I'll–"

A loud smack echoes through the room, and I gasp in shock. "Did you just *spank* me?" and do I *like* it?

He rubs the spot with his hand, soothing the sting. "Don't make me spank you again, pretty girl. Be a good girl and sit on my face."

Moving the pillows, Judd scoots down from the headboard and lifts an eyebrow at me. "Amelia."

I scramble to my knees and look at Judd, trying to figure out how to do this and *not* kill him. "Just put your knee here," he says, taking mercy on me and not punishing me for not moving fast enough and pointing to the spot by his face. "And straddle my face. Grab onto the headboard to steady yourself."

I do as he says. Once I'm kneeling over his face, Judd wraps both arms around my thighs and spreads me open. "Mmm, already *so* wet for me," he murmurs. "Widen your knees and lower yourself down."

"But I'll squish you," I croak out, already liking the feel of this new position.

"You won't Amelia, I promise. If I need you to get up, I'll tap this leg twice like this, got it?" he says, tapping my right leg twice.

I nod. "Got it." I spread my knees, lowering myself further onto Judd's face.

"Good girl," he mumbles into my pussy. His tongue sweeps out and gives me a long lick.

My hips involuntarily jerk forward, and I grind into his face. "Oh, oh my God." Being spread open like this on top of someone's face is not something I've experienced before.

Reaching up with his hands, Judd tweaks my nipples. Tightening my grip, I grind into his face again. He growls into my pussy, sending vibrations through me. "Keep riding my face baby," he says, voice muffled, then goes back to his meal.

I rock into him again and again, quickly finding my rhythm. My orgasm builds quickly and his pressure on my clit increases. "Yes, Judd. Just like that," I cry out.

Judd continues his assault on my clit as I chase my release. I can feel it building higher and higher. Judd reaches up again to tweak my nipples, sending me right over the edge. My thighs burn from kneeling like this, but the pain takes the back burner as pleasure rips through me. "Judd, I'm. I'm coming," I tell him, my body shaking uncontrollably.

Judd doesn't let up until my body is completely spent and I collapse onto the headboard.

"Holy fuck. I could wake up like that every morning," I say, rolling onto my back.

Judd sits up and props himself up on an elbow looking at me with a devilish grin. "I'm sure we could arrange that, Shortcake."

I grab a pillow and hit him in the face with it. He grabs it out of my hand and throws it to the floor, then gets to his knees and grabs one of my ankles, pulling me to him.

Right as he settles between my legs, we hear a muffled 'woof' outside my bedroom door.

Judd drops his forehead to mine. "Cock blocked by a dog."

Laughing, I bring my hands to his face, loving the way his scruff feels against my palms. "I'm sorry, but he's probably hungry and needs to go out."

He nods and helps me up. I throw on a pair of leggings and Judd's hoodie. My mouth goes dry when I look over at Judd in just his jeans. What is it about being barefoot in jeans that makes a man so damn sexy?

"Keep looking at me like that, Shortcake, and Bruno's breakfast will turn into lunch," Judd warns, stalking over to me. When he reaches me, he pushes my hair back from my face and grips my neck. Bending down, he gives me a kiss that quickly turns heavy. Bruno woofs at the door again, breaking us apart. "Okay, okay. We're coming," Judd grumbles.

I giggle and move past Judd to open the door. Bruno spins around excitedly, greeting me. I open the sliding door to my patio and Bruno darts out quickly, going over to where his potty area is and relieving himself. Tuning back to the living room, I leave the slider open so Bruno can come back in when he's finished.

"He goes to the bathroom out there?" Judd asks, coming up behind me while I'm scooping out Bruno's food.

"Yeah, I have a special area out there for him to go on."

"Huh, I wondered how you took him outside all the time. Now it makes sense."

I set Bruno's food dish down and when I stand back up, Judd turns me around and wraps his arms around me. Inhaling his scent, I return the hug. Relishing in the warmth of his embrace.

My stomach decides this is the perfect moment to declare

its hunger and rumbles loudly. Judd's body shakes with a laugh, and he pulls back, looking down at me. "Hungry?"

"What gave you that idea?" I ask, chuckling.

"Just a hunch."

I look at the clock on my stove and rub my eyes before looking at it again. "Holy shitballs. Does that say eight o'clock?" I ask, nodding to the stove.

"Yeah? Why? Are you late for something?"

I shake my head slowly. "No. It's just. I never sleep this late. And if I do, it's because I was up all night with panic attacks." Come to think of it, I can't remember the last time I woke up feeling as refreshed as I do.

"Do you get those a lot at night?"

I lift a shoulder. "Often enough I guess."

"But you didn't have any last night. Unless I slept through it?"

I shake my head. "No, I didn't." I give him a smirk. "Maybe all the exercise I got helped." Or the six orgasms he gave me. I've never had so many orgasms in one night in my life. Once I had one, I wanted more. It was like I couldn't get enough of Judd touching me, kissing me, tasting me. Judd gives me a smile, like he knows what I'm thinking.

My stomach growls again, but louder this time. Judd raises his eyebrows. "Let's get you fed before your stomach starts eating itself." He leans down, giving me a peck on the cheek before stepping back a few steps. "I'm going to run upstairs and change my clothes. I'll meet you back down here in...ten minutes?"

I dip my head in a nod. "Where are we going?"

"Wherever you want, Shortcake."

"Hazel's?"

Judd chuckles. "If that's what you want."

"Yes, please. She has cranberry white chocolate scones right now that I'm *obsessed* with."

"Can't deny my girl a sweet treat after she was so good for me last night."

"Hold up," I say, trying to ignore the delicious shiver that ran through my body at his words. "Who said I was *your* girl?"

His chest rumbles with a laugh as he steps back into my space and grips my chin, tipping it up so I'm looking into his green eyes that I can't seem to get enough of. "After what we did last night, there's no way I'm letting anyone else claim you. You're mine, I'm ruined for anyone else." He closes the space between us, leaning down and taking my lips with his, giving me a deep, slow kiss that leaves me breathless and wanting more. So much more. But he ends the kiss, much too early for my liking. Pulling back, he says, "So if that doesn't make you *my* girl, I don't know what does."

"Oh," I whisper, reeling from Judd's confession and soul searing kiss.

Dropping another kiss onto my lips, he turns and walks to the door. "Ten minutes, Shortcake," he calls over his shoulder.

I nod as he closes the door, even though he can't see me. Tracing my lips with a finger, I leave Bruno to finish his breakfast and head back into my room. It smells like Judd and sex, two things I never thought I'd be mixing together, but here we are and I realize I'm not upset about it. We may have started off not liking each other. Okay, *I* may have started off not liking *him*, but after unwillingly spending time with him, then willingly spending time with him, I've come to realize he's not the person the media has always perceived him to be.

He's more. So much more.

We get to the café just as the morning rush dies down. I only make it two steps in before I hear Hazel's fake southern twang accost my ears from behind the counter. "Well, well, well, look at what the cat dragged in. To what do I owe this absolute honor, Sugar?"

"Bite me, Hazel. Give me my coffee and four scones and no one gets hurt," I tell her, taking my jacket off and placing it on the back of my chair before taking my seat at the counter. I would order a coffee for Judd, but I'm not sure what he likes.

"Four scones? Jeez, someone's hungry. What did you do to work up such an appetite?" she asks, turning to make my coffee. "And where's Bruno?"

The bell jingles above the door and we both turn to see Judd and Bruno walking in, answering Hazel's question. I turn back to look at Hazel, who's now giving me a questioning look.

"Don't start," I tell her.

"Oh, ho, ho, I fudging knew it!" she exclaims under her breath. Keeping her words PG for the customers that are strung throughout the café.

Running a hand down my face, I suppress a groan. I'm going to be hearing about this later. Most likely with Charlie joining us. There better be alcohol for that interrogation.

She gives me one last look before turning her attention to the man now standing behind me. "Judd, how *lovely* to see you here. And with my best friend at that. What can I get you?"

Judd hands Bruno's leash off to me, giving me a peck on the cheek before taking a seat next to me, tucking his long legs under the counter. "Hazel, a pleasure. I'll take a medium Americano please," he says with a charming smirk.

"Coming right up," she says, handing me my plate of scones, then my coffee before moving to make Judd's order.

Judd eyes the scones and my drink before looking at me. "You're going to get diabetes."

I take a huge bite of my scone and moan in delight. "But they're just so good," I tell him around a mouthful of food, washing it down with my cold brew. "Try it."

I hold my scone out to him. Instead of taking it from my hand, he leans forward and bites off a corner. His lips brushing against my fingers. Keeping his eyes on me as he chews, he hums quietly. The sound travels straight to my clit, making me clench my legs together. "Mmm, so sweet," he whispers, his voice husky.

A throat clears and we both startle and look to see Hazel standing back in front of us with Judd's drink. "One medium Americano," she says, handing Judd the cup. "Can I get you two anything else? A room maybe?"

I break off a small piece of my scone and throw it at Hazel. "No, thank you. That will be enough, peanut gallery."

Hazel chuckles, dodging the piece of pastry.

"Actually," Judd says, looking at the menu behind Hazel. "Can we also get two cheddar, bacon, and egg breakfast sandwiches, please?" He turns to me. "You do like bacon, right?"

"Uh, yes? I already have my breakfast though," I tell him, gesturing to the plate of scones.

He snorts and shakes his head. "If you're going to ingest that much sugar, you at least need to consume some protein along with it." Reaching for the plate of scones, he takes one for himself and places it on a napkin, then sets the rest on the other side of him.

"Ooh, ballsy, Davis. Taking Millie's life blood from her," Hazel says, placing the breakfast sandwiches in the toaster oven to warm them.

Judd leans forward and whispers into my ear, "If you eat your sandwich like a good girl, I'll let you have the other one later and maybe this time I'll be the one feeding you."

Shivers race down my spine and my lady bits perk up at the suggestion.

My phone pings, interrupting the moment between us, and I grab it and unlock the screen, reading the text.

HAZEL

picture

My head whips up to Hazel. "Hazel Ann, you little shit."

Hazel just cackles and moves to the register to take another order.

Judd tips his head to my phone. "What'd she do?"

Turning my phone screen to face him, he takes it, looking at the picture Hazel secretly took of Judd and I. I'm holding the scone he took a bite of in my hand still, looking at him with pink tinged cheeks and hunger that food won't satisfy. He's looking back at me with the same look and something else I can't quite put my finger on. My phone pings again in his hand and he reads it before barking out a laugh and handing my phone back to me.

CHARLIE

Amelia Marie. You have some splainin' to do.

CHARLIE

GIF of Ricky Ricardo

CHARLIE

Hazel you owe me, I'll gladly take my payment in sugary sweets and coffee.

HAZEL

Deal

I look up from my phone to see Hazel grab our sandwiches out of the oven. "Why do you owe Charlie?"

Setting our food in front of us, Hazel wipes her hands on a towel and gives me a cheeky grin. "She won the bet."

"What bet?"

Hazel sighs. "Remember the bet we made last week? Well, from the looks of it," Hazel says, gesturing to me, "Charlie won."

"How did you know that?"

She points around my face. "You're glowing." She leans across the counter and lowers her voice. "Plus, you have beard burn on your neck and chest."

I gasp and pull my shirt open, looking down at it. Sure enough red, splotchy marks cover my chest. How did I not notice when I was getting dressed this morning?

Because he fucked you senseless.

I look at Judd, whose shoulders are shaking from laughter. Backhanding his arm I say, "You could have said something."

"But then everyone couldn't see that you're mine."

"Gah, why is it so hot when a guy gets all possessive?" Hazel asks, fanning herself.

I roll my eyes.

"Roll your eyes again, Shortcake, and see what happens," Judd whispers into my ear before placing a kiss on my temple. "I'm going to the restroom. Don't miss me too much while I'm gone," he says, giving me a wink and leaving the counter.

I watch him walk away, his dark wash jeans clinging deliciously to his toned ass.

"Oh girl, you got it bad."

I feel my cheeks redden and I grab my coffee, suddenly wishing there was alcohol in it.

"Don't be embarrassed, Millie. Love looks good on you."

I choke on my coffee mid swallow, spewing drops all over the counter in front of me. Once I've gathered myself and got my coughing under control, Hazel tosses me a wet rag to wipe up my mess. "When's the last time you had your eyes checked, Haze? I think you're seeing things that aren't there," I tell her, tossing back the rag.

"My eyes are just fine, girl. That fine specimen of a man is head over heels for you."

"But we're, we, we just started seeing each other. I mean, I think we're seeing each other?" I shake my head, confused. "I don't even know. He told me I 'ruined him for anyone else.' So, I guess that means we're...together?"

Hazel leans on the counter with both arms. "Oh. girl. That *definitely* means you're together."

I hum in acknowledgement while I pick at my scone.

"Is that not a good thing?" Hazel asks, seemingly confused by my reaction.

I tip my head, still staring at my scone. "I don't really know. You know how I am this time of the year. I just–" I blow out a breath. "I'm nervous? I guess? The closer it gets to the anniversary of my parents' death, the more unraveled I feel."

Hazel lays a hand over mine and I look up into her emerald-green eyes. "You know he would understand. He doesn't strike me as the type of guy to not care, especially about something like that. Just talk to him, okay?"

I nod.

Hazel's right. Judd has been nothing but caring since the beginning. He'd understand my struggles.

I make the decision to open up to him about my past. But not today. I don't want to ruin a good day by bringing up heavy things.

"So, what are you two up to today?"

"That's up to Amelia," Judd says from behind me, making me jump.

"It is?" I stare at him, squeezing back into his spot, letting my eyes wander over the body that I had my hands all over last night. Well, hands, lips, tongue... A shiver runs up my spine and I have to squeeze my legs together to ease the sudden ache that's appeared.

Judd takes a bite out of his breakfast sandwich and gives me a smirk, like he knows what's going through my mind. "Got something in mind, Shortcake?"

I feel my cheeks flush and clear my throat. "I might have an idea or two."

Hazel leans on the counter, dropping her voice. "Oh, please do tell. Inquiring minds want to know."

"Shut up, Hazel," I laugh, tossing my napkin at her.

She catches it before it hits her face and laughs. "I guess I can wait for girls' night to hear *all* the things," she says, giving me a wink.

Judd leans over and whispers into my ear, "I guess we need to give you a lot to talk about with the girls then, huh?"

My cheeks flame brighter, and I duck my head into my shoulder and whisper back, "I thought we did plenty of that last night...and this morning."

Judd chuckles quietly. "Oh, Shortcake, I'm just warming up."

My core clenches again as memories of last night flood my brain.

"Now be a good girl and finish your breakfast."

"And if I don't?" I challenge.

Judd grips the back of my neck and pulls me forward until I'm an inch away from his mouth. "Then I'm just going to have to fuck that attitude out of you later."

Before I can even respond, he takes my lips with his, giving me a slow, deep kiss. A kiss full of promises of what's to come later. A kiss totally not appropriate for public. But I can't bring myself to care because, for once, my brain is quiet, and my soul is at peace.

CHAPTER 22

Judd

"SO, what's the plan of attack for the day, Shortcake?" I ask Amelia as we walk out of Hazel's hand in hand and head down the sidewalk. It's rare we get a nice day with no rain in November, so we took full advantage of it by walking this morning.

She sighs. "I really should work on my book. But I'm just not feeling it today."

"Still stuck? Did talking to Lucy not help?"

"No, it did. It gave me some great ideas about where to go in the story. I'm just not ready to dive in yet." She gives me a sheepish smile. "I have a tendency to hyper focus when I'm writing. Charlie had to come over for signs of life one time because I was so sucked into my writing, I accidentally let my phone die and they didn't hear from me for like two days. Now I have to text them when I'm 'going in' so they know I'm not dead, just writing. I also keep a charger in my office now too, so they can check in and make sure I've eaten."

"Add me to that list."

"What list?" she asks, giving me a quizzical look.

"The list of people who check in on you. Add me to it," I

tell her, bringing her hand up to my lips and kissing the back of her knuckles.

Amelia shakes her head and laughs. "There's really not a list. It's just Charlie and Hazel. They're really all I have."

I stop in the middle of the sidewalk and pull her to me, her hands landing on my chest. She looks up at me with a grin as I cup her cheek. "And now you have me. I'm in this Amelia, however slow you need to take it. Whatever title you want to put on it. I'm telling you now and I'll keep telling you for as long as you let me. You're one of the most incredible women I have ever met in my life, and I know I don't deserve you, but I'll spend forever trying to be the man you deserve." A tear slips down her cheek and I brush it away with my thumb. "So please add me to your list," I tell her softly.

It scares me how gone I am for this girl. How, even though I haven't known her long, I want to give her everything she's ever wanted. I finally get it. What Kessler was feeling when he fell for Lucy. The connection. The need to protect her from everything bad in the world. But when I look into her sparkling blue eyes, the feeling I'm not ready to label yet pushes that fear away.

I'm not sure who moves first, but our lips find each other and there's a desperation in her kiss that hasn't been there before. We stand there in the middle of the sidewalk making silent promises with our lips that our voices aren't ready to say when we feel Bruno's head sneak in between our bodies, followed by a muffled 'woof'.

Amelia pulls back with a laugh, reaching down to scratch Bruno's head. "Sorry, bud. Are you feeling left out?"

Another woof.

"I'll take that as a yes," I say, reaching down and giving him a scratch too. Straightening, I clasp Amelia's hand in mine, and we continue our walk back to our building. "Anyway, back to our topic of what to do today. What do you like to do when you have a free day and don't want to write?"

Amelia gives me a sideways glance and bites the inside of her cheek. "Promise you won't laugh?"

I make an 'X' over my heart. "Cross my heart," I tell her, then give her hand a squeeze. "You can tell me anything, Mills."

"I like to snuggle up in my reading clothes, sit in my reading chair with my fluffiest blanket, get a tray of snacks and drinks all set up beside me and read. All day."

I clutch my chest. "A girl after my own heart."

She looks up at me, shock all over her face. "You, you're not going to make fun of me? Or tell me that's a waste of a day? Or tell me I shouldn't want to read after spending all my time writing?"

What?

"No? Why would I make fun of something you obviously enjoy doing? Anyone who has made fun of you for that is a twat and doesn't deserve you."

"You're too good to be true, you know that?"

I've never let anyone besides my family see this side of me. Never *wanted* anyone else to see this side of me. People see me as the hot shot playboy. Cocky and confident. But that's my public persona. The real me loves nothing more than spending time with my family and close friends, staying in and reading, normal things that I lost sight of when I played for my old team. "No, Mills. I'm just a regular guy."

We're about a block from our building when I see two guys walking in the opposite direction of us. The one in a Silverbacks baseball hat looks up and makes eye contact with me. Eyes widening, he nudges his friend, who looks up from his phone, his face replicating his friend.

Shit.

They know I've seen them and they've clearly spotted us, so there's no way to avoid them. It's not that I want to avoid my fans. I'm grateful for them, but this doesn't help prove my point to Amelia that I'm a regular person. We make it another couple of feet before they veer over to us.

"Hey, you're Judd Davis," the baseball hat guy says.

I chuckle. "I am."

He holds out his hand. "I'm Jake, this is my buddy, Craig. Do you think we could get a picture?"

I release Amelia's hand to give Jake and Craig a handshake. "Sure," I say, giving Amelia an apologetic smile. Amelia moves to get out of the way, but I quickly wrap my arm around her shoulders and pull her to me. "You don't mind if my girlfriend is in it too, do you?"

Amelia starts to protest, but the guys quickly agree. Jake asks someone passing by if they could take our picture and hands them his phone. We pose and the woman takes several pictures of the four of us.

She hands back the phone and they quickly look through them as she walks off.

"Thank you. These are great. Our buddies would have never believed us. Have a great day!" they both say, giving us a wave before continuing down the sidewalk.

Amelia bumps her shoulder into mine as we resume our walk. "Just a regular guy, huh?"

I bump her back. "Most of the time. The public gets a different side of me. My friends and family get the real me."

She hums, nodding her head. "I totally get that. My readers know I have a service dog for my anxiety, but they don't know the extent of it. I give them the version of myself I wish I could be all the time. Not the actual person I am behind closed doors."

We enter the lobby, and Marty greets us with a wave. We both wave back as we pass the front desk and head towards the elevators.

Hitting the call button, I turn to Amelia. "You know they would still follow you and support you, right?"

Nodding, Amelia sighs. "I know. Charlie and Hazel have said as much. It's just... I'm not always the bright, happy person they get. My readers bring me a lot of joy, them loving my stories brings me joy. But my anxiety and depression don't always allow room for that joy, and I don't want it to come off as ungrateful."

We step into the elevator, and I hit the button for her floor, then wrap her in my arms. "You don't have to do anything you don't want to do, Mills. But your readers could be going through similar things and showing them that you struggle too could be therapeutic for not only them, but you as well."

Amelia nods into my chest saying a muffled, "You're right."

"Tell you what. When you get into your apartment. Go get your reading clothes on, grab your fluffy blanket and whatever else you may need. Text me a list of all the snacks you want. I'll run to the store while you're gathering your things, and I'll meet you back here."

Amelia's head flies up, excited eyes meeting mine. "Really?"

"Yes, really."

"Wait. Why do I need to gather my stuff? We can just read at my place."

"No offense, babe. But my library and reading space is kinda hard to beat."

She snorts and pushes back from my chest when the elevator gets to her floor. "I'll be the judge of that, *babe,*" she says, as she backs out of the elevator with Bruno. Giving me a wink before she turns around and heads to her apartment.

Fuck, I love this girl.

CHAPTER 23

Amelia

HE CALLED ME HIS GIRLFRIEND. Not only did he call me his girlfriend to his *fans*, he said he wasn't good enough for me and he wanted to spend the rest of his life trying to be the man I deserve. My head is spinning by the time I gather all my stuff I want to take to his apartment and change into my reading clothes. I'm itching to text the girls, but I stop myself from reaching for my phone. I don't want anything to ruin this bubble of happiness I'm in. I know the girls will be ecstatic, but I want to keep this to myself a little longer.

Once I'm all packed and ready to go, I plop down on the couch and wait for Judd to get back from the store. I texted him a list of snacks and told him whatever he gets is good for me. While I'm waiting, I open up my notes app on my phone and jot down a few ideas for my next book that came to me while we were walking back from Hazel's. Writing down these ideas has the excitement building in me to get back to writing, something I haven't felt in a while. I should be writing today, while I have this feeling. But I really want to spend the day reading with Judd. He's the first guy I've dated that hasn't given me shit about my love of books.

Wow, even saying we're dating in my head feels weird and unbelievable.

I'm just finishing up my last idea when a knock sounds at my door. Bruno and I both bolt to the door and a look through the peephole shows Judd standing there with four reusable bags on his arms.

"Did you buy out the whole store?" I ask, opening the door for him.

"You sent me a long list," he says with a shrug. He looks my body up and down, stopping at my sweater. His mouth moves reading the words, barking out a laugh when he's done. "I'm digging the sweater, the whole outfit really. It screams comfort."

I look down at the sweater Hazel gave me last year for Christmas. It says, 'Your anxiety is a lying hoe.' "Thanks, Hazel got it for me, and don't change the subject. I sent you that list, so you had things to *choose* from, Judd. I didn't mean to buy it all."

"This way we'll have plenty of snacks for more reading days, or movie nights, or sleepovers." He wiggles his eyebrows up and down. "Not that there will be much sleeping," he jokes.

Shaking my head with a laugh, I grab my stuff and Bruno's leash, clipping it on him. "Ready when you are."

We head out the door and lock my apartment. Judd taps his phone to the elevator once we're in. "Remind me to set up your phone with my access key," he says as we ride the elevator up.

"Why?" I ask, not doing a great job of hiding the shock in my voice.

Judd chuckles. "Because Amelia, we're dating. I want you to come to my place whenever you feel like it." He lifts a shoulder. "Besides, once you see my library, you're never going to want to leave."

"We'll see about that," I tell him as we reach his floor.

"Ladies first," Judd says, motioning in front of him.

I walk out of the elevator and my mouth drops open.

Judd's penthouse is amazing. It's a modern design with sleek lines and wood tones. Dark hues of blues and blacks spread throughout the space. The white granite countertops pop against the black cabinets in the kitchen. It's an open concept layout so the kitchen and living room connect. Across one of the *two* large couches is a gas fireplace. And the back of the apartment is all windows, giving us the absolute best view of the city and mountain range in the distance. "Wow," I whisper.

This apartment screams masculine but lacks Judd's personality. It feels...incomplete.

"Make yourself at home," Judd says, walking into the foyer behind me and tossing his keys onto the side table next to us, then heading to the kitchen to set the bags of snacks down. Bruno must think Judd is talking to him because as soon as I unclip his leash, he runs into the living room and bounds up on the black leather couch, quickly turning a circle before plopping his body down.

"Bruno, that's not our couch!" I chastise him, running over to pull him off before he tears a hole in the butter soft material with his claws. "I'm so sorry."

Judd chuckles. "It's fine, Shortcake. He's just taking me up on my offer."

"But his claws," I start.

Judd doesn't let me finish. "He's fine, Mills. I'm not worried about it," he says, coming over to me and cupping my cheek. He closes the space between us and gives me a soft kiss. "Now, come on." He links my fingers with his and tugs me towards a room off to the right of the living room. Judd pauses at the door and turns around. "Close your eyes."

I narrow my eyes at him. "Why?" I ask, suspicious.

"Humor me."

I sigh and close my eyes. "Fine, but if I open them and it's just you naked in a room instead of books, I get to give *you* a surprise."

"Don't threaten me with a good time, babe."

I shake my head. I hear him turn the handle to the door, then feel his body behind me, guiding me forward.

I've taken half a dozen steps when he stops me. "Okay, you can open them."

Doing as he says, my eyes pop open and for the second time in five minutes, my mouth hangs open. "Holy fuck, Judd. This is amazing," I tell him as my feet carry me further into the room, where I make a circle.

The wall of windows has continued into the room, giving it tons of natural light, brightening the otherwise dark room. Floor to ceiling black bookshelves line two of the walls. Lights dotting the shelves every few feet. The shelves are filled with books of all kinds, mystery, thriller, fantasy. Special editions of books I've read myself. A ladder, *a freaking ladder,* with wheels is on the longest wall.

There's a smokey gray and white patterned area rug in the middle of the dark mahogany colored floor with an oversized brown leather couch and matching chair facing the window. A wooden coffee table with a black metal frame completes the look.

I keep turning, completing my circle facing where we came in. On the furthest side opposite the door sits a bulky wooden desk and leather chair in the corner. The wall behind it is lined with shelves holding various items of baseball memorabilia. This room is what I was expecting the living room to look like, not the sterile, cold vibe it gives off. He must spend a lot of time in here.

Judd's still standing where I left him, hands in his pockets. "I told you it was hard to beat."

As I'm walking back to him, I notice a framed sketch of a house on the other side of the door, opposite of where the desk is. "What's that?" I ask, passing Judd and walking over to the drawing.

The sketch is of a beautiful two-story house with charcoal gray siding and stone accents. The peaks of the house are all framed with wood to match the garage door and pillars of the porch. Matching wooden shutters also frames the black windows.

The bottom sketch shows what the back of the house would look like. It's the same as the front, but there's a black framed sliding door that takes up half of the back of the house.

"That," Judd says, coming up behind me and wrapping his arms around my middle, "is the house I hope to build someday."

"Why don't you build it now? I mean, you have the money."

Wow, rude Millie.

"Sorry, that was rude of me to just assume."

"No, you're right. I do have the money to build it now if I wanted to."

"Then what's stopping you?" I ask, turning in his arms to face him and linking my hands behind his neck.

He tips his head back and forth. "Well, for one, I'd like to live out near my parents and Kessler and his family. And right now, there's nothing available near them to buy."

"You're really close with them, aren't you? Not just your parents and Kessler, but Lucy and Hudson, too."

"I am. Lucy and Hudson were meant to be in our family. I could see that from the moment Kess brought them to the house." He smirks. "Plus, Lucy is always up to join me in giving Kessler a hard time."

I smile up at him. "Always the troublemaker, aren't you?"

He lifts a shoulder. "That's what little brothers are for."

"That was reason one. I'm assuming there's a second reason?"

"There is," he says, pausing to tuck a piece of my hair behind my ear. "I don't want to build a house by myself. I want to build a *home* with someone. Plan what the inside will look like. How many rooms we might need for kids. Fight over the color of the kitchen countertop or what color the living room should be."

My chest squeezes. The passion in his words flowing over me. The look of desire in his eyes, pulling me in.

"Oh," I whisper.

"Yeah," he whispers back. "And until my dream girl agrees to that, my dream *house* will have to wait. Because I can't have one without the other."

My heart speeds up, because I know he's talking about me and as much as my heart screams yes, the logical side of my brain chimes in, telling me no. It's too soon. He hasn't seen the worst of you.

"Anyway, enough about that. Do you want to see the rest of my place?" he says casually, like what he just admitted was no big deal.

Maybe it's not.

I write about this stuff all the time. Why can't it happen in real life?

Putting that thought away to mull over later, I give him a nod and we exit the library and up the metal staircase across from it.

"There's just a guest room and ensuite up here," he says, flipping on the light to a sparse guest room that only has a bed and a nightstand with a lamp on it. I guess you wouldn't need much if you were just a guest.

"Then out here," he says, turning the light off and leading me towards another door, "is the rooftop access." He opens the door, revealing a large, graveled area that we step out onto. There's a little area right off to our left that has what looks like a grilling station with a counter and barbecue that's been covered for the winter.

Judd points to an area that's bare. "I'm going to get furniture for that area next summer, not that I'll get to enjoy it too much with it being the middle of the season. But it would be nice to sit out here on warm summer nights."

"The view is amazing from up here," I say, taking a few steps further into the space. When I turn, I let out a gasp. "Is that a *hot tub?*"

Judd chuckles. "Yeah, I haven't really used it much since moving in."

I look at him in horror. "Why would you *not* use it?"

"I'll show you," he says, grabbing my hand and pulling me back through the door.

We make our way down the stairs and walk underneath them to a door. Turning the handle, he guides me in and switches on the light, revealing a huge king-sized bed with one of those floating frames. Wood and iron nightstands are on either side of the bed. Across the room is a large TV mounted on the wall. The wall with the bed is the only one in the room that has pitch black paneling, the rest of the room is white besides the thick black curtains that cover the windows. Other than that, there's really not much in here for decorations.

"How long have you lived here again?"

"I know. It's not really decorated. It kills my mom, trust me. She's been chomping at the bit to decorate my place, but I told her not to bother. This is just a place to live. I spend most of my time either at their place, at Kessler's, or in my library. Now, let me show you the second-best room in the place," he says, tugging me across the room and to the door to the right of the bed.

Judd hits the light switch, and the lights turn on revealing a bathroom I could live in. There's floor to ceiling windows in here too and in the corner of those windows sits a huge free-standing tub. I ignore everything else in the bathroom, heading straight to the tub of my dreams.

"It has jets too!" I say a little too enthusiastically.

Judd's deep chuckle sends shivers up my spine. "I told you it was the second best room. Plus, the shower has dual heads and can turn into a steam room."

I climb into the tub with my clothes still on and lay back, closing my eyes. "I'm moving in. You can just leave me here, maybe bring food and water every once in a while."

Judd kneels next to the tub and crosses his arms over the side. "You can stay here anytime you want, Shortcake."

I open one eye and look at him. "You say that now, but you don't know how *obsessed* I am with this tub."

"Hopefully as obsessed as you are with me."

I tap my chin. "Mmmm, I think the tub takes the number one spot," I tease.

Judd gets up and climbs into the tub with me, grabbing my hands and pulling me forward until I'm straddling his lap. His erection straining through his jeans. "You like that, Amelia?" he whispers into my neck. He moves his hips forward just enough to create some friction against my thin lounge pants, making me whimper. "Mmm yeah, you like that, don't you? You're a slut for my cock, aren't you, pretty girl?"

Judd repeats the motion. This time my hips move with him, hitting that delicious spot over and over. "Judd," I pant, clutching onto his shirt. He nibbles up my neck, sending goose bumps down my arms. "If we don't stop, I'm going to come," I warn, almost to the edge already.

"Then come for me, Mills. I want to watch you come apart in every room of this place," he says. His hands move to my breasts, his thumbs gliding over the nipples with the pace of my hips.

"Kiss me, Judd," I demand, taking his face in my hands and pulling him to me. He greedily takes my lips, sucking and biting as my orgasm hits me hard. His mouth mutes my loud moan, and he doesn't stop kissing me until the last of my orgasm fades.

"I take it back," Judd pants.

"Take what back?"

"This might be my new favorite room."

CHAPTER 24

Judd

KESSLER

Checking in fuckers. Everyone is coming for Thanksgiving right? Mom wants an estimated headcount even though we all know she'll make more than enough anyway.

REESE

Wouldn't miss it.

BRENT

I'll be there. We're doing Thanksgiving early since Lexi is due on Thanksgiving.

GARRETT

I don't know.

KESSLER

Yes you will. Mom will come over and drag you to her house by your ear if she has to.

ME

😂 Like she did when you guys were 12 and decided it would be a good idea to jump in the pond during the dead of winter to see who could stand the cold longer.

GARRETT

I couldn't feel my balls for a week. But I won. It was worth it.

KESSLER

You did not win. We both got out at the same time.

GARRETT

Nope. I was the last one to touch the water.

KESSLER

Bullshit.

GARRETT

Wanna re-match?

KESSLER

Oh it's on Seal boy.

ME

Jesus, mom should have let you both stay in there.

GARRETT

Fine. I'll be there.

ME

I'm sure Kara will be delighted to see you there.

GARRETT

Don't make me throw you in the pond.

ME

I'm not scared of you.

KESSLER

You should be.

REESE

You should be.

BRENT

I am.

GARRETT

What they said.

"What's so funny?" Amelia's sleepy voice asks.

"Just texting the guys about Thanksgiving and giving Garrett shit," I tell her, setting my phone on my nightstand and spooning her from behind.

She sighs and snuggles further into my body. "Always the troublemaker."

"Me? Never," I say, kissing a path from her neck down to her shoulder. Another sigh escapes her, and she arches her back, rubbing her ass along my already hard cock. "You like that?" I ask, biting the spot on her neck I know drives her crazy.

"Yes," she says with a breathy moan.

I rock my hips into her, my cock gliding between her naked thighs. "Are you already wet for me, Shortcake?"

Amelia reaches back and hooks an arm behind my neck, rocking back against me. Sending my cock between her slick pussy.

"You're such a good little slut for my cock, aren't you?"

Nodding her head, Amelia whimpers when I push forward again, rubbing the head of my throbbing cock against her clit.

"Judd," she cries, voice pleading.

Moving my hand from her hip, I reach up and tweak her nipple. "I know, baby," I tell her when she cries out again. "This is going to be hard and fast."

She pushes her ass against me again and lifts her leg,

inviting me in. In one swift thrust, I'm buried inside of her, both of us releasing satisfied moans.

My hand moves from her breast to her neck, gripping her firm, but not hard enough to choke her.

"Yes," she hisses, matching my thrusts.

"Such a greedy fucking girl, aren't you?"

A sheen of sweat quickly covers my body and the sound of our bodies joining together fills the room. Amelia's moans get louder the closer her orgasm gets. I pull out suddenly and get on my knees, flipping her onto her stomach.

Amelia lets out a surprise gasp, but quickly gets to her knees. I sink back into her, gripping her hips with both hands and driving into her hard and fast. The base of my spine starts to tingle, and I know I won't last too much longer like this. Her pussy starts to flutter around my shaft, telling me she's close, too.

"I'm close, Mills," I grunt out, trying to last long enough to get her there. "Reach down and rub your clit."

Amelia reaches down and touches herself, making her walls clamp down harder around me.

"Judd," she whimpers into the pillow.

"Come for me, Amelia. Give me what I want."

Amelia's whole body shudders, and a loud moan escapes from her lips. I thrust into her two more times before my own powerful orgasm follows. "Fuck, Amelia. You're perfect. So fucking perfect."

We ride out the last waves of our orgasm before both collapsing back onto my bed to catch our breath.

Amelia rolls over, snuggling into my chest. I reach down and pull the sheet over us to ward off the chill as our bodies cool, then tip her chin up. "Good morning," I say, placing a kiss on her lips.

She pushes against my chest, protesting. "Judd, my morning breath."

"How many times do I have to tell you, Mills? I don't care.

Now, let me kiss my girlfriend good morning." I lean down again and seal my lips around hers, giving her a long, slow kiss. When I finally pull back, she's breathless. "Good morning."

"I could wake up like that every day," she says with a giggle, tucking her head back under my chin.

She's said that every morning she's woken up next to me for the past four days and every morning I have to keep myself from asking her to move in with me. I've never asked a girl to move in with me, but I've never been as serious about someone as I am about Amelia. I know I'm moving fast, but it feels right. I just need to keep my feelings at bay until she's ready to hear them. The last thing I want to do is scare her away.

"Me too, Shortcake."

Her fingers trace a path over my tattoos on my right arm. The light touch sends goosebumps up my arm. "Can I ask you something?" Amelia says quietly.

My heart speeds up, but I try to keep my body relaxed. "Of course, Mills. You can ask me anything."

"It's nothing, really. I just noticed that since we've met. You always call me Amelia, or Shortcake." She pauses. Her finger traces faster over one of my tattoos. "Or Mills." There's a sadness in her voice on the last name. "But never Millie. I guess I'm just curious as to why? *Everyone* calls me Millie."

I pull back and reach under her chin, tipping it up so I can look into her eyes. "Because you're Millie to everyone else. To me, you're *my* Amelia, my Shortcake, my Mills. And I don't want to be just everyone to you. I want to be *someone* to you."

The one. I think to myself.

Her eyes widen and her breath hitches. "Why?" she asks, like she can't believe anyone would choose her.

"I think you know why, Mills. But we don't have to talk about that yet. Let's just spend time together and see where it takes us, okay?"

Her eyes flick down, and she pulls the corner of her lip into her mouth, worrying it with her teeth. My thumb pulls her lips out from between her teeth, and I trace over it, soothing the redness that's already there. "I mean it, Amelia. We will go at your pace. Whatever that looks like."

She nods her head, and I pull her back into my chest, wrapping my arms around her tightly. "What's on your agenda for today? Besides the library and interview this afternoon."

"I'm actually going to squeeze some writing in today after I shower. I'm finally feeling good about where I'm at with the story." She picks her head up and looks at me, resting her chin on her hand that's on my chest. "What about you?"

"Taking a shower with you and finishing the last few chapters of the book I've been reading."

"Who said I was showering here?" she teases, giving me a smirk.

I swat her ass, making her yelp. "I did. Now get in the shower, woman."

I'm about to throw her over my shoulder and carry her into the bathroom when we hear a 'woof' behind the closed bedroom door.

I drop my head and laugh. "Cock blocked again. Go get in the shower. I'll join you after I'm done taking Bruno out and feeding him."

She presses a kiss to my lips then, gets out of bed and walks naked to my bathroom. Pausing at the entrance, she looks back at me over her shoulder and says, "Don't take too long, or I'll have to take care of myself." Then gives me a wink before sashaying her hips the rest of the way through the door.

CHAPTER 25

Amelia

TWO ORGASMS and five hours of writing later, Judd and I arrive at the library just as the dogs are getting there. I almost didn't let Judd leave the house when he put that damn baseball hat on backwards. My vagina was screaming at me for one more round and I almost gave in. But the library needs us, so she can just wait until we get home later.

We make quick work of unloading and pottying the dogs, drying them all off the best we can with towels. The break in the weather was short-lived, and the rain is back in full force. But I can't seem to bring myself to care because the last four days have been some of the best days I've had in a long, long time. And I know it's because of Judd.

I've never been with someone who makes my soul feel alive and my heart at peace the way he does. The feelings I'm having both scare me and settle me all at once. Maybe, just maybe, Judd was right all along, and I've found my missing piece.

As if Judd knows I'm thinking about him, he looks up from where he's currently sitting with Ruby and gives me a wink before going back to giving Ruby belly rubs.

"That boy is smitten with you," Gladys says beside me, making me jump.

I bring my hand to my chest to slow the thundering of my heart. "Jesus, Gladys, you scared me."

"Sorry, hun, I said your name." She looks from me to Judd, and back to me. "Must have been distracted," she teases, giving me a wink.

I feel the result of my embarrassment climb up my neck and heat my cheeks.

Gladys waves her hand dismissively. "Don't be embarrassed, Millie. Young love is a beautiful thing."

I open my mouth to protest but my spit goes down the wrong tube and I end up choking. After a few minutes of coughing and a cup of water that Gladys brings me, my coughing spell finally fades enough for me to speak. "We just started dating, Gladys. We're not in love."

Gladys places a hand on my shoulder. "Millie, can I tell you something my mother told me when I was dating my Peter?"

I nod. "Of course," I tell her, patting her hand. Peter is Gladys' late husband. He died about a year after my program started. He was ten years older than Gladys, which wasn't as big of a deal as it can be nowadays. He was the sweetest man on earth and always brought Gladys fresh flowers every week and came to the library to volunteer when he could. When Peter was diagnosed with an aggressive form of cancer and knew he didn't have long, he asked me to help him set something up to make sure she still received her flowers every week after he was gone.

So, I did. I just never told either of them that I had the flower shop charge my account and I never will. She asked me once how Peter was able to do it because she didn't see the charges coming out of their account. I shrugged and told her some things are just better left a mystery. Gladys lights up every time a new bouquet arrives. She brings the bouquets from the previous week to the library to share with us and says it's like a part of Peter is still able to visit the library.

"I had only gone on a few dates with Peter when I started

feeling something for him. I thought it was just because the relationship was still new and exciting and would wear off over time." She pauses. "Do you mind if we sit down, honey? My hip is acting up now that the rain is back."

"Not at all Gladys."

We sit down on the couch nearest to us and she continues on. "Well anyway, my mother overheard me talking to Irene one day about it and she told us both that love knows no time, it can be fast, or it can be slow, but the length of time won't matter if it's the right person."

I glance over at Judd, who's taking pictures of Ruby. She's on her back, paws up in the air, with her tongue hanging out. Seeing Ruby, who has always been afraid of men, be this relaxed with Judd and hearing Gladys give me advice from her mother, sends my walls around my heart crumbling down.

I look back at Gladys, who's watching me with a knowing smile. "I hope it helps my, sweet girl." She gives the hand in my lap a final pat and gets up from the couch, going over to Irene to help her set out the snack table.

Judd looks at me again and gets up and walks over to me with Ruby, sitting in the seat Gladys just vacated. "Everything okay, Shortcake?"

Giving myself a mental shake, I smile at him. "Yeah, everything's fine. Gladys was just asking if I was feeling better. My migraines can hang on for days sometimes."

Not a complete lie, they do, but he doesn't need to know that's not what we were talking about. I need a minute to wrap my head around it first.

"Are you nervous about Jules interviewing you? You look a little flushed."

"No, I'm fine. I love talking about my program. I just hope between your foundation and the article, it'll help give the program the audience it needs to help us expand."

Judd grabs my hand and gives it a squeeze. "I have no doubt in my mind that it will, Mills."

He leans forward to give me a kiss when the door to the library opens suddenly, causing us to both look over our shoulders.

"Judd Davis! It's been too long!" a beautiful woman with long, straight glossy brunette hair says from the entrance, making all the dogs' heads pop up from their beds. Her long legs eat up the distance between the door and where we're seated on the couch. Judd gets to his feet, pulling me up with him just as the woman, who I'm assuming is Julie the reporter, reaches us.

"Julie, so good to see you again," Judd says, holding out his hand for a shake while still holding onto mine in his other.

"Judd, a handshake? Really? Give me a hug, I haven't seen you in what? A year?" she gushes in a voice I've quickly decided compares to nails on a chalkboard. Without waiting for Judd's response, she pulls him forward in an embrace. Giving him no choice but to let go of my hand to return the gesture. She's tall for a woman, probably 5'10" or 5'11", so she can easily see over Judd's shoulders while she's hugging him.

When she spots me, she gives me a wide smile and steps out of Judd's arms and comes over to me, offering me her hand. "You must be Amelia. I'm Julie, the lucky journalist chosen to write this piece for the Oregon Times." She gives my outstretched hand a shake before backing up a step and clasping Judd's arm with both of hers. "When I heard Judd was forming a foundation to provide kids access to literacy programs, I *begged* my boss to let me cover it." She grins up at him. "I've interviewed him a few times before and we just seemed to hit it off," she says, giving him a wink.

Judd clears his throat and steps out of her embrace, moving to my side and wrapping his arm around my shoulder. My body can't seem to relax since this human hurricane rolled in, so I stand stiffly under his embrace.

Bruno lets out a soft whine, sensing my discomfort, and I

can feel Judd's gaze bore into my head. "Mills," he starts, but I cut him off.

"Really nice to meet you, Julie. I'm glad my program will be getting exposure, hopefully enough to help us expand," I tell her, fighting off the sudden wave of anxiety that is building. "Should we start the interview? That way, we can hopefully get through most of the questions before the kids get here and you can focus on the parents and kids."

She looks between me and Judd, her wide smile never leaving her face. "Of course. Take a seat wherever you're comfortable and we can begin. Do you mind if I use the recording app on my phone? I like to focus on the conversation and listen to it while I'm writing up my articles."

I shake my head, feeling the muscles in my neck tighten from the tension. "No, go ahead."

Get a fucking grip, Millie. Judd's allowed to have a past. YOU have a past. Put your big girl panties on and get a grip.

Julie sets her recorder up on her phone and gets a paper out with a short list of questions printed on it.

"Okay, I'm going to ask the first question and let the conversation flow naturally and work the other questions into the conversation. Sound good?"

"Sure, whatever you think is best," I tell her, hoping this goes by quickly because I can already feel my tension headache starting.

"Great. First question. What gave you the idea of pairing dogs from the shelter with children who struggle to read? It's not exactly a common concept."

"Well, as you can see, I have a service dog," I start, gesturing to Bruno, whose head is on my lap. "He's trained to signal me by bumping me with his nose if he senses an increase in my anxiety. By doing that, he can usually distract me, enough to take my mind out of the spiral it's in. A lot of the kids in my program don't always have problems with reading. They have a problem with self-esteem. Just providing a child a safe space to stutter through words or get some pronunciations wrong and not having to worry about being made fun of by their peers helps boost their self-esteem. Dogs are great listeners, and they give unconditional love. It's been proven being around dogs can help increase our natural dopamine and oxytocin levels, or the 'feel good' chemicals in our brain."

"Fascinating," Julie replies, jotting down some notes on her paper. "But why shelter dogs? Don't they usually come from unknown backgrounds? What makes a dog deemed safe to be in the program?"

"That's where most of the expense of my program comes from. These dogs are thoroughly vetted and tested for their behaviors towards people, specifically children." I point to Ruby, who's asleep at Judd's feet. "Ruby is great with kids, actually prefers them over adults, but is the most shy with men. It took Jeremy, the lead handler from the shelter, months to get Ruby to come up to him without her cowering." I look up at Judd, who's looking down sadly at Ruby. "She actually wasn't a candidate for a while because we didn't think she would respond well to kids. If she feared adults, mainly men, that much, we figured she wouldn't tolerate children. But a kid walked by her kennel one day and instead of staying near the back like she usually does, she bolted forward and stuck her nose between the chain link. Jeremy saw it and told me about it and I immediately asked for her to at least be put through the testing to see if she had a chance."

The more I talk about my program, the more I feel my body relax. Maybe this isn't so bad after all.

"That's absolutely amazing. So she's better now?" Julie gestures to Judd. "I mean, she's sleeping on Judd's feet."

"No, Judd's the only man she seems to take to. She still tucks her tail when Jeremy walks up to her, even though he's been handling her for months. Ruby's been in our program the longest. All the other dogs that came through with Ruby have been adopted. Mainly by the families of kids who were previously in RUFF."

Julie's polite smile turns appreciative at my boyfriend. "Judd seems to have that effect on women, both two and four legged."

Hold the fuck up.

Judd clears his throat and looks at his watch. "The kids will be here soon, so we should probably get through a few more questions before our time is up."

"Of course," Julie says with a giggle. She peers down at her paper, then back up at me, slipping her professional smile back into place. "Amelia, you've made quite a successful career for yourself as a romance author. What inspired you to help children specifically? You don't write kid appropriate books."

I fidget with Bruno's leash, and he pushes into me further, trying to ease my discomfort. I knew there would be questions about me and what inspired RUFF, it's just never easy to talk about it.

"I grew up an only child and had a tough time in school making friends. I was diagnosed with generalized anxiety when I was a teenager. Reading was my escape and a love I shared with both of my parents." I pause and take a breath. Judd's hand covers mine, giving it a quick squeeze, easing the pinch in my chest. "I lost them the day after my 21st birthday."

"I did read that in an article when I was doing some background on you. I'm so sorry. They were killed by a drunk driver, right?"

I nod, my throat tightening. I feel Judd's body turn ridged beside me. I know I should have told him sooner, but I don't like repeating it, so it's better getting it out now.

I'll apologize to him later.

"They, uh, were hit head on. Killing them both instantly. The driver walked away with minor injuries. It was his second DUI in four years. He's currently serving 40 years in prison, with no chance of parole." My hand starts to tremble and Bruno whines, pushing into me.

"Maybe we should stop for the day? Finish the questions some other time?" Judd suggests.

I scoot closer to him, trying to draw strength from him. "No. I'm okay. I can do this," I tell him. Julie looks between us with raised eyebrows, shock, then realization crosses her face.

Yeah, lady, he's mine.

Taking a breath, I continue, just wanting to get this over with. "A while after that, one of my therapists suggested writing down my thoughts. Those thoughts became short stories, then books. One of my professors suggested I enter a contest with my writing. And I won." I leave out the part where I tried to take my own life. That's not something I'm ready to disclose to a complete stranger, especially one who would want to write about it. Plus, it's not fair to Judd to hear about it this way. "I found my love for books again, and when Gladys and Irene approached me to save their children's program, I jumped in with both feet. Books have always been my safe place and if I can offer that for children who need it, then at least some good will come out of my tragedy."

"That's such an inspiring story," Julie says with sincerity. "And the fact that you're with Judd after he was charged with the very thing that took your parents?" She shakes her head. "I don't know if I could do it."

What?

I leap up from the couch and turn to Judd. His face is in utter despair.

"No," I whisper. "Tell me it's not true."

"Mills," he says, holding up his hands like I'm a feral animal he's trying to calm.

"*Don't* fucking call me that," I bite out, taking a step back.

"Oh my god, you didn't know." I hear Julie whisper in the silence.

I look around to see Jeremy, Gladys, and Irene all staring at me with varying levels of shock. I suck it a breath, then another one.

I can't breathe. No, not now. PLEASE not now.

I take another step back, then another.

"Amelia!" Judd shouts as I turn around and run as fast as I possibly can out the back of the library and out to the parking lot, immediately getting drenched in the downpour. I dig the key out of my pocket and hit the unlock button. I open the front door and command Bruno in. He jumps in and quickly jumps into the back, like he knows I need to be as far away from here as quickly as I can.

"AMELIA!"

I take one last look over my shoulder and see Judd standing at the door. His hands are gripping the frame so tight I can see his knuckles turn white from here.

"Amelia, please let me explain."

I shake my head and climb into the driver's seat, letting the tears fall freely down my face. I see Judd start down the steps and I quickly turn the car on and pull out of the parking lot. I watch in my rearview as he runs after my car for a bit before falling back, realizing I'm not stopping.

I drive on auto pilot back to my apartment building. Realizing Judd's just going to go straight to my apartment. I speed past my building and call Charlie.

The phone's ring echoes through the car, setting me further on edge.

"Come on, pick up, pick up," I mutter to myself as I turn my car toward Charlie's.

"Hey, Millie. What's up? Aren't you supposed to be at the library?

"Charlie," I croak, a sob following.

"Amelia, what's wrong?"

"Judd, he, he."

"He what? Oh my god, is he okay? Are you okay? Where are you, Millie?"

Sucking in a breath, I choke out another sob. "I'm, I'm c-c-coming o-o-over," I manage to get out.

"Are you driving?"

"Y-yes, I'll be a-at your p-p-place s-soon."

"God, Millie. Be careful. I'm calling Hazel."

I nod my head even though she can't see me. The phone disconnects and I'm left with my racing thoughts in the silence of the car.

CHAPTER 26

Judd

"FUCK!" I scream out as I watch Amelia's car disappear down the street. This is not how I wanted Amelia to find out about my DUI. I grip the back of my hat and rip it off my head. Running my fingers through it and tugging at the ends. Rain beats down on me, soaking me instantly, but I can't bring myself to care. A horn honks behind me and I realize I'm still standing in the middle of the road. "Fuck," I mutter out again and jog back to the library.

When I walk back through the door, I notice a couple of the kids have arrived. Julie is talking to Irene while Gladys is getting the first few kids settled. Julie spots me and heads in my direction.

"Judd, I am so sorry. I didn't know," she starts, but I hold my hand up to stop her. I look around and motion for Julie to follow me to the office.

Once she's through the door, I close it behind us. "What the fuck was all of that, Jules?" I hiss out. Grabbing an extra towel off the table, I start to rub it over my head and down my arms, trying to dry myself off a bit.

She shrinks back at the venom in my tone. "What do you mean? I was just asking the questions from my list."

My fist curls around my hat that's still in my hand, bending the brim. "My DUI has nothing to do with Amelia's library program."

Julie drops her eyes. "No, you're right, it doesn't."

"Then why did you even bring it up?" I seethe.

"I, I guess after I saw how cozy and close you two were, I got jealous, and it just came out. But I swear I didn't mean to hurt her. I thought she knew."

I scrub a hand down my face. "Julie, we slept together once, *years* ago. What you did out there was not only out of place, but it was also unprofessional."

Julie swallows hard and nods. "I know, Judd. I'm sorry. So, so sorry. Please, what can I do to make this right?"

I shake my head. It's not all Julie's fault. I should have told Amelia about what happened, but I also didn't know that's what killed her parents. "Just go out there, interview some of the parents. Get all the information you need, pictures, whatever, and write the best damn article you've ever written."

She nods. "Of course. Despite what you may think of me now, I do think this program is a benefit to the community and I'll do everything I can to see it gets traction and funding to expand."

I nod. "Thank you."

She moves back to the door and pauses. "I truly am sorry, Judd. I hope I didn't ruin things between you and Amelia. You really are a great guy and I wish you nothing but the best."

I nod, again. Not trusting myself to lash out again.

Once the door closes, I plop down into the chair and lean forward cradling, my head in my hands.

How the fuck am I going to fix this?

A soft knock sounds at the door, and I look up, expecting Julie to walk back through. Instead, Gladys' face pokes in. "Mind if I come in for a minute?"

I make a move to stand, but Gladys puts her hand on my

shoulder, halting me. "Please don't get up. This won't take long," she tells me, leaning against the desk.

Dred fills my stomach. She's going to tell me I'm not good for Amelia and that I should find a different program.

"I've come to know Amelia pretty well in the last five years," she says. "She may be spicy from time to time, but her heart is in the right place."

I think back to our first encounter only a few weeks ago and chuckle. Knowing what Gladys is referring to.

"I lost my husband, Peter, the year after Amelia's program really took off. She was such a blessing to have during that dark time. She made sure I had everything I needed and even took over running the library for me, so I could take time to grieve."

"I know she's too good for me," I tell her before she has a chance to say it.

Gladys frowns. "No, Judd. You're perfect for her."

Huh?

"I don't understand?"

"You're the calm to her storm. She's run around here for the last five years, making sure everyone else was taken care of, that she's never had time to take care of herself. She helped my husband make arrangements to have flowers sent to me every week from my favorite florist, so I would still have fresh flowers long after he was gone because he knew I wouldn't buy them for myself." She swipes at her eyes and sniffs. "Anyway, my point is, Amelia has always been the pillar in our storms, standing strong, despite what's thrown at her. But even strong pillars get battered and beat up after a while. It's time someone stands beside her and helps bear some of the invisible weight she carries. She's known more heartache in her short time than most people experience in an entire lifetime."

"But what if she can't forgive me? What I did, what happened to her parents." I stop and shake my head.

Gladys walks over to me and places her hands on each of my cheeks. "You're her person. It may take time, but she will forgive you. But Judd, you have to forgive yourself too." She pats one of my cheeks, then moves away to open the door. "Go find our girl, Judd."

"But what about the kids and dogs?" I ask, standing from my seat.

Gladys waves me off. "We've got it handled today. You have something more important to take care of."

I lean down and give Gladys a hug. She gives me a quick squeeze and pats my back.

"Enough of that. Now get goin'," she tells me, opening the door.

I leave out the back door again and start jogging down the sidewalk towards our building. The rain is coming down harder, but I don't care. Because it's time for me to help Amelia weather the storm and this is the first step.

"Hey, you've reached Amelia. Leave me a message and I might remember to get back to you."

I hit the end button and tap out a text.

ME

Amelia. PLEASE answer your phone.

Read.

ME

or at least text me back to let me know you're ok.

Read.

ME

I can see you're reading these. Please, Mills. I just need to know you're ok.

Read.

ME

I'm sorry.

Read.

I sigh and throw my phone onto the couch. Plopping down beside it and pinching the bridge of my nose to ward off the headache that's developing. How did everything go to shit so quickly?

My phone starts to vibrate, indicating a call. I scramble to grab it and check the screen, only to feel a wave of disappointment wash over me.

MOM

I want to hit ignore, but the urge to talk to someone wins out. Sometimes a man just needs his mom, and this is one of those times.

"Hey, Mom."

"Hi, baby. I was just calling to check in and see if maybe you convinced Amelia to join us for Thanksgiving?"

The back of my eyes start to burn at the hopeful tone in her voice.

"It's just no one should be alone for the holidays, even if they're okay with it," she continues. "And I'm going through the final checklist to make sure I have enough food for everyone. Does Amelia even like turkey? It'll be fine. We have ham too if she doesn't."

"Mom," I choke out, voice cracking.

"Judd, what's wrong, baby?"

"Mom, I, we, she. I fucked up, Mom," I finally get out.

She doesn't chastise me for my language like she normally would, just asks me to tell her what happened.

It takes me some time to get through the story of what happened at the library, but I eventually do and when I finish, she's quiet.

"Mom?"

"I'm here, Juddson, just processing what you've told me."

Juddson, she used my full name, which only happens when she's mad or disappointed in me.

Fucking great.

I'm just letting people down left and right.

"Do you think I'm a bad person, too?"

"Oh, honey, no. You're not a bad person, you just made a bad decision. You are human and humans are allowed to make mistakes. Was your mistake worse than some? Yes, but the important thing is you *learned* from it and have grown tremendously since then."

"What if she never forgives me?"

Mom sighs. "Then you grieve what you had and try to move forward, but I hope you don't have to."

I can't lose her. "But she's my person."

"I know. I saw it from the moment you walked in with her. The same way I saw it with Kessler and Lucy. Give her some time Judd. Give her some space to sort through all the emotions she's probably going through. Just let her know you're still there for her if she needs you."

She doesn't want me. I saw the look in her eyes as she was getting into her car. The look of betrayal. She trusted me, let me into her closely guarded heart. And in an instant that trust was destroyed, and I have no clue how I'm going to rebuild it.

It's been three days since the incident at the library. Three days since I've heard from Amelia. Three days since I've held her in my arms. The longest three days of my life. I've slept on the couch the past three nights because Amelia's scent is all over my room.

The only thing keeping me from going completely insane is the text Charlie sent me letting me know Amelia was at her place and that she was safe. I asked her how she was doing, and Charlie just told me she needed time to process. I get the feeling I'm not getting the full story from her, and I probably never will, so I have to take what I can get from her for now.

The drive I usually enjoy passes in a blur on my way to my parents' for Sunday dinner. I almost didn't go, and I know Mom would have given me a pass, but I decided to go anyway. Maybe being around my family will help cheer me up and bring some normal back to my life. It beats sitting at home in my library that no longer brings me the peace it once did now that Amelia isn't there. She brought so much life to my sterile apartment, and now it's just bleak and empty.

I see Kessler and Lucy are already here when I pull into my parents' driveway. Shutting off my Jeep, I sit in the silence and stare out the windshield at the house I grew up in. I used some of the features of my parents' house in my own design for my house I hope to build one day. Hoping a little of the magic and love I experienced growing up here would grow in my own home.

A flash of movement from the curtain brings me out of my thoughts. Taking a deep breath, I get out of my Jeep and head inside, kicking off my shoes in the mudroom and opening the adjoining door.

The smell of my mom's cooking smacks me in the face. But instead of making my mouth water like it usually does, my stomach sours at the smell. I haven't had much of an appetite since Thursday. I've been living off protein bars and toast. Those seem to be the only things I can stomach.

Mom looks up from where she's chopping vegetables at the counter and sets her knife down when she sees me. Wiping her hands on her apron, she moves to come over to me. I meet her halfway and she envelops me in a hug. I squeeze her tight as she rubs my back like she used to when we were upset or sick as kids. I may sound like a pussy, but I don't care. I'm heartbroken and need a hug from my mom.

After a few minutes, Mom pulls back and looks up at me, taking my face in her hands. "Have you heard anything?"

I shake my head. "Just the text I got from Charlie."

"Mmm, it's only been a few days. Give it some more time," she says, patting my cheek with one of her hands and moving back into the kitchen.

I don't really have a choice. Amelia has completely shut me out.

I head into the living room where Lucy and Kessler are, taking a seat on the chair next to the couch.

"Hey, Judd," Lucy says, giving me a sympathetic smile.

"Hey, Luce. How's it going?"

She rubs her growing bump. "Fine. Just finalizing details for the wedding with Cass and getting fat. You know, living the dream."

A corner of my mouth lifts. It's the most I can muster at this point, but at least it's something.

"You're not fat. You're growing *two* of my babies, and I wasn't a small baby. Ask Mom," Kessler tells her, reaching down and rubbing Lucy's bump.

"He's right, dear. I hate to tell you, but he wrecked my vagina with his fat head. Took forever to heal."

"Ugh, Mom, I did not need to hear that," Kessler groans at the same time I mutter, "Gross."

"Oh, grow up you two, it's a part of life. Kessler, you're going to see it soon enough." Mom chastises us from the kitchen.

"Anyway," Kessler says, changing the subject. "How are you holding up, Judd?"

I lift my shoulders and let them drop. "Fine, I guess."

"You don't look fine; you look like someone kicked your dog," Kessler says.

"I don't have a dog."

"I meant if you had a dog."

The idea I had Thursday before shit hit the fan pops into my head. I dig my phone out of my pocket and unlock it, finding the pictures I took. "Speaking of dogs," I say, tapping on the screen and turning it to show Lucy and Kessler. "This is Ruby. She's three and one of the dogs in Amelia's reading program." My chest clenches when I say Amelia's name, but I push the hurt down. "She completely adores kids, actually prefers them over adults. She's been in the program the longest and is always sad when she has to leave the kids to go back to the shelter." I know I'm laying it on thick, but I want them to agree with my plan. "I was thinking since Christmas is coming up and Hudson has been bothering you guys for a while about getting a dog..." I trail off.

"You want us to adopt this one?" Lucy asks, not sounding sure, but not shutting me down either.

I nod. "I think she would be perfect. She's already potty trained. She knows the basic commands. She's spayed and is up to date on all her shots. Plus, you already know she would be good with kids because she wouldn't be in the program if she wasn't. The only thing she has a small issue with is that she's afraid of men, but she took to me right away, so she could be getting over that."

"Sounds like you should adopt her," Kessler says.

"If I didn't travel so much during the season, I would. But it wouldn't be fair for me to adopt her, then be gone all the time. Trust me, I've thought about it."

Lucy and Kessler look at each other. Lucy tips her head and shrugs a shoulder.

Kessler turns back to me. "Could Lucy and I meet her first? We'd feel better about saying yes if we knew she would be ok with us."

I nod my head enthusiastically. "Absolutely, I can give you Jeremy's contact information and you can schedule a time with him."

"We're not saying yes until we visit, so don't get your hopes up," Kessler warns.

"I know. I'm just happy you're considering it. She deserves a home."

I look over at Lucy, and she gives me a wink. I smile for the first time in days. If Lucy has anything to say about it, and she does, Ruby will have a home for Christmas.

Finally, one thing is going right.

CHAPTER 27

Amelia

"ARE you *sure* you don't need me to cancel my trip? You know I would," Charlie asks me again.

"Six."

"Six?" Charlie repeats. "Are you having a stroke? That's not at all what I asked."

Propping myself up on my elbows, I look at Charlie from where I'm currently laying on her living room floor. "You've asked me six times in the last," I tap my phone to look at the time, "Two hours. That's an average of three times per hour."

"Yes Millie, I know what six divided by two is. But that doesn't answer my question."

Flopping back onto the pillow, I grab another handful of Mike & Ike sours and shove them in my mouth. If I don't have cavities after the amount of sugar I've consumed in the last three days, I'm buying stock in the toothpaste I use. "No, Charlie, I don't need you to cancel your trip. Your mom has been wanting to do this for *years*. I'll be fine."

Probably.

"Have you had any more panic attacks?"

"Nope."

Yes. Several more, each one worse than the last.

But if I tell her that, she'll *definitely* cancel her trip. I've only had three in front of her since showing up at her place after fleeing the library Thursday. One as soon as I got here. One after Hazel showed up, and I was finally able to tell them what happened. And one yesterday morning when I thought she was still asleep. I've been able to surprisingly hide the other ones, or they've hit when she's been gone.

She eyes me suspiciously, like if she stares at me long enough, I'll crack.

I won't.

As much as I appreciate her and Hazel being here for me, crying with me, eating more ice cream than anyone should be able to consume, watching my comfort movies and shows with me. It's time for me to go home.

My phone pings with an incoming text. I don't need to look at it to know who it is. Judd has been texting me every day to check in and apologize. I've read every single text; I just can't bring myself to reply. Every time I think about texting him back, Julie's voice replays through my head. *"That's such an inspiring story. And the fact that you're with Judd after he was charged with the very thing that took your parents."*

I now understand what someone means when they say something feels like a slap to the face or a punch to the gut. I experienced both in that instant. The shock and sting of her words left me breathless and the only thing I could think of doing was run.

So, I did, despite my heart screaming at me to stop and go back. To let him explain that it's just a mistake, a misunderstanding. But the look of anguish on his face confirmed that it wasn't. That it was all true.

Sighing, I pick up my phone and unlock the screen, reading the new text.

SEXIEST MAN ALIVE

I talked to Lucy and Kessler… They're going to make an appt with Jeremy to go look at Ruby. I think the chances are pretty good of them adopting her.

SEXIEST MAN ALIVE

I miss you.

I gasp and sit up, getting worried looks from both Charlie and Bruno.

"What? What happened?"

The screen blurs from the tears building in my eyes as I read the text over again.

"Millie?"

I turn my phone around to show Charlie. She reads the text and looks back at me. "Oh Millie. That's great. They would be perfect for Ruby."

I nod and turn my phone back around, staring at the screen. My thumbs hovering over it, itching to text him back.

"How long are you going to shut him out? I know what happened was a shock to you, but if you can forgive me for not telling you, don't you think he at least deserves a chance to tell you his side of the story?"

I bite the corner of my lip. When Charlie told me she knew about the DUI, I felt betrayed, but she explained it wasn't her story to tell. I know Charlie would have never kept something like this from me to hurt me. So why can't I give Judd a chance to explain?

"You're right. I know I need to let him explain. I just, I'm so hurt." I stare down at my screen again. "How can I love someone who did the very thing that took my parents away?"

It's the first time I've admitted my feelings for Judd out loud.

"Oh, Millie." Charlie sits on the floor next to me and pulls me into a hug. She holds me tight while I let the tears fall. "I know nothing I say can make any of this better. But I can tell you one mistake doesn't define who a person is. Does Judd seem like someone who would do something dangerous like that on purpose?"

I think back to the moment I first met Judd. He was annoying and cocky in the beginning. But also kind, protective and sweet. He's never once done or said anything bad towards anyone. He doesn't strike me as a person who would ever do something that puts himself or anyone else in danger on purpose.

"No, he doesn't."

"So, what are you going to do?"

Pulling into my parking space, I turn my car off and sit in the silence. Charlie's question has been bouncing around my head all morning, and I still don't have an answer. Flopping my head back against the rest, I notice it's darker in here than usual. A light must have gone out. I make a mental note to tell Marty to let maintenance know and open my door, hitting the button to open the rear latch as I get out. I'm halfway to the back when something crunches under my shoe.

Glass. A lot of it.

Looking above me, I see that the light didn't burn out. It's been broken. A chill races up my spine and the hairs on my arms stand on end just as Bruno releases a low growl.

Turning in the direction Bruno is growling, I see a dark figure out of the corner of my eye before something strikes me in the head, causing my head to swim. The garage tilts sideways and my hand reaches out to grab something, anything to prevent myself from falling, but all I grab is air. I hit the hard, cold cement shoulder first, followed by my head. Black dots dance across my vision, and I try to blink them away.

I see the tall figure move closer when a streak of fur launches itself from the back of my car, grabbing onto the figure and snarling.

I hear someone yell "Fuck!" but it's muted, like I'm listening through cotton.

I push myself to my knees and crawl to the cement pillar, using it to brace myself as I get to my feet. My vision blurs and my head pounds horribly, but I push through the pain. I need to get to Bruno.

The sound of grunting and Bruno's growls gets louder as my senses come into focus. Pushing off the pillar, I stagger over towards where Bruno is still latched on to the person dressed in black. I see the man's arm hitting Bruno over and over again, but Bruno is relentless and refuses to let go. I'm almost to them when I see the man pull something out of his pocket and jam it into Bruno's side once, twice, three times before Bruno releases his arm with a yelp.

"Bruno!" I scream, blinking furiously through the wave of dizziness to get to him.

The man turns towards me and that's when I see that he's holding a knife. A knife with Bruno's blood on it. Rage overtakes my fear, and I charge the last few steps and slam my good shoulder into the center of the man.

I must take him by surprise because I'm able to knock him off balance, which causes him to stagger backward a few steps, crashing into the taillight of my car before hitting the ground. Unfortunately, I'm unable to stop my momentum and I crash down with him, landing on top of him. He throws his fists towards me, hitting me in the side of the head, once again making my head swim.

I've never punched anyone before. Never felt the need. But the rage I have for this man attacking me and Bruno has me balling up my fists and landing blows wherever I can. The shoulder I landed on throbs, but the adrenaline rush blocks most of the pain.

In between blocking my fists and trying to land his own, the man is able to get one hand around my throat and squeeze. I reach up, trying to pry his hand away, but his grip tightens. Now that I've stopped punching, he's able to get his other hand up and around my neck too, applying more pressure.

One last surge of adrenaline courses through me and I'm able to pry one of his fingers back, feeling the bone snap.

"AH! You fucking bitch!" the man yells, pulling his hand back.

I suck in what breath I'm able to with his other hand still wrapped around my throat and let out a scream that echoes through the garage. My vision starts to blur around the edges from the lack of oxygen and my strength starts to fade.

This can't be it. This can't be how I die. I still have things to do, like figure things out with Judd. Get married, maybe even have a family. This just can't be it.

Just as I'm about to succumb to the darkness, tires squeal behind me, and I hear my name.

"Amelia!"

CHAPTER 28

Judd

I FEEL LIGHTER on the drive back from my parents. Having one thing go right when everything else has gone terribly wrong in the past few days gives me a shimmer of hope that things are turning around.

I pull into the parking garage, but instead of turning left towards my section, I make a right. I don't know when Amelia is coming home, so I've been driving past her spot every time I return, just to check. Making a left, I'm halfway to her spot when I see her vehicle with the hatch open. My heart increases at the chance of finally being able to see her.

But what I see when I get closer makes my blood turn cold. Even with my window closed, the scream I hear coming from Amelia's throat will be one that forever haunts me. Slamming on my brakes, I throw open the door and leap out of my Jeep, barely getting the vehicle in park before exiting.

"Amelia!" I yell, making the short distance from my car to where she's fallen back onto the ground. Her chest is rapidly rising and falling as she tries to suck in as much air as possible.

The man, whose hands were around Amelia's throat just moments ago, is scrambling to get to his feet. There's no way I'm letting that asshole get away. I charge past Amelia and slam into his back, knocking him back to the ground. He struggles to turn over, but I place my knee into the middle of his back and wrench one of his arms behind him, then the other. He struggles to get free, but it's useless. He's about as tall as me, but I easily have a good thirty pounds on him.

"Let me go," he bites out, still trying to jerk from my grip.

"Not a chance, asshole," I growl back. "Amelia, talk to me. Are you okay?" She's not where I left her, but I can hear a whine and her crying.

"J-j-Judd, he, he stabbed Bruno."

Fuck.

"Mills, listen to me. Call 911 and try to put pressure on Bruno's wounds to help stop the bleeding."

I hear her say something to Bruno, then her face appears. Her lip is split and bleeding. Tears are streaming down her cheeks and there's a giant bruise forming on one side of her face.

I'm going to fucking kill this guy.

My knee presses down onto his back, causing him to scream.

"You're going to break my back!"

"I'd break every bone in your fucking body if I could, you piece of shit."

"Judd, I don't have my phone," she says frantically.

"In my car, center console, passcode is 1-0-3-0."

She dashes off to my car as I hear another vehicle approach, followed by voices, then footsteps. Two guys I've made small talk with in passing off and on since moving here come over.

"Holy shit, what happened?" John asks.

"I don't know the whole story, but I found this guy choking my girlfriend when I was driving by." I nod over to where Amelia appeared from. "He stabbed her dog."

Eric looks to the spot I nodded at and peels his sweater off, heading towards Bruno. I can hear him talking in soft, low tones to him.

Amelia rushes back over with the phone to her ear, talking rapidly to the dispatcher. She rattles off the address and tells them we're in the parking garage. I can see the tremor starting in her hands and moving throughout her body. Likely from the adrenaline crash.

I look up at Jake. "Got anything in your car that we can use to tie this asshole up?"

He nods and runs back to his car, returning a few seconds later with paracord.

"Perfect."

We work together, tying the man's hands and securing them to his feet, making it impossible to escape.

"Watch him. Just to make sure he doesn't go anywhere, will you? I need to check on my girl."

Jake gives me a nod and stands over the man, arms crossed.

I move around the back of Amelia's car and see her and Eric crouched next to Bruno a few feet away in an empty parking spot.

"He needs a vet now. He's losing a lot of blood," Eric tells Amelia. She's on her knees, leaning over Bruno's head, petting him and whispering to him.

"There's one a few blocks away, right?" I ask, crouching down next to them.

Amelia looks up at me and nods. "That's his regular vet."

"Let's go, we'll take my car. Mills sit in the back. I'll lay Bruno's bed in the back next to you and you can keep pressure on his wounds."

Amelia should see a doctor too, but we need to get Bruno help first.

Running back to my Jeep, I pull it forward next to where Bruno is. We make quick work of setting Amelia in the back and Eric, and I maneuver Bruno into the back next to her, trying not to hurt him more.

Sirens sound off in the distance, and I look at Eric and John. "Tell the cops we had to take Bruno to the vet." I grab a paper and pen out of my console and quickly write down my number, handing it to Eric. "Give them my number and tell them to call me." Eric nods and I get back into the driver's seat, looking in my rearview at Amelia, who is pale even in the dim light. "Hang on, Shortcake. We'll be there soon," I tell her, taking off out of the garage and going as fast as I can the few blocks to the vet's office.

Praying the whole way there, Bruno makes it.

CHAPTER 29

Amelia

AS SOON AS the tech's take Bruno back for emergency surgery, it starts.

The shaking.

The racing thoughts.

The uncontrollable heart rate.

"I, I can't breathe," I manage to get out before the room spins around me.

Strong arms keep me from face planting on the floor, guiding me to the nearest chair. Judd squats down in front of me, taking my face between both his hands. I stare into his eyes that are the shade of my new favorite color. "Take a deep breath through your nose and hold it," he whispers.

"I can't," I choke out.

"You can. Breathe with me. In," he says, inhaling a deep breath through his nose. I do the same, forcing air into my lungs.

"Good. Now, out through your mouth." His voice is low and soft. He slowly releases his breath, and I copy him.

We repeat the process over and over until I can feel my heart rate slow, but my body still shakes from a mixture of adrenaline and anxiety.

Judd's thumb traces a path back and forth over my cheeks. I grab onto his wrists, trying to anchor myself. "I can't lose him, Judd," I croak, my throat raw. The pain in my body increases now that the adrenaline rush has worn off. My shoulder screams at me. My knees burn and I look down to see my leggings torn and scratches litter my legs, dried blood coating the skin. But I can't leave Bruno. Not yet. Not until I know he's okay.

"You won't."

"How do you know? There was so much blood, Judd. Too much."

"He's a fighter, Mills. He's going to fight to stay with you."

"Will you stay with me? I know there are things we need to talk about but–"

"I'm not going anywhere, baby. I'm right here," he whispers, bringing his forehead to mine. I close my eyes at the contact, releasing his wrists and easing myself into his arms. Wrapping his arms around me, he picks me up and turns us around until he's sitting in the chair, and I'm curled up in his lap, face pressed into his chest.

He makes slow, soothing circles up and down my back, until I feel myself start to relax. I must drift off because the next thing I know, I'm waking up to the sound of two people talking.

I jolt awake, sitting up in Judd's lap. "Bruno?" I ask, ignoring the pounding in my head and the intense throbbing in my shoulder.

Bruno's vet nods and smiles. "He made it through surgery. He was lucky, and the knife missed all the major vessels. I'd like to keep him overnight for observation, but he should be fine to go home tomorrow."

My body slouches back into Judd with relief. "Can we see him?"

She nods. "Of course. Follow me back."

I stand from Judd's lap and hold my hand out to him. "Come with me?"

He takes my hand and follows me through the doors leading to the back. Bruno's laying in one of the large steel kennels on a pile of blankets, sleeping. There's a large ace bandage wrapped around his shoulder, chest, and neck.

Sinking to my knees, not caring about the pain, I softly stroke the top of Bruno's head. His big brown and blue eyes open and he softly whines when he sees me.

"I know, baby. But you're going to be okay. You just have to stay here for the night and then you'll be home tomorrow." Leaning forward, I place a kiss on Bruno's head. "I love you so much, Bruno. Thank you for saving me," I whisper. His eyes close again and I take that as our cue to leave.

Judd kneels down when I stand, taking my spot. He whispers something into Bruno's ear, then gives him a kiss and a pet before getting to his feet. He takes my hand, and we leave the back, making a stop at the desk to make sure they have both our numbers in case anything happens overnight.

I collapse into the passenger seat once we get to the Jeep. Exhaustion overwhelming me. Judd shuts my door and jogs around to his side, climbing in. Turning to me, he takes my hand and gives it a gentle squeeze. "Ready to get checked out?"

I roll my head in his direction, face scrunched. "I'm fine," I lie. All I want to do is go home and sleep.

"Amelia, you look like you went three rounds with a Tasmanian devil. There are scratches all over your hands and face. Your clothes are torn and bloody. And your face–" He pauses, gently touching my chin, turning it one way, then the other. The muscles in my neck scream in pain, making me wince. "See? You're in pain."

"I'm fine," I tell him, brushing his worry off with my hand.

"We're going to the ER."

"Judd, I'm fine. It's nothing rest and some ibuprofen can't fix." Lots and lots of ibuprofen, maybe a hot bath.

"It's not up for discussion, Shortcake. Besides, an officer called while you were sleeping. He's meeting us at the ER to get a statement and take pictures of your injuries."

My pulse ticks up, making the pounding in my head increase. The last time I was at the ER was when my depression took a turn for the worst. Judd's hand slides into mine, pulling me out of my spiraling thoughts. "I'll be there with you the whole time."

I nod, squeezing his hand tighter to hide the shake in mine, praying the panic attacks stay at bay.

CHAPTER 30

Judd

AMELIA HASN'T UTTERED A WORD, other than giving the lady at the registration desk her information, since leaving the clinic. She's been fidgeting in her seat, bouncing her leg up and down for the past ten minutes. "You doing okay, Shortcake?"

"Yeah, I'm fine, I'll be fine. It's fine," she says, sounding like she's trying to convince herself.

I open my mouth to ask her if she wants anything to drink when a nurse comes through the door and calls her back. Her body freezes and her hand tightens around mine.

"Do you want me to go back with you?"

Amelia nods her head jerkily. I stand, gently tugging on her to follow me. The nurse leads us back to an empty area with a bed and medical equipment. It's not really a room, just a space with two walls on either side and a curtain that can close to give the resemblance of some privacy.

"Go ahead and take a seat on the bed, honey. We'll get your vitals and then have you change into a gown so we can see the extent of your injuries."

Amelia climbs onto the bed, laying back. Her dark bruises look worse against the stark white sheet. I move to the opposite side from where the nurse is working, squeezing between the bed and equipment to be at Amelia's side. She immediately takes my hand, gripping it tightly.

"150/94," the nurse says, taking the blood pressure cuff off. "That's pretty high. But from what I can see of your injuries so far, understandable." The nurse's eyes flick to me. "Sir, can you step outside for a few minutes? I have to ask her some questions and then she can change into a gown."

"Oh, yeah, sure." I loosen my grip on Amelia's hand while hers tightens.

"No, he, he can stay."

"Are you sure, honey? It'll only be for a few minutes."

"He didn't do this, if that's what you're thinking. I was attacked in the parking garage of my apartment complex." Her raspy voice cracks. "My dog was st-stabbed. I was choked. Judd would never do that. He'd never do anything to hurt me." She ends on a sob.

Her words wash over me, relief flooding my system that she knows I'd never do anything intentional to hurt her.

I run my free hand over her hair gently, bending over to look her in the eyes. "Shhh, Baby," I croon. "It's okay, I'm here now. You're safe."

Once Amelia's sobs have subsided to a few shuddering breaths, the nurse hands her a gown and a plastic bag. She tells her to change into the gown and place her clothes in the bag and that the doctor should be in shortly.

After the nurse closes the curtain behind her, Amelia slowly maneuvers to the side of the bed, dangling her feet over. "Do you want me to step out?" I ask, because even though I've seen her naked several times, I'm not sure where I stand with her.

"No, please stay," she whispers, reaching for the hem of her long-sleeved sweater, pulling it up halfway, before she winces in pain, muttering a "Fuck" under her breath.

"Here, let me help," I tell her, reaching forward and

helping her get her sweater off the rest of the way as gently as I possibly can. When she's finally free, my blood boils at what was hidden by the piece of clothing.

"Jesus Christ, Amelia," I whisper.

Tiny scrapes and cuts litter the front of her body and there's a bruise on her shoulder that's already turning a deep blue and black.

"It looks worse than it feels?"

"It looks like you were laid out by a linebacker on cement with no padding," I deadpan.

"I've never experienced that, but it's probably an accurate description," she mutters, trying to pull down her thick, black leggings.

"Here, let me help." Crouching down, I pull them past her hips. "Sit down and I'll pull them off the rest of the way."

Amelia eases herself down on the edge of the bed, letting me pull her leggings down. I try to be as careful as possible with her knees, but they're pretty beat up and there are still little shards of glass in her skin. Her hisses of breath tell me they're more painful than she was letting on.

I'm finally able to get the leggings off, leaving Amelia in just her bra and underwear.

"Why are hospitals always so cold?" she asks, rubbing her hands over her arms to get rid of the goosebumps that have appeared before slipping on the hospital gown that swallows her body.

"I read somewhere that bacteria thrive in warmer environments so they keep it on the colder side to slow down the growth and spread of it."

The first smile I've seen cross her beautiful face appears, making my breath hitch. I could have lost her tonight. I could have lost her, and she never would have known how I feel about her. I've hinted and suggested, but never flat out told her I love her in fear she would run. That changes tonight. Not here, obviously. But when we get home. I'm laying everything out on the table.

I just hope she feels the same.

CHAPTER 31

Amelia

BY THE TIME pictures are taken of all my various injuries, my knees are debrided, wounds cleaned and bandaged, CT scan taken of not only my shoulder, but my head *and* I've given my statement to the officer that came to the hospital, I'm exhausted.

The doctor said I have to be screen free for at least a week due to my mild concussion and no driving for at least that long, longer if I'm still experiencing symptoms. My shoulder has a deep bone bruise and mild swelling in the joint space, which is why it's hard for me to lift it up. They gave me a sling to wear when I'm up walking so as not to aggravate it. My voice will be hoarse for a few days while my neck and throat recover from the trauma of being choked.

Basically, I'm a hot mess, but it could have been worse. So much worse. And on a good note, I didn't have a single anxiety attack. I completely expected to have at least one, since being here brought back a lot of hazy memories from my past. I think having Judd by my side the entire time helped keep them at bay.

"Are you going to tell Hazel and Charlie?" Judd asks from the driver's seat of his Jeep.

I sigh. “I will tomorrow. I don’t want to answer any more questions tonight. Besides, if Charlie found out, she’d fly right back home, and she deserves this vacation. So, if I wait until tomorrow, she’ll already be on the cruise ship by then.”

Judd’s mouth quirks. “You know she’s going to be pissed. Not only at you, but at me for not contacting her.”

I lift my good shoulder. “She’ll be fine. I’ve scared her enough for one lifetime. I don’t need to add to it,” I mumble, my eyelids growing heavy. Thank God we’re almost back to our building.

“What do you mean?”

The concern in his voice pulls me from thoughts of my fluffy blankets and pillows I want nothing more than to cocoon myself in and sleep in for days. “What?”

“You said you’ve scared Charlie enough for one lifetime. How?”

I don’t know what makes me say it, the trauma of the day? The concussion? The pure exhaustion? Whatever it may be makes the words slip through my lips before my concussed brain realizes what I’m saying.

“She’s the one who found me the day I tried to end my life.”

The rest of the drive home, Judd didn’t utter a word. The ride up the elevator to his place? Silence. Now he’s sitting on the bed watching me pull on clothes that I left here. Once I’m able to get my leggings and Judd’s hoodie that basically is now mine on, I pad over to the bed and gently climb up, sitting beside him. I take his warm, calloused hand in mine and wrap my other around the back of it.

"Remember when I told Julie I won a contest with my writing?"

Judd turns his head to look at me, shock and sadness reflecting back at me. The same look I've seen on Charlie and her parents' faces, Hazel's too, when I told her. A look I happily never want to see on any of their faces again.

"What I didn't tell her was, winning that contest sent me into a downward spiral. I picked up my phone to call my parents, and it hit me that I couldn't, because they were gone. I only won that contest because I wrote about the pain I felt losing them. It was too much. I felt too much and not enough at the same time. The intrusive thoughts in my head ran rampant. My depression told me I should just end it all, the pain, the suffering, that I was a waste of space."

Judd's hand tightens around mine, but he stays quiet, letting me get it all out in the open.

I focus on our hands clasped together and continue, "So, I went back to my dorm room and found a bottle of Charlie's pain pills she had left over from a procedure she had our sophomore year. I wrote her and her parents a letter thanking them for everything they've done for me and apologized for not being strong enough to bear the pain. Then I sat on my bed and swallowed pill after pill until the bottle was empty."

Judd squeezes his eyes shut, muttering "Jesus" under his breath.

I nod, still focused on our hands. "I know. I just wanted the pain to stop, my brain to be quiet for one minute, *one second*." A tear slides down my face and Judd uses his free hand to wipe it away. Our eyes lock, and he gently rests his forehead against mine. We stay like that for a few heartbeats, just being. Until Judd pulls back.

"Tell me the rest, Mills."

Nodding, I take a breath and continue. "Charlie came home from class early; she had a terrible headache. She found me on the floor, unconscious, barely breathing. She called 911, then her parents. While she was on the phone with her mom, she found the note and then the empty pill bottle. She told the paramedics as soon as they arrived what I had done, they gave me Narcan right away and I proceeded to violently throw up the whole trip to the ER. Everything was a blur for the next twenty-four hours after that, but I was placed into a facility for six months shortly after. I got the help I needed, learned coping mechanisms. They put me on medication for my anxiety and severe depression, which I still take and probably will for the rest of my life. I see a therapist regularly. I actually have an appointment with her on Tuesday because the holidays are always hard on me." I look up at Judd again, trying to gauge his reaction to all of this. "Do you have any questions?"

"No," he says, turning towards me and looking into my eyes. "But I am so damn glad Charlie left class early."

I smile, thinking back to what Charlie told me. "She told me later when she was visiting me that her headache came out of nowhere. One minute she was sitting in class and the next her head was throbbing so bad it was making her nauseous. She hasn't had a headache like that since."

"Like someone was trying to tell her something," Judd says the words I've always thought.

I nod.

Laying my head on Judd's shoulder, we sit in silence. I feel lighter getting my past off my chest. I've only ever told one of my ex-boyfriends what happened and that was only after I thought things were going somewhere with him. At first, he was sympathetic but when I was having a hard time around the anniversary of my parents' death, he became tired of me 'moping around all the time'. I quit dating after that. Until a cocky baseball player came into my life and showed me what it's like to truly care for someone.

Judd clears his throat, making me lift my head to look at him. "The night I was arrested for drunk driving was the night of Lucy and Kessler's engagement party. I didn't even realize I was drunk." He looks at me sheepishly. "I had been partying and drinking more before moving home. The drinking became worse after I moved home and saw how happy and content Kessler was. Don't get me wrong. I'm happy for Kessler and I can't imagine our family without Lucy and Hudson, but I was lonely."

I squeeze his hand this time, because I know that feeling all too well.

"All the women I met only wanted to be with me for my money or to say they slept with All-star pitcher Judd Davis, and I was tired of it. So, I just started drinking a little more to ease the burn in my chest."

He absently rubs at a spot on his chest like he still feels the pain.

"After I was arrested, Kessler came to pick me up. When we got into the truck, he reamed my ass. I've only ever seen Kessler that mad a handful of times, so I knew I fucked up."

I give him a smirk. "He definitely doesn't seem like someone who gets mad easily."

He shakes his head. "He's not. He made a good point, though. I could have killed myself or someone. And it would have ruined everyone's life who was involved."

"It was devastating getting that phone call. I called both my parents' phones after, thinking the police were wrong, they *had* to be wrong."

"But they weren't," Judd finishes.

"But they weren't."

"I haven't had a drink since that night. I–I'm afraid I won't be able to stop once I do. I don't *think* I'm an alcoholic. But I also didn't think I was drunk that night either. I just don't trust myself."

"There's nothing wrong with not drinking," I reassure him. "But if you do want to have a drink to unwind or just to have a drink, I'll be there with you. If you can't handle it, then we address it and get you help. Okay?"

He nods and glides his thumb back and forth over the back of my hand and he gives me a soft kiss on my head. "I am so sorry I caused you more pain, Amelia. I–I completely understand if you don't think you can be with me. If it's too painful. If–"

I cut him off, snaking my hand around his neck and pulling him to my lips. He's careful with the cut on my lip, letting me control the pressure. My fingers sink into his hair, and I open my mouth to let him in. His tongue tangles with mine as we get lost in each other.

When Judd finally pulls back, we're both breathless. He rests his forehead against mine. "When I saw you in the parking garage today, my entire world stopped. I've never been so scared in my life. I don't know what I would have done if I lost you."

"But you didn't. I'm right here and I'm not going anywhere, Judd. The saying 'life is short' hit home today and I don't want to waste any more time fighting my feelings." Lifting my head from his, I cup his cheeks with my hands, looking into his mossy green eyes that I want to get lost in forever. I tell him what I've never told another man before. "I love you, Judd Davis. And I want to spend the rest of my life loving you if you'll let me."

CHAPTER 32

Judd

"ARE you *sure* you want to go to my parent's house?" I ask Amelia again, coming up behind her and wrapping my arms around her bare middle, dropping a kiss on her shoulder. The one that's not bruised. It's been four days since Bruno and Amelia were attacked. The bruises around her neck and shoulder look worse, but she's reassured me multiple times that they look worse than they feel. While both of them are doing significantly better, I don't want the chaos and noise that are my family and friends to set back their healing.

She sets her makeup down, looping her arms around the back of my neck. "Judd, it's Thanksgiving. We're not missing spending time with your close friends and family."

"They would understand if we didn't make it." The day after the attack, I told my parents and Kessler what happened. My mom, being the amazing person she is, came over to my place right away to make sure Amelia and Bruno were really alright and to bring us dinner so we didn't have to cook.

Amelia had me do a group FaceTime to Hazel and Charlie so she could tell them what happened. Like Amelia predicted, Charlie was upset she didn't contact her right after it happened because she would have come home.

Amelia told her that's exactly why she didn't and reassured both her and Hazel she was okay. Telling them both she would be fine because she had me here and to enjoy their holidays.

She also had a session with her therapist and when she got back in the car after her session, she told me that's the first time she's left her office around the holidays without being in tears.

I hope I had some part in that.

Amelia rolls her eyes at me. "And I told you, Bruno and I are fine. The doctor *and* vet gave us both a clean bill of health yesterday at our re-checks. We're healing great and will be good as new in no time."

"You're lucky you're still sore or I would spank your perfect ass for rolling your eyes at me." It's hard enough keeping my hands to myself while she's in nothing but a black lace bra and underwear, wearing a blue silk robe that matches her eyes.

Her gaze turns heated, and she runs her fingers through my hair at the nape of my neck, giving it a small tug. My dick jumps in response. "Amelia," I warn. "If you want to make it to my parents' house, you better stop, or I'll spend all day and night eating my dinner right here in our bathroom."

Oh yeah, another thing that happened over the last few days was we decided to move Amelia in with me. It didn't make sense to have separate apartments in the same building. So, after Amelia starts feeling better, we're moving all her stuff in here, at least until we can build *our* dream house.

She gives me a seductive smirk and takes a step back, dropping her arms from my neck. "Maybe later, Davis. My hair actually looks good, and I'm almost done with my makeup. I don't need you ruining it."

"I won't ruin it," I tell her, backing her into the counter and dropping to my knees. "And you're beautiful with or without makeup, hair done or not."

"Juddson," she says in a warning that only encourages me.

"Hmm?" I hum, dipping my head down to kiss up one thigh, then the other.

A soft moan leaves her lips and when I look up, Amelia's head is tipped back and she's gripping the counter with both hands. I reach up and hook a finger on both sides of her underwear, dragging them down her legs. She steps out of them quickly and I toss them aside.

"Are you wet for me, Shortcake?" I ask, planting more kisses between her thighs. She spreads her legs wider, opening up for me. Using my pointer finger, I dip it into her center, feeling exactly how much she wants me and trail it up to her clit, tracing around the sensitive bundle of nerves. "You're soaked. Do you want me to help you with that, baby? I can get you all nice and clean before we have to leave."

She whimpers and nods her head.

"Say please."

"Please, Judd. Please, fuck me," she pleads.

"No time for that, baby. I don't want to hurt you. So, I'm going to have my dessert before dinner."

Wrapping a hand around her calf, I lift her leg and place it over my shoulder, giving me better access to her center.

"Hold on, Shortcake. I'm starving."

She runs a hand through my hair, gripping it tight when I take my first lick. "Yes," she whispers, grinding her hips into my face.

I quickly set a rhythm of licking and sucking. Applying more and more pressure to her clit with each pass, building her pleasure. Her thrusts soon become erratic as she chases her high. Her moans echoing through the bathroom.

I growl into her and add a finger, then two. Her pussy clamps down around me, welcoming the pressure. I match the strokes of my fingers with the strokes of my tongue, and it doesn't take long for her to come apart around me.

"Fuck, Judd. I'm coming."

Her pussy pulses around me, and she soaks my hand with

her orgasm. I stay down there, licking her clean as she comes down from her high. Once the tremors have subsided, I grab the underwear I tossed aside, helping her back into them and stand. "Fucking beautiful," I tell her, bending down and placing a kiss on her lips.

"I love you so much," she whispers when I pull back and rest my head on hers. My heart soars at her words, just like they did when she said them for the first time Sunday night.

"I love you too, Mills. I always will."

Dinner is loud and chaotic, and there's not an inch of empty space on the large dining table. Voices and laughter fill the air along with scents of the mouthwatering food Mom has cooked. Amelia is seated beside me chatting with Lucy, Kara and Kara's mom, Connie, about a scene in her next book, while we wait for Mom and Dad to finish carving the turkeys and hams. Kessler and I both offered to help, like we do every year, but Mom shooed us out of the kitchen, like she also does every year. Brent and his sister, Cass, are sitting on the other side of me talking in low whispers. Reese is sitting across from them, playing on his phone but looking uncomfortable. You bet I'll be poking that bear later.

Someone taps my foot under the table, and I tear my gaze away from Amelia to see Kessler staring at me. He tips his head to the sliding door that leads to my parent's backyard.

"I'll be right back." I tell Amelia, dropping a kiss on her head and getting up from my seat. She nods and gives me a smile before turning back to the girls to talk. Kessler does the same with Lucy.

The noise is muted as Kessler shuts the door behind him and heads over to the covered patio, taking a seat on one of the chairs. I sit down in a matching chair next to him. We both look out at the expansive backyard we were lucky enough to play in growing up. "How is she?" Kessler asks, propping his foot up on his knee. His breath puffs out in a white cloud in front of him. It's not raining, but it's cold.

I sigh and scrub a hand down my face. "She's actually doing okay. She had a nightmare the first night after it happened and a few panic attacks, but has been doing pretty good besides that. She had an appointment with her therapist on Tuesday and saw her doctor yesterday to make sure her wounds were healing properly and her concussion symptoms weren't getting worse."

"And how are you doing?" he asks, giving me his big brother stare down that means 'don't bullshit me'.

"I'm... okay. I know once she's able to drive herself, it's going to be harder to let her out of my sight, but I'll cross that bridge when I get to it."

"Have you thought about talking to someone?"

I give him a questioning look. "Like a therapist?"

He nods. "Yeah, or if you don't want to do that, you could always just talk to me about it, get it off your chest instead of bottling it up inside?"

"I'm not the one who was attacked, Kess."

Kessler drops his foot to the ground, sitting forward and resting his elbows on his knees. "No, but you witnessed some of it. You saw the woman you love being attacked. She could have lost her life. That has to be traumatic for anyone."

The image of Amelia fighting for her life flashes through my mind. "It was the scariest thing I've ever experienced in my life and I don't think I'll be able to get it out of my head for a long time. If ever," I admit.

"I don't even want to imagine what I would do if it had been Lucy. That guy is lucky he's alive."

"Trust me, I wanted to kill him. But the need to see if Amelia was okay overrode that urge."

The back door opens, halting our conversation, and Mom's head pokes out. "Everything okay?" she asks.

We both nod, getting to our feet.

"Well, dinner's ready, you two. Come eat."

We walk in and take our seats. Once everyone is seated, I notice one chair is empty. Just as I'm about to ask where he is, the mudroom door opens, and Garrett comes in. His long hair dirty-blond is pulled back into a low bun and his ice-blue eyes take in the room, staying a beat too long on Kara before continuing and finding Mom. "Sorry I'm late, Mom." His deep voice rumbles through the now quiet room.

"No worries, dear. There's a seat right next to Kara for you," Mom tells him. Lucy and Kessler share a smirk. And I cough a laugh into my fist. Leave it to Mom to play subtle matchmaker.

Conversations start back up and the buzz of voices once again fills the room.

"Wow, he is stupidly attractive," Amelia mutters, eyes not leaving Garrett as he takes his seat next to Kara, who's turned a couple of shades of red.

Lucy snorts into her water, making her cough while Kessler pats her back.

"I'm sitting right here, Shortcake," I mumble.

She turns and smirks at me. "Don't be jealous, Davis. I can look, It's you I'm going home with."

"Damn right you are," I tell her, giving her a wink.

"Alright, everyone," Mom announces, standing from her chair, "I just want to say how happy I am to have so many people joining us this year. My heart is full seeing all the love and laughter filling this house. For those of you who've never joined us before, we usually go around the table and say what we are thankful for this past year. Does anyone want to go first?"

Everyone looks around the table at each other, seeing who might go first. I clear my throat and start, probably shocking everyone because I'm usually one of the last people to go, but I have a lot to be thankful for this year.

"I have a lot of things to be thankful for this year, but I know Hudson and Kade are hungry, so I'll keep it short," I joke, getting chuckles from everyone. "First, I want to thank everyone for sticking by me a few months ago when I made the biggest mistake of my life. Your support got me through a dark time." I look at Amelia, taking her hand. "I'm also thankful for making that mistake because I may not have met my missing piece, if not for my stupidity."

Amelia squeezes my hand, giving me her sparkling smile and whispering, "I love you." I raise her hand to my lips, kissing the back of it.

Mom clears her throat, and I look down the table, seeing her dab at the corners of her eyes. Lucy sniffs and Kara swipes a finger under her eye. "Uh, who's next?" I ask, looking at Kessler.

"Yeah, sure. I'll go." He sits up in his chair, but keeps his arm draped across the back of Lucy's shoulders. "I'm thankful for meeting the love of my life this year and gaining a son." He ruffles Hudson's hair, then turns to look at Lucy. She nods her head and Kessler turns back to us. "We also have something we want to share with everyone. Well, two things actually." He pauses and Lucy reaches up and grips his hand on her shoulder. "This next season is my last year playing ball." Shocked gasps echo around the table, and he locks eyes with me. I know how hard of a decision this is for him and I know it's not one that was easily decided. But he's starting a new chapter in his life, one that involves being an incredible dad and loving husband, and when Kessler decides to do something, he never does it halfway.

"What's the second?" I ask.

Wide grins break out over Lucy and Kessler's faces. "If everyone could look under their plates, you'll see what it is," Lucy says.

Everyone picks up their plates. On the place mat is a picture of two baseballs, one pink, one blue. In the center of the baseballs are the names 'Aspyn' and 'Denver'.

"Does, does that mean you're having one of each?" Mom asks, voice tight from trying to hold back her tears. Lucy nods her head, her own tears streaming down her face. Getting up from her chair, Mom goes over to Lucy and Kessler, giving them each a hug.

Everyone takes turns telling them congratulations and once everyone is back in their seat, Mom asks if anyone else would like to share what they're thankful for.

"I'd be thankful if we could eat," Hudson says from the other side of Kessler.

"Hudson James," Lucy scolds, trying to hold back her laughter. Kessler doesn't succeed and chuckles along with everyone else.

"I want to say one thing, then we can eat, Hud," Mom tells Hudson. "I just want to say how thankful and blessed we feel to be able to share our home and food with you all today." She looks at Hudson and gives him a wink. "Now we can eat."

Dishes are passed around; plates are loaded, and a hush falls over the table while everyone eats. We're about halfway through the meal when some of the chatter starts back up.

"You doing alright?" I ask Amelia. She's only finished half of what's on her plate.

Leaning back in her chair, she groans. "My eyes were too big for my stomach."

I chuckle and run my hand over her thigh. "There will be *plenty* of leftovers and Mom will make sure she sends us home with more than we need." I look across the table and see Hudson reaching for seconds. "Or Hudson will eat it all."

"This kid is going to eat us out of house and home." Kessler laughs. His eyes flick to mine and he sits forward in his seat, leaning on the table. "Speaking of homes. I had an interesting conversation with Beau Miller the other day."

I set my spoon down and swallow my mouth full of mashed potatoes. "About what?"

"You know the lot next door to us?"

"I wouldn't call that a *lot*. It's 30 acres of overgrown pasture and trees."

"Same thing. Anyway, he's looking to sell. Wanted to know if I was interested before he officially put it on the market."

I sit taller in my chair. Kessler knows I've been looking for property near here since moving back home. "What did you tell him?"

Kessler smirks and leans back in his chair, lacing his fingers together behind his head. "I told him I wasn't interested. It's too big of a project for us right now with the babies on the way." He pauses and keeps staring at me with that stupid smirk.

"*And*?"

He lifts a shoulder. "I *may* have given him your number and told him you've been looking for property and might be interested."

I jump up, the scrape of my chair making a horribly loud noise against the floor. Everyone watches as I run around the table and give Kessler a hug from behind. "I could kiss you right now, big brother."

"Please don't."

"Oh, no. I think this deserves a giant smooch." Tightening my grip, so he can't get loose. Kessler struggles against me as I bring my face closer to his, giving him a loud smack on the cheek.

"Boys, not at the table," Mom chastises. "You'd think being adults, they'd quit picking on each other, but it still hasn't happened."

"I'm not picking on him, Mom. I'm thanking him."

Mom raises an eyebrow at us. "For what?"

I release Kessler and return to my seat, sliding my arm around Amelia's shoulders. "You know I've been wanting to build a house since being back. Well, Kessler said Beau Miller is looking to sell the property next door to him and gave him my number."

Amelia's head whips to the side to look at me, wincing slightly when she does. "Really?"

I nod. "Really. So, what do you say, Shortcake? Wanna build our home?"

CHAPTER 33

Amelia

"MARLENE, YOU REALLY OUTDID YOURSELF," Kara says, snuggling up next to Lucy on the plush couch in the living room. "I can feel the food coma coming on."

"Agreed. All I've been doing is sleeping and resting lately and I could even go for a nap," I tell them, yawning and burrowing myself deeper into the oversized chair.

Marlene waves us off. "It was my pleasure, girls. Cooking is my love language, and I love all the people here today."

My eyes flick to the kitchen where all the men are currently cleaning up after dinner. Apparently, that's the rule. Marlene cooks and the men clean.

Honestly, I'm here for it.

Kessler, Judd, and Garrett are doing the dishes. Judd's loading the dishwasher and Kessler is handing Garrett the pots and pans to dry and put away. Reese and Brent are putting all the leftovers into various containers for us to take home later. Henry escaped out the side door as soon as the table was cleared. Hudson and Kade were spared dish duty and are currently laying in front of the fireplace playing Hudson's

Nintendo Switch, with Bruno passed out in between them on the dog bed Marlene bought for him.

"So, Millie," Kara starts. "Things are pretty serious between you and Judd, then?"

"Well, I'm moving into his place and now we're buying property to build a house, so I'd say it's pretty serious. After what happened Sunday, we agreed life is too short to not go after what you want. And we both want this."

"No judgment here. I was knocked up and engaged all in less than four months." Lucy shrugs.

"You have such a way with words," Kara comments while she rubs Lucy's belly.

"I've gained two daughters and three grandbabies all in one year. I don't think I could get much luckier," Marlene adds.

"Well, we're not engaged yet."

Marlene winks at me. "You will be dear, in due time."

"When it does happen, I'd love to plan your wedding," Cass chimes in. I've learned Cass is Brent's youngest sister out of four and she works with one of the most prestigious event planning companies in the county. She's the force behind Lucy and Kessler's big day.

"She does great work. Ten out of ten recommend," Lucy adds.

"Plan whose wedding?" Judd asks, coming around from the back of the chair and lifting my legs so he can sit next to me.

"Ours apparently."

"Oh? And when might this wedding be happening?" he asks, grabbing a lock of my hair and twirling it around his finger.

I lift my hand, motioning to the women spread throughout the living room. "Ask the committee. They're the ones who brought it up."

"As long as it's not before Kessler and Lucy's wedding, I'm

ready whenever you are, Shortcake. I'd hate to show up my big brother and make him cry like the baby he is."

"Who the fuck are you calling a baby?" Kessler asks. He comes up behind Judd and puts him in a headlock before Judd can turn around.

"Here we go again," Marlene mutters, taking a sip of wine as she watches her two sons act like teenagers. She stopped telling them to watch their mouths about twenty minutes into the day. Apparently, when all the boys get together, it's a waste of breath.

"You're both babies," Garrett's deep voice booms from the kitchen island where he's currently standing with his arms crossed. His dark burgundy sweater is stretched around his thick muscles. The color makes his already mesmerizing eyes irresistible.

Kessler lets go of Judd and turns around, giving Garrett a mischievous grin. "Ready for our re-match, Seal Boy?"

Garrett's lips curl up into a smile as he stares Kessler down. "You sure you can handle it, old man?"

Kessler scoffs. "You're the same age as me, Dick Head."

Judd tips his head back against the chair, chuckling. "Oh fuck, this is going to be good."

I nudge him with my knee. "What is?"

"They challenged each other to a rematch to see who could last longer in the pond in Mom and Dad's backyard."

"Oh Jesus, not this again! You boys are going to catch hypothermia!" Marlene chastises them.

"It'll be worth it," Kessler and Garrett claim at the same time.

"Can I do it too?" Hudson asks, sitting up and finally tearing his eyes away from his video game.

"Uh..." Lucy says, looking from Hudson to Kessler.

Kessler shrugs. "I'm okay with it if your mom is."

"Mom, *please* can I? Dad's doing it."

Lucy's face softens and a slight sheen forms over her eyes. "Yeah Hud, you can do it."

"Yes!" Hudson yells, jumping up from the floor and fist pumping the air.

"Me too?" Kade asks, looking at Kara.

Kara bites the corner of her lip. "I don't know, Kade. You're not the best swimmer."

Kade's face falls and his shoulders droop.

"I'm sorry, Hun. I just–"

"I'll watch him," Garrett says.

Everyone looks from Kara, whose cheeks have tinged red, to Garrett, who's holding her gaze. "It's not that deep. He'll be safe," he reassures her.

Kade looks hopefully from his mom to Garrett and back again. "Please?"

Lucy places a hand over Kara's. "He'll be okay. Garrett won't let anything happen to him, and Kessler will be in there too."

Kara glances at her mom, who's sitting quietly in a chair next to Marlene. Her mom also nods her head in agreement. The room is silent besides the occasional crackling of the wood from the fire. Closing her eyes briefly and taking a deep breath, Kara opens them and looks Garrett in the eyes. "Okay. I trust you."

Kade and Hudson let out a whoop and race to the back door, leaving Kara and Garrett staring at each other for a few heartbeats before Garrett breaks eye contact and follows the boys out the door without another word.

"I'm gonna go grab some towels. You gonna watch your man win, Coach?" Kessler asks, winking at Lucy.

Lucy snorts. "Sorry babe, but my money's on Garrett."

Judd barks out a laugh and Kessler gasps, clutching his hand to his chest. "Lucy, I thought you loved me?"

She shrugs and pushes herself up off the couch. "I do, but I love winning more, and Garretts ex-Navy SEAL, babe. He's kind of a sure thing."

Kessler mutters something about marrying a traitor as he and Lucy go into the mudroom to grab towels.

"You gonna warm me up afterwards, Shortcake?" Judd asks. He lifts my legs again, then stands, holding his hand out to me.

Raising my eyebrows, I look at him. "You're going to do it too?"

He takes my hand and pulls me up gently from the couch, wrapping me in his embrace. "Sure, someones gotta make sure the children, big and small, play nicely."

Marlene snorts this time. "That's hilarious coming from the biggest child himself."

I giggle into Judd's chest, and he stares open-mouthed at his mom.

"But I thought I was your favorite!" he whines playfully.

"Lucy and Amelia are my favorites; I was just using you two goons to get them," Marlene teases.

"See if I give you any grandkids," Judd mutters. My stomach swoops with butterflies at the thought of having children with Judd. It's not something I've put a lot of thought into. But I can see it with him.

Kessler and Lucy return to the living room, arms overflowing with towels. Marlene and Connie get to their feet with Kara at their heels. Reese and Brent have already joined the boys outside. Sneaking out during the Kara and Garrett stare down.

"Well, if they're going to do this, we might as well go watch," Marlene says, taking the towels from Lucy as she passes.

Shuffling out the sliding door, we follow the gravel path down to the pond. It's a good size, about 12 feet in diameter, with plants lining the far side. The group jumping in already have their shoes and socks off when we get there, waiting for the last minute to shed the rest of their clothes.

"Alright Bitchachos, the person who can stay in the longest wins. Agreed?" Judd says, stripping off his sweater then the shirt under it, revealing the body that I still can't believe I get to worship. He hands me his sweater, and gives me a wink while everyone murmurs 'agreed' as they start to strip.

"You guys are crazy; I have a built-in heater," Lucy says, pointing to her stomach. "And I'm in a jacket and I'm *still* cold."

"No brain, no pain," I tell her, getting snickers from all the women.

"Are you calling us dumb, Shortcake?" Judd asks, prowling over to me in just his briefs. His thick thigh muscles ripple with each step, making my mouth go dry.

"Not at all, *sugar*," I retort in a sickly sweet tone.

He places his jeans in my hand and leans down to give me a hard kiss on my mouth. Pulling back, he whispers in my ear, "Better watch the sexy mouth of yours."

"Or what?" I challenge.

"Or I'll put it to work tonight."

My pussy clenches at the promise of his words and heat floods my body. "Don't tempt me with a good time, Davis."

He growls into my ear and pulls back, staring at me with heated eyes. "You're going to be the death of me, Mills."

I wink. "But what a way to go."

"Who's going to be the official timer?" Kessler asks, handing his clothes off to Lucy.

All the men are stripped down to their underwear and I have never seen as many toned and defined muscles up close.

"Lord have mercy," Kara murmurs, fanning herself in the forty-degree weather.

"That's an understatement," Lucy says. "These pregnancy hormones have me hot and bothered enough."

"Ew, my brother is among those you are drooling over," Cass says, pretending to gag.

"Sorry to break it to you, Cass, but your brother is *hot*," Kara smirks.

"Ugh, nope, nope, nope. That's going to give me nightmares."

"Hello!? Earth to the group of women standing there staring at us like we're an all you can eat buffet," Brent says, waving his hand in the air.

"Uh, yep, I can!" Cass answers, holding up her phone.

"Perfect." Kessler claps his hands together. "Let's do it! Coach, count us down."

All the guys, including Kade and Hudson, line up along the edge. I pull my phone out and hit the record button as Lucy counts them down.

"Three, Two, One... Go!"

Un-manly like screams and shouts fill the air as five grown men and two pre-teens surge forward into the frigid water.

"My balls!" Hudson screams, freezing as soon as he gets waist deep. "I think they're gone!"

Lucy brings her hand to her face, laughing and shaking her head.

Kade is further behind Hudson, only deep enough for the water to hit his knees. Garrett stands right next to him, letting him set the pace and decide how deep he's comfortable with.

"He's so good with Kade," Lucy comments, bumping Kara's shoulder with hers.

"I love you, but shut up," Kara retorts, glancing away when Garrett looks back over his shoulder at her.

"He's hot Kara. You should totally go for it," I say.

"Not interested."

Lucy snorts. "Oh, she's interested. She just won't do anything about it."

"I don't date."

Lucy places a hand on her hip. "You know, I recall saying

the *exact* same thing once. And a certain best friend of mine went ahead and meddled in my love life anyway." She levels Kara with a look. "Sound familiar?"

"That's different," Kara says, waving Lucy off. "Plus, I didn't meddle. I encouraged."

Lucy blows a raspberry. "No, it's not. It's the same. *Exactly* the same!"

Now it's Kara's turn to put her hand on her hip. "Not even."

"Please enlighten me on how this is different."

"The difference *is* you were interested; you were just scared to act on those feelings because of your past."

"And?"

"And I'm not interested because I already had the love of my life."

Stilled silence fills the air, the only noise now coming from the guys in the pond.

After a few beats, Marlene clears her throat. "You know, dear, there's no rule that says you can't have more than one great love in life."

Kara gives Marlene a sad smile. "I know, Marlene. I just don't think I have it in me to try again." Connie puts her arm around Kara, giving her a side hug.

"C-c-can we have a t-t-towel?" Hudson asks, running up to Marlene with Kade, their teeth chattering from the cold and breaking the heavy moment.

Marlene hands them both a towel and instructs them to go inside and sit in front of the fire to warm up.

Brent and Reese follow seconds after. Cass hands Brent a towel giving him a hard time for only making it a few more seconds than the children. When she hands Reese his towel, a shade of pink graces her cheeks that definitely isn't from the cold. Reese keeps his eyes on her a couple of beats longer than necessary as he takes the towel from her and wraps it around his body. Cass stares after them as they head into the house.

When she looks back towards the pond, she notices me watching her. I give her a smile and use my free hand to zip my lips. She gives me a small smile and turns back to the pond where Kessler, Judd, and Garrett are the only ones left.

Kessler and Garrett are splashing at each other, trying to get the other to give up first. Judd must have decided he's had enough because he gets out and heads towards me, goosebumps covering his body and his teeth chatter violently.

"Judd, your lips are blue," I tell him, handing him his towel.

"My balls probably are too, if I could find them. Might need your help with that later, Shortcake."

I gasp and backhand Judd on the arm. "Juddson Davis!"

"Ow, what?" he asks, rubbing his arm.

"Can you *not* talk like that in front of your mother?"

Marlene smirks. "I've read your books, dear. What Judd said is pretty timid compared to the scenes you write."

Judd snorts and I bury my face in my hands. "Oh, God."

"You'll be saying that later, too."

I smack him again, earning another yelp.

"How long have they been in there, Cass?" Lucy asks.

Cass looks at her phone. "Three minutes and forty-five seconds."

"Kessler Davis! You guys have proven your point. Get out of there before you get hypothermia!"

"Not yet! The bet was who could stay in longer. I'm not leaving until Garrett does."

"Listen to the missus, Kessler. You're not going to win this," Garrett taunts, not even looking a bit cold. Kessler, on the other hand, does.

"This is nothing, I d-do Ice baths all the t-time," Kessler says as his teeth start to chatter.

"Kessler Davis, if you don't get out of that pond right this second, the blue balls you're experiencing now will be nothing compared to what you're going to feel the rest of this pregnancy."

"Ooo, Lucy's cracking the whip." Judd teases.

"But, Luce!" Kessler starts to protest.

"Test me, Davis, and see where it gets you," she tells him, crossing her arms and lifting a single brow at him.

Kessler huffs out a sigh and trudges back towards Lucy, making Garrett the winner.

Marlene claps her hand. "Well, now that that nonsense is over, who's ready for dessert?"

CHAPTER 34

Judd

"YOUR MOM SENT us home with enough food to feed us for a week," Amelia says in the passenger seat on our way home.

I chuckle. "I told you. We *always* have tons of food. Mom doesn't know how to cook on a small scale. To be fair, she had to cook a lot of food for us when we were teenagers because we could put the food away. Plus, Garrett moved in with us the summer before he and Kessler started high school."

"I noticed he called her Mom when he came in."

"His parents...weren't the best. He came over one day and had scrapes, bruises, and a split lip. Mom took one look at him, grabbed Dad, and told us they'd be back. An hour later, they came back and told Garrett he would live with us from here on out if he wanted. It's the only time I've ever seen Garrett cry."

That day was the worst shape we had ever seen Garrett in. Kessler and I knew his dad hit him, but he always begged us not to say anything. I knew my mom suspected, but she didn't have any proof, and she never wanted to make things harder on Garrett. His dad always left marks that could easily be covered with clothing until that day.

"As sweet as your mom is, I don't think I'd ever want to be

on her bad side. She seems like she's a force to be reckoned with."

"Shortcake, you have *no* idea. Mom is scary when she's mad. She doesn't yell or scream. She's quiet, and she has this look that can stare right into your soul." A shiver runs through my body just thinking about it.

"I think our parents would have gotten along." She says quietly, staring out the window.

Ever since the night of the attack, she's been talking about her parents more. While I know it still hurts her to talk about them, it's been really good for her too.

"If they were anything like you, I know they would have, Shortcake."

I see her smile under the lights as we turn into the parking garage. I wave at the new security guard, then make a left towards my parking space. After the attack, security was increased, a guard was placed, and new cameras were set up. The guy who attacked Amelia had also broken into several other cars in our parking garage, along with a string of other apartment buildings. He'll be going away for a while.

Once we park, I send her upstairs with the leftovers, while I take Bruno out to do his business one last time before we turn in for the night. While he sniffs around, I take my phone out and send a group text to Hazel and Charlie.

ME

I need your help with something and you can't breathe a word of this to Amelia.

HAZEL

Sir, yes, Sir. What's the order sir?

I laugh and shake my head at Hazel's reply. I'm typing out what I need when a text from Charlie hits the chat.

CHARLIE

Whatever you need Judd.

I was hoping she would say that.

ME

She let it slip the other night that her birthday was coming up. I want to plan a surprise party for her. Just close friends and my family. It'll be at the penthouse. Do you think you can help with that? Decorations, food, desserts? You guys know her best.

HAZEL

Does a bear shit in the woods?

ME

Uh, is that a yes?

CHARLIE

Jesus Hazel, can you just say yes like a normal person?

HAZEL

What fun would that be?

I check on Bruno, who's still sniffing around, marking spots here and there before bringing my attention back to my phone and typing out a message I know will make both women lose their shit.

ME

Great. I appreciate it ladies. I also have to add one thing. The party won't JUST be a birthday party, but in order to make it work I'll need you two to help me with one more thing… You in?

CHARLIE

…Yes?

HAZEL

ooh this sounds interesting. Please enlighten us.

I blow out a breath. *Here goes nothing.*

ME

I need you to take Amelia to brunch at Cate's Bistro the day before her birthday. There's a jewelry store on the same block. I've already talked to the owner and gave him my card information. Take her in there to look at rings. He'll set aside the one she chooses. But don't make it obvious that she's picking out her engagement ring.

HAZEL

WHAT! OH MY GOD! JUDD DAVIS ARE YOU GOING TO PROPOSE?

CHARLIE

Holy shit, I did not see this coming so soon. Why so soon? Is she pregnant!?

ME

No she's not pregnant. In light of recent events we've decided life is short and we're going to start living in the moment. I know I want Amelia by my side for the rest of my life. So why wait?

CHARLIE

Wow. I'm really happy for you Judd. Leave it with us.

ME

Just don't make it obvious that this is what I'm planning.

HAZEL

We won't TRUST us. We won't let you down

ME

I know you won't. Oh and Charlie, I gave the jeweler your name and told him you would be the one to pick it up. I was hoping you could put together one of your 'Charlie Special' picnic baskets and tuck the ring box in it?

CHARLIE

You got it Judd.

With that taken care of, I stuff my phone in my pocket and clip the leash back on Bruno and head back inside. After we get inside our apartment, Bruno immediately heads for his bed, turning three or four times before he finally lays down. His strength has been coming back little by little each day, but all the excitement from today has worn him out.

I leave him to sleep and head into our bedroom, looking for Amelia. The suite is empty, but I hear water running in the bathroom. When I open the door, all the lights are off and candles are lit and set up around the tub, casting Amelia in a golden glow in the tub.

"There you are," she says when she sees me, reaching for the knob to turn off the water. Steam billows up from the lava-like temperature.

I step further into the bathroom and walk over to the tub, kneeling down beside it. "Here I am."

She gives me a sleepy, content smile. "Join me?"

Standing, I lean over the tub and lower my face to hers. She tips her head up to me, connecting our lips. She tastes like heaven. A mix of the dessert she had tonight and her, my favorite flavor.

"Is that a yes?" she asks when I pull back.

Reaching behind me, I pull my sweater and T-shirt over my head. Enjoying the way Amelia's eyes travel over my naked torso. "My eyes are up here, Shortcake," I tease.

"What's your point?"

Popping the button open on my jeans, I step closer to the edge of the tub. "I guess I don't have one. Are you enjoying the show?"

Her eyes flick up to mine, the candlelight reflects in her eyes, making them dance like a blue flame. "I'd enjoy it more if you had less clothes on."

"I think that can be arranged. Wanna help me out with that?"

She reaches for my jeans and tugs me forward, sliding the zipper down, never breaking eye contact with me. Tugging them down to my knees, she reaches into my briefs, her warm, wet hands warming my still cold skin. Wrapping her fingers around my shaft, she pulls my already hard cock out and gives it a long stroke with her hand. Getting onto her knees, Amelia leans forward and flicks her tongue over the tip, licking the drop of pre-cum that's leaked out.

Threading my fingers into her hair, I guide her mouth down my shaft until I hit the back of her throat. "Fuck, Amelia. You suck me down so well." She pulls back and repeats the motion, taking me to the back of her throat again, gagging. "Such a good slut for my cock."

She looks up at me with watery eyes, giving me a heated look as she sucks hard on the tip, then lightly traces her tongue along the ridge of my head. Reaching down with her free hand, she cups my balls and lightly massages them while continuing to switch up the pressure on my shaft, making my knees weak.

"Mills," I croak. "If you don't stop, I'm going to come."

She hums in response and increases her speed, sucking, licking and pumping my shaft with her hand. I tighten my grip on her hair as my balls tighten. My orgasm coming fast. "Amelia, I'm going to come. Where do you want it?"

Lifting her eyes to mine, she continues the intoxicating rhythm with her mouth. She scrapes her teeth along the underside of my cock, making spots appear in my vision. "Mills. Fuck. I'm coming," I groan, rocking my hips forward and spilling down her throat. She swallows every last drop, licking me clean as she pops off me.

I brace my hands against the edge of the tub, letting my heart rate return to normal before stepping out of my jeans the rest of the way. "Move forward and I'll sit behind you," I tell her, nodding my head for her to scoot forward.

I step one foot into the tub, hissing at that temperature of the water. "Jesus, Mills. This is fucking hot."

Amelia snorts and looks at me over her shoulder while I climb the rest of the way in and position myself behind her. "Don't be a baby. It just feels hotter to you because you're still frozen from your dip in the pond."

Sinking down the rest of the way, I position my legs on each side of Amelia. She scoots back and settles herself in between my legs, laying back against my chest. My arms wrap around her middle, securing her to me.

"It feels so good to finally be able to take a bath." She sighs, tracing the branches of the tree I have tattooed on my right arm.

"It feels even better having you naked in here with me," I tell her, running my fingers from her left knee up her inner thigh and back down again.

She sighs and tips her leg open further, allowing me better access to her center. I repeat the path multiple times, getting closer and closer to the spot she wants me to touch. She squirms as I make another pass up her thigh, growling in frustration when I still don't touch her clit.

"Juddson Davis, if you don't touch me, I'm going to do it myself."

"Is that supposed to be a threat? You know I love watching you touch yourself, Shortcake."

Reaching down, Amelia circles her clit, arching her back off my chest. Pushing her tits into the air. I bring my hands up and cup her perfect tits, sliding my thumbs over the tips of her hardened nipples.

She gasps at the sensation, arching further into my touch. "Judd," she whispers. Her hand moving faster.

"That's a good girl. Make yourself feel good," I murmur into her ear, then trail a path of kisses down her neck. I nip at the sensitive flesh between her neck and shoulder, getting a gasp of pleasure from her sweet mouth.

Her mouth falls open when I flick my fingers over her sensitive nipples. And a low groan sounds at the back of her throat. "Judd," she whimpers. "I need–I need your cock."

"Make yourself come first, then you can have it, baby."

Her breaths turn erratic, and her hand moves faster, chasing the orgasm I know is near. Her left hand reaches up and wraps around the back of my neck, anchoring herself to me. "Yes, yes, yes," she chants. I roll her nipples between my fingers, and her body stiffens, then shutters as her orgasm hits.

"Fuck," she cries, riding out the waves of pleasure.

I release her nipples and grab her waist. Spinning her around, I straddle her onto my lap. A shocked gasp leaves her lips, followed by a moan as I sink deep into her in one thrust.

"We fit together perfectly, baby. Like you were made just for me."

Her hands tangle into the hair at the back of my head. She tugs on the ends and swivels her hips slowly, staring into my eyes with each thrust. As much as we have had sex in our short time together, we've never made love.

Until now.

Our bodies meld together, matching each other's movements.

Amelia leans her forehead against mine, breathing me in as I am her.

"I love you so much it hurts," I whisper in between soft, slow kisses.

"I can't wait to build a life with you," she says, sitting up and changing the angle of her hips. Her mouth drops open, and her head falls back when she hits the perfect spot.

Increasing her speed just enough to create the perfect friction to drive us both over the edge without sloshing water out of the tub too much.

Not that it matters. She can make as big of a mess as she wants if it means I get to see her like this. Eyes dark with passion, skin flushed from the heat of the water and her previous orgasm.

"Fuck, Judd. You feel so good."

Her pussy flutters around my hard cock and I know she's getting close.

"I'm right there with you, baby," I tell her, then suck one of her nipples into my mouth, flicking my tongue across it.

"Yes," she hisses, grabbing her other nipple and rolling it between her fingers, riding me closer to our release.

I release her nipple and move to the other one, repeating the motion.

"I'm so close, Judd," she whimpers, bringing her hands to my shoulders to steady herself as her movements become erratic.

Grabbing onto her hips, I pin her to me and grind her pussy back and forth.

Her walls flutter, gripping onto my cock like a vice.

"That's it, Shortcake. You're almost there, aren't you, pretty girl?"

Amelia bites down on her lip and nods, a whimper escaping her throat.

"Just let go, Amelia. I'm right there with you." Moving a hand to her clit, I circle the sensitive nerves until she detonates. Spiraling out of control in my arms.

"Fuck, fuck. Yes, Judd," she screams, biting down on my shoulder to muffle her sounds.

I pump into her two more times before my own orgasm follows. Her pussy still flutters around me, milking the last of my orgasm out of me.

Amelia collapses against my chest, and I wrap my arms

around her back, resting my chin on her head. After a few minutes, she finds the strength to sit up and cups my cheeks, running her thumbs over my scruff while her eyes trace over my face.

"What's on your mind, Shortcake?"

Flicking her eyes to mine, she gives me a soft smile. "I was just thinking we need to get a tub like this for the master bath when we build our house."

Our house.

Two of the most beautiful words I've ever heard come out of her mouth.

"Anything you want, baby. Anything you want."

CHAPTER 35

Amelia

THE LAST THREE weeks have been like a dream. One I never want to wake up from. The gentleman who owns the property next to Kessler contacted Judd the Saturday after Thanksgiving asking if we wanted to come look and see if it's really what we want.

We went out the next day and walked around the part of the property that was accessible. It's overgrown with blackberry bushes, grass that reaches my hips, and trees that badly need to be trimmed or cut down all together.

It's perfect.

Judd took one look at me and the joy on my face and made Mr. Miller an offer right there on the spot.

We are now the proud owners of thirty acres right next door to Kessler and Lucy. We can't break ground until spring when the weather clears up, but that hasn't stopped us from going out to our property when the weather permits and think about where we want things to be.

If everything goes as planned, we should be in our new home by this time next year. If we can ever agree on a floor plan, that is. While we both agree that we like the drawing that's in the library and want the exterior of the house to reflect it. Our tastes differ on the layout, thus the multiple trips to the property.

"Good morning, Shortcake," Judd says, walking into the bathroom and carrying an iced coffee for me in one hand and a mug of hot coffee for him in the other.

I take the glass from him, taking a sip from the straw before setting it down on the counter and standing on my tiptoes to give Judd a quick kiss on his lips. Turning back to the mirror to finish my makeup.

"I bring you coffee and that's all I get?" he asks, pushing his bottom lip out in a pout.

I roll my eyes at him in the mirror. "You got *plenty* this morning," I tell him. Swiping mascara onto my lashes.

"Did you just roll your eyes at me, Amelia?" he asks, stepping up behind me so my back is flush with his front.

"And what if I did?" I challenge. Meeting his stare in the mirror.

"I guess you'll just have to find out later, huh?" he says, dropping a kiss to my hair and stepping back. "Wouldn't want you to be late to brunch with the girls."

Turning around, I lean against the counter, furrowing my brows at him. "Since when do you care if I'm late to meet the girls, if it means you get a chance to fuck me?"

He shrugs. "It's the first brunch since Charlie's been back. I figured you didn't want to be late." He steps forward and places a finger under my chin, tipping my face up to his. Green eyes boring into mine as he says, "Plus, that gives me more time to plan your punishment."

The promise in his words sends chills down my body.

Dropping a chaste kiss to my lips, he backs out of the bathroom, giving me a wink before disappearing back into the bedroom.

Leaving me suspicious, *and* turned on.

When Bruno and I arrive at Cate's Bistro, Charlie and Hazel have already been seated and a pitcher of mimosas is sitting in the middle of the table.

"Sorry I'm late!" I apologize when I reach the table. Charlie stands and gives me a giant hug before I take my seat and Bruno settles down at my feet. "What did I miss?"

Hazel pours me a mimosa and places it in front of me. "Well, for starters, you missed a spot riiiight here," she says, poking her finger into a spot between my neck and collarbone. The spot I tried, and obviously failed, to cover this morning.

I pull on the collar of my leather bomber jacket, trying to cover the spot. "I told Judd he better not leave a mark," I grumble, taking a huge drink of my mimosa.

"Looks like he didn't listen," Hazel says with a smirk, taking a sip of her own drink.

"Obviously," I say, taking another sip.

Charlie picks up her own glass, taking a drink. I do a double take. "Charlie, are you drinking *water*?"

Charlie sets her glass of water down and presses a hand to her stomach. "My stomach has been feeling off since we landed yesterday. I don't know if I ate something bad, or if I'm just feeling some weird effects of jet lag. But I wasn't going to miss catching up with you and Hazel."

"We could have rescheduled," I tell her.

She shakes her head and waves me off. "No, no. I'll be fine. I'm sure I'll feel better after some toast and more water."

"Okay, if you're sure."

"I am, I promise," she reassures me.

The waiter comes by and sets a fruit tray in the middle of the table, then takes our food order. Leaving as quickly as he came.

"So, let's get down to the good stuff," Hazel says, refilling our mimosas. "Charlie, you first. How was your trip? Meet any hot guys?" Hazel looks over her shoulders and lowers her voice. "Sleep with any hot guys?"

Charlie's cheeks turn red, and she plucks a grape off the fruit tray, popping it in her mouth.

Hazel and I both gasp, getting looks from patrons at other tables nearby.

"Charlotte Leigh Dixon, did you get laid on vacation?" I ask, scooting my chair closer.

"Will you *please* keep your voices down?" Charlie pleads. Her cheeks go from a blush pink to a deep red from her embarrassment.

Hazel flaps her hand in the general direction of the other tables. "They're fine. It's not exactly a secret that people have sex."

Charlie covers her face with her hands and groans.

I tap her leg with my foot, raising a brow at her. "Spill."

She huffs and takes another sip of her water. "Fine, but you *cannot* tell a soul. *Especially* my parents."

Hazel and I look at each other, then back at Charlie, both of us dragging our fingers across our lips like we're zipping our lips.

Charlie sighs. "I had sex with a man *fifteen years* older than me, not once, but *several* times, and it was the best sex of my life."

Hazel and I gasp again.

"Charlie, you little minx you," I say, wiggling my eyebrows up and down.

"Older men are *so* hot. It's truly not fair they get better looking as they get older," Hazel adds.

"But why the secrecy, Char? It's not like you'll ever see him again. Right?" I ask.

Charlie draws a pattern in the condensation that's formed on the outside of her glass, avoiding our gazes.

"Charlie?"

Her eyes snap to mine. "Does the name Grant Collins sound familiar?"

I wrack my brain, trying to think if we went to school with someone with that name, but come up blank. "No. Should it?"

Charlie lifts a shoulder. "Probably not. The only reason I know it is because I follow baseball. Not that I really have a choice, seeing as my dad's an MLB coach."

"Focus, Charlie," Hazel says, snapping her fingers in front of Charlie's face. "What's with the secrecy?"

Charlie takes a deep breath. "Because Grant Collins is a retired MLB player who used to play for my dad," she rushes out.

"Oh shit," Hazel says.

Charlie grimaces. "There's more."

I hold a finger up to Charlie and down the rest of my mimosa, reaching for the pitcher to fill it back up, then fill Hazel's, who also finished off her drink.

"Okay, please continue."

Charlie mumbles something under her breath.

I look at Hazel, who looks at me and shrugs her shoulders.

"You're gonna have to speak up, Charlie."

Heaving out a sigh, Charlie stares down at the table and says, "He's technically still married."

Hazel and I sit in stunned silence, staring at Charlie.

The waiter appears at our table, setting down our food, then asks us if he can get us anything else. I snap out of my shock when he speaks, thanking him and telling him we were good for now.

Once he leaves, I speak first. "What do you mean, *technically* still married?"

"Him and his wife have been separated for two years. He filed for divorce at the beginning of this year, but she's refusing to sign the papers."

Hazel puts a hand to her chest. "Oh, thank God. For a minute, I thought my best friend was a home-wrecker."

"No, but it still feels…weird."

"So, are you going to see him again? You said he's an ex-player for the Silverbacks. So does that mean he lives here?" I ask.

Charlie shakes her head. "We both agreed it was a vacation fling. Plus, he lives in Washington, so at least I won't bump into him by accident."

"Holy fuck," Hazel exclaims while looking at her phone, getting more dirty looks from people.

"Hazel," Charlie hisses. "You're going to get us kicked out."

Hazel turns her phone, showing us what she's freaking out about. On the screen is a very attractive, clearly older man with a close shaved salt and pepper beard and ice-blue eyes. He's wearing a black fitted long-sleeved shirt that looks like it's been painted on over his *very* defined muscle and baseball pants. To top off the already fine as hell image, the man also has a tattoo on the back of his hand.

"Woah, who is that?" I ask.

"Charlie's *lover,*" Hazel teases.

"I should have just kept my mouth shut," Charlie grumbles, shoving a slice of French toast in her mouth.

"No, you shouldn't have," I tell her, taking a bite of my bacon. "Teasing aside. I'm glad you had some adult fun on vacation. It's about time you let loose a little."

"You make it sound like I never have fun."

"You don't," Hazel and I respond at the same time.

Charlie points her fork at me. "I went out with you two on Halloween."

Hazel rolls her eyes. "When was the last time you had 'between the sheets' fun, *before* your vacation?"

Charlie pauses and squints her eyes in thought.

"If you have to think that hard, too long is the answer," Hazel says.

"Whatever, enough about me. What else is new with you two?"

"I moved in with Judd and we bought property next to his brother's place and are going to build a house," I say nonchalantly

Charlie drops her fork onto her plate. "What?"

Hazel raises her fork. "Knew that already."

Charlie looks at me, throwing her hand towards Hazel. "You told Hazel before me."

I lift a shoulder. "It's really not something I wanted to tell you through text. So, I'm telling you now."

"You could have done a video chat."

"It all sorta happened fast and when you were out at sea, so I just decided to wait until you got back." I place a hand over Charlie's. "I didn't mean to leave you out of the loop. I just wanted to tell you in person."

Charlie smiles and turns her hand slightly to squeeze my fingers. "I know. I'm just being sensitive. Must be the jet lag. I'm so happy for you, Millie. You deserve nothing but happiness."

I squeeze her hand back, then turn to Hazel. "What about you? Anything new since we last talked?"

Hazel shrugs and finishes off her second glass of mimosa. "I broke up with Jason."

It's Charlie's turn to gasp. "What? When?"

Hazel refills her glass and downs half of it before responding. "Two days ago."

"What happened?" I ask. Even though I never liked Jason, I know Hazel was head over heels for him.

"He cheated on me," she says, draining the rest of her mimosa, then adding, "with my cousin...over Thanksgiving."

More gasps, and a "Holy shit" from me, fly around the table.

Hazel laughs, which sounds a little on the manic side, and says, "Oh, that's not even the best part. The only reason I found out is because she showed up at my house when Jason was there and told me she not only slept with him, but that she's pregnant."

"No!" Charlie and I exclaim at the same time.

"Yep," Hazel confirms, making a loud popping sound on the 'P' and emptying the rest of the pitch into her glass.

I flag down the waiter and order another pitcher. It's a good thing Judd drove me, cause there's no way I'm leaving this place sober.

Thirty minutes later, Hazel and I are riding a happy buzz as all three of us leave the Bistro. Charlie suggested a walk up the block to sober us up a little and since it's currently not raining, Hazel and I agreed. Linking arms, we start our trek up the sidewalk.

"I've missed this," I tell them with a sigh.

"Missed what? Getting drunk before noon?" Hazel asks, then snorts and giggles. She's definitely more drunk than I am.

"No, hanging out with my girls. It feels like it's been forever since we've done this," I tell them.

"When *is* the last time we all hung out?"

We grow quiet trying to think when the last time actually was.

"I think it was when you found out about Judd," Charlie says.

"Almost a month ago?" Hazel shouts, making a few people on the sidewalk jump.

Wow, it has been almost a month since that day. So much has changed since then.

Charlie shrugs. "We've been busy, girls. Life's changing." She bumps my shoulder. "We're starting new chapters. Exciting ones. We'll still have girls' night; it just may not be as often."

"Have you ever thought about being a writer, Charlie? Because that was definitely something that I would read in a book."

Charlie chuckles. "I'll leave the writing to you. How's that coming, by the way? Still struggling?"

"Oh! In all the excitement at brunch, I forgot to tell you guys." I look over at Charlie and Hazel. "I finished. I sent it off to my editor yesterday."

"Oh my God, that's fantastic!" Hazel squeals.

I beam at them. It is fantastic. It feels so freeing to be done with a book that I struggled so much with. Being in Judd's library, well I guess it's mine now too, and spending time with Lucy and Kessler really helped with my creativity.

"I'm so proud of you for being able to work through your struggles this year, Millie. You went on your first book tour this year, *by yourself,* you were able to get enough funding to expand your program and help even more kids, you broke through the worst case of writer's block you've ever had since becoming an author." Charlie stops on the sidewalk and looks at me with glassy eyes. "And most importantly, you fell in love and found your person."

I look at my two best friends. The women who have been through it with me, who have picked me up when I've fallen, celebrated with me when I succeeded and gave me their strength when I couldn't find my own. I would have never made it this far without either of them.

"I have you two to thank for most of that," I whisper, my own tears threatening to spill over. "If not for you two, I never would have had the strength to keep going when I wanted to quit."

"I love you guys so much," Hazel sobs. "Who needs men

when I have the best two girlfriends anyone could ask for?" She sniffles then adds, "And vibrators."

We all burst into giggles and wipe away our tears before continuing on our stroll. We walk a few more feet before Hazel lets out a gasp and pulls us towards a store. "Let's go in here."

"What are you doing, Hazel?" I ask, looking up at the sign and see that she's pulling us towards a jewelry store.

"We're going in to look at rings."

I lift my eyebrow. "Uh, didn't you just break up with Jason?"

Hazel sighs and rolls her eyes. "Not for me, for you."

I give Charlie a questioning look. She just shrugs her shoulders and continues to follow Hazel like it's not the craziest thing to ever come out of her mouth.

"Uh, isn't Judd supposed to pick out the ring?" I ask as Hazel pulls open the door and leads us inside.

"That doesn't mean we can't look. That way, Charlie and I have an idea of what to tell Judd to get when the time comes."

"She's right. It's going to happen. We all know it. You might as well help us guide him in the right direction."

Ok, so they have a point. "Fine, but we're not breathing a word of this to Judd," I tell them as Hazel leads us to a display case.

An older gentleman who looks to be in his sixties comes out of the back when he hears the bell.

"Good afternoon. Is there anything I can help you ladies with today?"

"We were wondering if you could show us some engagement rings? Things are getting serious between our friend and her boyfriend, and we'd like to know what to show him when the time comes," Charlie tells him, pointing to me.

The man's warm smile brightens. "Certainly. Is there something specific you had in mind?"

"Um, I don't really know. I guess I never really thought about it."

"Not to worry. I'll pull a variety out and we can narrow it down from there. Let me just get my keys from the back and I'll open the cases."

While Walter, according to his name tag, disappears in the back, I turn to the girls.

"Is this weird?"

"No," they both reply, looking down into the glass cases.

Walter returns with his keys and begins opening cases. Taking tray after tray out for me to look at. My eyes wander over the sparkly diamonds. Nothing really standing out. Don't get me wrong, they're all beautiful, but nothing jumps out at me that I would want to wear for the rest of my life.

"See anything that catches your eye?" Walter asks after a few minutes.

I sigh. "They're all beautiful, but nothing really screams 'me'."

Walter taps his lips a few times with his pointer finger, then holds it up to me. "I'll be right back," he says, darting off to the back.

I give the girls a questioning look, but they just look at me and shrug their shoulders.

Seconds later, Walter comes out of the back with another tray of rings, with jewels in an array of different colors. He moves the other trays to the side and sets this one down in front of me. "Let's see if any of these speak to you."

I slowly look over the rings, each one more beautiful than the last. My eyes stop on one and a gasp leaves my lips. There's a beautiful green teardrop gem with deep green veining the color of Judd's eyes in the middle of a gold band. Little gold vines and leaves wrap around the band, reminding me of the leaves from one of the tattoos on Judd's arm. Diamond gemstones are scattered between the vines, completing the design.

"Find one you like, miss?"

I pick up the most beautiful ring I've ever seen and slip it onto my ring finger. It's a perfect fit. "This one. This is the one," I whisper.

Hazel and Charlie both ooh and awe over it, taking pictures so they know exactly what to tell Judd whenever the time comes. When we're done admiring the ring, I reluctantly slip it off my finger and place it back on the tray. Hoping one day it makes it back onto my finger.

CHAPTER 36

Judd

"HAPPY BIRTHDAY, SHORTCAKE," I whisper into Amelia's ear as I slide my cock into her pussy from behind. Her body is warm and languid from sleep, perfectly forming to mine.

Her eyes flutter open, a sleepy smile appearing on her face. "Good morning." She sighs, hooking an arm around my neck, anchoring herself to me as I start rocking into her. Tilting her face to mine, Amelia kisses me hard, biting down playfully on my lip.

Skimming my hand up her leg, and over her thigh, I apply firm pressure to her clit. I swallow the moans that escape her, quickly bringing her to the edge.

As much as I want to spend the day lying in bed making love to her. I have a full day planned for her, starting with breakfast at Hazel's and a trip to the tattoo parlor. I've wanted to take her ever since she asked me about how much they hurt. Her birthday is the *perfect* excuse to take her to get one.

"Judd," she moans as her pussy flutters.

"That's it, Shortcake. Come all over my cock."

Her hand slips from around my neck and she reaches

forward, gripping the sheet. Placing a hand between her shoulder blades, I push her body forward, bending her slightly at the waist and changing the angle.

"Oh fuck, Judd. Right there," she screams, burying her face into the pillow.

My hips piston into her faster, my own orgasm barreling forward. "Fuck, Amelia. Your pussy is gripping me so tight. Come for me, pretty girl."

I circle her clit a couple more times before she explodes around me. The walls of her pussy squeezing me so tight, my orgasm follows. We both lay panting on the bed once the waves of pleasure subside. My body curled around hers.

"Happy birthday to me," Amelia jokes once we've caught our breath.

"A *very* happy birthday to you."

"Mmm, can we just lay in bed all day?" she asks, stretching her arms over her head, pushing her perfect tits in the air.

Not being able to resist, I suck her nipple into my mouth, reaching over and rolling the other one between my thumb and finger. She arches her back, thrusting her fingers into my hair. "Yes," she hisses.

I sneak a peek at the clock on the bed-side table. We'll have plenty of time to make it to our tattoo appointment if I text Hazel on the way and make our breakfast to go.

Deciding I'd rather give my girlfriend, hopefully soon to be fiancée, another orgasm instead of eating breakfast at the café, I continue worshiping her breasts, trailing my fingers down her abdomen and to her sensitive pussy.

I flick my thumb over her clit, earning a sharp gasp from Amelia. Her hips push into my hand as I continue down, inserting two fingers into her soaking cunt. I quickly move them in and out, slapping her clit with the palm of my hand as I move. Her grip tightens on my hair, and her legs fall open, completely exposing herself, giving her body over to me.

"You like that, don't you, my little slut," I murmur.

"Yes, yes, yes," she chants as she thrashes her head back and forth.

"Come on, Amelia. I know you want to come."

"I can't," she whines. Grabbing her tits and pinching the nipples.

I curl my fingers slightly, hitting her G-spot and continuing my assault on her pussy. "Yes, you can." I whisper into her ear. Biting the spot on her neck she loves. "Come, Amelia," I command.

Her pussy clamps down onto my fingers at the same time she sucks in a deep breath, her back arching so hard it's completely off the bed. A sudden pressure pushes my fingers out of her and a rush of liquid follows.

"Holy shit, Amelia. Did you just squirt?"

Amelia's thighs slam together, her body continuing to convulse from her orgasm.

Once her orgasm subsides, her body goes completely limp. "Holy shit," she whispers, eyes closed.

"That was fucking hot," I tell her, leaning over to give her a kiss.

"I'm dead. How in the hell did you do that?"

I shrug. "I have no idea. But I *definitely* want to do that again."

She pats my bare chest and sighs. "There's no way I can go again. You've ruined me."

"I didn't mean right now anyway. We have to get in the shower if we're going to make it to your first surprise on time," I tell her, getting up from the bed and coming to her side of the bed. Holding out my hand to help her up.

"I told you we didn't need to do anything special today," she grumbles, taking my hand and letting me pull her up to her shaky legs and lead her into the bathroom.

I snort and wrap her in my arms before we get in the

shower. "Every day I get to spend with you is special. Today just happens to be extra special because it's your birthday." I kiss her again and cup her cheek. "Now *please,* let me spoil you."

"Fine," she sighs. "But I get to make a big deal for your birthday then."

"Whatever you say, Shortcake."

We pull up to the tattoo shop with just minutes to spare, breakfast in hand. I reserved the whole shop for the morning, so it would just be Amelia and me. Jade and Kris were more than understanding when I told them about Amelia's anxiety with new places.

Amelia looks at the building, then back at me. "Why are we at a tattoo place?"

"You're finally getting your tattoo today."

Her mouth gapes open and she looks at the building, then back at me again. "Really?"

I nod. "Really. I also rented out the whole place for the morning, so it'll just be us."

Her hand flies to her mouth and moisture gathers in her eyes. "I can't believe you did that for me."

Cupping her cheek, I look into her eyes. "Shortcake, I'd do *anything* for you if it meant seeing that beautiful smile on your face every day."

"I love you," she whispers, covering my hand on her cheek with hers.

"I love you too, Mills." I lean forward to give her a kiss when a cold, wet nose touches my cheek, followed by a tongue. I wipe my cheek and look at Bruno, who is panting and staring at us. "We love you too, Bruno," I tell him, earning me another lick.

Getting out of the Jeep, I take Amelia's hand in mine and walk through the door, the little bell overhead tinkling. Jade looks up from the front desk and smiles. "Welcome in." She nods her head to the door. "Do you mind flipping the lock? I don't want anyone to walk in while we're in the chair."

"Sure," I respond, locking the door before moving the rest of the way to the desk.

"Hi, I'm Jade," she says, holding her hand out to Amelia. "You must be Amelia."

Amelia takes her outstretched hand, giving it a shake. "It's nice to meet you."

"Likewise," Jade says, tipping her head towards me. "I've heard a lot about you. This is your first tattoo, right?"

Amelia nods. "Yes."

"No worries. We'll take good care of you. You're with me today. Kris will take Judd, but we'll sit you in chairs next to each other."

Amelia looks at me with a surprised expression. "You're getting one too?"

"Of course, Shortcake. Couldn't let you have all the fun," I tell her, giving her a wink.

"Do you have an example or drawing to show me of what you want, Amelia?" Jade asks.

"Oh, yes. Hang on." Amelia digs her phone out of her purse. Unlocking the phone, she taps on her screen and scrolls until she finds what she's looking for. "I was hoping to get this," she says, setting the phone down on the counter. "But instead of the stem the way it is. I want it to be this." Amelia digs a small, folded paper out of a pocket in her purse. She unfolds the paper and sets it down next to the phone. The word 'Breathe' is written on the paper in cursive writing. "Exactly in this writing. Is that possible?"

Jade picks up the phone and paper, looking at both. "That won't be a problem. Where do you want it?"

Amelia pulls the left sleeve of her sweater up. "Here," she says, tracing a path from her wrist down her arm.

Jade nods and smiles. "Let me go draw up a sketch and see if it's what you want. I'll be right back."

She hands Amelia's phone back then retreats to the back to sketch. I peer down at the phone screen, it's a picture of a dandelion that's gone to seed and some of the seed pods are floating away.

"Why a dandelion?"

Taking the paper off the counter, Amelia traces the word with her finger. "It's for my mom. She's the one who taught me to breathe through my anxiety. She told me to 'picture blowing the seeds off the wisher', that's what we called them."

Wrapping an arm around her shoulders, I pull her body into mine and place a kiss on the top of her head. "Is that her handwriting?"

She nods. "She gave this to me the day they dropped me off at college. She told me to carry it with me and if I found my anxiety to be too much to look at it and know that she was breathing with me." Amelia swipes at her eyes and whispers, "I miss them so much."

"I know, Mills," I whisper into her hair, wrapping my other arm around her and hugging her tightly. "I wish I could take your pain away."

She looks up at me, tears silently falling down her face. "You loving me for who I am, for all my flaws and struggles is more than I could ever ask for. Your unconditional love helps ease the ache."

I place a kiss on her soft lips, then wipe her tears away with my thumbs. "I didn't mean for this to make you cry. I wanted this to be a happy day."

Amelia laughs, swiping at her face some more. "It is.

You've already done more than enough. No more crying today, promise," she says, crossing her finger over her heart.

I suspect there will be a lot more crying today, but I can't tell her that without ruining the surprises.

"Now, we know what I'm planning to get, but what are you getting?" she asks and motions to my arm. "Are you adding to your sleeve?"

I shake my head. "No, I actually need your help with mine."

She gives me a confused look, but before she can say anything. Kris pops out of the back. "Hey, Judd. How's it going?"

"Great," I tell him, giving his outstretched fist a bump. "Amelia, this is Kris. Kris, this is my girlfriend, Amelia."

"Good to meet you," Kris tells her, holding his hand up in a wave.

"Likewise."

"Alright," Kris says, clapping his hands together once. "Should we get down to it?"

I nod and look at Amelia. "I need a favor, Shortcake."

"Um, okay?"

Kris lays an inkpad on the counter and a blank piece of paper. "Can you touch the ink pad with your thumb, then press it to the paper?" I ask.

"Why?"

"Because I can't get my tattoo without it."

Amelia stares at me, eyes widening a little. "You're getting *my* thumb print tattooed onto your skin? Why?"

I smirk. "You'll see once it's done."

Amelia lifts a brow at me but rolls her thumb in the ink and puts it to the paper.

"Perfect. I'll go get it drawn up," Kris says, passing Jade on his way to the back.

"Ok, Amelia. How does it look?" Jade asks, setting her

sketch down in front of Amelia. "If you don't like anything, let me know and we can tweak it."

Amelia stares down at the paper, her fingers tracing over the sketch. "I love it," she whispers, trying and failing to blink back another set of tears

"You're positive?"

Amelia nods and swipes at her cheeks. "Yes, it's perfect."

"Great!" Jade says brightly. "Let's get you in a chair, then. Judd, you can sit in the seat next to her while you wait for Kris to get done with yours."

We follow Jade back, and she settles Amelia into her chair. I take the one to her right. She preps Amelia's arm, then places the stencil onto her skin, checking the placement. Once Amelia gives her the 'OK,' she starts, telling Amelia to let her know if it's too much so she can give her a break.

Ten minutes into Amelia's tattoo, Kris comes out of the back and motions me over. "Be right back, Shortcake," I tell her, getting up from the chair.

"How's it look?" Kris asks, handing me his drawing.

"It's perfect."

"You like the size?"

I nod.

"Great, let's do this," Kris says, leading me back to his station. Taking my shirt off, Kris preps my chest.

"You're getting it on your chest? Can I see the design?" Amelia asks.

"Not until it's done."

She sticks out her bottom lip in a pout.

"It'll be worth the wait, Shortcake. Trust me."

"Alright, you're all finished," Kris says, passing me a handheld mirror.

"Looks great man. Thanks again."

Amelia sets her phone down and turns towards me. "Can I look now?" she asks, standing from her chair. She was done thirty minutes ago and has been messing around on her phone waiting for me to get done.

I lower the mirror as she steps up to my side and looks down at the tattoo. Her thumb print is enlarged and makes up one side of the tattoo. "*Ergo dum me diligis.*" She reads the words that complete the other side of the heart. "What's it mean?"

I lace my fingers between hers. "It says 'So long as you love me' in Latin. Because as long as you love me, Mills, we can get through anything."

Her eyes flick to mine. "Judd," she whispers. "It's beautiful." Her eyes mist over, and she blinks rapidly to hold back her tears, then smacks me lightly on the arm.

"Hey! What was that for?"

"You made me almost cry, and I said *no more* crying today."

"It's not my fault you're emotional today," I joke, earning another whack. "What was that one for?"

"For calling me emotional," she says, giving me a smirk.

"Note to self, don't call Amelia emotional, even when she is being emotional," I mutter, pulling my shirt over my head once Kris has covered my tattoo.

"What was that?" Amelia asks, glancing back over her shoulder at me as we walk to the front.

I give her a cheesy grin. "Nothing, Shortcake. Just saying how much I love you."

"Right," she replies, not believing me one bit.

"All set?" Jade asks once we get to the front.

"Yep, thanks again, Jade. I really appreciate it."

"Happy to do it. Plus, it's been a while since I took someone's tattoo virginity."

Amelia chuckles. "Thank you for being gentle with me."

Jade gives her a wink and waves at us as we leave the shop.

"Wait," Amelia shouts after we get in the Jeep. "We forgot to pay." She moves to unbuckle her seatbelt when I lay my hand over hers to stop her.

"I already paid," I tell her.

"When?"

"When I booked the appointment," I explain, starting the Jeep and pulling out of the parking lot to our next stop.

"But how did you know how much to pay? You didn't even know what I was going to get." She pauses and looks at me, narrowing her eyes. "You paid an obscene amount for us to have the shop to ourselves, didn't you?"

Lifting a shoulder, I keep my eyes on the road. "Depends on what you think is an 'obscene amount'."

Amelia snorts. "That answers my question."

Chancing a look at her, I take my eyes off the road and throw her a wink before focusing back on the road. Flicking my blinker on, I change lanes and take a right at the next intersection.

"So, what's next on Judd's birthday extravaganza list?"

Butterflies take flight in my stomach as we get closer to our next stop. Doubts race through me, wondering if it's too soon, if she's going to hate where I propose to her, will she even say yes?

Amelia's hand lands on my forearm, jerking me out of my thoughts. "Judd? Did you hear me?"

"I'm sorry, Shortcake, I zoned out for a minute. What did you say?"

"I asked what was next on your list of birthday surprises."

I grab her hand and bring it to my lips, kissing the back of her hand. "You'll see shortly."

My heartbeat increases the closer we get until I'm convinced it's going to beat right out of my chest. I make the last turn and pull into the parking lot, instantly feeling Amelia's body go still.

I put the Jeep in park and turn off the engine, filling the cab with silence.

"Why are we here, Judd?" Amelia asks, voice barely above a whisper.

Clearing my throat, I take a breath and let it out. "Because I want to tell your parents about the girl I've fallen in love with."

CHAPTER 37

Amelia

JUDD TAKES my hand in his and leads me down the path towards my parent's graves. The path that will forever be ingrained in my memory.

Eight rows down, three plots to the left.

After their funeral, I found myself here almost daily. No matter the weather, I'd sit in front of the fresh piles of dirt for hours, and just stare. Trying to will the piles away and my parents back into existence.

Bruno trots beside me, looking up at me every few steps as the memories of those days run through my head.

My feet slow when we approach the eighth row. Judd notices and stops, turning around to check on me. "Are you okay?"

Instead of answering I turn my head to the left and let my eyes drift down to the headstone with 'Morgan' engraved across the top and my parents' names written on each side.

"We don't have to go if it's too hard."

"No, I want to. I just didn't expect to come here today." I tug on Judd's hand and lead him over to their graves, running my hand along the top of the smooth marble when we get there. "Hi Momma, Hi Daddy. I'm sorry it's been a while," I say, kissing my fingers and laying on their headstones.

Judd sets the giant bag he somehow hid in the Jeep down and starts pulling things out of it. First is a potted mini Christmas tree that's no bigger than a foot tall. He sets it on Mom's side of the headstone and dives back into the bag, producing a large wool blanket with a buffalo plaid pattern. "Are you alright with me laying it down here?" he asks, pointing to the grassy space where the large piles of dirt used to be.

I nod, and Judd shakes the blanket out, laying it down over the grass. He pulls a variety of containers out next, placing them in the middle.

"Are we, did you? Are we having a picnic?" I finally get out. Watching as Judd places a bottle of chilled wine and tumblers next to the containers.

How is the wine still chilled?

"We are," he says, reaching into the bag *again,* this time pulling throw pillows out.

"Do you have a stove and a fridge in there too, Mary Poppins?" I joke, stepping forward to look into the bag.

"Ah ah ah," Judds says, closing the bag when I get near. "My eyes only."

"Well, now I really want to see what else you have in there," I say, reaching around, trying to grab the bag from behind him. He holds the bag up over his head, knowing there's no way I'll be able to reach it. "Not fair," I pout, crossing my arms over my chest.

Judd chuckles and sets the bag back down, taking me in his arms to keep me from going after the bag. "It's not my fault you're the size of a gremlin."

"Feed me after midnight and see what happens."

Judd wiggles his eyebrows up and down. "Sounds kinky."

I laugh, the first laugh I've ever had while standing in a

place where I've only known sorrow. And it's all thanks to the man I never saw coming.

"There she is," he says, looking down at me in his arms and cupping my face. "There's *my* Amelia." I close my eyes as he places a soft kiss on my forehead, a sense of peace falling over me. "Let's sit," he whispers.

We settle onto the blanket facing the headstone. Bruno plops down to my right and Judd starts taking the lids off the containers, revealing some of my favorite foods. Pasta salad, blueberries, sweet and sour chicken that's warm. I look up at him when I see the steam rising from the last one. "How did you keep this hot and the other things chilled?"

Judd smirks. "I have my ways." Judd reaches behind him in the bag and produces a bone for Bruno to enjoy, and hands me a fork. "Now dig in before it gets cold."

We eat in silence, the only sounds coming from Bruno and the birds that are flying from tree to tree nearby. Judd is the first to speak after we've made a dent in the containers. "Tell me about them," he says, nodding to where my parents' names are engraved.

Eleanor Grace & Jonathan Lee

"Uh, let's see. Dad was a contractor, mainly for custom homes. He hated 'cookie cutter' houses. He said there was no character to them. He was really handy and could fix *anything*. For my eleventh birthday, he built me my own little reading shack in our backyard. Mom decorated it with cushions and blankets and put a string of twinkle lights around the ceiling." I sigh, leaning back onto my hands. "I used that thing until the day I went off to college."

Judd smiles, staying quiet while I dig into my memories.

"Mom was a teacher. An English teacher. She's where I got my love of books from. I remember *always* coming home with at least one book after a shopping trip, no matter how many I had in my pile that I hadn't read yet." I chuckle at the happy memories playing in my mind. "Dad joked that one day he would open the fridge and instead of food, it would just be filled to the brim with books." I sit up and grab a handful of blueberries, popping one into my mouth. "So, one year for April fools, my mom and I got up really early and took *all* the food out of the fridge and placed as many books as we could in there. When dad came down that morning for breakfast, he opened the fridge, and a mountain of books greeted him. The look on his face was priceless." I sigh a contented sigh. "Wow, I haven't thought about that in years."

Judd places the lids back on the pasta salad and chicken, sticking them back in the bag before scooting closer to me, wrapping an arm around my shoulders. "They sound like they were great. I wish I could have met them."

"They were the best," I say, laying my head against Judd. "And they would have really loved you."

"I mean what's not to love," Judd jokes and I poke a finger into his rib. He grabs my finger and brings it to his lips, placing a kiss on the top before lacing my fingers with his.

"Thank you for bringing me here today. For asking about them. You're the only one I've ever dated who's made an effort to get to know them, even though they're gone."

"None of the other guys deserved you, Mills."

I look down at our linked hands. "You know, the only other person who has ever called me Mills was my dad."

Judd clears his throat. "I didn't know. If you want me to stop–"

"No," I say quickly. "I love it. The only two men who have ever mattered in my life have only called me that." Bruno plops his head into my lap and looks up at me, releasing a heavy sigh. "Excuse me, the only two, *two-legged men*," I correct.

Bruno sighs again and closes his eyes.

Judd and I share a smirk. "I swear he knows exactly what we're saying," Judd muses.

"You'd be surprised what he understands."

"Speaking of surprises," Judd says, dragging the bag of wonder to his side. He reaches in, producing a plastic container with a large cupcake inside. Handing the container to me, he turns back to the bag and pulls out a candle and lighter. He takes the cupcake back from me and opens the lid. Sticking the candle in the middle of the frosting, he lights the wick. "Make a wish."

"Aren't you supposed to sing 'Happy Birthday' to me first?"

He lifts a shoulder. "If you want."

"You know what, on second thought. Never mind, I've heard you sing," I tease.

He bumps me with his shoulder. "Keep it up and I won't give you your present," he warns.

I lift an eyebrow at him. "I thought the tattoo was my present."

Judd snorts. "You can have more than one present."

"Judd, the tattoo was more than enough."

"Just blow out your candle and make a wish."

I close my eyes, trying to think of what to wish for. If I'm being honest, there's not much more I could ask for. I have the most amazing friends in the world. A successful career doing something I love. A service animal who is worth his weight in gold. And last but not least, a boyfriend who I'm building a life with. The only thing that could make any of this better was if my parents were here to witness it, but I know they're watching and knowing my mom, she had something to do with Judd and I finding each other. Taking a deep breath, I send them a thanks instead of making a wish and blow out my candle.

When I open my eyes, Judd is in front of me. Down on one knee. With the ring I picked out at the jeweler's yesterday.

I gasp, my hands flying to my mouth and my eyes instantly filling with tears. "Judd, what, what are you doing?" I ask, my voice coming out in a squeaky whisper.

"I'm asking the love of my life if she would do me the honor of becoming my wife."

"But isn't it too soon? What are people going to say? What are your parents going to say?" I ask, dropping my hands from my mouth.

Judd grabs both my hands in his, the one that's not holding the ring box. "I don't care what anyone thinks. My parents love you. And if we've learned anything in the last few months, it's that life is short. We're building a home, a life together. The only thing that's missing is me being able to call you my wife. I know the cemetery isn't an ideal place for a proposal, but it's the only way I knew how to have your parents involved, since they can't be with us."

I shake my head, tears streaming down my face from his words. "It's perfect Judd. Everything is perfect."

"Almost," he says, clearing his throat. "Amelia Marie Morgan, will you please make me the happiest man on earth and marry me?"

"Yes," I choke out, launching myself into his arms. "A million times, yes."

He slides the ring onto my finger, exactly where it belongs.

CHAPTER 38

Judd

AMELIA HASN'T STOPPED STARING at the ring on her hand since we left the cemetery. She wanted to video call Hazel and Charlie as soon as we got back to the Jeep, but I convinced her to wait until we got home. I didn't want her catching on that they were already at our place, setting up for Amelia's surprise birthday/our engagement party.

"I can't believe you put all of this together, even getting the girls to trick me into picking out my own ring."

I grin. "Not going to lie. I thought you might get suspicious when they took you into the jewelry store."

"I probably would have if I had been sober, but thanks to Hazel and her break-up with Jason, I was tipsy enough to not give it a second thought."

Amelia told me all about what happened between Hazel and her shitty ex-boyfriend when she came home last night. I messaged Hazel later, telling her she didn't have to help set up for the engagement party if she didn't feel up to it. She messaged me back, saying she wasn't going to let Jason's wandering dick get in the way of celebrating me and Amelia.

"What do you think your parents are going to say?" she asks, picking at her nails.

I lay a hand over hers. "They're going to be extremely happy for us. They already think of you as family. This," I say, holding up her hand with my ring on it, "just makes it official."

She blows a breath through her lips. "You're right. Are we going to tell them tomorrow at Sunday dinner?"

I smile, knowing it's going to be sooner than that. "Whatever you want, Shortcake."

Once we park, Amelia takes Bruno out to do his business while I grab the bag Charlie made. I meet her back at the elevator and we ride up together.

Amelia leans back against the elevator wall, letting out a contented sigh. "This has been the craziest, best day I've ever had."

I tower over her in the elevator, bracing an arm above her head and tucking a strand of her hair behind her ear with the other. "And to think, you hated me only a few short months ago."

"I wouldn't say *hate,*" she says, running her hand softly over where my new tattoo is. "It was more strongly dislike."

"Well, I'm glad I was able to win you over."

She gives me a wicked grin and grabs the lapels of my jacket, pulling me closer. "Did you though? Maybe I'm just using you for your big dick."

I close the distance, capturing her lips in a deep, slow kiss. She snakes her hands around my neck and tugs at the short strands of hair, making me growl into her mouth.

The ding of the elevator brings me to the present, and I pull back just as the doors open and shouts of 'Surprise.' surround us.

Amelia jumps, letting out a surprised squeal. She stands there, looking back and forth between me and the room full of people. "What are you all doing here?"

Charlie and Hazel step forward, each taking one of Amelia's arms and pull her out of the elevator and into the living room. "We're here to celebrate you and your fiancé," Charlie tells her.

"And your birthday, of course," Hazel adds.

I step out of the elevator looking at the decorations Charlie, Hazel, my mom, and Lucy set up. Next to the entrance is a balloon arch with gold and pink balloons with a banner that says 'Congratulations' in the middle and 'Happy Birthday' below that. Streamers in the same colors as the balloons are strung throughout the room. Meat and cheese trays, fruit trays, and a variety of other types of finger foods are laid out across the kitchen island.

Everyone who was at Thanksgiving, plus Coach Dixon and his wife, are there to celebrate with us. Mom and Dad come up to us first. Mom pulls Amelia into a hug while Dad pats me on the back. "Congratulations, Son. I knew when you brought her to the house, that was it," he says, giving me a wink.

"Thanks Dad."

Mom moves over to me while Dad trades her, hugging Amelia. "Oh Juddson. I knew you two were meant for each other."

I give Mom a hug. "Thanks for always being there for me, Mom. I don't tell you how much I appreciate you and what you've done for me over the years enough. I love you."

Mom cups my cheek. "Of course, Judd, that's what parents do."

Hazel and Charlie drag Mom and Amelia off to the rest of the women to fawn over my beautiful fiancée and her ring. I head over to where the guys are. "Congrats, little brother. Now you can stop hitting on *my* fiancée," Kessler says, slapping my back, then pulling me into a hug.

"Thanks, Kess. And not a chance," I say, returning the hug.

Kessler shakes his head and laughs, then looks around and lowers his voice, "I also wanted to tell you, Lucy and I went to look at Ruby yesterday. We're going to adopt her. Lucy fell in love the minute Ruby laid her head on her lap."

"I knew she would be a perfect fit."

Kessler nods. "We're going to take Hudson to meet her tomorrow and sign the official papers."

"That's great, Kess. I'm glad Ruby will finally get a home."

I move onto Reese and Brent both humming 'another one bites the dust'.

"You just wait, you two are going to fall hard for someone and I'm going to be there every step of the way telling you 'I told you so'."

Garrett holds his hand out for a shake. "Can't say I ever thought you'd find someone to put up with your dumb ass, but I guess I've been proven wrong."

"I love you too, Garrett," I tell him, returning the shake.

I look around and spy Hudson and Kade on the couch.

"I'll be right back," I tell the group, walking over to where the boys are. Hudson sees me first and gets up from the couch to give me a hug. "Mom says I'm supposed to tell you congratulations."

I laugh and give him a hug back. "Thanks dude. I know this isn't fun for you guys, but it means a lot to have you here," I tell both him and Kade. They just shrug their shoulders, quickly returning to their game once they've greeted me.

Looking around, I spot Amelia over near the drink table. Making my way over there, I sidle up to her. "Excuse me miss, has anyone told you you're the most beautiful woman here?"

She giggles and takes a drink. "Sorry, but I'm engaged," she says, holding up her left hand. The ring looks like it was made just for her.

"Who's the lucky guy?" I ask, looking around the room then back at her.

She flaps her hand at me. "Just some cocky baseball player. You wouldn't know him. He's not even that good."

I snake an arm around her waist, pulling her to me. "Oh, is that so?"

"Okay, you two, you can celebrate later," Charlie says. "It's time for a toast." Charlie grabs a glass of water and turns towards our small group of friends and family. "If everyone can grab a drink. Judd has something he wants to say."

Charlie directs us to stand in front of the arch while everyone grabs their drinks. Once everyone is settled, she gives me the go ahead.

"I just want to start by thanking everyone for coming today. I know it's a busy time of the year, with Christmas and Kessler and Lucy's wedding a week away, so thank you for taking the time to celebrate with us." Turning to Amelia I continue, "Amelia, thank you for trusting me with your heart. I know it wasn't easy, but I am so grateful you took a chance on me."

"Well, you didn't exactly give me a choice. Everywhere I looked you seemed to pop up," she quips.

"Like a bad penny," Kessler adds.

The group chuckles.

"Jokes aside. You are the absolute best thing to happen to me this year, and I can't wait to see what the next fifty-plus years bring. I love you."

"Kiss her!" Mom shouts.

I lean down, giving Amelia a tender kiss. Her blue eyes look into mine as I pull back. The promise of forever reflecting back at me.

"A toast," I say, lifting my glass. "To finding your puzzle piece."

EPILOGUE

Amelia

THE ENERGY in the air is palpable.

Excitement and uncertainty hang all around us.

I guess that's to be expected in the ninth inning of Game 7 of the World Series. It's been a grueling six games against the Wilkesboro Wolves, both teams putting up a fight for the title. Judd started tonight and is still going strong. I know he's determined to make the last game of Kessler's career memorable.

Lucy and I are sitting in our usual spot behind home plate, one sleeping twin strapped to each of our chests. I swear she's more superstitious than Kessler. He tried to convince her to sit in the suite for the series games because of the utter chaos that can happen, but she wouldn't hear of it. She said she's sat behind home plate at every home game of his she's ever been to and she won't be changing it in the last games of his career.

So here we sit with our very large group of family and friends, watching the men we love play the best game of their life. Judd hasn't walked one batter tonight, making each man who gets on base earn it. They're leading the game by one run, and if they can hold off these last few batters, it's game over.

"I think I'm going to be sick," Lucy mutters as our guys

take the field, hopefully for the last time tonight. Kessler takes his position behind the plate and before he lowers his mask, he sends a wink to Lucy and taps his chest plate three times. She kisses three of her fingers and holds them up to him in return.

The crowd's cheers grow louder as Judd takes the field, but instead of heading towards the mound, Judd jogs to Kessler. They exchange a fist bump and a laugh, then both of them embrace each other in a back slapping hug before Judd sends a wink towards me and jogs off to the mound.

Lucy and I both look at each other with matching red-rimmed eyes. We've grown close over this last season with the guys being on the road half the year and Lucy needing help with the twins. Not only have I gained a friend over these last few months, but I've gained a sister I never knew I wanted.

A wave of nausea hits me, making me suck in a slow, steadying breath. I have a surprise for Judd when he gets home tonight. One we brought back with us from our trip to Sisters during All-Star week break. One only Lucy knows about because she and Kessler were with us on that trip and announced a surprise of their own last month. It wasn't until their announcement that I realized I had missed my period.

"Are you okay?" Lucy asks, leaning into me and lowering her voice.

I nod. "The nerves aren't helping, but I'll be fine. I haven't tossed my cookies for a few days, so I think I'm on the upside of this."

"Upside of what?" Charlie asks, returning to her seat on the other side of me, her own surprise securely in her arms.

"Uh, finishing up the decorations for the house," I say quickly.

It's not that I don't want to tell Charlie. I just need to tell Judd first. Seeing Lucy every day meant I wasn't able to hide my morning sickness from her. And seeing as she's pregnant for the second time in a year, she guessed it right away.

"Oh, that's great. I can't wait to see it once it's done."

Charlie and Hazel have come over during different stages of building, but we haven't had anyone over to see the final product. There's one room I've been hard at work on, not even Judd knows about, but he will tonight.

"We'll have everyone over for a housewarming party soon," I assure her.

The volume of the crowd increases, making us all turn our attention to the field. The first batter of the inning has taken their position. Judd already struck him out twice tonight, and I'm praying he does it again.

His first pitch goes straight through the strike zone, but the batter was behind in his swing, earning Judd a strike. The second pitch is the same, adding another strike to the board. Before the next pitch, the batter takes a timeout and steps out of the box, taking a couple of practice swings and blowing out a breath before returning.

"Hit him with your changeup," Henry shouts from his seat behind us.

Lucy shakes her head and turns to Henry. "No, the guy has been behind on his swings all night. Judd needs to either keep throwing the fastball or give him a slider."

"It's killed you not coaching this season, hasn't it," I tease Lucy, bumping her shoulder with mine.

She groans. "You have *no* idea. And now I won't be coaching next year either, thanks to my not-so-great timing." She lifts a shoulder. "But Kessler will be retired, and I think the boys will have no qualms about being coached by him."

I look at where Hudson and Kade are standing in the dugout with the Silverbacks. Kessler arranged for them to be the official bat boys for the World Series games and they have eaten up every second of it.

"Are you still going to be the assistant coach, Kara?"

She pokes her head out from the other side of Lucy with a Red Vine clamped between her teeth. She rips off a bite and chews for a minute before replying. "Fuck no, that's what this one is for," she says, nodding to Garrett, who's sitting to her left.

He looks down at her, giving her a smirk that could melt the panties right off of you. "Is that the only reason you want me? For my coaching skills?"

Kara lifts a shoulder. "You might have a few other uses."

Garrett leans down and whispers something into her ear, making Kara's entire face flush a bright red. I've only known her for a short while, but Kara is not one who blushes easily, so I have no doubt whatever Garrett just said to her is something dirty and I couldn't be more happy for her. The start of their relationship was anything but easy. Everyone knew they were meant for each other. They just both had high walls that they needed to dismantle for each other. Seeing them now happy and at peace tells me the journey was worth it.

Cheers grow louder around us, and I turn back to the game to see Judd has struck out the first batter.

"One down, two to go," Lucy mutters, twisting the ring on her thumb faster.

"They've got this," I say, not sure if I'm trying to reassure her or me at this point.

Batter number two steps up to the plate and Lucy groans.

"What?" I ask, not really sure if I want to know the answer.

"He's made it on base every time tonight."

I grimace. "Maybe he won't this time?"

The crack of the bat quickly diminishes my optimism as the batter sends a line drive between first and second. Brent dives for the ball once it hits the ground. He's able to scoop it up, but the guy is fast and makes it to first just before the ball hits Duke's glove.

"Or maybe he will."

"It's ok, it's just one runner," Lucy reassures me, or herself. Honestly, could be both of us at this point.

The next batter hits a pop fly that Reese catches for an easy out.

Lucy jumps to her feet with the rest of the crowd. If we get this last batter out, it's game over.

Kessler lifts his mask and calls for time, then jogs out to the plate. He and Judd place their mitts over their mouths as they talk to keep the opposing team from reading their lips. A few head nods and a butt slap later, Kessler returns to home plate and takes his position.

The first pitch is outside for ball one. Kessler tosses the ball back to Judd, who catches it, then wipes the sweat from his brow with his arm. Setting himself back up, he throws another pitch for an inside corner strike.

I reach down and grab Lucy's hand. Aspyn stirs from inside her carrier strapped to my chest and I start to bounce and sway softly, soothing her and my nerves slightly.

Judd sets up again and checks over his shoulder at the runner on first who's taken a big lead off the base. Judd fakes a throw to the batter and spins to throw to Duke. The crowd grows silent as the runner slides back into the bag, touching it right as the ball hits Duke's glove.

The first base umpire gives us the safe signal, and the crowd moans in unison.

"That was his last throw he's allowed if he doesn't want to get charged with a balk," Lucy says, gripping my hand tighter.

"He won't chance it being this close to the title." I think.

Judd sets himself up again. A grin breaks out over his face, and he nods his head once at Kessler.

"They're planning something," Lucy comments.

Judd checks over his shoulder again. The runner on first is taking his lead off of first, inching closer and closer as he watches Judd. Judd turns his head back to the batter and sends a pitch to the plate. The runner takes off, legs and arms pumping wildly to gain speed. The ball makes a loud popping sound as it hits Kessler's glove. Kessler jumps to his feet and Judd ducks as Kessler sends the ball down the center to Brent. The ball and the runner make it to the base milliseconds within each other and the runner collides with Brent, who's crouched down to catch the ball and knocks him backwards.

A collective gasp fills the stadium at the impact. Brent holds the ball up, still laying on his back and the umpire holds his fist to the sky indicating and out. Players run onto the field. The noise of the crowd grows to a deafening level, and Lucy and I look at each other before both bursting into tears.

Judd

Holy fuck, we did it.

The thought kept replaying in my head through all the interviews and pictures and celebration in the locker room. I was able to see Amelia and my family briefly when they were eventually allowed onto the field, but that was hours ago, and I want nothing more than to go home and see my beautiful fiancée. We haven't set a date for the wedding yet since we've been so focused on getting the house built. And with the library getting the funding it needed, Amelia has been working hard with Gladys and Irene on building the reading program.

I pull into our driveway and am slightly shocked to see the soft glow of a lamp still on in the living room. It's a little after midnight and while Amelia is usually a night owl lately, she's been in bed and passed out shortly after eight. Getting out of my Jeep, I jog up the steps and open the front door, where Bruno greets me excitedly.

"Hey bud, where's your mama?"

Bruno turns and jogs through the living room and down the hall where the master suite is. Kicking off my shoes at the door, I follow him down the hall. When I catch up to him, he's sitting outside the door of the spare room down the hall from ours. The door is cracked open, and a light is on.

"Is this where your mama is?"

I move into the doorway and push the door the rest of the way open. My breath catches in my chest at the sight in front of me. The once white walls are now painted a soft sage green. There's a light gray crib on the far wall with a baseball themed mobile above it. Pictures of baby jungle animals with various pieces of baseball equipment are hanging throughout the room. A matching dresser and changing table sit on the opposite wall of the crib.

In the corner next to the window, I spot Amelia in a plush gray rocker, sleeping soundly. My feet move across the space and I'm kneeling at her side in a matter of seconds. My eyes roam over my beautiful, smart, feisty fiancée as questions and elation course through me. Picking up the hand closest to me, I gently kiss the back of it, causing Amelia's eyes to flutter open.

She stares at me sleepily before her eyes widen and she sits up. "You're home!" She looks around. "No! I wanted it to be a surprise. I must have fallen asleep," she cries.

"So, you're really, it's not. You're pregnant?" I finally choke out.

Tears fill her eyes, and a smile breaks out over her face as she nods.

I reach forward and pull her into me, hugging her tight. She sniffles into my chest, and I feel my own tears silently roll down my cheeks. We sit here on the floor, wrapped up in each other, when Bruno's cold nose bumps my cheeks as he licks my tears away.

A laugh bubbles out of my chest and Amelia pulls back

from me. Bruno takes that opportunity to move onto her. She takes his face into her hands and rubs his ears as she looks up at me. “This didn’t go how I had planned.”

I scoot over to her and wrap my arm around her shoulder and pull her into me. I tip her chin towards me and take her lips with mine. We’re breathless by the time we break apart. Resting my forehead on hers, I whisper, “The best things never do.”

ACKNOWLEDGMENTS

Wow! Book 2 is well... in the books. I couldn't have done it without an amazing group of people behind me.

I'm going to thank my husband first this time, HAHA! Babe, I literally would not have finished this book without you giving me all those child free days/weekends to get this story out. I know you've sacrificed a lot to get me here and I could never thank you enough.

Savannah! My forever hype girl turned best friend and instagram guru. You've kept me going when I wanted to quit. Your encouragement that it's OK to take a break and reset, kept me and this story going. I will forever be grateful for our friendship. And our group chats with Taylor James.

That leads me to my next acknowledgement...

Taylor freaking James. Who knew I'd have an author bestie? I am so fucking glad you decided to jump into my DM's, and forever grateful for your friendship. I can't tell you how glad I am to have you and Savannah in my circle. I can't wait to do some book signings with you... hopefully soon!

Amber and Jess, my go-to BETA readers. Your feedback and SCREAMING over Judd and Amelia's story makes me so excited to put them out there into the world. I can't thank you enough for sticking with me on my author journey.

Kate and Erica! I am so happy to be working with you again on book two. Thank you for fitting me into your schedules as always! Can't wait to see where the future takes us with the next books!

And last, but certainly not least...

Thank you so much to all my readers who have popped into my DM's since the release of Catching the Coach to tell me how much they loved Lucy and Kessler's story and to scream their excitement over Judd and Amelia's. I wouldn't be doing this without your support and I am so grateful for every single one of you.

ABOUT THE AUTHOR

D.B. Axtell has loved to read since her Great-Grandmother taught her how at the age of three. Although the type of stories she likes to read has changed dramatically throughout the years, one thing that has stayed the same is her love of getting lost in others stories. In 2023 she finally decided to take a chance and write a story of her own, with hopes of providing a story other readers will love getting lost in.

When she's not arguing with her characters on whose story is next or encouraging them to speak to her, she's living her best life in the northernmost part of Oregon as a wife and stay at home mom of two very active boys and their trusty sidekick Gunner. Her favorite pastime is drinking Starbucks and spending time at the barn with her four legged baby, Phoenix.

Keep a lookout for her future books because there is plenty more to come.

Printed in Great Britain
by Amazon